BROTHERS
OF THE
BUFFALO

A NOVEL OF THE RED RIVER WAR

FULCRUM

JOSEPH BRUCHAC

© 2016 **Joseph Bruchac**

Library of Congress Cataloging-in-Publication Data

Names: Bruchac, Joseph, 1942- author.
Title: Brothers of the buffalo : a novel of the Red River War / by Joseph Bruchac.
Description: Golden, CO : Fulcrum Publishing, [2016] | Summary: "In 1874, the U.S. Army sent troops to subdue and move the Native Americans of the southern plains to Indian reservations, and this chronicles the brief and brutal war that followed. Told from the viewpoint of two youths from opposite sides of the fight, this is a tale of conflict and unlikely friendship in the Wild West"-- Provided by publisher.
Identifiers: LCCN 2015039450 | ISBN 9781938486920 (paperback)
Subjects: LCSH: Red River War, 1874-1875--Juvenile fiction. | CYAC: Red River War, 1874-1875--Fiction. | Cheyenne Indians--Fiction. | African Americans--Fiction. | Soldiers--Fiction. | Friendship--Fiction. | West (U.S.)--Fiction. | BISAC: JUVENILE FICTION / Historical / Military & Wars. | JUVENILE FICTION / Action & Adventure / General. | JUVENILE FICTION / Historical / United States / Civil War Period (1850-1877).
Classification: LCC PZ7.B82816 Br 2016 | DDC [Fic]--dc23
LC record available at http://lccn.loc.gov/2015039450

Printed in the United States
10 9 8 7 6 5 4 3 2 1

Fulcrum Publishing
4690 Table Mountain Drive, Suite 100
Golden, Colorado 80403
(800) 992-2908 • (303) 277-1623
www.fulcrumbooks.com

ALSO BY JOSEPH BRUCHAC

Dog People: Native Dog Stories

*The Girl Who Married The Moon: Tales from
Native North America*

*Keepers of Life: Discovering Plants through
Native American Stories and Earth Activities for Children*

*Keepers of the Animals: Native American Stories
and Wildlife Activities for Children*

*Keepers of the Earth: Native American Stories
and Environmental Activities for Children*

*Keepers of the Night: Native American Stories
and Nocturnal Activities for Children*

Long River

Native American Animal Stories

Native American Games and Stories

*Native American Gardening: Stories, Projects,
and Recipes for Families*

Native American Stories

Native Plant Stories

*Our Stories Remember: American Indian History, Culture,
and Values through Storytelling*

Rachel Carson: Preserving a Sense of Wonder

Roots of Survival: Native American Storytelling and the Sacred

CONTENTS

AUTHOR'S NOTE

Many years and many people went into the writing of *Brothers of the Buffalo*. One of the first people I have to mention—and sincerely thank —is Lance Henson, Cheyenne poet, Dog Soldier, and loyal friend for more than three decades. It was Lance who first opened my eyes to much of the history in this tale and told me many of the stories that I retold in the book. For example, it was Lance who introduced me to the epic story of Sweet Medicine as we sat on his back porch in Calumet, Oklahoma. Wolf's side of this story would never have been possible without Lance and other Cheyenne friends and elders over the years who were extremely generous in sharing their knowledge. Special thanks go out to Gordon Yellowman, teacher and contemporary Cheyenne peace chief, who reviewed this entire manuscript and offered invaluable assistance.

But I also have to reach farther back than that in terms of acknowledgments—back to the years 1966 to 1969, when I was a volunteer teacher in Ghana and found myself immersed in African culture, something that no amount of books or online research could ever match. Whatever understanding I have of the depth, power, and sophistication of the many cultures and oral traditions of West Africa began then. The African proverbs interspersed between chapters— which are my own translations from the Hausa language—came out of those years and the years that followed in which I've had continued contact with West Africa and African writers from across the continent. Chief among them is the late Chinua Achebe of Nigeria, who was one of the advisors for my PhD, and a true friend and mentor.

In a similar way, I need to thank my many African American friends and teachers—friends and teachers in every sense of those words, who've opened my eyes to so many aspects of American history of which far too few are aware.

In fact, my own awareness began before I went to Ghana, in the '60s when, as an eager—but very ignorant—young man, I was blessed to be a tiny part of the Civil Rights Movement, and marched in Missis-sippi alongside Martin Luther King, Dick Gregory, Stokely Carmichael, Jesse Jackson, and so many other incredible, dedicated visionaries.

In the years since then, my understanding of the complexity of African American history in the nineteenth century—the period of this novel— has only deepened thanks to the help of more people than I can mention in this brief space. So, let me just list a few authors, whose books should be in every school library: Julius Lester, whose *To Be A Slave* is a classic; Patricia McKissack, author of *Christmas in the Big House, Christmas in the Quarters*; and Christopher Paul Curtis, whose notable titles include *Elijah of Buxton*.

I'm no longer sure who first directed my attention to the accomplishments of the African American soldiers, many of them former slaves, who made up the 10th Cavalry when it was formed after the Civil War. It may have been Dick Gregory in a conversation I had with him years later, when he was invited to Skidmore College, where I taught courses in African and African American literature in the '70s. Or the visionary novelist Ishmael Reed. Or maybe my very close friend Ron Welburn, whose life and writing span both the African American and the Native American worlds. What matters is that they, and the contemporary African American historians and reenactors who keep that legacy alive, are determined that the 10th should always be remembered and honored.

The incredible story of the men of the 10th Cavalry, and the important roles a large number of African Americans played in the "settling" of the American West are topics that should be taught in every school. It should be noted that the distinguished, truly heroic role the Buffalo Soldiers played in America's wars did not end in the nineteenth century but continued on. Our history would have been far different without them. For example, during the Spanish-American War, when president-to-be Theodore Roosevelt made his famous charge up San Juan Hill in Cuba, his life was saved by the 10th Cavalry.

In a strange sort of way, this book also owes its genesis to Jim Thorpe, the greatest athlete in American history. I've now written two books about Jim: *Jim Thorpe, Original All-American* (Dial) and *Jim Thorpe's Bright Path* (Lee & Low). I also co-wrote and produced with Tom Weidlinger a documentary film entitled *Jim Thorpe: World's Greatest Athlete* that aired on PBS.

My research into Jim's life led me not only to the Carlisle Indian School but to its well-meaning, but deeply opinionated founder, Richard Henry Pratt (1840–1924). The idea for the Indian boarding schools and residential schools in the United States and Canada came from Pratt's experiment in "civilizing" the Fort Marion prisoners. Those schools impacted the lives of every Native American, often in tragic ways, for decades (in Canada, the residential schools did not end until 1992), and their effect is still being felt—and recovered from.

WOLF I AM
WOLF I AM

WHEREVER I SEARCH
IN DARKNESS
IN LIGHT

WHEREVER I RUN
IN DARKNESS
IN LIGHT

WHEREVER I STAND
IN DARKNESS
IN LIGHT

EVERYTHING WILL BE GOOD
FOR MAHEO PROTECTS US

WOLF I AM
WOLF I AM

— CHEYENNE SONG

THE MAN WITH ONE EYE
LEARNS TO THANK GOD
WHEN HE MEETS A MAN
WHO IS BLIND.

BOWING TO ONE
WHO IS SHORTER THAN YOU
DOES NOT PREVENT YOU
FROM STANDING STRAIGHT AGAIN.

A MAN'S FAULTS
ARE LIKE A HILL.
WHEN HE STANDS ON THEM
HE SEES ONLY THOSE
OF OTHER PEOPLE
AND TALKS ABOUT THEM.

IT IS NOT THE EYE
THAT UNDERSTANDS
BUT THE HEART
AND THE MIND.

— HAUSA PROVERB

The land is lit by the full moon, us just passing into Kansas. Most people are asleep, but me, I'm still awake, feeling as if every mile that passes is taking me further into a freedom I never knew back East.

As I stare out the window of the train, I feel a prickling at the back of my neck. Mama told me that feeling may mean you're being touched by an ancestor's hand, that something powerful may be about to happen. Even if you can't yet say what, or why.

The wide plain is almost bright as day, wide and free in a way it never is in Virginia. Then it changes. A dark mass just rises up out of nowhere and covers the land, like the earth itself has come alive. Takes my breath away. Then, though the engine is chugging noisier than a cotton gin, the rails clanking and clattering louder than a ton of chains, I hear a new sound. Thunder. A thunder that never seems to end, but just keeps rumbling and rolling.

And suddenly I know what it is. It is the hooves of thousands of buffalo. Animals I have never seen before save in pictures.

I hear excited voices shouting. Everyone else on the train is waking up now. From us negro recruits to the finer folks in the higher class cars farther back, away from the smoke of the engine, folks are wide-eyed and staring out at that moonlit herd. Men leaning out their windows, pointing, mouths open. They are yelling at the top of their lungs, but their human voices can barely be heard over that drumbeat of about as many hooves as there are stars in the sky. The great herd floods right up to the tracks, flowing like a black river with no beginning nor end, running alongside the train but not crossing over the rails. That sound of their hooves pounding the prairie seems to come not from outside but from deep in my heart.

Then there is a popping sound. One of them buffalo goes down, suddenly limp as a hung man cut down from a tree limb. More popping sounds. More buffalo falling whilst others tumble over their bodies. I lean out my own window. Hot cinders and smoke stream past my face as I see what I feared I'd see. Those popping sounds of rifles being fired are coming from the cars behind us. A dozen or more white folk all dressed up in suits, businessmen fresh out of the East, shooting through their open windows. The smell of blood is whipped in the wind—like when a lash cuts again and again into a man's back.

Tears from the engine's harsh smoke fill my eyes as they empty their guns into that mass of buffalo, reload, and keep firing. All of them laughing as they kill and kill for no reason at all other than to see those big black beasts fall.

I sit back down and close my eyes. Yeah, I'm finally in the West. But despite my dreams of finding a new life here where I can be a man, it seems most things are still the same.

THE BUFFALO IS OUR MONEY.

IT IS OUR ONLY RESOURCE WITH WHICH
TO BUY WHAT WE NEED AND DO NOT
RECEIVE FROM THE GOVERNMENT.

THE ROBES WE CAN PREPARE AND TRADE.
WE LOVE THEM JUST AS
THE WHITE MAN LOVES HIS MONEY.
JUST AS IT MAKES A WHITE MAN FEEL
TO HAVE HIS MONEY STOLEN AWAY,
SO IT MAKES US FEEL TO SEE OTHERS
KILLING AND STEALING OUR BUFFALOES,
WHICH ARE OUR CATTLE GIVEN TO US
BY THE GREAT FATHER ABOVE
TO PROVIDE US MEAT TO EAT
AND MEANS TO GET THINGS TO WEAR.

— KICKING BIRD
KIOWA PEACE CHIEF
1835–1874

GET ON
THE TRAIN

St. Louis, Missouri
March 4, 1872

Dear Mother,

I hope all is well with you and Pegatha. I am well. I have finished my training and I was told that I did well. Now I am about to go by train from St. Louis to my post. I have seen so much of this great country already. It is a fine thing to be a free man and a soldier. I think you would be proud of how fine I look in my uniform of the 10th Cavalry. I am in D Company.

I hope this letter is being read to you by either Pegatha or Preacher Williams. I hope that he will help you write a letter in reply to me. I am eager to hear from you and to know that you are doing well. You will soon receive some money from my pay.

Give my love to Pegatha and tell her that her brother expects her to do well and apply herself at the new school for colored children.

I send you my love and my good wishes.

Your devoted son,
Washington Vance

9

Even out here, Wash thought, *looks like there's still no safe place to be a colored man.*

Standing with forty other new cavalrymen on the platform in St. Louis, he and the other black recruits for the 10th were being given a taste of what sort of respect they might expect where they were going.

"Once you boys get on my train, you better mind your manners, assuming you ever learned any," the middle-aged white conductor with the big belly said.

From his eastern accent and the way he limped, it seemed likely he'd fought on the side of the North—just like some of the black men he looked down on from the ladder he'd climbed to address them. But there was no sympathy in his sneering voice.

"Now you better make sure you do not move about at all. You hear me. You stay in your own car. Unless you want to get your thick woolly heads broke."

As if we hadn't all figured that out already, Wash thought.

It would have been impossible not to notice the looks he and the others had gotten as they neared the tracks. Despite the fact they wore US Army uniforms, the mean-looking white men had given them the sort of squint-eyed stares that showed they'd as soon shoot a colored man as spit on him. They'd glared at Wash like he was lower than the dirt caked on their boots.

A surprising number of them were former Confederates. It didn't take much guesswork on anyone's part to know that. Some of them were actually still wearing parts of their sessesh uniforms. That was part of the quick education Wash was getting about what life might be like on the far side of the mighty Mississippi River. It looked as if there would be no shortage of unreconstructed rebels, rough-edged men ready to make a new life in the West and bringing their animosity toward the entire negro race with them.

I would bet a dollar against a dime, he thought, *that few of you rebs boys have ever read Shakespeare like my daddy and me. I wonder just how many of you can even write your own names.*

Then, out of the corner of his eye, Wash noticed something.

One of those Southern gentlemen, a skinny white man with a full-face beard who was eyeing him from the window of the car just behind the one they were boarding, appeared sort of familiar.

Now where have I seen him before?

The thought tugged at Wash so much that he just stood there as the train started to move.

"Don't you be looking back at them, brother," a voice with a thick Mississippi Delta sound to it said from above him. "You just be asking for more trouble than a man can load into a wagon. Get on the train."

Wash tried to turn his gaze down at the ground, cussing himself for being so foolish.

Look a bad man in the eye, you asking to die.

But a bell had been rung in his head by something about that cadaverous white man. Maybe it was those eyes of his, as black and beady and full of death as a rattlesnake's. Or the way he was holding the gold chain that hung across his vest, as if he was about to pull out a watch and check the time.

One foot on the step, his hand grasping the rail by the door, Wash was frozen. He couldn't move, even as that skinny ex-rebel stood up and leaned even closer to the window and Wash saw that he had let go of the watch chain and now was reaching for the ivory-handled pistol in the holster hung across his chest.

A big brown hand wrapped itself around Wash's arm and yanked him up off the platform and in through the door. A smiling, good-looking face that was as brown as fertile soil and about as round as a ball was thrust down in front of him.

"Charley Smith is my name," the soldier who had hoisted him up said, "and fighting Indians is to be my game. Now you tell me who you be. That ways I can notify your next of kin if you goes agitating any more mean white men."

Wash looked up at him. Charley Smith's head was a full foot above his. The big man had lifted up his solid hundred and fifty pounds into the car with no more effort than pulling a carrot out of sandy soil.

This Charley Smith looks to be the sort of fellow to have by your side in a ruckus. If only to hide behind like an oak tree once the shooting starts, Wash thought.

He lifted up his right hand. "Washington. Washington Vance Jr."

"Aw right," Charley Smith said, making Wash's sizable hand disappear into his bear-sized paw. "You play cards? Throw dice?"

"Some."

"Aw right," Charley Smith said, slapping him so hard on the shoulder that it made Wash's teeth rattle. "You and me, we are going to be fast friends."

The young Cheyenne man sat up quickly. With his right hand he grabbed for the rifle that was never far from his side. He looked around inside the lodge. In his dream he had been shouting loudly. But no one else seemed to be awake.

Did I just shout? The light of the full moon came in the open door, showing him the sleeping forms of his mother and little sister.

No. If I had shouted outside my dream, they would have wakened. Their sleep is always as light as mine. That is why we are still alive.

He wiped his hand across his forehead. It came away wet with sweat, but not from the heat of the windless night, the heat that had led his mother to prop open the lodge flap to allow the air to come in and cool them.

The dream had brought the sweat to his brow. If it was a dream.

A dream, yes.

But only a fool would ignore it, would turn away from what was seen or heard in a dream.

He lifted the rifle, moved slowly to the door of the lodge, and paused. Then he looked outside. All he could see in the moonlight were the other lodges of his people.

We should be safe here. We are no longer alone out on the prairie. This is a quiet night. It is not filled with the barking of dogs and

gunshots and the shouts of white men and the screams of wounded
horses. There are no smells of smoke and blood.

He let out a slow breath. They were safe. They were at the
Cheyenne and Arapaho Agency, under the protection of Friend Darlington. All of their Wutapio band were here. All those still living.
All those remaining of the people who had followed the peace road
of his grandfather Moketevato.

He stepped outside. The black horse tethered in front of the
lodge next to theirs turned to look at him. It was the horse belong-
ing to Dirty Face, his best friend. The horse turned to look at him,
moonlight glittering in its eyes. It shook its head and nickered softly.
Wolf sighed. He leaned back against the lodge and slid down into a
sitting position.

There is nothing to fear in this night.

But his heart would not stop pounding. Another sound was
still echoing in his mind. That sound had been an awful scream, a
scream so long and loud that it could have come from no human or
animal throat.

Then he remembered. But the memory brought him no peace.
He had first heard that terrible, voiceless howl when he was still
small and eager. He had been out hunting with his second father,
Pawnee Killer. Pawnee Killer had still walked then among the living.
Pawnee Killer had been by his side when that sound tore the air like
a knife cutting through the wall of a lodge.

Wolf had been frightened. He had started to turn and run, but
Pawnee Killer had grasped him by the arm. "Wait," he had said in
his kind voice.

Wolf had looked up at his second father. There was a smile on
Pawnee Killer's face. But that smile was sad.

"What was that?" Wolf had whispered. "It is a monster? Will it
chase after us? Will it eat us?"

He had been very young. Not a grown man of fifteen winters.
That was why he had asked such questions. But he had been old
enough to know that he should ask in a whisper. He had been old
enough to have learned the important lesson that every child of the

Striped Arrow People needed to remember. That lesson was to be quiet when danger is near.

Pawnee Killer had made the sign for *yes*. It is danger. Then he had made the sign for *no*. He beckoned for Wolf to follow him.

They crawled to the top of the hill in front of them. The terrible scream had come from the other side. They looked over the top. There they saw the strangest thing Wolf had ever seen. A road made of stones and logs had been laid across the land. On top of that road rested two metal bars. Those bars were so long, they had no beginning or end. On top of the metal bars was the monster he had heard. It was as black and shiny as a beetle. It was so huge that it made the men who rode on its back look like ants. Its front end was on fire! Then, as more smoke billowed up from it, it screamed again.

Pawnee Killer held his arm to keep him from fleeing.

"Be calm, Following Wolf. It cannot chase us," Pawnee Killer whispered. "See. It is stuck to those rails. But it is still a monster. It has cut our buffalo herds in half. It brings men who kill our sacred animals. If we cannot stop them, our world will end."

Following Wolf looked out at the quiet village around him. It was beautiful, so quiet in the moonlight. But there was no quiet in his mind. There was a lump in his stomach. It was as tight as a knot in a horsehair rope.

My dream has warned me. Something bad is coming.

Great-Grampa Hausaman, he was a prince. A real African prince. That is what my daddy told me. When Great-Grampa came into town, they would shout out his name, dancing and playing the drums and singing praise songs.

> *Here he comes, he is the lion.*
> *When he roars, the enemies do tremble.*
> *Here he comes, he is the elephant.*
> *When he steps on the ground, that ground shakes.*

He would ride a fine horse, all black with silver reins and gold on the saddle. He had traveled all the way to Araby, visited the sacred places there and come back. That made him what Daddy called a hajee, a man who had made the big pilgrimage to Mecca. He was not a tall man. He was short, as we black Vances are today. But no man's heart can be measured by his height. In his hand he carried a big iron sword, blade as wide as a man's hand, sharp enough to cut a hair in half down the middle. When he raised that sword, they all called out his honor name, all the people.

Daddy, he never said what that honor name was. When they took Great-Grampa Hausaman captive, put him in chains, walked him down to the coast to the castle of El Mina, he left his name behind. Left it strong in Africa. Left it for his people, even if his body was taken. He just called himself Hausaman from that day on.

It was his enemies who took him, Daddy said. They were men jealous of him because the people loved him so much. They ambushed him as he rode his fine horse on his way to meet with the prince of another town. They jumped out into the road, pointed their guns at him, and told him to stop. He rode through them, cut down three of them with his sword before they shot his horse and threw a net over him and caught him. Then they sold him to the slavers. My, my. Think of that. Men as black as my great-grampa, selling their own people to the white men.

That slave ship was about as close to hell as a man can get on earth. I heard that not just from my daddy telling Great-Grampa's tale, but from older slaves whose parents came across the wide ocean that way. But Great-Grampa Hausaman was tough as leather. Not being as big as many of the others, he was able to get by on less food and water. He was also not about to surrender to despair like so many did who just quit, just gave up and died.

According to Daddy, old Great-Grampa stated that life is a gift from the Great God of all. So we need to hold onto it as best we can and not just throw it away. My, my, Daddy said, he was a strong one. He was strong enough to help others as much as he could, keeping up their spirits, singing to them and the like. Even shared his food so as to keep some of the weaker ones living.

He also was a magic man, sort of like Moses in the Bible. He was slow to use that power. But when the captain of that slave ship went to whip him for no reason at all, Great-Grampa lifted up his chin and pointed his finger at that captain. Then he said in African, "You whip me, you never use that arm again."

The captain took just one cut with that whip. Then his face drained of blood and he clutched his arm and dropped that lash. They carried the captain back to his cabin. He'd had some sort of stroke. The right side of his body just stopped working.

From then on, those white men on the ship, they gave Great-Grampa Hausaman a wide berth. They started to feed him and the other slaves better, too. That story about him being magic got around fast. When the time came to sell him at the auction block in Richmond, at first not one white man dared to bid for him. They saw the look in his eye. They knew that a man like that, they either had to respect him or kill him. None of them wanted to waste their good money on such a slave.

Finally, he was bought by Master Vance's old Gran-daddy who, being an educated man, found Great-Grampa Hausaman interesting. Old Master Vance even gave thought, Daddy said, to sending Great-Grampa back to Africa, except Great-Grampa turned out to be too valuable a worker, seeing as how he knew so much about farming. Great-Grampa Hausaman had owned his own big farm back in Africa, a whole lot bigger than the Vances' plantation. Also, once he found a wife here in Virginia, he decided to make his life here. He even said the red earth here made him think of home.

This is part of Africa now, he said. He had decided himself not to spread his wings and fly back home with his magic.

They never needed an overseer as long as Great-Grampa Hausaman was alive. Folks just did their work well enough with no whippings at all. Of course, things changed some after old Master Vance and Great-Grampa Hausaman both passed on. That old African prince's life just became a story people told. That power he had was never passed on to any of us who come after him. Except for the power of his story, which now that I think on it, is considerable.

CAMP SUPPLY

Camp Supply,
Indian Territory
March 15, 1872

Dear Mother,

I hope all is well with you and my little sister, Pegatha. I have not yet heard from you. However, I have been told that it may take some weeks for mail to arrive from the South. So I am eagerly awaiting news from you. I hope that the crops you planted have done well. I hope Pegatha is in school and studying hard.

As for me, I am well. I am at my post. It is called Camp Supply. It is not a large army post, but it is a good place and I am learning how to be a proper cavalryman. I have also made a new friend. His name is Charles Smith. He is from Mississippi and a new private like myself. We are fast friends. There is also another man who I think will be a good friend. He is named Joshua Hopkins and he is a Virginia boy like myself. He has already been in the 10th Cavalry for a year and so I am learning from him. The three of us are now "bunkies," which is the term used in the 10th to describe best friends.

It is quiet here. You do not have to worry about me. I have not seen even one hostile. And if we did see any hostiles, you can rest assured that our Company D would be equal to the task of fighting them.

That is all I have to say for now. I hope to hear from you soon. Give my love to my little sister, who has probably grown taller than her brother in the months I have been gone. Ho ho.

Your loving and obedient son,
Washington Vance

"My, my." Charley Smith swung his big hand in a half circle to encompass the military camp they were approaching that was to be their new home. "Camp Supply sure enough ain't much to write home about, is it?"

Wash nodded. Hard to argue with something as obvious as that. What they saw of the main buildings of the camp as they passed the enlisted men's canvas tents set up outside—carefully segregated, with one area for the colored soldiers and another for the whites—was little more than a series of dirt-floored log cabins linked together by porches on either side, making the structure a big rectangle. The only doors in those cabins opened into the center of the rectangle.

Maybe even smaller than the slave cabins I grew up in, Wash thought. *Matter of fact, we had plank floors, which is a step up from dirt. Wonder how the wives of those white officers are liking it here?*

He could see some of those women standing on their little bitty porches, watching the arrival of the new recruits. None of them were smiling.

Mind your manners, Wash. Don't look their way. Just keep your eyes straight ahead.

But then a darker countenance among those worn and tired-looking white ladies caught his attention. He could not help but turn to look.

And his heart did something he had read about in books but never experienced. It skipped a beat. For there, looking back at him, was the prettiest, most perfect brown face he had ever seen. Even prettier than his mama, who when she was young had been said to be the most beautiful woman on the plantation—white or black. Wash took a deep breath as he took in the vision before him. She was not dressed as fine as the officer's wife standing in front of her, but Wash could not imagine anyone in creation looking as elegant as that lovely girl. She appeared to be about his age, and she didn't look worn or tired, despite the fact she had a bucket in one hand and a wet rag in the other. She looked as full of life and as graceful as a fawn. Seeing her, he couldn't help but smile.

But she did not smile back. Instead, she just gave a little sniff—as if she was smelling something three days dead. Then she lifted her chin, turned around, and disappeared with her bucket and rag back through the door.

The corners of Wash's mouth turned down as if they had weights on them.

Next to him Charley Smith chuckled.

"Uppity little thing, ain't she?"

Wash said nothing. What had passed between him and the girl had lasted no more than a few seconds, but he felt a whole lifetime older and sadder.

"I reckon I know who that girl is," Charley said in a low voice as they tied their horses. "The beauty of the camp, I heard the corporal say. Has so much book learning that she holds a high opinion of herself. The only reason she is here is that she is the niece of our sergeant, whose wife is her only surviving kin. And even though she may be working as a maid for an officer's wife, Sergeant Brown and his wife treat her like a princess and watch over her like a hawk! Know what that means?"

Wash shook his head.

"It means that even if she had smiled back at you and not turned up her nose, you'd have less chance with her than a rabbit trying to court a fox."

Wash nodded.

"And if I do not miss my guess, here is the man himself," Charley whispered, pointing with a little waist-high gesture of his index finger at the six-foot-tall, stocky black man walking toward them, wearing sergeant's stripes on his shoulder and a look like a storm cloud on his face.

"AH-TEN-SHUN!"

Almost every one of the twenty new men snapped up straight and clicked their heels together. Almost—because just then Wash's heel chose to catch itself on a little clump of dirt pushed up by some horse's hoof, and he took one stumbling half-step forward before catching himself.

First Sergeant Samuel Brown glared down at him. "Trooper," he growled, "you know what it means to wear the uniform of the 10th?"

What was the right answer? Yes? No? Wash felt like a man who just dove into water so deep he couldn't tell which way was up or down. He took a deep breath and said the only thing he could think to say.

"Sir?"

"Huh! It means you act like a soldier. You don't go staring about and tripping over your own feet like you was some little baby."

"Yes, sir, sir." Wash squared his shoulders and stared straight ahead, trying not to show how intimidated he was by the fact that Sergeant Brown was now leaning so close that their noses were about touching.

"Ah-huch!"

At the sound of that cough from Wash's left, the sergeant straightened up and turned, fast as an eagle striking.

"What?" Sergeant Brown barked, pointing his finger like a dagger at the chest of the man who had coughed.

"Sorry, sir," Charley Smith said, his eyes focused over the top of the sergeant's head. "Got me some dust in my throat, sir."

Sergeant Brown shook his head and took a step back.

"You staring, stumbling, coughing lot are the saddest excuse for cavalrymen I have ever seen," he said, sweeping his hand in front of them in a wide dismissive gesture. "But I am going to make you into men of the 10th. You understand me?"

"YES, SIR," they all answered.

Sergeant Brown grinned.

But not like a man who's happy, Wash thought. *More like a fox who has just found its way into the chicken house.*

"But you ain't going to enjoy it," the sergeant said. "Now march, double-time, round the camp and back and keep going till I tells you to stop."

LONG AGO, LONG AGO, THE PEOPLE LIVED
IN THE PLACE OF MANY LAKES.
WE DID NOT HAVE THE BUFFALO THEN.
FOOD WAS NOT EASY TO GET,
AND WE MOVED OUR CAMPS OFTEN.

ONE DAY, IT IS SAID, THE PEOPLE WERE CAMPED
NEAR A LARGE SPRING FLOWING FROM
THE SIDE OF A MOUNTAIN.

THE MEN BEGAN PLAYING THE HOOP GAME.
THE GAME WAS SO CLOSE THAT THEY HARDLY NOTICED
A YOUNG MAN WALKING INTO THE CAMP CIRCLE
FROM THE DIRECTION OF THE SUNSET.

AS SOON AS THEY SAW HIM,
SAW THE WAY HE WAS PAINTED,
SAW THE WAY HE WAS DRESSED,
THE HOOP GAME WAS FORGOTTEN.

EVERYONE IN THE CAMP GATHERED ROUND.
WHO ARE YOU? THE PEOPLE ASKED.

I AM SWEET MEDICINE, THE YOUNG MAN REPLIED.
THIS MEDICINE PAINT AND WAY OF DRESSING
WAS GIVEN TO ME BY MATAMA, OLD WOMAN.

WHERE DOES MATAMA LIVE? SOMEONE ASKED.

SWEET MEDICINE LOOKED TOWARD THE SPRING.
SHE LIVES JUST THERE BEHIND THE WATER.

NOW, HE SAID, I WILL RETURN TO HER
AND BRING SOMETHING BACK.

THEN SWEET MEDICINE WALKED INTO
THE FALLING WATER AND DISAPPEARED
FROM THE SIGHT OF THE PEOPLE.

HE CAME TO THE PLACE,
THERE INSIDE THE MOUNTAIN,
WHERE AN OLD, OLD WOMAN
SAT BEFORE A FIRE.

MY GRANDSON, THE OLD WOMAN SAID,
WHY HAVE YOU COME BACK TO ME?

I NEED SOMETHING, SWEET MEDICINE SAID,
TO TAKE BACK TO THE PEOPLE.

GRANDSON, SIT DOWN, MATAMA SAID.
SWEET MEDICINE SAT DOWN ON HER LEFT.

THEN MATAMA FILLED A BOWL WITH FOOD.
HERE, SHE SAID, THIS IS BUFFALO MEAT.
THEN SWEET MEDICINE BEGAN TO EAT.
AS MUCH AS HE ATE, THAT BOWL STAYED FULL.

MATAMA LIFTED THE BOWL OF MEAT
AND HANDED IT TO SWEET MEDICINE.
TAKE THIS AS A GIFT FOR THE PEOPLE.

SWEET MEDICINE WALKED BACK THROUGH
THE WATERFALL
TO WHERE THE PEOPLE WERE WAITING.

SOMETHING GOOD IS COMING,
HE SAID TO THE PEOPLE.
WATCH, BUT DO NOT DO ANYTHING.

THEN, AS ALL WATCHED, A COW BUFFALO
PUSHED HER HEAD THROUGH THE WATERFALL,
LEAPED OUT FROM THE WATERFALL, AND RAN AWAY.

ONE BY ONE, MORE BUFFALO CAME OUT.
FIRST ANOTHER COW AND THEN HER CALF
AND A BIG BULL BUFFALO.

SOON MANY BUFFALO WERE COMING,
UNTIL A GREAT HERD HAD PASSED THROUGH.

WHEN THEY WERE ALL DONE COMING OUT,
SWEET MEDICINE SPOKE AGAIN.

NOW YOU CAN HUNT THOSE SACRED ANIMALS.
BUT YOU MUST ALWAYS FEED THE OLD PEOPLE
AND THE ORPHANS FIRST AND WASTE NOTHING.
AND YOU MUST ALWAYS SHARE THE MEAT
WITH ALL THE PEOPLE IN THE CAMP.

SO SWEET MEDICINE BROUGHT THE BUFFALO.
AND AS LONG AS THE PEOPLE RESPECTED
AND SHARED, THEY NO LONGER WENT HUNGRY.

POLISHING BOOTS

Petersburg, Virginia
April 15, 1872

My Dear Son Washington,

I your mother writing to you. We have got two letters from you and those letters made me happy. They made your sister happy. We love you. We miss you. We know you do your best.

We are well. Weather has been dry. We have been given help by Mr. Moses Mack. You remember him. He went away after his wife die and was gone 8 years. He just come back. He was good friend, good friend your daddy. He help in the field. We will have a good crop.

This is Pegatha writing what Mama say. I am good in school. We love and miss you. We know you be a very fine soldier.

Your loving mother,
Mama

"Private Washington Vance Jr.," Wash asked himself, pausing to run his hand back through his short hair, "why you ever leave Virginia and join the 10th Cavalry?"

Shut your mouth, Wash. Best to just concentrate on polishing—seeing as how opening your yap is what earned you this extra duty from Sergeant Samuel Brown during inspection.

"Private, your boots is a disgrace," Sergeant Brown had said in his slow Georgia drawl.

Those scornful words had made Wash mad. Just an hour before parade, he had shined his boots till they gleamed like the bright morning sun. He'd planned to be praised for the way he looked, not made to feel like some ignorant field negro. He was wearing his proud new uniform—made of lighter blue and coarser cloth than the more expensive broadcloth worn by the officers, but handsome nonetheless, and made more so by the yellow trim showing he was cavalry, different from the white trappings of the infantrymen and the red of the artillery. Standing at the end of the line, which had been arranged by height, he'd imagined that though he might be lacking some in stature, he surely looked as fine for his first inspection as any man on the post, black, white, or red. Surely he would prove to the sergeant that he was a real man of the 10th and not some stumbling baby.

Then the white captain had trotted his horse past, spattering mud all over Wash as he was lining up at attention. If he had just kept his mouth shut as he should, that might have been the end of it.

"My boots was clean before that old white man's horse near run me down," he mumbled softly under his breath.

But not softly enough. Sergeant Brown turned to him, his ears pricked up like a cat that just heard the squeak of a mouse.

"What you say, Private?"

"Nothing, Sergeant, sir."

"No-o-sir," a big grin that was far from friendly spread over Sergeant Brown's face. "You said more'n that, Private. Enough to make me wonder if you are anywheres near the right material for our 10th."

And that was how Wash had ended up polishing not just his own footwear, but the boots of every non-com and officer in the fort.

Of course, such work as Wash was doing was not unusual for one of his station. In the short time he'd been at Camp Supply, he'd learned that black soldiers had to do more than double duty. They were expected to serve not just as fighting men, but as handymen and laborers, lugging and toting, hammering and nailing. Also, when picked to be strikers—personal servants for the white officers—they had the additional job of acting as house men and valets. True, if a man got picked to be a striker he did earn extra pay, just as the wives of the colored soldiers who were married made cash money for cooking and doing laundry.

But being a dog-robber—the name the other black soldiers called a striker, seeing as how he got to eat the extra food from the officers' tables that otherwise would have gone to the officers' dogs—was not to his taste, even though those selected did get finer chow than was served to the enlisted men.

I did not join up to take the place of any white man's pet—even if I was to make extra money I could send back home to provide for Mama and Pegatha. Nossir. I mean to prove myself as good and proud as any man.

Wash shook his head.

Maybe a little too proud. Stuck doing a striker's job as punishment duty with no extra food or pay.

He sighed and picked up another boot. Spit, rub the polish in, buff it with the cloth. Make it so shiny it reflects your face.

Wash paused and studied his reflection. The face looking back at him from the side of that boot was dark and shadowy. But in the light of day he knew his skin to be nigh the same color as that of the Indian scouts at the fort.

The old Powhatan blood shows in me just like in Mama. That is why I am so light. And I have got high cheekbones just like her. My hair's like hers, too, more wavy than kinked up. But mine is kept cavalry short, not long like the full-blood Indians here at Camp Supply.

Wash thought about those full-blood scouts. Osages, he had learned. The only red men he'd been able to see close up thus far. There were, he knew, a passel of other Indians not far away. Most of them were at the Cheyenne and Arapaho Agency. But none of them had come in to the fort in the week he'd been here.

There was considerable tension at Camp Supply about that. Just what was the present intent of those Indians? Would they remain peaceful or go again on the warpath as they had so often done in the past? No one seemed to know. Even the Quaker agent, Brinton Darlington, no longer seemed sure of himself when he had stated to all and sundry that surely the way of peace and not the path of war was the road his savage charges were going to follow.

What was it Sergeant Brown had said as they lined up on their arrival at Camp Supply?

"You men best assume that the Indians is always watchin' us. Even if you not layin' eyes on them. You doubt my word, just walk out onto that peaceful-seeming prairie by youself. Once you get past that little hill there, you might could run into as many Indians as any man'd want. 'Course, you won't live to tell about it. No-oo-osir."

Wash turned his gaze toward the open gate of the fort. For all anyone really knew, the hills out there might just be crawling with renegades. During the two times Wash had been sent out with a wood-cutting party, he'd kept expecting to feel an arrow in the back at any minute. On his way back there was such a tightness in his belly that he felt as if he had to climb down off his horse to relieve himself. But he didn't dare do that. The thought of getting punctured by an arrow while unbuttoning his pants was a sight more distressing than just getting shot in the back.

Wash sighed. All this thinking about being killed was not doing him any good. Best to concentrate on the task at hand rather than writing his own obituary.

"Shining boots," he said to himself. "That is what you need to be about right now, Private Vance. Cogitating on other concerns is just going to confuse you and get you into more trouble."

"Uh-huh. Amen to that," an amused voice replied. A long-fingered hand reached over to pass Wash another boot.

"Thank you," Wash said.

"You welcome, my man."

Private Josh Hopkins leaned back against the post with his hat over his eyes, his long legs stretched out in front of him.

Having no duty assigned him till supper, Josh didn't have to assist Wash with his task. True, his help consisted of little more than handing over each boot when it came time to polish it. When it came to being lazy, Josh Hopkins was the match of any man Wash had ever met. But, lazy as he was, Josh was also seasoned. Though still a private like Wash and Charley Smith, Josh had a good year on them in the 10th, having enlisted back when they were still using the hair-trigger Spencer.

"And I do not miss those guns at all. They was as like to kill the one carrying 'em as anything a man might aim at."

Wash was glad of having the benefit of all of Josh's experience, nearly as glad as he was for the companionship of Charley Smith, who had just about adopted him as kin.

"You 'mind me of my own little brother," Charley had told Wash. "He had that same Indian hair as you. Simon was his name. Simon." Charley had paused then, swallowed hard, and looked out the window. "That boy and I never let a hair come between us till he was sold down the river by our old master."

True, Charley had used those dice to take the little bit of cash Wash had in his pocket during their train ride. But Wash chalked that up to experience and didn't hold a grudge. Gambling looked to be in Charley's blood. In the few days Wash had known him, it had become clear that whether it was luck or skill...or something else, Charley Smith always came out on top in any game of chance.

What was it Mama said about gambling? Only way not to lose is to never play.

So when Charley had proposed after reaching Camp Supply that they play a few hands of cards, Wash simply smiled and shook his head.

"I'll just watch, if you don't mind."

From the way Charley had raised an eyebrow and then nodded back at him, Wash had known it was all right between them if he declined to gamble. There were plenty of other men eager to hand over their pay to Charley.

Now Josh ran his hand back through his hair. "Know why they calls us Buffalo Soldiers?" he asked.

Wash shook his head.

"Indians give us that name."

"Indians."

"Uh-huh. Now there are some as say it is because most of us have this hair. Pretty much like those buffalo the Indians love so much. But that is only a part of it. It is also because those Indians saw right off that we black cavalrymen is a tougher and more stalwart breed—like those big animals. Buffalo will face into the storm and not let anything turn them around. Buffalo Soldiers. A name we have been proud to adopt ourselves."

Buffalo Soldiers, Wash thought. *Sure has a better sound than "brunettes"—or any of the other names the soldiers in white companies call us. Despite the emancipation of our race and the fact that so many men of our color serve not only in the army but in state legislatures and the United States House of Representatives, there are still those who despise us—including some in uniform—even more that they hate the red men. 'Course, Indians aren't actually red. Those I've seen range from a tawny hue to a deep brown. Not that the shade of their skin makes any difference. Just two colors here. White on the top and everything else underneath.*

That thought brought another image to Wash's mind, one that had been troubling him ever since the train ride that brought him west. It was the thin, mean-looking face of that bearded white man, the one who had stared with murderous eyes at him through the train window. Though he had little doubt that the man had gotten off the train at the same depot where Wash and the other new recruits had disembarked, he hadn't seen the man either then or since. But that man's face kept coming back to him. Wash had a feeling deep in his gut that he knew the man. That was why he had gawked at him like a schoolboy seeing an elephant for the first time. Or maybe more like a rabbit staring at a snake. But from when or where he knew that dangerous man, Wash could not quite say. And what was it about that gold watch chain that had drawn his attention? Wash shook his head. The answer was just staying out of reach, like a box on a shelf so high there was no way to get it without a ladder.

Maybe it was the beard. Maybe that is what's throwing me off. Now how would that man look if he was clean-shaven? Who would he look like then, maybe...?

"Wash."

Wash opened his eyes. Another pair of boots was being dangled in front of him.

"Take special care with these here. They are the footwear of none other than our commanding officer, Mister Lieutenant Colonel John W. Davidson hisself. You get any scuff marks on these, you be carrying the log all night for sure."

Wash took hold of those boots carefully. He'd seen how strict their commanding officer could be. And how unpredictable. One day he'd be ignoring everyone, and the next he'd have a man with one little loose button sentenced to carry the forty-pound punishment log for two hours.

Wash rubbed his shoulder. It still ached from when he'd lugged that rough piece of pine himself three days earlier. All for accidentally stepping on the little patch of grass Colonel Davidson was trying to nurture on the parade ground.

"Yessir," Josh said. "You have got to watch yourself ever' minute with them white officers. You know, every one of them is still smarting over the way they was demoted once the Civil War was over. Colonel Davidson hisself was a major general. Head of the cavalry for the whole Department of the West. But when the army was cut back from two million to just twenty-five thousand men, he was dropped in rank like a rock in a pond. Only about seven or eight generals left in the entire army. And our old colonel is about as far from being one of them again as the earth is from the moon in the sky. You know what that means?"

"Walk on eggs whenever Colonel Davidson is around?"

"Better than to walk on his grass," Josh chuckled

Wolf looked across the fire at the sleeping faces of his mother and sister. Their faces, like his, had grown thin from the lack of food. It had been days since a real meal. Once again, the promised rations had not been given. If other families had food they would have shared it with them. That was the way the Real People lived. But now every lodge in the village was suffering the same.

Come in to the agency. Give up fighting. You will be safe here. You will be fed. That is what was promised. That is what they wrote on the papers they signed.

But we cannot eat promises or paper.

The Animal People, he thought, *are like us Real People. When they sense the presence of ve'hoe soldiers, they flee. As soon as the ve'hoes built their fort, the buffalo moved away. Then the deer and antelope left. Even the rabbits and prairie chickens disappeared.*

So it was that their only source of food had become the government rations, solemnly pledged to them in exchange for their land, in exchange for peace. But though their Quaker agent, Friend Miles, tried his best to keep the government's promises, he was not the one who had the final say as to when that food would arrive, how much there would be, and what condition it would be in. If it was late, or scant, or mostly rotten meat and stale hardtack, there was nothing he could do. And if it did not come at all, all he could do was write more words on paper to complain.

It had not taken long for the Real People to see that the agency was not a good place. They had been told to farm. But they saw what had happened to their cousins, the Cloud People, who had arrived at the Darlington Agency for the Cheyenne and Arapaho tribes ahead of them. The Cloud People had tried hard. But they had little luck in growing anything. It was too hot and dry. Even when some rains did come, the earth was too poor. It was nothing like the rich river bottom soil in which their old people used to grow corn.

Despite the broken promises of plenty of food for everyone, despite their empty bellies, the Real People were still forbidden by the army to leave and go look for game. Anyone seen outside the agency boundaries was to be shot on sight.

But now, Wolf thought, *to hunt—or raid—is our only choice.*

He shook his head as he hefted his rifle. *I will not raid. I do not want to hurt any innocent people—even ve'hoes. But I must keep my mother and my sister from starving, I have to find food.*

Now was the time. It was a dark night with no moon, a good time to leave without being seen.

He put down the rifle. The noise of a gunshot could be heard from far away out on the plains. He took down his quiver of arrows from the place where they hung high in the lodge poles. He took down the war bow that Pawnee Killer had helped him shape during his twelfth winter. On the day Wolf was born, his first father had cut a strong Osage orange sapling and hung it in the rafters. There it had cured in the smoke of one winter's fire after another. Each time the lodge was moved, the sapling was wrapped and taken along. Each time the lodge poles were set back up, it was put back in its place. His father did that again and again until he died. Then his second father did the same until it was ready. That bow was strong, strong enough to send an arrow deep into the side of a running buffalo and reach its heart.

"My son."

Wolf turned toward his mother. She was not asleep after all. Her eyes were open. She had propped herself up on one elbow to gaze across the fire at him. The firelight reflected from her dark eyes. She looked up at him. She looked into him.

My mother knows me well. She knows what I intend. Will she ask me not to risk leaving the agency?

There was a long silence between them. His mother nodded her head.

"Following Wolf," she whispered, "be careful."

A STORY, A STORY. LET THIS STORY COME.

IN THE TIME OF BATA-MUSA IN THE KINGDOM OF KABI,
A BOY WAS BORN WHO COULD NOT WALK.
HE WAS STRONG AS A LION, BUT HE COULD NOT STAND.
HE DRAGGED HIMSELF ABOUT ON THE GROUND.
SOME MADE FUN OF HIM, BUT THEY DID NOT DO SO WHEN
THEY WERE CLOSE ENOUGH FOR HIM TO TAKE HOLD OF THEM,
FOR ONCE HE GRASPED SOMEONE WITH HIS HANDS
THEY COULD NOT ESCAPE HIM.
STILL, FROM A DISTANCE THE OTHER BOYS
THREW STICKS AND BALLS OF MUD AT HIM.

A LEARNED HOLY MAN CAME TO KABI.
HE WAS ONE WHO FOLLOWED THE GREAT GOD
BUT HE WAS ALSO ONE WHO COULD SPEAK WITH THE DJINNIES.
HE SAW THAT BOY AND THOUGH
THE BOY WAS COVERED WITH DIRT,
THOUGH HE CRAWLED ABOUT LIKE ONE OF THE BEASTS,
HE SAW SOMETHING IN THAT BOY'S EYES.
SO HE MADE A STAFF OF WOOD AND GAVE IT TO THE BOY.

"LEAN ON THIS AND STAND," HE SAID.

BUT WHEN THE BOY LEANED ON THAT STAFF
AND TRIED TO USE IT TO LIFT HIMSELF UP,
THE STAFF BENT BENEATH HIS WEIGHT AND THEN BROKE.

THEN THE HOLY MAN GAVE THE BOY
A STAFF MADE OF BAMBOO, BUT THAT STAFF SPLINTERED
WHEN THE BOY TRIED TO USE IT TO STAND.

SO THE HOLY MAN WENT TO THE BLACKSMITH AND HAD HIM
FORGE A STAFF OF IRON. IT WAS SO HEAVY THAT IT TOOK
THREE STRONG MEN TO CARRY THAT STAFF BACK TO THE BOY.

THE BOY TOOK THAT STAFF WITH ONE HAND.
HE STRUCK IT UPON THE GROUND

AND THE EARTH SHOOK. HE GRASPED IT WITH BOTH HANDS
AND PULLED HIMSELF TO HIS FEET
AND NOW IT COULD BE SEEN
THAT HE WAS TALLER THAN OTHER MEN.

THEN THE HOLY MAN GAVE HIM FINE ROBES
AND HE PUT THEM ON.
HE GAVE HIM A SHARP SWORD AND BELTED IT TO HIS WAIST.
HE BROUGHT HIM A STRONG HORSE THAT NO ONE HAD EVER
BEEN ABLE TO RIDE AND THAT BOY CLIMBED ONTO ITS BACK,
A BOY NO LONGER.

NOW HE WAS A GREAT WARRIOR.
OTHER MEN BOWED THEIR HEADS BEFORE HIM IN RESPECT.
FODIO-MUSA WAS HIS NAME. HE WAS THE GRANDFATHER
OF MY GRANDFATHER'S GRANDFATHER.

AS LONG AS WE KEEP HIS MEMORY,
WE WILL REMEMBER THAT WE HAVE
GOT A WARRIOR'S BLOOD.

THAT IS WHAT MY DADDY SAID.

OFF WITH THE OLD RAT'S HEAD.

CHOOSING MOUNTS

Camp Supply,
Indian Territory
June 1, 1872

Dear Mother,

I received your letter. It made my heart leap to hear my name called and to have your letter handed to me from the company mail pouch! I am so glad everything is well. I am glad that Pegatha is doing well in school. I am sure she is reading this to you right now. So I say to her a big hello. Hello, my little sister.

I am glad to hear that Mr. Mack is helping out. I remember he was one of Daddy's best friends and went fishing with Daddy and me. I remember how sad he was not to be able to join the army and march off with Daddy when word came that black men were needed. Mr. Mack had to stay with his wife because she was sick, as I remember. I do remember how sad Mr. Mack was when word came to us of Daddy's death at the Crater. As were we all.

Let me speak now of happier things. I am now doing even better than before. Josh and Charley and I are best of friends.

The Indians call us Buffalo Soldiers. Is that not a fine name?

There is still no action, no fighting at all. But we are being well prepared.

I send you my love and warmest wishes. Write me again soon.

Your loving and obedient son,
Washington Vance

"That is one mean piece of horseflesh, soldier. You want to keep your distance 'less you want your arm tore off."

Wash looked over at the stable master. Blood was still seeping through the cloth bandage wrapped around the man's arm where the big black stallion with the white blaze on its chest had bitten him.

"Best we could do," the man growled, "is put a slug in that devil's brainpan."

Charley Smith tugged at Wash's sleeve. "Come on, brother. There's a nice little gelding down the line there would be jes' right for you. It is jes' as black as this one and ten times as gentle."

A black horse. That was what Wash needed. Every man in their company had to be mounted on a horse of that color. It was part of what made the cavalrymen of the 10th stand apart. Not only did they aspire to be twice the horsemen of their white counterparts in other units like Custer's 7th, they also aimed to look twice as sharp. That was why each company made sure to ride matching steeds. And now every new recruit had his horse except for Wash.

"Why you being so picky?" Josh Hopkins had asked him the day before when Wash had passed by one horse after another from the herd of blacks that had just been driven into Camp Supply by a hostler. "Me, I just took the first horse I saw that fit the bill far as color went. And old Midnight and me gets along fine."

Wash hadn't answered that question. Maybe it was because he didn't know himself for sure what it was that he wanted. Or that it was too hard to explain that it wasn't just his eyes that had to tell him a horse was right for him. It was something more, something that had to do with his heart and his gut. Or maybe—and he knew this would have made his two friends bust a gut laughing—he needed a horse that needed him.

And that was why he was back standing there, staring at that black stallion rearing up, screaming, and flailing its hooves in the air, trying to break free of the rope that held it.

Wash felt another hand on his shoulder. He turned to look at the stable master. The anger was gone from his face, replaced by something akin to regret.

"Son," the man said, the growl gone from his voice. "Don't you think I don't care about my horses. I love them like they was family. But that one there is as different from the rest as the night from the day. If you think he could be yours, you are just fooling yourself. That horse would as soon kill you as look at you."

"You sure?" Wash said, turning his gaze back to the black, which had settled down some and was just standing there now. But the fire was not gone from its eyes, and its ears were laid back flat against its skull in a way that told Wash, who had been around horses since before he could walk, it was ready to flare up at a moment's notice.

"You know something about horses, boy?"

"A little."

"What you see about that one?"

"It's smart."

"You right about that." The man tapped the bandage on his arm. "No dumb horse could have done this to me. But what else you see?"

"Strong. Broad chest, sturdy legs. A man could ride that horse all day without it wearing out."

"Un-huh. If it'd let a man get up on its back. So fine looking an animal you'd think one of our officers would have claimed it for his own. But not a one of them gave it a second glance. Now why in the name of all the Saints was that? What else you see about this beast, what one thing?"

Wash studied the stallion. He crouched down low on the ground and walked around the front of the animal slow, not getting within range of its hooves or teeth. Then he saw it. There it was on the left flank. US.

"That," Wash said, pointing at the brand.

The stable master shook his head in surprise. "Boy, you pretty good. My Lord. Never expected you to see that. But what it is that you see, and what you think it means?"

Wash bit his lower lip. "Wellll," he said in a slow and careful voice, "that is a new brand, even though that horse has to be at least four years old. Though I'd have to look at its teeth to see how much they are wore down to be sure. And there is no other brand on it, which is strange for a four-year-old horse. So I guess what it means is that it was never branded until just before you got it."

"And who rides horses with no brands?"

"Indians," Wash said. "This was an Indian pony."

The stable master chuckled. "Good thing I am not a betting man, or I would have lost my bankroll betting against your ever figgering out a thing like that. Yessir, by the Jeezus, that is an Indian horse. Likely one stolen by those rustlers what have been raiding all the Indian herds hereabouts for the last few years."

"I thought it was Indians who was the big horse thieves out here," Charley said.

"Huh," the stable master sniffed. "Shows how much you know, soldier. I would wager that these days there's four horses taken from our Indians for every horse they might steal. Lordy, Lordy! That is one of the things that has them Cheyennes all het up, having those horses they cares so much about rustled in the night and then drove down to Texas or up to Kansas to be sold. Not that I sympathize so much with the Indians, but I can sort of understand why every now and then some young brave decides to go off on a little horse-taking venture of his own. Half the time they are trying to steal back their own steeds."

"My, my," Charley said.

"My, my indeed," the stable master echoed, dusting his hands off one against the other. "So that is why what you see here," he waved a hand toward the stallion, which shied back from him at the gesture, "is a certain kind of horse that is no good to us. The army was cheated when they bought this animal, not noticing anything strange about it seeing as how it was in a herd of similar critters."

"What kind of horse?" Charley asked.

The stable master turned a pitying glance his way. "Young man, you might pay attention to your friend here. He may be half your size, but he has twice your horse sense." He patted Wash on his shoulder. "You want to tell him?"

"I guess," Wash said, "that horse has decided that it just likes Indians and will abide nobody else."

"That is right," the stable master said. "And that horse is not about to change its tune. Lord knows. Nossir."

As the man spoke those words, a thought came to Wash's mind. He turned back to study the black stallion again, dropping back into a crouch.

Charley took a long look at Wash. Then he lifted his hand up to his chin. "You said you was not a gambling man," he said to the stable master, taking him by the arm and drawing him away. "You sure about that? 'Cause I do have a little bet I would like to make with you."

As the two of them walked away, Wash began to draw a pattern in the soft earth between him and the big horse. A song began to sing itself in Wash's mind, an old song that his father had taught him.

As he heard it, he remembered the words his father had said to him before singing that song for the first time.

"This is a song from your mama's grandfather, Great-Grampa Hausaman. He was an old, old man when I knew him and he gave me that song. But he was born free in Africa on the banks of old River Niger. He was a prince there, rode a great black horse and carried a lance and a sword like one of the knights of the round table. He could make a horse do anything for him. He knew the Horse Song. And though we are not free, we have his blood. We have his song."

The song had made its way to Wash's lips now. He ran his hand back through his short wavy brown hair, then opened his mouth and let the song free, soft at first, no louder than the whisper of fingers across the top of a drum.

Fodio-lay, Gunba
Gaban-gari, Kanta.

The black stallion's ears lifted an inch and its head turned to look down at him as he continued to draw the pattern he had been taught by his father. Circles and lines intersecting and swirling. Wash moved forward as he continued to sing.

Fodio-lay, Gunba
Gaban-gari, Kanta.
Fodio-lay, Gunba
Gaban-gari, Kanta.

A little louder now, his finger still drawing in the dirt, extending the pattern of crisscrossing lines and sweeping circles. Now his side was toward the stallion, whose head was lowered, its ears raised as it gazed at the pattern. Still singing, his back now to the big horse, Wash could feel its hot breath on his neck and cheek. He stood up slowly, reached one arm out, reached up so that he was embracing the neck of the black stallion, its cheek now pressed against his.

Wash stopped singing. He turned, placed his hands on either side of the horse's big head, and looked it in one eye and then the other. Then he closed his eyes and leaned close.

"I'm Wash. You know me now," Wash whispered into the horse's right ear. "You are Blaze. Wash and Blaze. We belong to each other."

"Holy jumping Judas priest!" a voice said from a few yards away. "I do not believe it."

"Believe it, my man. And pay what you bet."

Wash opened his eyes to look. The stable man was shaking his head in disbelief as he counted out coins into Charley Smith's outstretched palm.

"Huh!" said a deeper voice from behind him. Wash turned. It was Sergeant Brown. "Trooper," he said, pointing a big finger at Wash's chest, "seems I might have been wrong 'bout you."

MAMA'S STORIES ALSO WERE ONES THAT YOU HAD TO THINK
ABOUT, BUT NOT THE SAME WAY AS DADDY'S. HIS WERE OF THE
PAST. HERS WERE OF THE WAY THE WORLD IS TODAY.

OLD ROOSTER WAS ROOSTING HIGH IN A TREE, WAY UP WHERE
BROTHER FOX COULDN'T GET HIM. BROTHER FOX CAME BY AND
CALLED UP TO OLD ROOSTER.

"MORNING, BROTHER ROOSTER."

"MORNING, BROTHER FOX," ROOSTER SAID BACK.

"COME ON DOWN HERE. I HAVE GOT SOME GOOD NEWS THAT
YOU ARE GOING TO WANT TO HEAR."

"NO SIR," OLD ROOSTER REPLIED. "IT IS WAY TOO EARLY IN
THE MORNING FOR ME TO COME DOWN. YOU JUST GO AHEAD
AND TELL IT TO ME FROM WHERE YOU ARE. I CAN HEAR YOU
REAL GOOD."

"WELL," FOX SAID, "IT IS FINE NEWS, INDEED. THE LAW HAS
BEEN CHANGED. FROM NOW ON IN, THE LAW SAYS THAT HOUNDS
ARE SUPPOSED TO RUN NO MORE FOXES AND FOXES ARE
SUPPOSED TO EAT NO MORE ROOSTERS AND HENS. SO COME
ON DOWN HERE."

BUT OLD ROOSTER, HE JUST COCKED HIS HEAD LIKE HE WAS
LISTENING TO SOMETHING.

"YOU HEAR THAT?" OLD ROOSTER ASKED.

"WHAT YOU HEAR?" FOX SAID BACK.

"WHAT I HEAR IS THE HOUNDS. THEY ARE GOING AH-WOOO, AH-
WOOO, AND THEY ARE ALL HEADING THIS WAY."

"WELL," FOX SAID, "I DO BELIEVE I HAD BETTER GET GOING DOWN THE ROAD."

"WHAT ARE YOU SCARED OF?" OLD ROOSTER SAID. "NOW THAT THE LAW BEEN CHANGED, HOUNDS NOT SUPPOSED TO RUN NO MORE FOXES."

"YES, SIR," FOX SAID BACK. "BUT SOME OF THEM HOUNDS ARE AWFUL LAWBREAKERS."

OLD LANDRIEU

Petersburg, Virginia
June 8th, 1872

My Dear Son Washington,

The money you send us came here. Thank you so much. It was more than we expect. I hope you save enough to take care of yourself. I use some of the money to buy new tools and also a bonnet for myself and dress for Pegatha. She has grown so much she needed a new dress.

Washington, this is Pegatha. I have grown. I am now taller than you. Does that mean I am now your big sister and you are my little brother? Ho ho!

I hope your sister Pegatha is writing just what I say. I am.

She promises me she is taking down ever word I speak. It is a warm spring and summer. We think the crops will be good. We are eating well. Poor Mr. Moses Mack was thin as a starved horse. Now he is putting some weight on his bones.

We glad you safe and doing well. Be brave, but do not risk yourself. Please. We want you home when you are done being a cavalryman.

Say hello to your friends Charles and Joshua from your mother.

And your BIG sister!

Your loving mother,

Mama

A man could fry an egg on a flat rock out there in that sun.

Wash wiped his forehead with the end of his bandanna. From the shady place near the blockhouse where he was walking back and forth on duty, he could see the wide expanse of land to the west of Camp Supply. Nothing moving out there, unless you counted the dry earth itself, which seemed to ripple in the heat.

Not much to look at.

But neither, Wash thought, *is Camp Supply*.

His first impression of the square of rough-made buildings and stockade walls of logs had changed little since his first sight of it, of the long rows of officers' cabins connected one to the other by the little porches on the sides—if you could use the word *porch* for a passageway so narrow that a man could stretch out his arms and reach from one cabin to the other. Add in the blockhouses built into two of the facing corners, the tents set up along the inner east wall for the use of the white non-coms, the outside stables, and the other tents for enlisted men, and there you had it. The whole of Camp Supply.

Frontier living, for sure, not that much better than the tipis the Osage scouts set up over the rise on the prairie.

"In some ways," Josh had said when they climbed that rise and he pointed out the Osage lodges to Wash, "them Indians have got it better than us. Indian tipis stays cooler than cabins in summer, and I have heard that with a good fire and the flaps closed they be a sight warmer in winter than our tents and log quarters. You never hear none of them Indian women complaining like the wives of our white officers, wailing about their quarters being more like shed barns than proper houses."

As Wash turned on his heel to walk back the way he had come, he cast his eye toward the nearest of those officers' quarters. Its walls were indeed naught but rough logs running vertically with mud chinked in between. Even the beds were cobbled out of rough boards nailed together with government bed sacks filled with straw for mattresses. Those mattresses, like the soldiers' bedrolls, required daily shaking to be rid of the centipedes, spiders, and scorpions that found their way into every tent or cabin just as regular as sunrise followed sunset. Floors of packed dirt. Roofs of sod. Mud falling from the ceilings when heavy rains came.

But Wash had already seen that, despite what Josh said, most of those white ladies seemed to know what it meant to be married to the cavalry and seemed determined to make the best of it. Take Captain Nolan's wife, for example. Wash had been asked by the captain to carry a message to her just the day before. When he had reached the cabin, the door had been open.

"Hello?" he'd called out.

No one had answered, and he had peeked inside to see a place as neat as a pin. Thick straw lay over that dirt floor, covered by layers of newspaper over which she had placed a fine ingrain carpet. Tent sheets tacked up on the ceiling kept whatever water might come through to a minimum. She'd even painted some of the chairs nailed together out of boards by the post carpenter.

But that was all he had time to see before someone had grabbed him by the arm and spun him around.

"What you think you are doing here, Private?" a scornful voice that made his rank sound like an insult had demanded.

He found himself face to face with none other than the young woman who was the personal maid of Captain Nolan's wife. Sergeant Brown's niece, Bethany.

"Message, Miss," he'd said, lifting up the piece of paper like it was a shield against her disdain.

"Hmmmphh," she'd sniffed, crinkling that little nose of hers, which was nevertheless still pretty to look at. Then, snatching the paper from his hand, she had pointed across the parade ground. "Now you get back where you came from, soldier!"

"Yes, Miss," he'd said.

Then, hoping he didn't look too much like a whipped pup with its tail between its legs, he had bowed to her, turned on his heel, and got.

The prairie sun beating down on Camp Supply was like a blacksmith's hammer on iron. Out of the corner of his eye Wash made out someone sneaking along the side of the buildings across the square. Private William Landrieu Jefferson, keeping in the shade. Even at a distance Wash could see the look that always seemed to be on the man's face. A contemptuous sneer.

Despite the short time Wash had been at Camp Supply, he had made the acquaintance and quietly taken the measure of every other Buffalo Soldier at the camp. Wash prided himself on being able, like his mama, to size up a person soon after meeting them. And though there were some here he liked more or less than others and one or two he might even already call true friends, he'd concluded his fellows to be nearly universally a good lot, men who seemed to be trying to do the best they could and bring credit to their race. Almost without exception they seemed to be soldiers you could expect to rely upon when the chips were down. The one exception was William Landrieu Jefferson.

"Old Landrieu," as Josh called him, was a man who enjoyed a high regard for himself in contrast to his obviously low opinion of most of the rest of humanity. It wasn't just, as he frequently stated, that his quadroon background, being only one-quarter black, made him superior. He was also the company bugler and played that role to the hilt—as if *he* was telling everyone else what to do with his bugle calls and not just passing on commands from the officers. He carried the bugle with him everywhere he went, like a badge of high office.

Landrieu paused, took off his hat, looked furtively one way and then another.

Like a yellow weasel about to sneak into a chicken coop, Wash thought, standing still. *Sun in his eyes, he can't see me here in the shade.*

Landrieu slowly ran the fingers of his left hand back through his brown hair, then replaced his hat, a thoughtful look on his face. Then he turned and disappeared behind the further blockhouse at the other end of Camp Supply.

Now where is he going?

Wash turned at the sound of steps coming from behind him. It was Emmett Branch, another of the privates in his company come to relieve him.

It took only a few moments for Wash to cover the distance to the place where Landrieu had vanished behind the blockhouse. He flattened himself against the wall, bent low, and peered down around the corner of the structure. And there the bugler was, no more than a hundred feet ahead of him, moving slow as a heron stalking through the shallows. But it was no fish he was after. There, all alone and bent over a washtub was none other than Sergeant Brown's niece. In another few steps Landrieu would be upon her and then...

What's he got in mind? Just say a polite hello? Not likely, the way he's creeping and crawling, low down now almost on his belly like a snake. Grab hold of the girl and steal a kiss? Or something far worse than that?

Wash was not about to wait to find out. The distance between him and the bugler was too great for him to cover quickly enough, but that did not mean there was nothing he could do. Wash forked the two outside fingers of his right hand, stuck them in the corners of his mouth, and blew hard.

WHEEEEET.

It was a whistle loud enough to wake the dead—and make Old Landrieu try to jump to his feet and turn around all at once. It was clearly not something the man had ever practiced before, seeing as how he tripped over his own legs and ended up on his back, kicking up a fair-sized cloud of red dust as he landed.

"Wha—? *Sacre!*" Landrieu sputtered as he stumbled up, trying to free the one arm tangled in the lanyard of his bugle as he tried to see who had just whistled. Wash, though, had already slipped back out of sight—but not far enough so his voice could not be heard.

"PRIVATE JEFFERSON," Wash shouted, putting enough of a growl in his voice to make it sound like Sergeant Brown, "REPORT TO THE COLONEL, DOUBLE TIME!"

Then Wash slipped inside the blockhouse, his eye to a shoulder-high crack. Sure enough, no more than half a minute later, Private Jefferson, still brushing the dust off his clothing, hustled past in the direction of the colonel's office.

With a wide grin on his face, Wash walked toward the back of the blockhouse and peered through another crack. And there, fifty yards away, was Bethany Brown. Still alone amidst the clotheslines, she was bent over her washtub, scrubbing Mrs. Nolan's blouses as if nothing had happened. Wash shook his head.

That fool girl will never know what almost happened to her, he thought.

And because Bethany Brown's back was turned to him, he did not see the little smile on her face—or the long, lethal hatpin that she reached up to stick back into the bun of brown hair held on top of her head by her scarf.

IN THE OLD DAYS, NO ONE EVER STOLE.
THOSE WHO WERE WELL OFF
ALWAYS SHARED WHAT THEY HAD.

IF THERE WAS ANYTHING SOMEONE WANTED,
THAT PERSON HAD ONLY TO ASK THE OWNER
AND THAT THING WOULD BE GIVEN.

BUT THE COMING OF THE SACRED ELK DOGS,
THE HORSES, BROUGHT SOME PROBLEMS.

IT WAS NOT SO EASY TO GIVE AWAY A HORSE,
UNLESS IT WAS A SPECIAL OCCASION.

SO SOME PEOPLE BEGAN TO BORROW HORSES
THAT BELONGED TO OTHERS WITHOUT PERMISSION.

THEY WOULD BRING THEM BACK,
BUT SOMETIMES MANY MOONS
PASSED BEFORE THAT HORSE WAS RETURNED.

SO THE MATTER WAS BROUGHT TO THE ELK SOCIETY,
AND THEY PUT FORTH A NEW RULE FOR THE PEOPLE.

FROM THIS DAY ON, THERE WILL BE NO MORE
BORROWING OF HORSES WITHOUT PERMISSION.
IF ANYONE DOES SO, WE WILL FOLLOW THEM,
TAKE BACK THAT HORSE, AND GIVE THEM A WHIPPING.

PAWNEE WAS YOUNG, AND HE DID NOT LISTEN
TO WHAT WAS SAID BY THE ELK SOLDIERS.
HE BORROWED A HORSE WITHOUT PERMISSION.
THE BOWSTRING SOLDIERS TOOK OFF AFTER HIM.
THREE DAYS OUT ON THE TRAIL THEY TRACKED HIM DOWN.

THEY TOOK BACK THAT HORSE.
THEN THEY BEAT PAWNEE, DESTROYED HIS CLOTHES,
BROKE HIS SADDLE AND GUN, TOOK ALL THAT HE HAD,
AND LEFT HIM THERE, ALONE AND NAKED ON
THE PRAIRIE.

HIGH BACKED WOLF THEN CAME UPON POOR PAWNEE,
SITTING THERE AND WAITING TO DIE.

"NOW," HIGH BACKED WOLF SAID, "I AM GOING
TO HELP YOU.
THAT IS WHAT I AM HERE FOR, FOR I AM A CHIEF.
BUT FROM THIS DAY ON YOU MUST BEHAVE RIGHT."

HE TOOK THE YOUNG MAN BACK TO HIS LODGE.
"HERE IS YOUR NEW CLOTHING,"
HIGH BACKED WOLF SAID TO HIM.
"OUTSIDE ARE THREE HORSES. TAKE YOUR PICK OF THEM AND
THAT HORSE WILL BE YOURS.
HERE IS THE SKIN OF A MOUNTAIN LION.
I GIVE IT TO YOU.
WEAR THIS SKIN AS PROOF THAT YOUR HEART IS GOOD."

HIGH BACKED WOLF WAS TRULY A CHIEF.
AND FROM THAT DAY ON, PAWNEE'S HEART WAS GOOD.

FIRST
PATROL

Fodio-lay, Gunba
Gaban-gari, Kanta.

Wash hummed his great-grandfather's song as he ran the curry brush along Blaze's back. As he stroked the animal's fetlocks, the big stallion whickered in pleasure and then turned its head back to nuzzle Wash's chest.

A fine steed to ride into war, Wash thought, a picture coming into his mind of himself riding across imagined African plains, his clothing shining with gold. And now they were about to go out on patrol, his first patrol. The thought of it filled his senses, but not so much that he was unaware that someone had just come up very quietly behind him.

The smell of the grease told him that it was an Indian. Only Indians lathered their bodies with buffalo fat like that to prevent them burning in the sun and to keep the bugs away.

He felt a gentle tug on his hair. It took less than a second for Wash to spin, swat the hand away, and reach for his revolver. But the tall man had already stepped back and folded his arms. It was the biggest of the four Osage scouts. Wash had seen him from a distance. That was easy to do because of his great size, which seemed characteristic of his tribe.

He looked even taller now. The top of Wash's head barely came up to the man's chest.

"Excellent hair," the scout said in a slow, deep voice.

"Huh?" Wash replied. No other words came to his mouth.

"Short," the Osage man said. "Yet it would be prized," he gestured toward the small hills and stand of scrubby trees about three hundred yards out, "by some of those out there. A worthy scalp to hang from a warrior's lance."

Wash stared up at him, his mouth open as if he was attempting to catch flies, as surprised by the huge man's good English as by the import of the words he had spoken.

The tall Indian nodded, as if Wash had just uttered something halfway intelligent.

"That song you sang," he said. "Medicine song, no? It will protect you."

Then the Osage scout nodded and wandered off, leaving Wash to thinking about how his hair would be a real coup for one of those red men out there that he was just as likely to run into on that day. And somehow the prospect of his first patrol seemed a bit less pleasant.

"You thinkin' again, Wash?"

Josh Hopkins, who had been grooming his own horse a few yards away, put down his brush and walked over. He put his hand on Wash's shoulder and gave it a companionable squeeze.

"Never did see anyone who ever seemed to be in a brown study as much as you."

Wash shook his head ruefully. "I suppose," he said.

Josh looked in the direction where the Osage scout had walked.

"That is one big Indian, ain't he? They call him Baptist John. Heck of a name for an Indian."

"I suppose."

"Heard some of what he said to you."

"Uh-huh."

"I wouldn't worry about it none. I believe that is just the way Indians show you they like you. They tease you like that. And I doubt we will see more than dust and sagebrush out there on patrol."

Josh sat down on a wooden stool and watched as Wash continued to run the comb over the big black horse's body. "You know," he said, "Sergeant Brown has taken note of the way you have with that animal of yours. Seems to have softened him a bit toward you. Where you learn so much about horses?"

"Back home."

As Wash spoke those two simple words, he felt a wave of emotion. It surprised him to the point that his legs felt a little weak. Of all the reasons he had joined the 10th, which included proving himself as a man and being able to send money back home to care for his widowed mother and his little sister, perhaps the most important reason he'd had for leaving Virginia had been to get away from that place where he'd been nothing more than another piece of property until emancipation. A place where, even now, he doubted he would find any white man who would ever view him as a real person. How could he think of that little cabin as home? Yet he now realized that he did.

"You never told me much about where you come from. What was it like?"

Wash took a deep breath. If he started talking about it the way he felt at the moment, he wasn't sure he'd be able to stop talking.

"Like most every place else, I suppose. You know how it was, being owned and all."

Josh picked up a piece of straw and bent it back and forth in his long fingers. "I suppose so. But was it a big plantation like where I come from, with a Big House the size of a king's palace and all? Rose Hill, they called it."

Wash let out the breath he'd been holding. "Not so much," he said. "The Vances had a nice Big House—least it was big before the Yankees burned it. But they never named it. It was just called Vance Farm. Had a nice library. More than a thousand books in there. One of my daddy's jobs was to keep that library clean and dust those books." Wash smiled. "Not that any of the Vances read them. Master Philip had inherited Vance Farm from his uncle, who had been some kind of professor."

"So what kind of folks was they? They the kind to do this?" Josh stood up and slipped his shirt halfway down. Wash looked at the long lines of scar tissue across his friend's back. "Stealing apples from the orchard," John said. "Didn't matter I was but ten. Stealing was stealing, my old Massa said. Said that was in the Bible. He was a righteous man, for sure."

"No," Wash said. "Master Philip was kind and never whupped his slaves. We were treated decent—or so the neighbors said who were scandalized that we darkies were allowed to marry like my daddy and mama did. No jumping over the broom on our planta- tion. Black couples wedded proper in the little negro church we had been granted permission to build out of scrap lumber down by the river, in whose warm waters we babies were baptized. We were even allowed to use the Vance last name as our own."

Wash put down the curry brush, picked up three straws from the ground, and sat next to Josh.

"Unlike some owners, the Vances suffered a man and his wife to stay together—unless they misbehaved. The Vances hardly ever sold off any of us children, at least until they were thirteen or so. Truly, as slaves to the Vances, our cup did runneth over." Wash chuckled. "Or so, I am certain, the Vances told themselves."

He held up the three straws he'd plaited together. "We had it better than some, being house slaves and also with Daddy being in charge of the horses. Our cabin was closest to the Big House, not way down in the quarters. But Mama and Daddy were not like some house slaves who thought themselves better than anyone else. They never made it seem that we were too good to mix with the field negroes, those men and women working rain wet and sun dry whilst we were inside. Whatever extra victuals was left over did not just go into our bellies. Mama made sure that it got out to the quarters down by the lower fields. And whenever Daddy could find the time he was teaching anyone, old or young, the reading and writing he had learned, even though it would have gotten him whupped by the over- seer had he been caught. Mister Tom frowned on darkies reading."

Wash looked up. "I didn't mention him yet, did I?

Josh shook his head. "But there was always one of them, weren't there?"

"Yup. And he was the one who did the whipping that Master Philip was too kind to do himself. Mister Tom Key. He was tall and bony as a skeleton. The cheeks on his smooth-shaven face stuck out like wings above his long chin. And he was meaner than dirt. He always 'knowed what he was doing,' indeed, he did. How can a man who swings a whip until your father's back looks like a skinned calf not know?"

Wash tossed the straws down onto the ground.

Josh nodded, saying nothing.

Wash took another deep breath. "'Don't you worry none,' he said, that day they left. 'I will stay here till the last dog is hung. I will defend this house like it was my own. Your loyal Tom Key will shed every drop of his blood before any Yankee foot ever steps over your sacred threshold.'

"Mistress Vance paid him no heed, but I recall how Master Philip Vance took out his watch and studied it as Mister Tom was talking. Then Master Vance raised one eyebrow and shook his head. He reached down to open the strongbox at his feet and pulled out a twenty-dollar gold piece. 'For your loyalty,' Master Philip said as he pressed it in the overseer's hand."

Wash paused, raising one hand to run it back through his short hair. The picture of that parting was as clear in his mind as if it had been yesterday. And for some reason he was seeing things that he didn't recall having noticed at the time. Like the way Master Philip lifted his hand to run it back through his wavy brown hair as he stared at Mama as if he was trying to catch her eye. His wife glaring at him as he did so. And Mama keeping her gaze down toward Wash and his sister.

"What happened next?" Josh said.

Wash took a breath and shook his head. "Not that much," he said. "Master Philip looked over to where Daddy, straight and neat in his butler's uniform, was standing next to Mama while we two children looked out from behind her skirts. 'Washington,' Master

Philip said, his voice slow and careful, 'I thank you for your years of service, you...and your good wife.' Then, thankful or not, Master Vance did not hand a gold piece to my daddy. Nor did my daddy smile or say anything back. He just held harder on to Mama's hand and stood there like that, until Master Philip looked at the time on that watch of his that always hung by a gold chain from his vest. Oh—my Lord!"

Wash looked down at his hand as if he was holding that watch. The realization that had just come to him took the air out of him as if he had been hit in the gut.

"What is it? Josh said. "You all right, Wash?"

"They said it was Yankees killed the Vances on the road and stole their gold," Wash said slowly, his memories putting things together in a way they never had been before. And it all made such sense.

The Vances had been gone for no more than a few hours before Mister Tom had ordered them all to assemble in front of the Big House. "Now all you," the skinny overseer had said, "you all listen up here. You all stay right here and protek this here plantation on account of I'm a-going off to get help. I'll soon be a-coming back with a big Southern army to drive off and kill all those damn Yankees, and I will take real close notice of what you all done whilst I was gone. Now don't you be thinkin' about runnin' away to join them damn Yankees, neither. What they will do to you is a lot worse'n anything we ever done here, where we is kind and cares for your wants. Nossir. Them damn Yankees, they will starve you and they will hitch you to their wagons and make you pull them like you was oxen. That's if they don't shoot you or sell you off to Cuba or do wust things to you. They is all cowards, them damn Yankees, and they will run when us strong Southern white men come back at them. You all mark my words."

He might have said more, but then they'd all heard distant sounds like thunder. Yankee guns. Mister Tom had spurred his horse hard and galloped off in the opposite direction of those sounds of battle. Galloped off in the same direction the Vances had taken on their wagon, the sack over his back clanking from the silver candlesticks and tableware he'd taken from the dining room of the Big House. But Wash realized now that that had been only the start of the unfaithful overseer's stealing.

Just as he realized why his eyes had been drawn to the watch chain—that had once belonged to Master Vance—and the deadly eyes of that man on the train, the full beard disguising the mean, thin face of Mister Tom Key.

SWEET MEDICINE WAS GIVEN FOUR LIFETIMES
TO REMAIN WITH THE PEOPLE.

HE CHANGED WITH THE SEASONS.
EACH SPRING AND SUMMER HE GREW YOUNG
AND STRONG.
EACH AUTUMN AND WINTER, HE BECAME FEEBLE.
HIS HAIR TURNED WHITE AND HE ALMOST DIED.
OTHERS WERE BORN, GREW OLD, AND PASSED
AND STILL SWEET MEDICINE LIVED ON.

FOR FOUR LONG LIFETIMES, HE LIVED WITH THE PEOPLE.
BUT THEN THE DAY CAME WHEN SWEET MEDICINE KNEW
HIS TIME AMONG THE PEOPLE WAS DONE.

HE CALLED THEM ALL TOGETHER.
HEAR ME, HE SAID.
THEN HE TOLD THEM AGAIN THE GREAT STORY
OF HOW THE SPIRIT PEOPLE HAD TAUGHT HIM, AND
WHAT THE PEOPLE MUST DO
TO STAY STRONG AND SURVIVE.

THEN HE GREW VERY SAD.
HE TOOK UP HIS PIPE AND POINTED IT WEST,
NORTH, EAST, AND SOUTH, POINTED UP TO THE SKY
AND DOWN TO THE EARTH SO ALL THE SACRED BEINGS
MIGHT LISTEN AND HELP HIS PEOPLE UNDERSTAND.

HEAR MY VOICE, HE SAID. HEAR MY VOICE,
NEW PEOPLE YOU HAVE NEVER SEEN
ONE DAY SOON WILL COME AMONG YOU.

THEY WILL BE PALE PEOPLE WITH HAIR ON THEIR FACES,
THEIR DRESS WILL BE STRANGE, EVERYWHERE THEY GO
THEY WILL LOOK FOR CERTAIN STONES.

THEY WILL OFFER YOU GIFTS.
AT FIRST YOU WILL REFUSE THEM,
FOR THOSE GIFTS WILL BE BAD FOR
THE PEOPLE TO TAKE.
BUT THE TIME WILL COME WHEN YOU ACCEPT THEM.

THESE NEW PEOPLE WILL KILL ALL THE BUFFALO,
ALL THE ANIMALS THAT HELP US TO SURVIVE.
THEY WILL NEVER BE TIRED OR SATISFIED.
THEY WILL GO EVERYWHERE, OVER ALL OF OUR LAND.

THE WASHITA

Camp Supply,
Indian Territory
August 1, 1872

Dear Mother,

I hope all is well. It is very hot here. It is hotter than any hot day in Virginia. It is so hot that it is hard to think, but it has been a little while since I have written to you, so despite the oppressive heat, I have taken pen in hand.

I am not complaining. Unlike some here, I am very happy to be a soldier. I now have a fine horse, the finest in all of the company, I believe. I have also met one Indian who is something like a friend to me. He is one of our scouts and his name is Baptist John. As you might expect, he is a Christian.

I have been thinking lately of what life was like during the days when we were owned by the Vances. Even though they were slave owners, they did not treat us that badly as I recall. But I would never again wish to be a slave. That is why Daddy did as he did and gave his life to fight for our freedom.

I have met a young woman here who seems to be a very admirable person. She reminds me of you and of my sister. She is very lovely but also seems to be a strong person. Just like you and Pegatha. She is the niece of our sergeant and is working at Camp Supply, as do a number of respectable women, doing housework for the families of our white officers.

Still no action here. My friend Charley says it is boring, but my friend Josh says that it is good luck.

I am rather going on in this missive. I have not asked how you all are doing. Has the money I sent home reached you? I know you received one payment but two more should have come to you by now.

I trust that Pegatha continues her studies. Hello, sister! Have the crops been good? I know that this letter will reach you at harvest time. Is Mr. Mack still assisting? Tell him that, as the head of our little household, I extend my sincere thanks for his help.

I send my love and warm wishes and await your next letter.

Your loving and obedient son,
Washington Vance

Hot as Hades, Wash thought.

He lowered his chin and pulled down the brim of his hat as yet another gust of wind whipped up dust from the plain, throwing it back into the faces of the twenty men in the column.

"Does it ever cool off round here?" Wash asked as Josh brought his horse up between him and Charley. The three of them surveyed the hazy landscape ahead of them, where dust devils chased each other back and forth. Two days of riding and all they had seen was dust and more dust. Having crossed the Canadian River some ten miles back, they were now far south of Camp Supply, which was located at the northwest edge of the big reservation that had been set up for the three thousand Cheyennes and Arapahos. Five million acres between the Cimarron and Arkansas River was supposed to be theirs. Now, though, the Indians were not allowed make free use of it, having been ordered to stay close to the Darlington Agency, southeast of Camp Supply. Keeping the Indians from leaving the confines of the agency was one of the reasons for their patrol through this dry, deserted land.

"You all jes' wait till January," Josh replied, a rueful chuckle in his voice. "There will be plenty of cold then. Near cold as the North Pole. Snow will do a fine job then of replacing this here dust so as you can freeze and choke at the same time."

"Hah," Charley snorted. "Hard to believe it has ever been cold here. Hotter'n any August back home in Virginny. I feel like a strip of bacon in Lucifer's frying pan."

"Here come the lieutenant," Josh said. "Look sharp."

Wash looked back down the column. Sure enough, it was their commander, Lieutenant Richard Pratt. His sharp eyes, staring like those of a hunting hawk out of his scarred, rugged face, seemed to take in everything around them as he approached.

The three men saluted, but Lieutenant Pratt paid their gesture no mind as he reined in his horse and leaned in their direction.

"Drought," the lieutenant said. "It does make this land seem at times like the Valley of Dry Bones, does it not, men?"

More like Jeremiah, Chapter Fourteen, Verse Four, Wash thought. But all he said out loud was "Yes, sir, it does!" as the wind kicked up in the little dip in the ground ahead of them—as if to illustrate those lines from the Good Book that Wash had pretty much memorized from cover to cover.

Lieutenant Pratt nodded, his face so close that his hooked nose was almost touching Wash's cheek. Unlike most of the white officers, Wash had noticed, Pratt always spoke to his colored soldiers as if they were men and not monkeys. And when he spoke to them, he called them "men," a word some white troopers never used when addressing anyone with dark skin—even a fellow solider.

"Buffalo wallow down there," Pratt said, pointing. "Can you imagine what it was like to see them rolling there?" He shook his head. "No, imagination is the only place we are like to see such a sight. No buffalo here now. The hide hunters have killed so many that those great beasts are scarce as hens' teeth. Years past, this land was black with herds so big it might take a day for them all to pass at full gallop." He waved his hand in a wide circle. "When there were buffalo, our Indians did not have to come in for supplies. They lived off the meat and used the hides to purchase trade goods."

Lieutenant Pratt wiped sweat off his long nose with the back of his gauntlet and sighed. "When this dry weather began back in '53," he observed, "it could not have come at a worse time for the tribes. Water holes and streams drying up or being claimed by white home-steaders. Cattle are now eating up the forage that the buffalo herds depend upon. A perfect recipe for conflict."

"Yes, sir," Wash agreed, thinking to himself as he did so that not only was their lieutenant a man who did not mind talking to his col-ored troops, he was also a man who surely liked to hear himself talk.

Pratt nodded. "Indeed," he said. "And so, now that their buffalo herds have grown thin or gone entirely, the only nourishment our Indians may obtain is what the agencies dole out to them. It does not make them happy, most especially when those promised rations are scant or late, which of late they always are. Our aborigines are also far from pleased about the white desperadoes who regularly steal our Indians' horses and drive them up to Kansas. To add to the poor Indian's displeasure, the buffalo hunters from Dodge City have again begun poaching on his lands, despite our best efforts to exclude them. It may not be long before the hunters wipe out what few buffalo are left, despite the fact that no white men are supposed to venture south of the Arkansas River. Then, to add the icing to the cake, the whiskey traders come in with their helpful wares." Pratt shook his head sadly.

"One of the main tasks we cavalrymen from Camp Supply have is to protect the reservation from the bad influences of white men. Worst are the whiskey dealers. Bringing in big wagons loaded with clanking bottles and thumping barrels of cheap whiskey—mixed with gunpowder and turpentine. There is an endless supply of that rotgut whiskey, and our Indians provide an endless demand. They will even trade their ponies and mules and buffalo robes for that whiskey when they do not have enough food to eat. Add to that the sad fact that the whiskey dealers are constantly selling our Indians guns and pistols and ammunition, surplus left over from the Civil War. When our poor savages are intoxicated, they fall into senseless arguments and stab and shoot one another."

Interesting, Wash thought. *So instead of fighting Indians, we men of the 10th are now supposed to save them.*

Wash looked up at the long-nosed lieutenant, who seemed lost in thought. Yet and still, Wash had to admit to himself, superior though his tone of voice might be, the lieutenant's unprejudiced attitude applied as much to the colored troopers as it did to the Indians. Being able to see a man as a man and not just judge him by the color of his skin made Pratt far different from most other white men.

Pratt stirred from his reverie with a long sigh. "Alas," he said. "Too little food, too many horse thieves, too few buffalo, and too much whiskey make a witches' brew."

"Double, double toil and trouble," Wash said out loud before he could stop himself.

Pratt leaned back and looked hard at Wash.

"What was that, trooper?"

"Nothing, sir."

"No, that was from the Scottish play, was it not?"

Caught, Wash thought, *but at least it is by a white man who may not resent me for being uppity enough to educate myself a little.* So he nodded. "Yes, sir."

"You know the Bard's plays?"

"I know a bit of Shakespeare, sir."

"Ah. At some point in the not too distant future," Lieutenant Pratt said, "we must talk."

"Yes, sir," Wash answered. *And at some point in the not too distant future I must learn to keep my mouth shut.*

Pratt pulled back on his reins to wheel his horse as he raised his right arm.

"Move out," he shouted.

More clopping along through the wind and the dust with it. Wash pulled his bandanna over his mouth and returned to humming his great-grandfather's song beneath his breath.

Fodio-lay, Gunba
Gaban-gari, Kanta.

But even as he sang that song he couldn't keep from thinking. Quieting his mind was a trick he had never learned. And this time his thoughts returned to the home he had left behind, to the place where he had learned to read from a father who defied the rules that forbade slaves to become literate. The place where he had, indeed, read and loved the plays of William Shakespeare, the Bard of Avon.

In his mind he saw himself again in the little cabin his family had occupied behind the Vances' Big House. The best thing about that one-room shack was that it had a shelf with no fewer than eight books on it. They hadn't always been there. They came from the Big House, where his mama was cook and his daddy was butler. When the Vances ran off, the first thing Wash's father had done was rescue his favorite books from that library. The collected works of Milton and the collected plays of Shakespeare, the *Lives of the Saints,* the Greek myths, Plato, *Le Morte d'Arthur, Beowulf,* and the Bible.

"Wash."

Josh Hopkins had brought his black horse up next to Wash's. Like Wash, he now had his neckerchief tied up over his mouth and nose. Not that it helped much.

"Well," Josh coughed, "ain't hardly no need for us to eat tonight. I figures we both gonna gain about ten pounds with all this dust we eating."

Wash nodded. Opening his mouth would mean swallowing more of the dirt caked on his face.

I imagine I now appear more red than a Cheyenne, he thought.

Josh pointed down toward a small ribbon of water barely visible in the dust-filled wind.

"Know what that is yonder?"

Wash shook his head.

"Been this way once before. Recognize that hill and the way the stream it bends here. That is the Washita. Where Custer whupped them Cheyennes to a fine fare-thee-well in November of '68. I surely would have liked to have been there."

Josh started to chuckle, a chuckle that turned into a hacking cough. He spat out a dust-flecked glob of phlegm. "'Course," he continued, leaning close so that Wash could hear him over the wind, "there is not a snowball's chance in hell that I or any other colored man could have ever been riding among Custer's 7th Cavalry—unless he was a cook or laborer of some sort in the following supply wagons."

Wash nodded. He had not been with the 10th more than a week before he began to hear Custer stories. How the colonel had threatened to resign his commission when they attempted to put him in charge of colored troops. How his wife was even worse, threatening to shoot any negro soldier that came within fifty yards of her home. Colonel George Armstrong Custer—one of a good many white officers who believed they knew a colored man's rightful place. If such men as Custer had their way, every negro soldier would have his gun and uniform and horse taken away.

"Camp Supply," Josh said. "It was built for old Massa George. It was from our very own Camp Supply that he set out to attack those Cheyennes here on the Washita."

"Custer!" Wash said, shaking his head. "Custer," he said a second time, just as the wind died down a bit so that the colonel's name went echoing out across the land. Just then Wash thought he heard something. Something other than the howling wind.

"Did you hear that?" he asked.

"Huh?" Josh said

They scanned the land around them. Numerous small bushes that appeared to have been born dead, and below them, on the other side of the nearly dry streambed, a line of small stunted cottonwood trees, limbs lifted up like defeated enemies trying to surrender.

"Did you hear a wildcat or some such creature growl?" Wash asked.

Josh shook his head. "Don't you let that imagination of yours carry you off. Ain't nothin' here but old Indian ghosts."

A shiver went down Wash's spine. Then he nodded. The two men rode at a slow trot down the hill. The hooves of their horses cracked through the eggshell-dry surface of the thick gumbo mud, then splashed through into water that rose up to their fetlocks. There was a flash of silver as a long-bodied fish twisted out from under the hooves. A few more steps and they were up and out of the creek, beginning to pass through the little cottonwoods. Though the trees had seemed dead from a distance, close up it could be seen that they were alive enough to hold on to a few green leaves that shook as a hot breeze, like the exhaled breath of a giant creature, washed over them.

They reached the hilltop and came in sight of the rest of the company, which had reached the other side before them. As they rode down the hill, Wash untied his bandanna to shake out some of the red dust that had coated it.

"Look there," Charley yelled, pointing behind them to their left and reaching for his rifle. Something brown and quick had leaped up and was running out of the clump of rabbitbrush below Blaze's feet.

I'm about to get shot or stuck by an arrow, Wash thought.

Pulling at his reins with one hand and grabbing for his gun with the other, Wash let go of his bandanna, which was taken by the wind to go flying up and over the hill.

"Whoa up, son!" a voice shouted.

Wash turned to look. Sergeant Brown, of course.

"Don't go shooting that muley," the sergeant said, amusement in his voice. "It never done nothing to you."

Wash dropped his gun back into its scabbard, feeling like every kind of fool in the book. The big mule deer he'd spooked from its hiding place leapt up over the hill and disappeared from sight.

Probably not an Indian within ten miles of us, Wash thought.

The dust was thick. The bush Wolf lay behind was no bigger than a war shield. But because of the dust, he was sure the troop of bluecoat soldiers could not see him. He could see them well, though. Their leader was a tall, hook-nosed soldier chief. A second white man rode by his side. The other sixteen were all black white men. Buffalo Soldiers.

Some of those brown-skinned bluecoats had eyes keener than those of their white leaders. So Wolf had heard. That did not worry him. Even a five-winters-old child of the Real People could still see twice as well as they could.

What troubled him now was not the ve'hoe soldiers. What made him feel ill at ease was this place. It had once been a favored place for the Cheyennes to set up camp with their brother friends, the Cloud People. Now it was inhabited only by the memory of death. No one had stayed here since the coward's raid, the raid on their peaceful camp led by Long Hair Custer. It had not mattered that they had flown an American flag above their lodges.

Wolf had intended to stay farther to the east. But the deer had led him here. It was the only large game animal whose tracks he'd been able to find after days of hunting. He had finally gotten almost close enough to try to bring it down with an arrow. Then the deer had raised its head in alarm and looked away from him. Wolf had lowered his bow. As the deer bolted over a hill, he had taken shelter behind that friendly bush.

Soon, he thought, *soon they will move on.*

Then he began to hear something. Was it real? Or was it one of the bad dreams that came to trouble him every night? Was one of those dreams somehow finding him in the half light of this dusty day? It was a faint, distant sound at first. Then it came closer. It grew louder. It was so loud that he thought surely the ve'hoe soldiers must also hear it. The despairing voices of dying women and children swirled in the red wind around him. The dust began to take on human shapes. People falling in front of their lodges as the hail of bullets struck them.

Then he heard his mother's voice. It seemed as close and real as it had been on that day. "Run, my son, run."

He did not run. His legs trembled. He forced them not to lift him up into the view of the ve'hoe soldiers. Those men would surely shoot him. *No*, he said in his mind to the treacherous vision. *No. I will not run. I will not join you. I will not allow you to kill me.*

He tried to think of other things as the ghost voices continued to urge him into flight. He thought of the preparations he had made for hunt. He had made a small fire. He had cleansed himself with sage smoke. He had prayed to the spirits of the game animals. He had asked that one of them might give itself. An antelope, a deer, a buffalo. Give itself to him so that his family might survive. The big mule deer had answered that prayer. It had walked out of the cottonwoods. Before the soldiers came, it had been about to offer itself. That deer. Its gift. The preparations he had made. The ghost voices began to fade. Though the red wind still swirled, the sounds and shapes were gone.

"Thank you," he whispered.

The game animals were protecting him. Their spirits had been helping him all along. They had sent him a deer rather than a buffalo. If it had been a buffalo he would have been on horseback. Buffalo will allow a man using a bow and arrows to ride up to them. But deer are more wary. To hunt them, you must dismount. So he had left his horse three hills back. The bluecoats were poor at seeing anything in front of them but their own big noses. But a hunter on horseback would have been hard for even them to miss.

"Thank you," he whispered a second time.

The wind was quieting down now. Three of the mounted black ve'hoe soldiers were so near that he could hear their words. Wolf had learned some English at the agency. Perhaps he could understand some of what they said. He listened closely. They were talking about a battle. Then the smallest black white man said a word that Wolf understood very well. It was a name he hated.

Custer.

In spite of himself, a low growl escaped from Wolf's throat. He bit his lip back into silence. The smallest brown bluecoat cocked his head. He put one hand over his forehead to shade his eyes. He squinted and looked hard. His gaze swept over Wolf's hiding place without stopping. Then he kicked his heels into the side of his big black horse. He and the others continued on down toward the creek.

Wolf watched as the ve'hoe soldiers quickly crossed the nearly dry creek and went up the buffalo trail that led up the hill. They seemed as eager to leave this place as he was. Did they, too, feel the presence of the dead? Could they see and hear those slaughtered innocent ones? Might they feel some shame about what was done here? The small Buffalo Soldier who mentioned the name of Yellow Hair had sounded angry.

Yellow Hair Custer, Wolf thought. *You brought death to our peaceful village. You attacked our seventy-five lodges set up here near the Big Sandy. Around that bend, my grandfather and grandmother died.*

Wolf's thoughts of Yellow Hair were interrupted. Hooves were coming his way. He nocked an arrow to his bowstring. As he did so, a gust of wind came over the hill. It carried with it a yellow neck cloth. The cloth twirled and danced in the air and then landed at his feet. He did not pick it up right away. It was followed by the one whose hooves he had heard.

The mule deer had crested the hill. It had come down and stopped by the creek bed. It was no farther from him than a strong man could hurl a lance. It was a large young buck, one with much meat to give. Its side was toward Wolf, its head up.

"Thank you for the gift of your life," Wolf whispered. "My family and I will eat."

He let fly his arrow.

MY MAMA ALWAYS SAID, "CHILDREN, YOU SHARE WHAT YOU GOT AND YOU WILL SURE HAVE ENOUGH."

THERE WAS A RICH MAN WHO WENT UP TO HEAVEN, SURE THAT A FINE FELLOW SUCH AS HIM WOULD BE WELCOMED IN. GOD AND SAINT PETER STOPPED THE MAN AT THE PEARLY GATES.

"I HAVE COME TO GO TO HEAVEN," THE RICH MAN SAYS.

"MMM-HMM," GOD SAYS. "WHAT HAVE YOU DONE FOR YOUR NEIGHBOR?"

THE RICH MAN, HE HAS TO THINK SOME ABOUT THAT. "WELL, HE SAYS, "ONCE I SEEN A LITTLE BOY CRYING. I ASKED HIM WHAT WAS WRONG AND THAT LITTLE BOY SAID HE HAD LOST HIS NICKEL AND IT WAS ALL THE MONEY HE HAD IN THE WORLD AND HE WAS GOING TO USE THAT NICKEL TO BUY BREAD FOR HIS HUNGRY LITTLE BROTHERS AND SISTERS. SO I REACHED RIGHT INTO MY POCKET AND PULLED OUT A BIG HANDFUL OF MONEY AND I COUNTED OUT THREE WHOLE PENNIES AND I GAVE THAT LITTLE BOY THAT THREE CENTS."

"HMM. LOOK THAT UP IN THE GREAT BOOK OF GOOD DEEDS," GOD SAYS TO SAINT PETER.

SO SAINT PETER, HE DOES THAT. IT TAKES HIM SOME TIME, BUT FINALLY HE SAYS, "YES, THAT IS RIGHT. IT SAYS RIGHT HERE HE GAVE THAT LITTLE BOY THREE CENTS."

"MMM-HMM," GOD SAYS TO THE RICH MAN. "IS THERE ANYTHING ELSE YOU HAVE DONE?"

THAT RICH MAN, HE REALLY HAS TO THINK NOW. BUT THEN HE SNAPS HIS FINGERS AND SMILES. "YES, THERE IS. I ONCE COME ACROSS A LITTLE GIRL CRYING. WHEN I ASKED HER WHAT WAS WRONG SHE SAID THAT SHE, TOO, HAD LOST A NICKEL. AND SHE WAS GOING TO

USE THAT NICKEL TO BUY MEDICINE FOR HER SICK OLD MOTHER. SO I REACHED RIGHT INTO MY POCKET AND PULLED OUT A HANDFUL OF CHANGE AND GAVE THAT LITTLE GIRL TWO PENNIES."

"PETER," GOD SAYS, "CAN YOU FIND THAT IN THE GREAT BOOK OF GOOD DEEDS?"

THIS TIME IT DON'T TAKE OLD SAINT PETER NO TIME AT ALL.

"YES, SIR," SAINT PETER SAYS. "IT SAYS RIGHT HERE THAT HE GAVE THAT LITTLE GIRL TWO CENTS."

"MMM-HMM. ANYTHING ELSE?" GOD ASKS.

"NO SIR," SAINT PETER SAYS. "THOSE ARE THE ONLY TWO GOOD DEEDS THAT MAN EVER DONE FOR HIS NEIGHBOR."

GOD, HE TURNS TO THAT RICH MAN AND NODS HIS HEAD.

"SON, I GOT HAVE SOME BAD NEWS AND SOME GOOD NEWS FOR YOU," GOD SAYS. "BAD NEWS IS THAT YOU ARE NOT COMING IN THROUGH THESE PEARLY GATES. GOOD NEWS IS THAT YOU ARE GOING TO GET BACK YOUR NICKEL. IT IS WAITING FOR YOU DOWN IN HELL."

PRACTICE

Camp Supply,
Indian Territory
September 1, 1872

Dear Mother,

I hope all is well. I am learning something new every day. I think I am well suited for this life, though I miss you and Pegatha very much.

I have not heard from you for some time. I hope that Pegatha is continuing her studies with diligence. Diligence is the key, little sister.

Pegatha, you do not need to read this paragraph to our mother. Please know I am counting on you to see that she takes care of herself. Our mother is always thinking of others so much that I fear she may neglect her own health and happiness. Please do this for me.

Your loving brother and son,
Washington

"Can't I hold the gun this way?" Wash asked.

"No!" Sergeant Brown said, reaching down to adjust Wash's hands on the rifle. "Show me a soldier with an original idea, I show you a man wants to be dead." He pressed one palm on Wash's back. "Down lower on your belly. That's it. Prop up the rifle just so. And remember, breathe in once, then out, take careful aim, press and not jerk at the trigger, then pull through. But count to ten before you shoot. That way you make every shot count."

Count every shot, too, Wash thought.

Unlike in the Great War of Emancipation, where the Union had more guns and ammunition than you could shake a stick at, the new army of the western frontier had to watch every penny. That was one reason why they had the new Springfield .45 carbines that fired just one shot at a time before you had to reload. The Spencer repeating carbines that the army had stopped using a year ago were the sort of guns that encouraged a soldier to waste bullets.

As did the Indians, who wasted their bullets as freely as if they were water. Thanks to the whiskey traders and the gun runners, the Comanches and Kiowas, Arapahos and Cheyennes now owned not only much ammunition, but also all sorts of small arms left over from the war. They had .50 caliber Spencers that could fire seven shots before reloading and .44 caliber Winchesters and Henrys holding up to sixteen rounds.

"When a passel of them well-armed Indians come charging at you with repeating rifles," Josh had explained, "it is near like the Fourth of July. Bammity-bam, bam, bam." Then Josh had let loose one of his deep throaty chuckles. "But most of them shots is fired so high you might think they were making war on the sky. Amongst our Indians, putting on a good show is more important than killing enemies. War's more like playing tag than our idea of fighting. They would ten times rather hit you with one of their coup sticks or be the first to touch an enemy—live or dead—with their hand than put a bullet into him."

Wash thought about Josh's words as he took careful aim again. Somehow they hadn't reassured him that much. He had yet to see any sort of battle—unless you counted the war every man waged against the bedbugs and fleas that counted coup on the soldiers' poor itchy carcasses every night. What would it really be like when someone was charging at him shooting a weapon that held ten times as many shots as his own? He held back a sigh. All he could do now was try to follow the sergeant's instructions, especially with Brown leaning over his back and watching him like a hawk hovering over a henhouse.

Breathe in, then out. Steady. Pull through.

Pow! he felt the kick of the gun against his shoulder.

"Good shot," Sergeant Brown said in his preacher's voice. "Son, you have got a good eye. Man who can hit the enemy with one shot from three hunnad yards away is a man who wins battles. Umm-hmmm. Even when outnumbered ten to one. Which we may expect to be."

Wash nodded without looking up as he reloaded. Out of the corner of his eye he could see the line of other men practicing. Most of them were doing like Wash and trying their best, even though he'd noted that no one was hitting the dead center as often as he was. One at the far end of the line, though, showed little interest in target practice, not even looking at the target when he pulled the trigger. Only when Sergeant Brown was watching did he make any real effort.

Private Landrieu Jefferson.

If he wasn't valuable as the company bugler, Wash thought, *I suspect he would be in the guardhouse right now.*

It was plain to everyone that Landrieu Jefferson had a lackadaisical attitude about everything except eating and drinking. The man was the biggest chow-mouth at the post, always wanting more than his share. There was one other thing he was good at: bragging about his conquests. The way he spoke about the ladies bothered Wash. Wash had been brought up by parents who demanded that he be a true gentleman and show respect for everyone, especially those of the fairer sex. No gentleman would ever say such things as Landrieu did, even if it was likely that the only women he had actually known were those he'd paid for their favors. But he had a fine opinion of himself and clearly imagined that others must feel only either admiration or envy when they saw him.

You can see that in the way he behaves whenever he catches sight of Bethany, Wash thought. *Acts as if he is the cock of the walk. Strutting and puffing his chest out.*

But Bethany had paid no mind to Private Landrieu Jefferson, aside from walking away from him—and patting her hair for some reason—whenever he came anywhere near her. The thought of that made Wash smile. Then he shook his head.

Pay attention to what you are doing, Wash. You will be the kind of soldier Sergeant Brown wants you to be. Take every word he says as the gospel truth. Keep your mouth shut. Practice and then practice some more. And when the time comes, make every shot count.

Wolf's mother smiled as she and his sister cut up the big deer.

He was tired. There was a good feeling inside him. There was enough meat on this deer to feed his family for a week. But it would not last that long. They would share its meat with those too old and weak to provide for themselves. During the days he had been gone, no rations had been given out. Wolf's deer was the only food any of them would have for a while.

"The ve'hoe soldiers are patrolling more often?" his mother asked.

She and his sister pulled the skin from the deer. It made a popping noise as the hide separated from the muscles.

Wolf nodded. "But their eyes are still blind."

His little sister laughed. "My brother is the best hunter. He is truly a wolf!"

Wolf grinned back at her.

But it is not as easy as I make it out to be. I came too close to being discovered by the bluecoats. But I must continue to take this risk. That is what it means to be a man. The life of a hunter or a defender of our people is never without danger.

Wolf's mother nodded.

She always seems to know what I am thinking.

"My son," she said, amusement in her voice. "You've done well. You have come a long way from the first time when you went out to take horses. Remember?"

Wolf nodded.

It was just like his mother to mix teasing in with praise. She was reminding him to remain humble by bringing back that memory.

It was the first time he had tried. He did not do so alone. He went with his four best friends, Dirty Face, Skinny Legs, Cougher, and Eats Fat. They all agreed that he should lead their party. Even though he was the littlest of them, he was the best wrestler. He also had the best weapons. They assembled under the big cottonwood.

"Now we go to take horses," he had said to them. "Taking horses is an honorable thing to do. We must make our way quietly into the enemy camp. The owners of those horses are more numerous and stronger than us. They will be vigilant and keeping watch against thieves."

"Uh-huh," Dirty Face said, nodding his head seriously.

"It will not be easy," Skinny Legs said.

"If this was easy," Wolf said, "it would not be worth doing. Accomplishing something hard makes people praise your success. When we were little children we heard stories told by our uncles and fathers. They told how they led raids on such enemies as the Pawnees and the Crows. They told how they sneaked in under the cover of dark. They cut the best horses from the herds. They vanished into the night with their prizes. How they did this?" Wolf paused. "Do you know the story of how Pawnee Killer got his best horse?"

"Yes," Eats Fat said.

Skinny Legs glared at Eats Fat, motioning for him to be quiet. "Tell us the story," Skinny Legs said.

"Yes," Cougher agreed. "Tell us."

Wolf nodded. "It was a great deed. Pawnee Killer crawled into the center of the Crow camp. There the leader of the Crow Warriors Society had his lodge. That man's best horse was a beautiful broad-chested roan. It was tied to a rope that led right back to its sleeping owner's wrist. Pawnee Killer undid that rope without waking the man. Then he fastened that rope to a large white dog sleeping next to the tipi. That was a great joke. It was also a sign of the power of his horse-taking medicine. To slip into a hostile camp and not be barked at by the dogs was amazing."

"Powerful," Skinny Legs said.

"Such a deed will make a man's name remembered," Cougher said.

Eats Fat said nothing. But when Skinny Legs poked him in the side, he nodded his head.

So the five of them had been ready to set out. But not before two more tried to join them.

Those two were twin brothers, alike in looks and dress. Too Tall and Too Short. No one could really tell them apart. Thus their nicknames were a good joke. Too Short and Too Tall were not fond of their nicknames. But there was nothing they could do about it until they earned or were given better ones. Everyone thought that might not be soon. The joke was that the brothers had only half a brain between the two of them.

"Take us with you," one of the brothers said. Probably Too Tall. He usually spoke first.

The others in the raiding party looked to Wolf for a decision. He did not hesitate.

"No," he said. "Not two, only one."

"Why?" both asked at the same time.

Wolf made a circle with his hand. "Count how many of us are here."

The brothers counted, using their fingers to do so. It was a slow process.

"Six," the one who was probably Too Tall finally said.

"Six," his brother agreed.

Wolf sighed. "Each of you, count yourself as well."

"Oh," both brothers said. "Seven."

Wolf nodded and for emphasis made the hand sign for yes. Seven. As all Cheyennes knew, that was a very unlucky number for raiding or going off to war. Seven people could spoil their luck.

In the end, neither of the brothers went along. They were not talented at thinking, but they were loyal to each other.

At first all went well. The five raiders had blackened their faces so that they would not be seen in the night. They had crept on their bellies, only a finger's width at a time, closer and closer to their objective. No one had seemed to take any notice of them. Wolf had almost laughed at how easy it was. Because he was the leader, he was the first to try to take his prize.

But as soon as he reached for the one he had chosen, strong fingers closed on his wrist.

"Ah!"

He could hear his companions running away back behind the lodges.

"Short Legs," his mother had said, "leave that meat on the drying rack."

Wolf smiled at the memory of how he and his faithless companions had failed. None of them had gotten in trouble, though. What they had done was expected of them. It was one way a group of six-winters-old boys could practice the skills of stealth. One day they would need such skills when the horses they tried to take were real ones and not pieces of dried buffalo meat.

"Here," Wolf's mother said. Her voice brought him back to the present.

"Hahoo."

He looked at the fine piece of meat she had thrust out toward him on a sharpened stick. The lines of fat in the venison sizzled. It smelled wonderful.

"I do not need that much."

His mother shook her head. "No, you must eat and stay strong."

Wolf nodded. *She is right,* he thought. *I feel weak and tired. Food in my belly will help me stay awake. Dirty Face has the job tonight of guarding our horse herd. I have promised to help him.*

OLD MASTER PRIDED HIMSELF ON BEING THE SMARTEST MAN
AROUND. HE HAD BEEN OFF TO SCHOOL AND KNEW FOR A FACT
THAT HE HAD BEEN THE SMARTEST MAN THERE.

HE RECKONED THERE WAS NO MAN ALIVE WHO COULD ASK HIM
A QUESTION ABOUT READING OR WRITING OR ARITHMETIC THAT
HE COULD NOT ANSWER.

SO OLD MASTER SAID TO HIS SLAVES, "IF ANY ONE OF
YOU CAN STUMP ME, ASK ME A QUESTION THAT I CANNOT
ANSWER, THEN I WILL SET THAT MAN FREE."

THAT WAS WHEN JOHN SPOKE UP.

"MASTER," HE SAID, "YOU GIVE YOUR WORD ABOUT THAT?"

"I AM A MAN OF MY WORD," OLD MASTER SAID.

"IF I ASK YOU A QUESTION THAT YOU CANNOT ANSWER RIGHT,
WILL YOU SET ME AND MY WHOLE FAMILY FREE?"

OLD MASTER THOUGHT ABOUT THAT SOME.
JOHN HAD A BIG FAMILY, NIGH ONTO A DOZEN.
AND JOHN WAS KNOWN TO BE CLEVER.
BUT THERE WAS SURELY NO SLAVE WHO KNEW MORE THAN HE DID.

"YES," OLD MASTER SAID. "AS LONG AS IT IS A QUESTION ABOUT
READING OR WRITING OR ARITHMETIC, I WILL SET YOU AND YOUR
WHOLE FAMILY FREE IF I CANNOT ANSWER IT RIGHT. AND JUST TO
PROVE THAT I AM A MAN OF MY WORD, I WILL BRING THE JUDGE
ALONG WITH ME WHEN YOU ASK ME THAT QUESTION."

SO, THE NEXT DAY, OLD MASTER BROUGHT THE JUDGE OUT TO THE PLANTATION. HE CALLED ALL THE SLAVES TOGETHER, GLAD TO HAVE A CHANCE TO SHOW THEM JUST HOW SMART HE WAS. THAT WAY HE FIGURED THEY WOULD NOT TRY TO GET OUT OF DOING WORK OR PLAY ANY TRICKS ONCE THEY SAW HOW HE BEAT JOHN BY ANSWERING HIS QUESTIONS RIGHT.

"ALL RIGHT," HE SAID TO JOHN, "YOU ASK YOUR QUESTION."

"WELL, SIR," JOHN SAID, "I GUESS MY QUESTION IS ABOUT THAT ARITHMETIC. AND MY QUESTION IS THIS. IF THERE ARE TWENTY-SIX PIGEONS IN A TREE AND YOU SHOOT ONE, HOW MANY PIGEONS WILL BE LEFT IN THAT TREE?"

OLD MASTER LAUGHED. "THAT IS THE EASIEST QUESTION I HAVE EVER BEEN ASKED. IF YOU SHOOT ONE PIGEON, THERE WILL BE TWENTY-FIVE LEFT IN THAT TREE."

JOHN GRINNED. "NO SIR," HE SAID. "THAT IS NOT RIGHT. THERE WOULD NOT BE EVEN ONE LEFT. IF YOU SHOOT ONE PIGEON, THEN ALL THOSE OTHERS ARE SURE AS GLORY GOING TO FLY, FLY AWAY."

AND THAT WAS HOW JOHN AND HIS WHOLE FAMILY WAS SET FREE.

HORSE THIEVES

It had been a long ride from Camp Supply to the Darlington Agency. They'd traveled more than a hundred miles, farther than their patrol had planned to go. They'd been seventy miles from Camp Supply and about to circle back when the rider sent by the agent found them.

"Mr. John Miles...needs you...at Darlington," the rider gasped, wiping the dust from his face with a shaking hand. He was a young man, a Quaker like the agent and just come from the East. The miles he'd ridden had taken a toll on him. His lips quivered as he spoke, and he took a series of breaths before managing to deliver the rest of his message. "Horse thieves," he said, "drove off and stole the whole Cheyenne herd last night."

As they rode into the Cheyenne camp, slowing from a trot to a walk, Wash looked first one direction and then the other. Tipis set up in a big circle. Cooking fires burning in front of them. Everything here you would expect from an Indian camp except for horses. Not a one to be seen.

But plenty of Indians. All of them as silent as the grave.

And not eager to get close to the men of the 10th. Indian children running away like they'd seen the boogeyman. Women covering their heads with their blankets. Old folks going into their tipis and closing the flaps behind them. Even the men looking away. All except one.

The only one staring at them, at Wash in particular, was a tall young Indian man, wearing what looked exactly like a cavalry scarf around his neck. He was looking at Wash so hard it seemed as if he was trying to burn a hole with his eyes. Among the Plains people, Wash had learned by now, staring at someone that way is meant as a challenge. To be polite, you looked down at a man's feet.

Nossir, Wash thought. *You will not buffalo me.*

He looked right straight back at the tall Cheyenne. To Wash's surprise, the ghost of a smile came to the lanky Indian's face—to his lips, at least. But not his eyes. His eyes still looked angry.

Likely one of those who had his horse stolen, Wash thought. The young Indian followed them on foot as they proceeded out to where the herd had been grazing. *Now nary a horse in sight.*

Lieutenant Pratt slid off his horse. He walked over and held out his open hands to an old Cheyenne fellow, who nodded back politely. The old Indian was not dressed in buckskin. Like a good many of the other Cheyenne men around them, he was wearing an old gray cloth shirt, likely cast off by some white family back East and given to missionaries to be passed on to the Indians. He also had on a gray felt hat.

If not for his long hair and brown skin, Wash thought, *you mightn't know he was an Indian. Unless you looked below his waist, where he has got no pants on.*

Wash was unsurprised that none of the Cheyennes were painted up and wearing feathers like the noble savages on the covers of dime magazines. Back when he had first got to Camp Supply he had wondered if he was seeing any Indians at all. They'd appeared more like poor sun-tanned farmers.

As usual, Josh had been the first to explain it to him.

"Just as we puts ourselves in our best clothes when we goes to church, Indians get dressed up only for special occasions," Josh had chuckled. "And their most special occasions is when they goes to war."

As they had ridden through the camp, Wash had not been able see into the Cheyenne tipis. But he had no doubt that in every warrior's lodge was a box or a bag or whatever packed full of such apparel as would be needed to look fine for fighting. Eagle feather headdresses, buckskin shirts with designs of birds and arrows and such, and painted, beaded moccasins. Even war lances and quivers all decorated and made special to look their best when they rode into battle.

"But not beforehand," Josh had said. "When our Indians be on the way to make a fight, they carry all their necessaries in a bundle—like some salesman with a carpetbag of goods. They get close enough to where their enemies live, they dismounts from their horses and spends a good long time getting ready, putting on their finery, painting designs on their faces, braiding their hair just right. Even painting up their horses and braiding their tails and their manes. My, my! They look as pretty as a picture. A picture 'at might put an arrow through your heart. Lemme tell you, Wash," Josh added, "you see a pretty Indian comin' your way, best get out of the way."

Lieutenant Pratt was now using an interpreter to talk to the old Indian in the gray shirt and hat.

"Gray Head," Josh whispered in Wash's ear. "Big Cheyenne chief. And that interpreter is Mr. George Bent. Dressed like a white man, pants included. Father was a trader, but that dusky skin of his comes from his Cheyenne mother."

Wash watched as the lieutenant, the interpreter, and the chief spoke. Though he was too far away to hear more than a word or two, he watched the motions of the old man's hands acting out the events of the night before.

Last night, no moon. White men came, Gray Head signed.

As the old chief pointed out some of the hoof marks in the soft earth, Wash understood. The horse they rode wore shoes. So they were not Indians because Indian ponies were unshod.

Wash looked at the four Cheyenne youths now standing off to the side by the tall one wearing the bandanna. All five with arms folded, faces grim. Ready to light out after those white rustlers on foot. Track them down and come back not just with their horses but with seven scalps. That'd be a problem, seeing as how one of the jobs of the 10th was to prevent Indians from injuring white men, even horse thieves.

As Gray Head finished speaking, the Indian agent arrived. More talking. Agent John D. Miles gesturing at the five young men, shaking his head. The interpreter translating. Then Gray Head sighing and nodding.

A pleased look on his face, Lieutenant Pratt shook hands with the chief, the agent, and the interpreter and then walked over to Sergeant Brown, who had stood holding the reins of Pratt's horse and his own, patiently watching, a few feet in front of Wash and the other mounted members of the company.

"Chief Gray Head is in agreement," Lieutenant Pratt said, taking the reins and vaulting up into the saddle. "We men of the 10th shall pursue the horse thieves, and the Indians will not interfere with us."

As they rode out onto the wide treeless plain south of the Canadian River, Wash chanted his great-grandfather's riding song under his breath.

Fodio-lay, Gunba
Gaban-gari, Kanta.

Finally, he thought, *finally there's going to be some action.*

Something more than riding across a dusty plain seeing little more than hills and sky and stunted brush and trees. Folks might think the lot of a cavalryman was all action and danger. But they would be wrong. Wash now knew there was more drudgery and boredom than anything else in a cavalryman's life.

True, things did get a little exciting when a man discovered one of those big browns in his bunk—nasty eight-legged spider the size of your hand! Or found a prairie rattlesnake crawling into the tent. Or when a rabid wolf came drifting into the camp and started chasing everyone around, trying to bite them. That happened just last week. Josh had to take shelter up on top of the cookhouse, calling out for someone to shoot the damn critter. Which Wash did do, right between the eyes from forty yards away. And even though most everyone said it had been needful, Wash had then found himself trying to justify to Sergeant Brown the use of a perfectly good bullet. Though it had been Private Landrieu Jefferson who had ended up being ordered by the sergeant to carry the punishment log for one hour for daring to laugh at Wash's plight as he was being dressed down, and for an additional two hours for swearing when he was given his sentence.

Private Landrieu Jefferson. That man was a bad egg, for sure. Since the episode with Bethany, Wash had been keeping an eye on the man and found himself wondering how he ended up in the 10th. Aside from his bugle playing, it was hard to see how he was of any use. Six foot tall, lantern-jawed, loud-mouthed, and the lightest-skin man in the company. Narrow shoulders, but with a belly that made up for it. Ate more sugar and drank more coffee than any other man in the company. Lazy, greedy, self-centered, and a bully. The definition of a coffee cooler, slang in the 10th for a lazy trooper. If there was ever a person not made for this sort of life, it was the big Creole. And he was proving it more every day.

Wash looked up ahead to where their head Osage tracker was conferring with Lieutenant Pratt, indicating the direction they should go. Old Landrieu Jefferson had just reined up close to them, holding his bugle in his hands. Trying to look important, hoping to be asked to sound that bugle. As if they would want to announce their approach to a band of horse thieves!

The lieutenant shook his head, motioning for Landrieu to fall back and put his bugle away. Landrieu yanked angrily at his rein, a poisonous look on his face. But he wheeled his horse wide before he passed Wash, turning the bruised side of his face away.

Wash still kept an eye on the man—the one person in Company D he did not want behind him if a shooting fight took place. Bullets were been known to go astray during a battle. Though Jefferson was avoiding him now, Wash had no doubt that what had happened between them two days before was far from forgotten.

"You not going to eat that, eh, little man?" Landrieu had been looking at Wash over the top of his third cup of coffee loaded with sugar, his New Orleans drawl more sneer than question. He'd plainly expected Wash, being half his size, to hand over the food he had just started to eat. Instead, Wash stood up with his mess tray and walked away from the big Creole without a word or a backward glance.

It hadn't pleased Landrieu to be ignored. So the next evening, when he saw Wash and his friends Josh and Charley about to sit down together, Charley taking out a deck of cards, he had immediately ambled over.

"I play a hand or two, eh?" Landrieu said, shoving himself down onto the nail keg upon which Wash had been about to sit.

Charley raised an eyebrow, but Wash merely stepped back and nodded his head.

"Well," Charley said, scratching his forehead, "I allow that there's room for you here. And seein' as how this is jes' a friendly game for nickels and dimes and whatnot, it won't do no harm."

It took little longer than two shakes of a lamb's tail for Landrieu to realize that Charley was not the hayseed he played himself up to be. Half an hour later, the New Orleans sharper had been cleaned out of every cent in his pocket.

Wash had not been able to hide the smile on his face as Landrieu stood up, kicked the nail keg over, and walked off without a word.

"Watch out for him, Wash," Charley whispered as Landrieu disappeared into his tent. "That Creole man is a mean one. I might have taken his money, but it's you he has got it in for."

"I reckon so," Wash replied.

"You know that he is carrying a straight razor in his right back pocket?" Josh asked.

"I do now," Wash nodded.

Early the next morning Wash had gone looking for something he remembered seeing. Turned out it was right where he had observed it, just outside the stable. He picked it up. It fit fine into his sleeve, and he carried it throughout the day, even though he knew that whatever trouble Landrieu had in mind for him would not likely occur till after taps.

Wash sat down in front of the tent he shared with Josh and Charley. *Soon*, he thought. He could feel the moment coming.

Sure enough. The torches had just been lit when Wash saw Private Landrieu Jefferson heading straight for him like a fox that had sighted a rabbit.

"Little man," he snarled. "No one laugh at me."

"Take it back of the barracks," Wash said, standing up and walking quickly away from the big man. Camp Supply was built in a square, and the troopers billeted outside in tents. The doors and windows on the officers' quarters inside all faced into the square. Once the officers retired for the night, they neither saw nor cared much about what went on among the enlisted men outside. Back of the barracks was where enlisted men went when they wanted to settle something between themselves.

As soon as they reached that spot, where just enough light made it possible for the men to see each other, Wash turned around.

"Now," Jefferson said, "we fight fair. No weapons, eh?"

But halfway through saying that, the lanky Creole swung the arm that he had been holding behind his back in a wide arc. The glint of light off the blade of the razor showed Wash that what was coming toward him was not just a punch. Landrieu meant to cut him badly. Wash stepped back, throwing his arm up so that the razor sliced into his sleeve. It could have been a fool move, the razor cutting right through the cloth and opening up an artery. But it did not.

Clang! The razor hit the long piece of discarded iron Wash had picked up from near the blacksmith's shed and hidden up his sleeve. It hit so hard that the iron broke the blade and jarred the razor right out of Landrieu's fingers. The big Creole stepped back, shaking his numbed hand in disbelief. Wash let the iron slide out of his sleeve, showed it to Landrieu, then tossed it aside.

"*Sacre!*" the big man spat, clawing out his long-fingered hands with the intent of snatching up Wash like a hawk grabbing a mouse.

What he didn't count on was what Wash's father had taught him, after noting how his son was always going to be smaller than the other slave children on the plantation, boys—and girls, too— who could play rough.

"This is an old way of fighting, from your Great-Grampa Hausaman. If someone is taller than you," Daddy said, "it just means he has farther to fall when you grasp him like so and then bend."

And that was exactly how, when Private Landrieu Jefferson tried to take hold of him, Wash grasped, bent, and heaved the much bigger man high over his hip—and onto the ground so hard that a cloud of red dust flew up about him.

"Hoo-wee, Bunkie. That was some throw!"

Charley's shout was followed by the sound of four or five men laughing. Charley and Josh and the others had seen Wash head back of the barracks with Jefferson and followed to take a look-see.

After a moment of gasping on his back like a catfish out of water, Private Landrieu Jefferson got up slowly. He did not look at any of them. He dusted himself off, picked up his bugle—which now had a small dent in it—and disappeared into the night without a word.

It had not surprised Wash that the fight ended with that one throw. He remembered his father's words. Bullies do not come back at you when you stand firm. Even the big river must flow around an island.

But yet and still, he was not going to let the big Creole get behind him in a fight.

Hours passed as they trotted along in a loose formation. The rustlers' trail was an easy one for the Osage scouts to follow, led by Baptist John. The huge Indian rode along as easy on his horse as if he was sitting in a rocking chair. Sensing Wash's eyes on him, Baptist John turned back and smiled. Wash touched the brim of his hat with one finger, and the Osage man did the same.

Osages, Wash thought. *Almost as much strangers to this part of the plains as us army men.* From what he'd learned, the whole Osage tribe had been uprooted by the government from their old homeland in the Indian Territory to make room for Cherokees who'd been likewise uprooted from the South. Plopped down in the middle of land other tribes like the Cheyennes saw as their own, the Osages had to fight to stay in their new lands. Moreover, for lack of any work, a good number of Osages had ended up being employed by the army as scouts. As a result, the Osages did not get along well with the other western tribes. It was Osage scouts who led Custer to the Washita, where they did about as much Cheyenne killing as the 7th Cavalry troopers that day.

Baptist John fell back next to Wash.

"Ho, Little Friend."

"Ho, Baptist John."

"Good horse."

"He surely is," Wash replied, smiling as he remembered their last conversation in the stable. He had been tightening the cinch on his saddle when he smelled the grease in the Osage man's hair and knew that once again the big Indian had come up behind him as quiet as a small breeze. A hand holding a small piece of sugar had then been thrust in front of him.

"Me give?"

"Go ahead."

As Baptist John gave Blaze that sugar, he had leaned forward to whisper something in the black horse's right ear. The big animal leaned its head against Baptist John as it never had done before with anyone but Wash, then nodded its head up and down. Baptist John had turned and smiled.

"I told your horse to take care of you," he said. "It has agreed."

Baptist John, Wash thought. *I wonder what his real name might be. Whenever he introduces himself, John always taps the little Bible in his breast pocket and says "Baptist." Hard to imagine a man with all the hair shaved off his head but for a little fringe on top as a Baptist. But that is the fashion for him and all the fighting men of his tribe.*

The two rode along for a while in silence. Wash looked around. Josh and Charley were behind him, Old Landrieu way off to the left. Everyone tending to their own business, which was mostly trying not to eat too much dust from the riders in front of them.

"Can I ask you a question?"

Another long silence. Then Baptist John nodded.

"You always have your Bible with you?"

"I do. As do you."

Since Wash was patting his mother's Bible in his breast pocket as he asked his question, he was not surprised at the big Osage's answer.

But a little smile did come to his face as he thought of just how good Baptist John could talk English when he put his mind to it. Better than a good many white men out here, and formal as a preacher. Coming, no doubt, from the missionaries and from all his reading of the Bible. Wash had observed how now and then as Baptist John rode along, he would take out the Good Book and hold it open before him, his lips moving as he silently read the words.

Baptist John reached over, lazy-like, to pat Blaze on his neck.

"Your horse is a fine, spirited steed."

"I do agree."

Baptist John chuckled. "As thy friend, wilt thou give me thy horse?"

Teasing me, Wash thought. *And testing me.*

He'd learned that when an Indian complimented you on something and said he liked it, if that Indian was your friend then the polite thing to do was just to give it to him. But this time the answer was an easy one, and likely one that Baptist John fully expected.

"Sorry, my friend. My horse, he belongs to the 10th."

"Ah," Baptist John smiled. "Like unto thee and me?"

No reply needed to that.

As the soldiers rode off, Wolf watched with a very heavy heart. He had not been asked to keep watch over the herd. It had been the job of his equally disconsolate friend, Dirty Face, who stood now by his side. Both of them had fallen asleep. For Wolf it was a deeper sleep than he had known in years, untroubled by the dreams that usually woke him in the middle of the night. When he had opened his eyes again, it had been to see the sun lifting up over an empty plain where no horses were grazing.

Now a hand came to rest on his shoulder. Wolf turned to look into the gentle face of Chief Gray Head.

"Do not blame yourselves," Gray Head said. "Look."

Wolf and Dirty Face looked down toward the hoof mark by their feet.

"You see that raised mark left by the shoe? Only one ve'hoe horse thief has such a curved mark on the shoes of the horse he rides. Jack."

Jack. Wolf had heard stories about him. The white rustler who had become friends with their old enemies the Pawnees. Adopted by the best Pawnee taker of horses, Jack had been given a special horse medicine. It was one that made eyes go blind and ears become deaf.

"It was strong medicine," Gray Head said. Wolf nodded. It made him feel a little better to hear such words from him. Gray Head was a leader of sixty lodges, a man everyone admired.

Dirty Face shook his head. "I am going to throw away my name. I vow that I am going to do something that will give me a new name. I shall do things that will make my family proud. Even if I must die."

Wolf looked over at his friend. The serious look on his face showed how much he meant those words he had just spoken. It worried Wolf. Making your family proud was a good thing. However, if one did not stay alive, then who would care for them?

Gray Head pressed his hands together. "I still have two horses," he said to Wolf. "They were tied behind my lodge." His voice was soft, but deliberate. Wolf listened closely. Though Gray Head always seemed calm, when he made up his mind, he never hesitated.

"You are a Kit Fox."

Wolf made the sign for *yes* with one hand. Though young, he had already earned a place among that honored society. The job of the Kit Foxes was to take care of the people.

Gray Head pointed with his lips toward the dust cloud left by the departing cavalrymen. "Two horses tied to the back of my lodge," he said. "You take the black one. And you...," he turned to Dirty Face, whose expression had changed from despair to eager hopefulness, "you take the brown one."

DEATH SEES NO DIFFERENCE
BETWEEN THE BIG HOUSE
AND THE QUARTERS.

THE BUZZARD DOES NOT
JUST CIRCLE IN THE AIR FOR FUN.

DON'T TELL A WHITE MAN
HE HAS FORGOT HIS HAT.
HE WILL JUST TELL YOU
TO GO AND GET IT FOR HIM.

THE WAGON THAT MAKES
THE LOUDEST NOISE
IS THE ONE
THAT GOES OUT EMPTY.

JUST TALKING ABOUT FIRE
DOES NOT HEAT THE POT.

ONE GOOD SHOT

They had made up some of the distance between them and the
horse thieves, who were heading north toward Kansas. They had
been moving fast for half of a day since coming on their trail. But it
was clear they would not overtake them before night.

Sergeant Brown rode back along the line.

"Make camp there," he said, waving his arm toward a little
fold in the prairie out of the wind where a few stunted trees grew.
"No fires."

Cold as it was now getting, Wash understood that order. Those
horse thieves were a crafty bunch. One of them might have been left
to trail behind the others. The glow of a fire could be spotted from
miles away out on these plains. Let them think there's no pursuit
coming after them. He took off Blaze's saddle and tied him to the
rope that had just been run between two of the sturdier trees.

"You hear what I said?" a stern voice said from behind him.
It was the voice of Sergeant Brown, but it was not directed at
Wash. The sergeant was standing almost nose to nose with Private
Landrieu Jefferson, who was holding up his coffeepot.

"Just a small fire, Sergeant. No harm to that," Landrieu said in a
wheedling tone. "I need my coff-ee."

"What you need is to learn to listen, boy," the sergeant said,
knocking the pot out of the big man's hands. "No fire, and no java,
none at all!"

A mean, snaky look came over Landrieu's face. Then he reached into his pocket and defiantly pulled out his corncob pipe.

"I just smoke some, no?"

"No!" Sergeant Brown snatched the pipe from his hand, broke it, and tossed it to the side. "We get back to Camp Supply, you either going to be carrying the log or on the chimes, trooper."

Landrieu clenched his fists. Wash watched. It seemed as if the big Louisianan was about to swing on the sergeant. But Brown did not move. He just stared at the tall man until Landrieu dropped his eyes.

"Uh-huh," Sergeant Brown said. "You on picket duty, Private. Now."

Though he looked angry enough to chew on nails and spit out tacks, Landrieu shouldered his rifle and marched out to his post.

Wash almost managed to stifle a laugh. But not quite.

Sergeant Brown turned to him and smiled. "Thank you for volunteering, Private Washington," he said. "You on picket next."

Six hours later. Though Wash kept moving his feet in a steady walk, it was a struggle to hold his eyes open.

You'd think a man would have trouble falling to sleep out in the cold wilderness, but you'd be wrong. A day of riding tires you to the bone. Enough sand in my eyes to fill an hourglass.

The full moon cast a faint shadow. Wash had cleared a path around the camp, kicking aside sticks and small stones as he'd walked the perimeter, so there was less chance of stumbling, falling down, and shooting himself. He'd learned that more men shoot themselves by accident than get hit by enemy fire out here, especially when they're green as Virginia grass.

Josh had told him about seeing that very thing happen. It was one of the new recruits last year, a clumsy boy from Georgia who had never handled any tool more complicated than a hoe. Dropped his Spencer while loading it. When it hit the ground, it fired off a shot through his knee and put an end to his military career.

"Makes a man glad," Josh had said, "we no longer got those hair-trigger Spencers. Springfield .45 is a weapon you can trust." Then he had grinned. "Thanks to the traders, it is now our Indians who are enjoying the blessing of guns with minds of their own. Making it possible for our red men to up and shoot themselves rather than waiting for us to do it."

Did something out there on the prairie just move? There atop that little hill maybe a hundred yards away? There was enough light from the moon for Wash to almost make out something.

AWROOOO!

The howl that came out of the darkness seemed so close that Wash nearly jumped out of his skin. He struggled to regain his balance and raise his gun at the same time.

"Whoa-up, son," a low, husky voice said from right behind him.

It was Sergeant Brown. "Jes' a coy-o-te, trooper," he said, a hint of amusement in his voice.

"Yessir," Wash said, putting his rifle back up on his shoulder. "I guess I knew that."

Sergeant Brown chuckled. "Umm-hmmm. 'Course, it might also be one of them Cheyenne boys from back at the camp. Don't you doubt that they sent one or two to track behind us. But we be more likely to see a coyote at night than one of our Indians. Got to admire the way they can stay hid. Back when I was first fighting 'em eight years ago, we called 'em kite people. Every time we thought we was about to catch them, we'd just find an empty camp. Like they up and flew away."

"Yessir," Wash replied, wondering why the sergeant was talking to him this way.

The most he has ever said to me. Most I ever heard him say to anyone.

As Wash continued walking his round, the sergeant paced along beside him, both of them outwardly silent for the moment, though Wash's mind was far from quiet.

Why has he picked me out to talk to like this? And why now? Does the darkness make talking easier? Whatever the reason may be, I better listen close. If there's any man out here on the frontier I'd wish to emulate, it is our sergeant.

Sergeant Brown cleared his throat and spat into the darkness. "Our Indians. Now we figure we got 'em all cooped up on that agency like they was chickens—though chickens is a sight better fed than our Indians."

There was an angry tone in his voice that Wash thought he understood. The sergeant was not the only army man with more than a little sympathy for the Indians. The government had promised them food and clothes if they gave up and came in. But all they got were moth-eaten surplus blankets and scraps.

If I were in their place, Wash thought, *I would doubtless sneak off my reservation to hunt for meat for my starving family.*

And then the trouble would start. For though it was not the army's responsibility to provide the necessities of life for the Indians, it was their charge to keep them cooped up and then to go get them if they strayed. When the Indians were up in arms, it would not be the politicians who would have to fight them. Nor would it be the dishonest traders who did such things as selling a herd of cattle to one reservation, collecting the money, giving the Indian agent a cut of the cash, and then driving that very herd off to sell it to another reservation down the line.

Wash growled under his breath.

"What's that? You thinkin' 'bout, somethin', son?" Sergeant Brown asked.

"Nothing much of note, sir," Wash answered, cursing himself for not being able to keep quiet.

"You a thinker, ain't you, Private?"

"Yessir, I suppose."

Brown stepped in front of him and stopped. He leaned close to look into Wash's face.

"Son," the sergeant said, "way you talk at times, using words I never heard from any negro before, makes me wonder. You read books, don't you? Just like my niece does."

Wash took a breath, surprised by the turn in their conversation.

"Y-yessir," he managed to stammer, trying to choose his words carefully. "But that does not mean I believe that I am any better than any of the other men, sir."

"Umm-hmmm," the sergeant said. "Now why am I not surprised you would say such a thing? So answer me this, why you here and not in school, trying to better our race? I look at you, I see school."

This time Wash could not hold back his feelings. "What school, sir? There's no schools for coloreds. All I want is to be a soldier. That way I can hold my head up like a man. I can earn an honest day's pay and send money back home to take care of my mama and my sister and…"

Wash swallowed hard to stop himself, certain he was saying far too much.

But Sergeant Brown just nodded. "Uh-huh. I seen what you does with your money, Private. Don't spend it on foofaraws or liquor or gamble it away. And you never on the bum and trying to beg or borrow from your messmates. But why you have to be sending so much back home? Don't your papa take care of your family?"

"My father's dead, sir. Died at the Crater. And even though he served in the war, there's never been a penny of pension sent to support my mother and Pegatha, my little sister."

"Hmm."

The sergeant turned and took Wash's free arm to start them walking once more. They were halfway around the perimeter before he spoke again. This time, to Wash's relief, it was no longer about him or his family or any foolish notion of being something thing other than a soldier.

"You know," Sergeant Brown mused, "two years ago, there'd be buffalo here. Don't see none now, does you? How we supposed to keep our Indians from going out and killing those buffalo hunters who slaughters ever' animal in sight? But we got orders to leave the buffalo hunters alone, even though they be breaking the treaty by hunting on the land south of here was supposed to be Indian forever. You watch. Faster than the Word of God, we are gonna be sent to protect them damn buffalo hunters from our Indians."

They'd now perambulated all the way around the camp and were starting on a second round. The coyote—or Indian—out there in the dark had not howled again. As they reached the tethered horses, Blaze nickered softly. Wash patted the big animal once as they walked past.

"Love that horse, don't you, son?" Sergeant Brown's rough voice softened.

"Yessir, I surely do. He's a fine animal."

"Umm-hmmm. When I first joined up, you should have seen the horses they give us. What you would expect a white man to give a darky. They was all cast-offs from Custer's 7th, knock-kneed, spavined, bony, and old. All about on their last legs. But we took care of them steeds. Nursed 'em back to health and rode 'em with pride. That was why they allowed us better horses every year. And now we even able to match every troop to horses of the same color, like our black ones for D Troop."

"Yessir."

Sergeant Brown put a big hand on his shoulder. "Son, you do talk better than most, but you are not uppity. Good with horses, real good. And you are a decent shot, too. Make ever' bullet count on the firing range. Hit dead center ever' time. Saw how you shot that rabid wolf. Now you say all you want is to be a soldier, even though old Sergeant Brown still sees you doing something more with your life. Think you can shoot that good in a real fight?"

"I can try, sir," Wash said, standing up as straight as he could and squaring his shoulders.

"Ever fire a Sharps?" the sergeant asked, slapping the butt of the long gun he had slung over his shoulder. "I confisticated this one off of a buffalo hunter las' month."

"Yessir," Wash said. Which was true. He'd had the chance back in St. Louis at the barracks. Though its kick was that of a mule and had bruised his shoulder, he had placed a hole in the center of a paper target set at 500 yards.

"Hmm. Then let's see how good a soldier you can be," the sergeant said, walking away until he disappeared into the night.

Wash thought him gone, but then Brown's voice came back out of the darkness. "Soon as there's light, you report to me."

The place they had chosen to conceal themselves was high on a small hill. The soldier camp was to the southwest. The camp of the horse thieves was farther down the trail to the northeast. Their hiding spot was at the head of the little box canyon into which they had driven the stolen Cheyenne herd. By moving only a little, they could see into one camp or the other.

Perhaps, Wolf thought, *we might slip in on foot before the sun rises. We might free some of our horses.*

He shook his head. They could be silent going in. But coming out, the sound of horse's hooves on the hard ground would be loud. It would surely waken some of the sleeping thieves.

"We could cut some of their throats," Dirty Face suggested.

He was only half joking. Wolf shook his head no.

The thought of killing sleeping enemies bothered him. And to try such a thing when there were so many enemies would be foolhardy.

Courage makes a name for a man, Pawnee Killer had said. But behaving fearlessly does not mean acting like a fool. It does not mean risking the lives of those who follow you.

My friend, Wolf thought, *might do something foolhardy on his own. But he is not alone. I am the leader. His safety is more important than my own.*

"We wait. Watch both sides."

"Ah." Dirty Face did not look happy, but he nodded.

"Good. Just because those soldiers were sent to help us, it does not mean they won't shoot us."

The night passed slowly. The two young men waited. They could see the soldier camp below them.

Maybe, Wolf thought, *these soldiers will behave wisely. Maybe they will take back our horses.*

The ve'hoes were off to a good start. Their scouts had located the rustlers. But they had waited. They had quietly set up camp before the horse thieves knew they were close. They had made no fires to give themselves away. And now, as the sun began to peer over the hills, they were doing something else. They were sending out two small parties, one to each side of the box canyon. Each party was made up of three people, one Indian scout and two black white men.

Dirty Face tapped Wolf's arm. He pointed with his chin toward the party to their left.

"Long gun."

One of the black white soldiers was carrying a Sharps rifle. Wolf recognized that man. Easy to do so. He was the smallest blue-coat Wolf had ever seen.

Our paths cross again, Wolf thought.

The first time had been along the Washita. Wolf tugged at the bandanna around his neck and smiled. The second was when the ve'hoe soldiers rode into the Cheyenne camp. The little black white man had ridden well. His legs were short, but he had cinched his stirrups up high.

If I stood next to him, Wolf thought, *his head would reach the middle of my chest.*

The two groups of flankers were taking their time. Sun had now lifted the width of three more fingers above the horizon. Finally the men stopped. Good places. The ve'hoes could now look down into the thieves' camp.

In the camp below, some of the rustlers were awake. Smoke rose from their cooking fires. They were making breakfast. The air was so clear that Wolf could see smiles on the bearded faces of Jack and his men. They had no idea there were enemies above them.

Dirty Face grinned. "Soon?"

Wolf nodded. The soldiers had just called down into the rus-tlers' canyon. The wind was blowing away from him. So he had not heard the soldiers' voices. But the thieves in the camp below had heard whatever was shouted at them. Their complacent grins had been replaced by looks of surprise. One of the bearded men had spilled his coffee over his chest. Another had kicked his foot into the pot of beans hung above the fire. Others were scrambling to grab their guns.

Perhaps the words shouted at them had been a command to surrender. They were not surrendering. Wolf heard the pop of a rifle over the wind. Then another, as smoke exploded from the barrels of the rustlers' guns. But they were firing wildly. Nowhere near the two flanking parties of soldiers and scouts.

"Ahh," Dirty Face said. "Good show."

The shots being fired by the rustlers were now doing damage. But it was to their own camp. One horse thief blew the heel off another's boot. That man, as he went sprawling, fired off a shot that knocked down one of their own horses. Only the big man that Wolf took as their leader, Jack, was not panicking. The head horse thief was sighting his rifle in the direction of the first party of blue soldiers. Wolf turned to look at the second group of flankers. It was the one that included his little Buffalo Soldier. The small man was on his belly. He was looking down the sights of that long gun. A little spurt of flame burst from the barrel.

The shot was well-aimed. The heavy bullet knocked Jack's gun from his grasp. Wolf's keen vision showed him that it took something else. Some of the rustler's fingers on his right hand were gone. Jack dropped to his knees, clutching his hand. The other six men dropped their weapons. A third party of ve'hoe soldiers rode into the camp, their weapons pointed at the thieves. All the rustlers except Jack—who was moaning on the ground—raised their hands. The fight was over.

Dirty Face and Wolf backed down the hill toward their two horses. The blue soldiers had done well. Now all the two young Cheyennes needed was to ride back to report what they'd seen.

Dirty Face looked up at the sky. He raised one eyebrow.

Wolf nodded to him. He saw the shape and movement of the clouds. He saw the changing color of the sky to the north. Hard weather would be coming in soon. It was warm now. But after another sunrise or two the land would be covered by Winter Man's blanket.

They mounted and began to ride. They went down a draw and over another hill. Side by side, they started to pass through a narrow gap.

Dirty Face reached back to grasp Wolf's wrist. "Look!" Dirty Face said. His voice was excited.

Wolf saw it. Another box canyon was just ahead of them. Its mouth was closed by a rough fence made of brush and logs. The wind blew out of the canyon as they approached. The sharp smells of sweat and dung floated on that breeze.

This is good, Wolf thought.

It was better than good. He and Dirty Face slid off their ponies. They looked over the brush wall. There inside were horses. Many horses. Horses that they did not know. The small canyon was full of Indian ponies. They were not the ones that had been stolen from the Cheyennes. The rustlers had probably taken them from the other tribal nations around them. Wolf counted. At least two hundred fine horses!

Dirty Face grabbed Wolf. He hugged him hard. "Yes," he yelled.

"Yes!" Wolf shouted, hugging his friend back.

We are acting like crazy people, Wolf thought as they laughed and jumped up and down and rolled on the ground. *It is right that we should. How our people will welcome us when we drive these new horses into our camp!*

They got up and dusted themselves off. They climbed over the brush fence. They walked into the canyon. Horses circled around them as they walked.

"Look," Dirty Face said. "There's more."

"More horses?"

"No. There."

Wolf looked. Next to one of the steep walls of the narrow canyon was an outcrop of rock. It had formed a protective roof. Beneath it was a big wagon. As they walked over to it, the sharp odor coming from it made their eyes water. The wagon was loaded with casks and boxes covered with crisscross marks. Bad medicine. Whiskey.

Wolf ran a hand over one of the kegs. It was moist from the strong liquid inside. He pulled back his wet palm and licked his hand. His tongue burned. He climbed up on the wagon and, using his knife, pried open one of the wooden crates. Inside were black bottles. Each was in a nest of straw. Each was filled with that fiery liquid.

Wolf looked down at Dirty Face. "Poison for our people," he said.

Dirty Face nodded. He made the sign for *fire*.

They gathered dry brush and piled it around the wagon. Wolf took flint from his pouch. He used the steel of his knife to strike it.

As they drove the horse herd from the canyon, a voice roared hot behind them. It was the voice of the fire they had started. That fire would consume the wagon and its load of death.

SWEET MEDICINE TOLD THE PEOPLE,
THOSE NEW PEOPLE WILL BRING NEW ANIMALS
WITH THEM,
ANIMALS WITH NO SPIRIT, UNLIKE OUR BUFFALO.

THEY WILL BRING GREAT SICKNESS
AND A KIND OF DRINK THAT WILL MAKE YOU ALL CRAZY.

I AM SAD BECAUSE MY HEART IS HEAVY.
I CHOSE FOOLISHLY FOR I WISHED TO BE HANDSOME.
NOW I MUST DIE AND LEAVE YOU, MY PEOPLE.

YOU WILL FORGET MY WORDS,
YOU WILL LEAVE THE OLD WAYS.
YOU WILL DRINK THEIR DRINK AND YOU WILL BE CRAZY.
YOU WILL TAKE UP THE WAYS OF THOSE
FROM FAR AWAY.
YOU WILL TEAR UP THE EARTH AND YOU WILL GROW WEAK.

SWEET MEDICINE LOOKED AROUND AT THE PEOPLE.

BUT PERHAPS SOME OF YOU WILL REMEMBER
MY WORDS.
YOU WILL STILL DO HONOR TO THE SACRED ARROWS.
YOU WILL STILL BE FAITHFUL TO OUR OLD WAYS.
YOU WILL STILL SPEAK OFTEN OF ALL THAT I TOLD YOU.
IF YOU DO THIS, THEN YOU WILL BE STRONG.
IF YOU DO THIS, THE PEOPLE WILL SURVIVE.

AND THEN SWEET MEDICINE DIED.

TRADE

"The Indian," Lieutenant Pratt said, "may be made to be just as civilized as the negro."

Wash nodded, even though he was not sure if the lieutenant was speaking directly to him or just saying his thoughts out loud as he seemed prone to do.

Never met a man liked to hear his own voice more than our lieutenant, Wash thought, pulling his coat tighter around himself as the lieutenant continued on into the officers' quarters and shut the door behind him, leaving Wash outside on duty. It was a bitter day, just as unpleasantly cold as it had been unbearably hot mere days before. On the Great Plains, he'd learned, a man could never tell what the weather would be from one day to the next. A week ago, when they got back from taking the rustlers briefly into custody and returning the stolen horses, every man had been sweating.

Briefly into custody because every mother's son of them, Jack included—now known as Three Finger Jack—had been released by a sympathetic judge after being turned over to civilian authority. And as for *sympathetic*, one might just as well substitute the words *easily bribed*.

"All that riding and dust eating and sweating and for what?" Wash had asked. "Just to set them free to rustle again?"

Josh had shrugged his shoulders at Wash's complaint. "Just the way it is out here," he said. "Our job is to catch 'em, not be judge nor jury. But maybe next time they will come across a hanging judge and it will be a different story."

Wash blew into his hands to try to warm them. Twenty below zero and heavy blowing snow everywhere. He stomped his feet, the rough boards of the porch cracking with frost as he did so.

This weather turned faster than a squirrel running around a tree.

The door opened again and Lieutenant Pratt came out, the kind of smile on his face that Wash had come to recognize.

Oh my, we are about to be sent out again.

And indeed they were.

Whiskey dealers. That was who they were after this time. As they rode through the increasingly deep snow, Wash stayed close to Lieutenant Pratt—on the leeward side so that he was partially sheltered from the wind by the huge buffalo coat worn by the tall white officer. It had not been his choice to remain at Pratt's side, but a direct order from Sergeant Brown.

"Private Vance, you are to stay close to the lieutenant. Seems to have taken a liking to having you listen to him talk." Sergeant Brown had grinned. "Better you than me, boy."

But at the moment the fact that the lieutenant was serving as a windbreak made the fact that he hardly ever shut his mouth more than bearable. Plus, even though it took Pratt a hundred words to say what most could express in a sentence, most of what he said made sense. It was, Wash had to admit, educating. And right now that education was about Indians and alcohol.

"Our Indians will trade anything they own for that whiskey. They will give over all of their buffalo robes for a few bottles. A whole string of horses for a single keg. It does not matter if such uneven trading leaves them with nothing to keep them warm or take care of their families. All that matters is getting the firewater. But the trouble does not end with making our Indians poor."

Pratt looked over and down at Wash. Though his collar was turned up and his face was so fully wrapped in a scarf that only his eyes were visible below the brim of his cap, Wash had still heard every word and had an answer ready.

"Why not, Lieutenant, sir?" he said.

Pratt pressed his lips together and nodded like a schoolteacher pleased that his class was paying attention. "The barrels of rotgut those unscrupulous traders peddle to the Cheyennes might as well be gunpowder. As a matter of fact, actual gunpowder is sometimes mixed in to give the drink more of a kick after the traders have watered it down. When our poor Indians begin drinking whiskey, it is much like starting a prairie fire that may burn in any direction. With whiskey in their bellies and an angry confusion in their minds, they may attack anyone who crosses their path and have been known to murder their best friends and family members."

Pratt paused again, in part for emphasis and also because the gust of wind that had just swept over them was too strong for even his stentorian voice to be heard over it. But as soon as the wintry blast had passed, he took up his lecture again.

"No, it is not even over when the Indians sober up. For they then must find some way to get new horses so as they can go buffalo hunting and get new robes and meat and whatnot. Thus they go raiding the other tribes or the white folks to get their mounts. And at that juncture they are also usually better equipped for raiding after trading with those whiskey sellers. For the other items those traders offer in ample supply to our Indians are guns and ammunition."

Wash nodded, thinking back to the words spoken by the Indian agent, Mr. John Miles, who had given them this errand to apprehend the miscreant whiskey traders and sent along with them one Mr. Hoag, an Indian superintendent, to do the official arresting.

"Thou must do your best," Agent Miles had said to their party as they set out. "I have been told that there are now more than half a dozen of those pestilential whiskey ranches set up, just south of the Kansas border within the reservation line. Those men who sell that whiskey to our Indians are the cause of most of our troubles."

That might be so, Wash thought, but as he hunched his shoulders against yet another blast of wind that bit like a wolf, it seemed that most of their trouble right now was this weather. Fifteen degrees below zero, heading straight into the teeth of a blue norther'.

A blue norther', he'd learned, was the name for a wind that roars down from arctic regions. So hard, so cold, so full of snow that the air looks blue. And if a man was fool enough to stand out in it for more than a few minutes, he would soon be blue himself.

Wash reached up a gloved hand to tap his brow and brush his face to break off the ice that had formed on his eyebrows and eyelashes. Otherwise, his eyes might freeze shut, even with a lined hood and a woolen scarf like the one he had pulled over much of his face.

Thanks to Lieutenant Pratt, always one for planning ahead, they were all as well dressed as anyone could be for such an expedition. Every man had on double underwear and buffalo-lined overshoes, beaver caps with earflaps, and beaver gloves with long wrists nearly up to their elbows. However, Wash had quickly discovered, sitting on a horse you grow twice as cold as when walking on your own feet. As they plodded along, he leaned forward to get as close as he could to the body heat coming up from Blaze. Three hours after dawn now, though you would hardly know the sun was in the sky. It showed as no more than a small glow off to the east.

The first leg of their journey would be thirty-six miles. That would take them to an abandoned fort on the Cimarron River. The plan was to get there before dark—which came early and sudden in February. Thus they had to press on without pause, but not at a gallop. They had to do no more than a slow trot at best, for the four wagons to keep pace, and be wary of places where drifts were so deep they would overtop both horse and rider. Lost in such deep snow, a man might not be found till spring when his frozen carcass was exposed by the melting snow.

The lieutenant seemed to have finished his soliloquy. The two of them were now riding close to the west side of the second wagon. That cut the wind enough for it to feel the tiniest mite warmer.

Thank the Lord we have these wagons, Wash thought. *They are about all that is going to keep us alive once the night comes on, seeing as how they carry not just our tents, but Sibley camp stoves and a good supply of wood.*

Except he had to survive until then. He tried thinking about those Sibleys to take his mind off of freezing.

Just imagine, Wash, how warm it is going to be, holding your hands close to that little stove and soaking in its heat.

A blast of wind lifted a double handful of snow off the wagon to land right in his face and trickle down his neck, wiping away the image of that hot stove.

What else could he think of that might warm him inside, keep him going? A face came to mind. Bethany, the sergeant's niece. Her pretty, perfect brown countenance looking right at him. And smiling, not frowning.

Bethany's aunt was Sarah, the wife of Sergeant Brown. She and Bethany were brought up on the same plantation in west Louisiana. When Emancipation came, they took off for the West and ended up in Kansas, in one of the numerous new towns made up of freed slaves. It was there that Sarah met and married Sergeant Brown, one of the first members of the 10th Cavalry. When she traveled farther west with him, they had left Bethany behind in the care of other cousins, feeling that army life on the frontier would be too dangerous for a small child.

As Camp Supply had grown there had been more work than Mrs. Brown could handle on her own, acting both as a laundress and as cook for the Pratt family. So, since their niece was now old enough and in need of employment, the Browns had sent for her to come lend a hand. But her plan was to stay only through the end of spring. So Wash knew there was little hope of his having anything more to do with her than perhaps, one day, a polite hello as they passed.

Yet he'd kept thinking of her. Thinking of her as he was doing right now. Her smooth, even features. Her skin a gentle brown color that set off her green eyes. Her smile fine and smart. The intelligence gleaming from her eyes, showing that she had not just good looks, but a good head on her shoulders. But it was her pride, so much like that of his own mother, that attracted him the most to Bethany Brown. The way she always stood up straight, even when she was carrying a load of laundry through the snow. Even when she paused to wipe her arm across her forehead when working, she never lost her dignity. He couldn't help but watch her.

Of course, Wash had always been careful to turn away when she looked in his direction. Not wanting to seem bold. In no way like the way Landrieu had behaved before he up and deserted. But that little smile of hers had almost seemed to be turned up his way the last time he passed her. Up because he had been on Blaze's back and riding past her. Had he been on his own two feet, she would have been looking down, her being half a head taller than him.

But it is not through height that a man sees the moon.

"Wake up, Private!"

The voice of Sergeant Brown jolted him out of his reverie. Wash had almost ridden into a drift. Thoughts of Bethany Brown vanished as he pulled back on the reins as the wind sent a slash of sleet across his cheek.

Camp Supply was now fifteen miles behind them. Despite the storm, they were still on the trail toward the Cimarron. Or so their Osage guides assured them. Forward, always forward, undeterred by wind and weather. Chilled to the bone, but well-mounted.

"Good boy, Blaze," Wash whispered in the big horse's warm left ear as he leaned to pat him on the neck.

Sergeant Brown fell back as another trooper came up to ride beside Wash. All that could be seen of the man was one eye peeking out from behind a double-wrapped scarf, but the amused light in that eye and the way he tilted his head was enough for Wash to recognize the well-swathed rider as Charley. Wash nodded. No attempt to converse. Words would be lost in the wind whistling about them. A blizzard was howling loud as ten war parties of Indians. And no matter how many layers of clothing they had on, a knife could not do a better job of cutting through to their skin than that cold-whetted wind. Heads down, plodding on. Making slower time now. Hours passing in a numb haze. At last, with the weak glow of the sun in the west, the signal came to make camp. They were short of the old fort on the Cimarron, but deep cold and dark were upon them and they had no choice.

"This hill and those trees will shelter us somewhat," Lieutenant Pratt shouted, waving an arm. "Half a loaf is better than none,"

More like half alive, Wash thought.

But they all worked as one. No time for tents. Pulled the wagons together. The metal of the stoves so cold that fingers would have frozen to them if they'd touched them bare-handed. One match after another failing to catch. But, somehow, a faint flame growing and then the logs catching. All of them huddling close, shoulder to shoulder, hip to hip. No matter if a man's skin was black or red or white. It was the heat of life that mattered.

In this wagon it was Private Thorny Hamms, the new bugler, on one side of Wash and Lieutenant Pratt on the other. Josh next to him, then their young Osage guide, whose name Wash had not yet learned, then Charley and Sergeant Brown and half a dozen other men hard to recognize in their thick clothing. All shivering, despite the stove, the buffalo robes and layers of clothing. Feeling in their bones it would be a miracle if they made it alive through the night. But somehow sleep found them.

And then it was morning. Hamms, the new bugler, had not dared blow his horn for reveille. The metal would have frozen to his lips. But someone was pulling at their blankets.

"On your feet, troopers."

Wash felt as stiff as a board and ready to splinter if he so much as breathed hard. But he forced himself to follow Sergeant Brown's orders. He sat up along with Charley and Josh and the other men of the 10th still in the wagon who were groaning and complaining as they roused from the rough sleep they'd shared. No sign of Lieutenant Pratt or the Osage guide, who both must have risen before dawn.

Wash gritted his teeth and forced his legs to work, crawling past the cold Sibley to stick his head outside.

The wind had died and the new day was clear. The sun was a piece of steel nailed in the southeastern sky. Less warmth seemed to come from it than from the chill face of the moon visible low in the west. Clouds of smoke from their breath wreathed the horses where they stood tied together inside the small circle formed by the wagons.

The only good thing about the weather was that it had pinned down the whiskey traders they were seeking. They'd plowed through the drifts no more than two hours before they sighted a pillar of smoke rising high in the sky above a small fold in the prairie.

Pratt held up his hand, pointing to the front of the cabin as they came close. Next to it was a small barn with a wagon parked next to it under a lean-to roof. From where they were, the boxes of whiskey marked with big Xs were easily visible. The right place, all right. The lieutenant nodded to the sergeant before making a downward slash in the air and a circling motion.

"You men," Sergeant Brown barked, signaling to the soldiers on his left, including Wash. "We take the back."

Once again, neither a bugle call nor a charge of any kind. Just a slow slog through the deep snow until they were in position, then equally slow progress through the white mounds that grew deeper as they approached the windward side of the cabin's back door. They were close enough to almost touch the cabin's walls before Sergeant Brown gave the order to dismount.

Wash let Josh and Charley go ahead of him, certain that if he was first he'd disappear in the deep snow. Let them beat a path to the door, which was mostly raised up above the level of the snow because of the rickety back porch tacked onto the building like an afterthought.

The four of them stood together on the porch, boards cracking under their feet so loud that Wash wondered if anyone in the cabin was alive, much less awake and aware they were about to be busted in on.

"Now!" came a shout from the other side of the cabin. Pratt's command for the two parties to break in.

Charley raised up one huge, snow-crusted boot and kicked. The back door burst open so easily that Charley took two stumbling steps in the room, almost falling onto his face had it not been for Sergeant

Brown grabbing his collar and following him in close. Wash came in low behind them, his rifle leading the way, ready to fire.

But there was no need. The whiskey traders' pale faces looked up from where they were huddled together on the south side of the cabin, their cots pulled together for warmth. It was only a little less cold in the cabin than outside, seeing as how not a one of them had gotten up the gumption to rise and stoke their cold stove.

As Wash and Josh held their guns on the seven men, all but one of whom had put up their hands, Lieutenant Pratt and his party came bursting through the front door, which had been twice as stout as the back.

"Ah, Sergeant, check them for weapons," Pratt ordered, the look on his face saying to Wash that he was a mite embarrassed at his tardiness into what might have been a fight.

"Yessir," Sergeant Brown replied, not bothering to mention that he and Charley had been about that task for a solid minute before his superior's late arrival and had already gathered up three Remington carbines, an 1867 model Sharps, two army colt pistols, and a shotgun.

"And stoke up that fire," Pratt added, pulling the blankets from the windows that had been hung up against the cold and to keep the light out of the cabin.

As Hamms and their Osage tracker worked to bring the embers in the stove back to life, Wash studied the faces of the six prisoners who had bestirred themselves and now stood against the wall with their hands raised. Hoods or blankets around their heads and every man jack of them so dirty that it was hard to tell one from the next.

But none of them was tall and lanky enough, and even that amount of dirt could not hide skin of the color Wash was looking for.

"Looking for Landrieu?" Charley asked.

Wash nodded.

On their raid against the rustlers, Private Landrieu Jefferson had finally decided military life in Company D was no longer to his liking. The last anyone had seen of his high yellow hide was the back of his neck as he high-tailed it over a ridge half a mile away, bugle bouncing against his back, a sack of coffee tied to one side of the saddle and all their sugar to the other. He had, in the most literal sense of soldier slang for deserting, gone over the hill.

Scouts sent out to bring back the deserter had returned empty-handed. And all that had been heard of him in the days since the big Creole had skipped had been rumors. He'd made it all the way back to New Orleans. He had joined up with renegade Indians. He was running with Three Finger Jack's rustlers. He'd joined a party of whiskey traders.

Wash reached up one by one to pull down the hoods and blankets that obscured the hair and half the faces of their prisoners. Every one a white man. Every one a stranger. And some looked scared enough to soil their britches.

Might be, Wash thought, *it's because we are the ones who have caught them. Likely most of them are unreformed rebs. A white man with a guilty conscience might view being in the hands of black soldiers as a fate worse than death.*

Wash looked back over his shoulder at his fellow troopers. Looks on their faces about as grim as the Reaper. Wash almost chuckled.

After having to come out in the weather to find these bastards, I guess all of us would have been just as glad to plug a few of them for our troubles.

"Ah, ahem!" One of the white men was clearing his throat. He drew himself up like a politician climbing onto the stump. His face, more clean-shaven than the rest of the miscreants, was about as round as a ball and as pink as a sow's belly. He pointed a chubby finger at Lieutenant Pratt.

"You have no business here, sir," he declaimed. "We are legitimate businessmen. I am the son of a United States senator."

Charley, who had moved to the back doorway to try to prop the broken door into the shattered frame, hawked loudly and spat a brown goober the size of a walnut back over his shoulder. The glob of tobacco-stained spit froze hard as a rock before it hit and went bouncing along the snow crust.

"Do you hear me, sirrahs?" the senator's son said. As he stepped forward he twitched the blanket off his shoulders and let his right hand fall to his side. A Colt single-action revolver, the one weapon their quick search had missed, was strapped backwards in a holster on his side, meaning he was either a fast draw or, more likely, a would-be gunslinger who had seen it pictured that way on the cover of a dime store novel.

Wash stepped forward and shoved the barrel of his rifle forward so that it touched the end of the pink-faced man's nose.

"I am no sirrah," Wash said. "I am a private in the United States 10th Cavalry. Unless you want me to blow a hole in you big enough to see to Kansas, you will move your mitt away from that hogleg, shut your mouth, and reach for the sky."

The moment of silence was broken by a chuckle from Wash's left. Lieutenant Pratt.

"I would suggest you do just that, sir," Pratt said. The senator's son shot both hands up into the air, his face pinker than before.

"Gentlemen," Pratt continued, voice as dry as a crust of day-old bread, "you are all under arrest."

"This one here dead or playin' possum?" Charley was pointing at the seventh cot, where a figure wrapped in blankets had not moved when the other six stood up.

"Private Vance," Lieutenant Pratt said. "See if you can rouse that man."

Wash kept his rifle leveled at the inert figure as he edged forward past the other six men, who had been herded against the other side of the cabin, their hands still raised in surrender. He reached out one hand, yanked free the blanket, and stepped back.

"Get up now!"

The man who lay with his face down slowly lifted himself up, slid his feet onto the floor, and began to turn toward Wash, his right hand near his waist, his fingers twitching.

"Hold it! Hands high! Josh, check his belt."

Josh reached a long arm down and grabbed something hidden along the man's side. He came up with an ivory-handled revolver.

"Man," Josh said, stepping back so the man would have no chance to grab at him or the weapon he'd just taken, "you born stupid or just studying hard at it? You pulled this thing, you would have been a dead man."

"Stand up," Wash ordered, his heart pounding so hard after seeing that ivory-handled gun that he could barely hear his own voice. The man slowly unfolded himself, his back still turned. His head almost brushed the low ceiling of the cabin, even though his shoulders were hunched as much in resentment as against the cold.

"Now turn around."

The man turned his head first, his skeletal face covered by the full-face beard that did not hide those familiar eyes or the look of pure hatred held in them. A coiled whip hung from his belt.

"Tom Key," Wash said, his voice calmer than he felt.

"You know this man?" Lieutenant Pratt said, stepping forward.

"Ain't my name," the former overseer snarled. "Your boy done got it wrong. Ulysses S. Lee, that's me."

Lieutenant Pratt shook his head. "This man is no boy. He is a soldier in the 10th Cavalry. And you, Mr. Grant or whoever, are his prisoner."

Wash motioned. "There," he said. "See what's at the end of that chain."

Pratt leaned forward to grasp the chain that hung from the man's vest, pulling out a gold watch. "Ah," he said.

"That there is mine, I done worked for it," the skeletal man whined.

Pratt opened the watch and studied what was inside.

"Private Vance, can you tell me what I am looking at here?"

"Unless he took it out, there will be a photo of a man and his wife and their two children. All four looking serious. And the name of Philip Vance. My old master back when Mister Tom Key was the overseer and near beat my father to death with his whip. Last time I saw that watch, Master Vance had it on his vest when he and his family drove off from the plantation before they all got waylaid and killed." Wash looked again at bony man whose hands were trembling and whose gaze was dripping with malice. "The same vest Mister Tom Key is wearing now."

"Ah," Lieutenant Pratt said again. He closed the watch and handed it to Wash. "Well, Private, I suggest that you hold onto it for now, for safekeeping until we ascertain just who our Mr. Ulysses S. Lee is." Pratt smiled. "Or is it Mr. Robert E. Grant? You may face more charges than just whiskey trading."

You a dead man, boy, Tom Key mouthed silently as he stared at Wash.

But Wash returned his stare, his face calm, and in the end it was the bony man who looked away before he was pushed over to join the others.

There were horses for each of the prisoners in the barn out back, as well as a great pile of buffalo robes and crates filled with enough rifles, pistols, and ammunition to start a small war. With the storm wind gone, they could also see a corral behind the barn holding thirty head of cattle and a number of mules and horses.

"Buying firewater with what they needed to keep themselves and their families alive," Lieutenant Pratt said. "It makes me shake my head in sorrow."

After dumping twenty barrels of booze so foul that the scent of it alone might kill a horse, the party began the journey back to Camp Supply. Although they made better speed without the wind in their faces, the trip was nearly as painful and cold as had been the journey out. By the time they entered Camp Supply they felt more like icicles than men. The surgeon took one look at them and sent them all straight to the hospital. Seven of the troopers and three of the whiskey traders, the senator's son among them, ended up hospitalized for frostbite.

Wash, perhaps because being smaller there was less of him exposed to the elements, was not among those who needed to be treated. But Charley's hands and toes were no longer brown but bright blood red. The surgeon had him stick both hands and feet into buckets of cold water. Frostbitten parts needed to be thawed out slowly. Hot water would have hurt more than helped.

As fast as it had come in with its deep drifts and freezing blasts of arctic air, the weather changed again. The snow melted away. Within a week, it was sixty degrees warmer.

"More fickle than a pretty woman," Josh said as he and Wash strolled past the parade grounds and out the gate toward their tents.

Wash shook his head. "Don't know if I'd say that."

Josh looked down at him and raised an eyebrow.

"How's that, Wash? You thinking about someone? Some little brown-eyed girl?"

Wash felt his cheeks begin to burn. Why had he said that? Why couldn't he just keep his mouth shut and his thoughts to himself? He pressed his lips together and looked down at the ground as they walked, not wanting to meet Josh's eyes.

Josh chuckled and patted his friend on the shoulder. "Is something starting to happen between you and that little girl?"

Wash stopped and turned to look up at Josh, his fists clenched. "There is nothing happening between me and Bethany. Just talking, that is all."

Josh held up both his hands, palms toward the sky. "Whoa, pardner. Now, now. Don't you get riled up. I'm just joshing you. Miss Bethany seems like a fine young lady to me. Don't mean nothing bad."

Wash took a deep breath, more surprised at his own reaction than his friend had been. "All right, then."

It had been only a week since he had found himself on real speaking terms with Bethany Brown. A week since he'd worked up the courage to say a polite "Howdy-do, Miss," when he saw her and be answered by her equally polite but far sweeter voice saying "I am well and how are you?" back to him. It was such a change from his being tongue-tied when he saw her that Wash could hardly believe his good luck.

But a day ago that had changed even more.

As he stood on attention outside the officers' quarters, Sergeant Brown had come up to him.

"At ease, trooper."

"Sir."

"You been speaking with my niece?"

Wash's heart sank lower than a stone dropped into a deep well, sure that what was to come next would be an order from the sergeant to stop bothering Miss Bethany.

"Yes...sir," Wash replied, his voice tight. "Just a polite hello now and then. That's all."

Sergeant Brown smiled. "It's all right son. I ain't about to bite your head off. Now you like to read, don't you?"

"Yes, sir, I suppose I do," Wash answered, as confused by the question as by the way the tone of Sergeant Brown's voice had changed.

"I know you do," Sergeant Brown chuckled. "And unless I miss my guess, you a young man who knows what good manners is." Sergeant Brown shoved his face close to Wash's. "Don't you?"

"Ah, yes. Yes, sir."

The sergeant leaned back. "I expect so. I do expect so. So, how would you like to come by this evening after mess when you off duty and chat with my niece about those books?"

Wash caught his breath, trying to make words come out of his mouth, even more tongue-tied than he had been those times when he had tried to say hello to the sergeant's niece, when she seemed as distant and bright and unreachable as the morning star.

"Well?" Sergeant Brown said.

"Ah, yes, sir, that is, if Miss Bethany would like me to, sir."

Sergeant Brown put both hands on Wash's shoulders. "Son, you just don't know nothing about womenfolk, do you? You suppose I would be asking you this if she hadn't asked me? So you be there after mess, right?"

Wash nodded.

"Good. Me and my wife—who will be right in the room whilst you two talk about books—and my niece will be expecting you."

Wash shook his head at the thought of the way Bethany looked as she sat on that straight chair with a book in her lap. Himself not two feet away from her in his own chair, leaned close enough so they could both look down on the same page as she held the book in her small, perfectly shaped hands. Hands made as fine as the Good Lord could make any pair of hands. The two of them talking about Shakespeare and, truth be told, Wash enjoying the fact that he could once again talk with someone about a book—the way he and his father had talked—nearly as much as he enjoyed the sweet sound of her voice.

Her saying, "Why, Private Vance, what an intelligent way you have of describing the plight of the Prince of Denmark!"

Him replying, "Revenge is something that can drive a man or drive him insane."

And then her lifting a hand to tap her index finger thoughtfully against her chin before turning the page.

"I do hope we'll have time to talk about every one of the Bard's plays."

I do hope so, indeed, Wash thought now as he and Josh ducked into their tent.

Charley had gotten there ahead of them. As he often did since being discharged from the infirmary, he was sitting on his cot with his left shoe and sock removed, looking at the foot that was now missing the little toe that had turned black as a burned piece of meat and had to be lopped off.

"Charley," they both said.

"Boys," Charley replied, still staring down, his voice grim as a grave digger. "Y' hear the news?"

"What?"

"Them white men we arrested, the ones they shipped up to Topeka, Kansas. I jes' overheard the lieutenant talking 'bout them. And what do you suppose happened up there to them SOBs?"

"They get tried and throwed in jail to rot?" Josh asked.

"Nope."

"Hung?" Wash ventured, seeing in his mind the evil eyes of Tom Key glaring at him from that wolfish face.

"Hah!" Charley rolled his eyes. "Not in Kansas. The white men on that jury and that old white judge took pity on them. 'Specially since one of them was a senator's son. Gave 'em a lecture on mending their ways, fined 'em each fifty dollars, and then set 'em as free as jaybirds. Bet you a dollar 'gainst a dime that they go right back to selling whiskey to our Indians. Want to take that bet, Wash?"

Wash shook his head, feeling as glum now as his friend and remembering the words that were mouthed at him in the freezing cabin. You're a dead man.

Revenge, he thought, tapping the watch in his pocket.

"Nope," he said.

Charley went back to staring at his foot.

"Wish we had shot at least one of them. That might have been a fair trade for a toe."

"Do you know the story of Porcupine Bear?" Gray Head asked.

Wolf shook his head. He was too ashamed to speak.

Next to him was his best friend whose name was no longer Dirty Face. His best friend also shook his head.

"It was Porcupine Bear," Gray Head continued, "who spoke strong against the evils of firewater. He spoke of how it makes us so weak that we cannot even pull back our bowstrings. He spoke of how we become fearful to our own families. Do you remember now?"

The two young men nodded, their eyes turned down.

It is less than one moon since we returned with that herd, Wolf thought. *It is less than one month since we were given great praise. Less than one moon ago my friend was honored with a new name. He became Horse Road. But now...*

"Then what did Porcupine Bear do?"

Wolf reached up. He touched the bruise on his forehead where Horse Road had struck him with a heavy stone. Next to him, Horse Road was feeling his own bloody lip. Wolf had kicked him there.

After finding that hidden herd, they had done good things. They had driven the horses out of the box canyon. They had set fire to the whiskey wagon. But before setting that fire, Wolf had done something else. He had picked up one of those bottles and slid it in the parfleche bag slung over his horse. His friend smiled at him as he did it.

Both had forgotten about that bottle. There was so much excitement that followed their triumphant return. Dirty Face's old name had been thrown away. The new, strong name Horse Road had been bestowed upon him. The two of them had been seen as heroes.

Until last night. That was when Wolf noticed the parfleche bag that he'd placed against the back wall of the tipi. He had picked it up. He had felt the weight of the bottle within it.

He had hefted the bag. As he did so, he had remembered the tingling of those drops of whiskey on his tongue. It had not harmed him. Maybe the stories were exaggerated. Maybe his own mind was too strong to be made foolish by whiskey. He had put the bag under his arm and gone to the tipi of Horse Road's family. He had scratched softly on the door. His friend was a light sleeper. Only he would wake.

Horse Road had come crawling out.

"What?" he whispered.

Wolf held up the dark bottle.

"I am curious about this medicine water. Shall we try it?"

Horse Road looked over his shoulder. None of his family had wakened. Then he grinned the way he had when they were small children and sneaking out to do mischief. His teeth shone white in the darkness.

"Hee'he'e. Good idea."

They wrapped warm robes about them and walked out onto the calm snowy prairie. Above them was the bright full moon. Sentries had been posted, watching over their now much larger horse herd. But those watchers were on the far side of the herd, and everyone else was asleep.

"We will celebrate," Wolf said. He opened the bottle.

The first drink had been hard to take. Wolf coughed and his eyes watered. His mouth and tongue were on fire.

Horse Road laughed. He grabbed the bottle.

"Do it like this," he said. He tipped it up and took an even bigger drink than Wolf. Then he let out a great cloud of breath from his mouth. It looked like smoke in the cold air.

"Epeva'e," he said. "It is good."

He handed back the bottle. Wolf drank again. He did not choke this time. The more they drank, the easier it became. Then they began to act like children.

"I am happy," Horse Road shouted. "Happy, happy!" He belched and shook his head. "Are you happy?"

"I am a human being," Wolf shouted. The prairie was spinning around them. The moon was dancing up and down in the sky. The next thing he knew, he had hold of Horse Road's neck. The two of them were rolling in the snow. Wolf was laughing.

Then Horse Road hit him. He hit so hard that Wolf found himself on his back, arms splayed out.

"Your head is an egg," Horse Road said. His voice was serious. He picked up a rock. "I am going to break it open."

Wolf kicked him in the leg. As Horse Road fell, Wolf leaped. He began to kick his friend. He kicked him again and again, laughing like a crazy person. He would have kicked him more times but their fighting had been so noisy that the horse herd was stampeding. People were shouting. Hands had grabbed hold of them as other hands tied them up to keep them from killing each other.

Wolf put his own hands up to either side of his head. Horse Road had been right about it being an egg. It felt like an egg. It was a cracked egg with a dead chick inside it.

"Listen," Gray Head said to them now. There was sadness in his eyes. He was seeing the story he was about to tell. "It was back before the Kiowas became our allies. Forty-eight of our Bowstring Soldiers were killed by them. We had to make the Kiowas cry. Porcupine Bear was then chief of the Dog Soldiers, a man of great honor. So it fell to him to bring together the war party. He traveled from one camp to the next, seeking volunteers. At last he came to a village where he had many relatives. It was by the South Platte River, not far from Fort Laramie. Traders from the fort had just visited that village and brought some useful things. But they also brought whiskey. Porcupine Bear's relatives were already drinking. It would have been an insult to refuse to drink with them. Just one drink. Then one more. And one more. Soon he was sitting propped up in the corner of his relatives' lodge. He was singing Dog Soldier songs, ones not meant to be sung unless one was going into battle. That was shameful. What happened next was worse."

Gray Head paused. He looked at Wolf. Though it hurt his head to move it, Wolf nodded.

"Two of Porcupine Bear's cousins were very drunk. They began to fight each other. Just as you two were doing. One of them, Little Creek was his name, managed to get on top of the other one, whose name was Around. Little Creek pulled his long knife and tried to stab Around to death. Around called for help. Porcupine Bear took the knife away from Little Creek. Then, because he, too, was crazy with drink, Porcupine Bear stabbed Little Creek many times and killed him."

Gray Head stopped talking again. His gaze turned away from the two young men who kept their heads lowered in shame. Gray Head sighed.

"So it was that Porcupine Bear became outlawed. And the Medicine Arrows were not carried against the Kiowas by Porcupine Bear's Dog Soldiers, but by what was left of the Bowstring Society. That is why his part of the Dog Soldier Society began to camp away from the rest of the people. All because of the firewater."

"Why?" Wolf asked. "Why did he drink after speaking such clear words against drinking?"

Gray Head did not reply. He looked at Wolf. Wolf saw the question the elder was asking with his eyes.

Why did Horse Road and I get drunk?

Wolf felt his face grow flushed.

"Ah," he said.

The three of them sat for a long time. It was a silence that Wolf thought might never end. Then Gray Head sighed again.

"Even Sweet Medicine made mistakes," Gray Head said, his voice soft. "We human beings are all weak. We all make mistakes. Even those whose names are great may make mistakes. But Maheo takes pity on us when we humble ourselves, when we try to do better. Can you two do better?"

"Hee'he'e," the two young men answered, their voices small.

Gray Head slapped his palms together, so suddenly that both Wolf and Horse Road jumped.

"Aahto! Listen," Gray Head said. "Mistakes may be forgiven, but they must not be forgotten. I do not mean that you must carry guilt. If the water in your cup has gone bad, you must pour it out, not carry it around with you. Instead, use what you have learned to help find a better path next time, a path that will make your life of worth to the people. Do you understand?"

"Hee'he'e," Wolf answered, his voice louder this time.

Horse Road paused before he spoke. "Hee'he'e," he agreed.

His voice sounded less certain. That worried Wolf. Was Horse Road truly going to set aside his guilt? If not, he might be inclined to do foolhardy things to prove himself.

Gray Head did not seem to notice. "Good," he said. "You both have good hearts. I have seen this in you. So I have work for you to do. You will be my wolves. You will scout around and come back and tell me what you find. I will trust you. Even though the agent is a good man, no food comes for us. So, my wolves, scout about and see if there are still buffalo—or any game at all—to be found. I know you can do so without the ve'hoes catching you, but be careful. And harm no one. Do you understand? Your job will be to help the people, not start a war. "

Wolf nodded. Despite his aching head, his spirit had been lifted by Gray Head's words.

Yes, he thought. *To help the people. That is what I want more than anything else. I want to help our people survive.*

ONE TIME, MAMA SAID, FOOLISH JOHN GOT A BOTTLE OF
RUM. HE STOLE IT FROM OLD MASTER
AND WENT DOWN TO THE CREEK BOTTOM THAT NIGHT
TO DRINK IT.

THE FULL MOON WAS SHINING BRIGHT AS HE SAT THERE
DRINKING. PRETTY SOON THE FROGS OUT ON THE POND,
THEY BEGAN TO SING.

BRRUM, BRRUM, BRRUM, THE BIG FROGS SANG.

FOOLISH JOHN, HE HEARD THEM.

"YOU WANT SOME OF MY RUM?" HE SAID. "I BE GLAD
TO BRING SOME OUT THERE AND SHARE IT WITH YOU.
BUT I DON'T KNOW HOW TO SWIM. HOW DEEP IS
THE WATER HERE?"

THEN THE LITTLE FROGS STARTED SINGING.
NEE-DEEP, NEE-DEEP, NEE-DEEP.

"WELL," FOOLISH JOHN SAID, "IF IT IS ONLY KNEE DEEP,
THEN I CAN COME RIGHT ON OUT THERE."

BUT AS SOON AS HE WADED IN, HE WENT IN OVER HIS HEAD,
LOST THAT BOTTLE, AND JUST ABOUT DROWNED.

INDIAN FIGHTING

The Texas frontier.

My, my, Wash thought as he walked the parade ground perimeter, careful not to step on the recently seeded but already browning lawn. *Am I really here?*

"Wash," Charley had said when word came of the transfer of their company, "bet you a dime it is goin' to be hotter in more ways than one where we goin'."

Wash had not disagreed. It was not just because no one ever won a bet against Charley Smith—to the point where no soldier, no matter how good he believed his luck to be, would sit down to play a game of chance with Charley. It was also because the past three months had convinced Wash that anywhere on earth would be warmer than Camp Supply. Heading south sounded like a blessing and a relief.

They'd been told it was also likely to be hotter in Texas in another way beyond mere weather. And that excited those in Company D who had joined up to shoot at something other than targets and jackrabbits.

"You men been jawin' about not havin' seen any Indian fightin' yet," Sergeant Brown had growled as he passed on the orders. "You soon goin' to have to find something else to grouse about. We are going to Fort Griffin, Texas. Down there is the Texas frontier. That is right on the route what the Kiowas and Comanches and Cheyennes and Arapahos take in their raiding. Plus there are more than enough bad white men and buffalo hunters down there to stir up trouble—some of them just about within spittin' distance of the fort."

It took less than a week for Wash to learn just what the sergeant meant. The Flat. That is what they called the little town that sprung up below the fort. The buffalo hunters used the Flat as their base of operations, but the army could not go after them as they had the whiskey runners. Nothing illegal about hunting buffalo unless it was on Indian land.

And there was no way for anyone to say if the hides the white hunters were getting came from Indian land or not. Though it was a safe bet, as Charley put it, that the majority of those hunters were risking their scalps for every hide they peeled off a dead buffalo. The only places where the big beasts remained plentiful were on the Indian lands to the northwest.

The buffalo hunters were only part of the potential for trouble in the Flat. There dwelt more than the usual amount of lawbreakers in the hastily constructed settlement, a good many of them unreconstructed rebels. Shifty looks in their eyes and big hogleg pistols strapped on their belts. Pretending to be law-abiders during the day but out rustling cattle after dark.

Of course, not all of those among the five thousand folks in the Flat were lawbreakers. There were ranchers, farmers, and cowboys coming through on drives to Dodge City. Those cowboys were the big reason that there were more dance halls and saloons than restaurants. And the Flat was still growing, getting bigger and more out of control every day seeing as how there were no reliable peace officers.

"Sooner or later," Sergeant Brown said, "we going to have to declare martial law and clean that place up."

Despite the sergeant's words, the Flat did hold some who were more kindly disposed toward colored soldiers because they were also black. Some were cowboys, but even more were farmers, teamsters, or ordinary tradefolk. It had surprised Wash how many from the East that had come to settle the West were former slaves and their families, chasing a new life away from the old ways of the past. Some saloon owners would even serve drinks to black men.

And allow them into their card games—which Charley Smith had mentioned to Wash on three separate occasions thus far.

"Man," Charley had said, "first chance I get, I am going to try my luck down there."

Bad idea, Wash had thought. But he'd said nothing. Telling Charley not to do something would just set his cap even more in that direction.

Sergeant Brown had also, thus far, not been exactly right about Indian fighting being more likely in Texas. Raiding parties often passed close to the fort. In the last few weeks they had twice gotten word of such renegades and set out after them. But it had been to no avail. Such parties moved like the wind and were just as hard to catch before they would swing northwest up onto the buffalo range. Up there, there was no chance of tracking them. Whatever trail they might have left was obliterated by the buffalo herds they passed through.

But there were, for sure, more red men to be seen at Fort Griffin. There were double the number of Indian scouts they'd had at Camp Supply. In addition to the Osages who'd accompanied them, there were Indians of another sort. Tonkawas. And not just a few of them. Their whole tribe was living right next to the fort.

Tonks, Sergeant Brown called them.

"Our Tonks," he said, "are not exactly well liked by the other red men down here. Matter of fact, they are just plain hated. Back in '62, the other tribes hereabouts, Kiowas, Comanches, Shawnees, Caddos, Seminoles, Delawares—even some Osages—got together a war party and about wiped the Tonkawas out. When they got done, only 250 Tonks was left."

The surviving Tonkawas had taken refuge at Fort Griffin, where some had already been employed as scouts. Unlike the other southern Plains tribes, the Tonks had a long history of working for the white man better than fighting him. That was one of the reasons why the other tribes didn't like them. But not the only reason.

"You know why else the tribes don't cotton to our Tonks?" Charley asked a week after their arrival.

"Why?" Wash asked.

"Corporal Waller, he say it is on account of the fact that they eats them."

"Who eats who?"

Charley let go a deep chuckle. "Our Tonks is cannibals. Corporal Waller, he say that whenever Tonkawas are riding with the cavalry and there's a fight, as soon as one of the Indians from another tribe gets killed those Tonks make sure they get to that body first. They cuts out the best parts and eats them right there. Just like having a picnic lunch."

"No!" Wash said.

Charley chuckled again. "Want to bet?"

"Never mind."

There were no fewer than twenty-five Tonkawas working as scouts at Fort Griffin. Soon after his arrival, Lieutenant Pratt, due to his liking for Indians and their ways, was put in charge of them. Wash watched as the lieutenant strode across the yard, his hand extended toward the head Tonkawa scout, a pleasant look on his face. It was something like the face he showed to his black soldiers. A way of looking at them that was different from most white officers. Pride, but not the sort of pride their former slave owners had shown about those few men and women who'd became their favorites, the same pride of ownership felt toward one's best horse. No, Lieutenant Pratt's pride in his black underlings was of another sort. Pride, perhaps, that they were proving to be just as good soldiers as any white man.

His feeling toward the Indians, though, seemed to be a more complicated kettle of fish. Sometimes he seemed to be looking at them with the expression of a father seeing his firstborn child. Or like he wanted to adopt them into his family. Wash had learned that there were some white men on the frontier who seemed to love Indians. They dressed like them, married Indian women, let their children be raised as Indians. But that was not Lieutenant Pratt, even though he seemed to like nothing better than to be in their presence. But not to learn from them.

As he watched the lieutenant take the Tonkawa scout's hand and pump it, a thought came to Wash.

Maybe it's more like he wants to take them up like handfuls of red clay and mold them into some other shape.

That was a curious thing. But any man who served on the frontier generally had more than one thing about him that the civilized world would call curious.

I need to take my mama's advice. Just look the other way when it comes to the strange behavior of white men.

Strange behavior or not, Wash was more than glad that Lieutenant Pratt had come to the Texas frontier with Company D. Not just for his treating negro soldiers like men and not "mud turtles"—which is what the local white Texans, mostly unreformed rebels, called the black cavalrymen. It was especially because wherever Lieutenant Pratt went, he brought along his wife and his children and their whole household staff, including Sergeant Brown's wife and Bethany, who had formerly worked for Captain Nolan. Their weekly conversations about Shakespeare's plays had been able to continue, a discussion that was about to bring them to Romeo and Juliet.

Wash shook his head at that. It seemed as confusing as it was pleasant. His simple goal of proving himself to be a man and providing for his family back home was getting more complicated every day. First Sergeant Brown had put those ideas into his head about someday being able to go to school. And foolish as such an ambition was for a negro soldier to have, it stayed in his head, buzzing about like a gnat through his dreams. And now, since his meetings with Bethany, an even more impossible possibility had begun coming up again and again in the back of his mind. That somehow, some way, she might be a part of his future and more than just a ship passing in the night.

Impossible, Wash thought. And even as he thought that, along she came, a little parasol over her head.

"Good morning, Miss Bethany," he said.

She smiled back at him, sending a shiver down his back. "Good morning, Private Vance."

Just his name. But the nice way she spoke it, made *Vance* sound almost as pretty as her smile. If Wash had been a dog he would have rolled over on his back and wagged his tail.

But even though he wanted to say more, like commenting on the weather, he kept his mouth shut. A man on duty was not to engage in idle conversation with a civilian. One who got caught doing that would find himself on a punishment detail. And there were those who would give a trooper harsh punishment quicker than you could say Jack Robinson.

Lieutenant Pratt was not the only officer who was sent to Fort Griffin with them. They had also been blessed with none other than the former commander of Camp Supply, Lieutenant Colonel John W. Davidson, who had finally been given a larger command than that little understaffed outpost.

Openings for advancement were as scarce as hen's teeth in the Army of the West. However, the man formerly in charge at Fort Griffin, Colonel Benjamin Grierson, who was the first man ever to command the black 10th, had been promoted to superintendent of the Mounted Recruitment Service in St. Louis. Davidson had been the next former general in line.

The first thing Colonel Davidson had done was to impose a passel of strict new commands. No frivolity. No talking while on duty. No card games. No walking on the grass! As at Camp Supply, the commander loved his fresh-planted lawn more than all his black and white soldiers put together. Anyone seen putting one toe on the grass of the parade ground would get sent to the guardhouse.

Wash gently shook his head as he continued around the parade ground's perimeter. Davidson's orders had made the new commander even more unpopular than he'd been with the enlisted men at Camp Supply. Even the officers beneath him disliked him. His first order on arrival had been to dismiss the entire staff that Colonel Grierson had left in place. That staff change had lasted less than a week. When the Adjutant General's office for the Department of Texas got word of it, the colonel had been informed that he could do no such a thing.

So Davidson took out his frustration on the enlisted men, looking for any opportunity to bedevil them with new rules that made no real sense.

We may not be walking on the colonel's grass, Wash thought as he finished his round and saluted to the private who was taking his place, *but we are all walking on eggs.*

As he entered the main barracks, Charley and Josh beckoned Wash over to join them where they'd saved him a seat. The show was about to begin. They had a special visitor, one of their own 10th Cavalry, but serving in Company H, which was stationed elsewhere. He had been sent to Fort Griffin as a courier. He'd be there for only one night before returning to his own post, but there was time enough, he'd declared, to share a story.

It was one the men were eager to hear. The grizzled veteran, whose name was Corporal Reuben Waller, had played a part in the great rescue at Beecher Island.

"Think of that," Josh had said. "Beecher Island. Where some of our own negro cavalrymen rescued the survivors of that grim fight."

Charley was grinning from ear to ear as Wash took his seat. He looked happier than if he'd won three pots in a row.

"Wash," Charley said, bouncing his legs up and down like he was about to get up and start a jig, "you here just in time." He pointed at the far door. "Here he comes. The man of the hour!"

Wash looked where Charley was pointing. Two men of about the same size and age were walking into the barracks. The one on the right was Sergeant Brown. The other had to be Reuben Waller. They were alike enough to have been twins, aside from the abundant white hair of the one who had to be the Beecher Island hero.

"Men," Sergeant Brown said, "you ready to hear a story?"

He swept the crowd with his eyes as if he expected someone to disagree.

No chance of that. Everyone was as awed and silent as a bunch of farm boys seeing an elephant for the first time.

"The corporal here joined up when the 10th was first formin', back in '67. Already knowed a bit 'bout war, having seed it from the other side. His old master was a general in the reb army and took him along as a body servant. Twenty-nine battles he saw!" Brown paused to let that number sink in. "Twenty-nine. And you know what one of them was? Fort Pillow."

A few men gasped at that. There was not a black man alive who had not heard of that infamous engagement. The Union fort in Tennessee had been manned by black troops and a few white officers. The white officers were spared when they surrendered the fort to General Bedford Forest, but the unarmed colored troops were massacred by the rebels. "Remember Fort Pillow" had become the battle cry of black men in blue for the rest of the war.

At the mention of Fort Pillow, Corporal Waller dropped his head for a moment and closed his eyes. Then he lifted his gaze again to look at the men arranged around him with hard eyes like those of an eagle and shook his head. There would be no further talk of Fort Pillow that night. Instead it was time for stuffing the tenderfeet, telling grisly stories about Indians to the rookies.

The room was silent as the grizzle-haired veteran lowered himself into the camp chair set in front for him. He flopped his hat into his lap and settled back.

"Well," Waller said, his voice surprisingly high and thin. He paused, pulled a corncob pipe from his pocket, held it up, and looked around.

Immediately, a dozen sacks of tobacco were offered to him. He chose one, slowly filled his pipe, put the sack in his pocket, pulled out a match, and struck it on his boot. It was still so quiet in the assembly hall that everyone could hear the flaring of the flame and then the pock-pock-pock of his indrawn breaths as he puffed the pipe into life before letting out a hiss of white smoke.

"Beecher Island," he said. "Beecher Island." He looked around. "You want to hear about that one?"

"Yes, sir!" at least a dozen men answered.

The corporal allowed a grim smile to visit his lips. "Beecher Island. Uh-huh, uh-huh. It was one great sensation. Beecher Island on the Arickaree Crick in Colorado. September 1868 it was."

He raised his pipe, looking down the length of it as if it was a telescope showing him that scene.

"Them hostiles had surrounded Major Forsyth and Lieutenant Beecher and their brave men. Most of them was grave wounded and compelled to live on the flesh of horses for nine days on that small island out there in the middle of the crick."

Another dramatic pause as he let this sink into everyone's imagination.

"One of Forsyth's men, Jack Stillwell it was, he slipped through the Indians, rode to Fort Wallace, and brought word of the terrible fix they was in. Right away it was boots and saddles and we was entered in the race for the island. Twenty-six hours of hard riding and then Colonel Louis Carpenter and myself, being his hostler, rode first into the rifle pits they had dug out. What a sight we saw. Thirty dead and wounded men surrounded by dead horses that had lain in the hot sun for ten days. Those poor men were in a dying condition when the colonel and myself dismounted and began to rescue them. Before long the rest of the men of Company H were all in the pits, and we began to feed those men from our haversacks. They were eating all we gave them. If the doctor had not arrived and bade us to desist, we would have killed them by feeding them to death. And then when they was strong enough, they began to tell their tale."

Waller drew deep on his pipe, expelling a ring of smoke that hung above his gray-haired brow like a halo over a saint.

"God bless the Beecher Island men," Corporal Waller exclaimed, raising his hands as if he was in church and praising the Lord. "There were two thousand Indians attacked them. All under the great Cheyenne chief Roman Nose. Those murderous hostiles were preparing to raid Kansas and Colorado before they ran into Major Forsyth and his brave crew. There were no other soldiers within miles. All that Roman Nose had to oppose him and his thousands of braves was Major George Forsyth, Lieutenant Fredrick Beecher, and their scouts. The Indians had them surrounded. Every one of their fifty horses was shot by the Indians in less than an hour. But seeing how outnumbered they was, those brave men started to dig rifle pits in that sand, using spoons and pocketknives. Five men were killed as they dug, Beecher among them, and many wounded, but they dug out good deep rifle pits in the sand. Then old Roman Nose fixed up for a grand charge he thought would be fatal to the white men. But that was the greatest mistake Roman Nose ever made."

Waller looked round the rapt circle and cleared his throat. "A bit dry here, boys," he said.

Six canteens of water and three bottles containing something stronger were thrust out to him. Despite his other strict policies, Colonel Davidson was a heavy drinking man and did not mind at all if others did the same. There was never a problem finding whiskey at Fort Griffin.

Waller carefully selected the largest of the bottles, swigged back a good slug, corked it, and slid it into his breast pocket next to his new tobacco pouch. Then he lifted his hand to his chin, leaned forward, and held out his pipe as if it was a sword.

"Well, now to the fight!" He slapped his free hand hard against his hip like a man whipping his horse into a charge.

"Here they come from a hundred yards away. Two hundred Indians, three hundred Indians, a thousand Indians. Then opens up the Spencer carbines of them thirty-five remaining brave scouts. Firing and loading again and again. Renegades falling off their horses like leaves from the trees in fall! Roman Nose and his grand charge is wiped off the face of the earth."

The corporal settled back and rubbed his hands together as if dusting them off.

"Hurrah," someone shouted from the crowd of men.

Waller nodded in the direction of that shout. "Hurrah, indeed. By that brave stand made by the Forsyth and Beecher scouts, hundreds of settlers was saved from massacre and destruction."

The corporal looked around as if to judge if any of the men gathered around him might measure up to be the equal of those famous souls. Wash stood up straight as he could and met the veteran's eyes. Waller nodded back.

"Now, boys," Waller continued, "I have had many fights with the Indians in the ten years after that Beecher fight. But never have I seen anything to equal what was done that day. I say it was the greatest fight ever fought by any soldiers of the regular army at any time. And I do say further that in all the fights we had with the Indians, we never killed as many. A year later I heard Lone Wolf, who was there, say that the Cheyennes lost four hundred killed and fatally wounded in that one charge at Beecher Island."

"Imagine that," Charley said under his breath. "Four hundred killed."

Four hundred killed in one charge? That number bothered Wash and gave him pause. With only thirty-five rifles being fired at them?

"Well, we stayed on the island for three days after the fight and rescue. We buried the five men was killed. Lieutenant Beecher, Dr. Mooers, Louis Farley, and others, all with military honors. Used the funeral flag of Company H, which flag I have in my possession. Though I feel honor bound out of respect for the dead not to bring out that flag and just flaunt it around."

Waller raised his hand, two fingers held up. "However," he nodded, reaching into his pack. "I do also have in my possession these items to show you lads. A scalping knife and a horseshoeing knife, both that I picked up on that very battlefield."

Putting away his pipe, the corporal held the blades out. Most stared, wide-eyed. But Wash, who was in the front row, was close enough to reach out and touch the two weapons. Neither was sharp or at all impressive to look at. The red stains on them might have been blood...or rust. They look suspiciously like any old knife a man might obtain in trade.

"Tell you what, boys," Waller said, a look on his face that seemed to Wash more sly than generous, "I have been thinking that it is selfish of me to keep these two blades for myself. If you was to take up a collection, I might see my way to leaving one of them here in the safekeeping of your company. Just to bring you luck."

Wash looked over at Sergeant Brown, who was looking up at the ceiling and not reaching into his pocket like most of the other men who were excitedly bringing out whatever coins they could find to drop them into the old corporal's hat, which Josh was passing around.

When the hat reached him, Wash followed the sergeant's lead and just nodded as it went by, despite the look Josh gave him. Charley Smith, though, eagerly dove into his own pockets to add to the considerable stack already amassed.

"My, oh my," Charley said, coins clinking as he dropped them in one after another. "What a story! I just hope that when my time comes to face the enemy I may prove as worthy as them heroes of Beecher Island."

The minister was just getting warmed up.

"Your Cheyenne beliefs are foolish, ignorant, and pagan. This is the one way. Otherwise, when you die, you will fall into a lake of fire and burn in it forever. The Christian way is the one way of the spirit that you must now follow."

Everyone was listening patiently. They listened first to the white man's excited words spoken in English. Then they listened to the calmer voice of the translator as he put those words into human language.

That lake of fire is interesting, Wolf thought. *It sounds like something that would happen to Wihio.*

Wolf looked over to his left. Too Tall and Too Short had just stood up. They were walking away, shaking their heads. Wolf understood their feelings. Why would anyone who had lived a good life be punished? If one shared with others and was kind to his family, why would he be set on fire forever just because he was not a Christian? It was silly.

And why, instead of giving them the food they needed, had they been gathered by their agent to listen to foolish talk? But Gray Head was still politely listening. The old peace chief's family was just as hungry as his. He knew how nonsensical the preacher's message was. But it was important to be polite to a guest. So Wolf stayed where he was. He kept his face impassive as the white man's voice rose to a shout. The Cheyenne translator, though, remained calm.

"Their Jesus god is the most powerful," the translator said. "So he says. Their Jesus god was born of a woman who never slept with a man. So he says. He did many miracles. He turned water into wine and cured bad sicknesses. So he says. Then their Jesus god died. But he came back to life."

Out of the corner of his eye, Wolf saw Gray Head nod. It was possible their Jesus did all those great and wonderful things. In their oldest stories Sweet Medicine did things just as wonderful.

If this Jesus was so powerful, why were his enemies able so easily to kill him?

An elbow poked into Wolf's right side. Horse Road leaned close to whisper into his ear.

"Do you think Hook Nose had better medicine than his Jesus? Could his Jesus god make himself bulletproof?"

It took an effort, but Wolf managed to not grin. Horse Road's thoughts were much like his own. Why didn't Jesus protect himself?

Holy men among their people and other nations of the plains knew great medicine. Such medicine could protect a man from enemies. It would work not just against spears and nails. It could also make someone invulnerable to gunfire. Of course, such medicine worked only if you followed its rules.

The white preacher went on and on, repeating himself. Wolf no longer listened. He was thinking about how one could get medicine. It could be given to you. Or you could go and seek it on your own. Spend a long time alone on a hilltop crying for a vision. Go without food or sleep for days. Then you might get a medicine that would protect you.

That was how it had been with the great man Horse Road had mentioned. Wo-oh-ki-ni, Hook Nose, was his name. He was known by everyone for his bravery. Even the white men knew him, though they called him by the strange name of Roman Nose. He was an honored member of the Crooked Lance Society. But he was never a chief or a headman of any sort. Whenever such honors were offered to him, he refused them.

The fight in which he died was not an important one. The Striped Arrow People remembered it only because it was where Hook Nose lost his life. Three villages had been set up along the Republican River. Two were Lakota villages. The third village was Cheyenne. Hook Nose was there. He was visiting friends. Just before dawn, a small party of Lakotas coming from the south saw a column of fifty white soldiers. Those Lakotas hurried back to the villages farther up the river.

"The Long Knives are coming," they shouted as they rode through the three camps.

Criers went from lodge to lodge.

"Make ready to defend our women and children. Make ready to defend our old people."

Boys ran out onto the prairie to drive in the horses. Men got out their paint, their weapons and coup sticks, their war regalia.

The war leaders of all three camps came together. They agreed to attack as one. This was a good plan. Things often went badly when fighting the ve'hoes when small groups of young men slipped away from the main party to be the first to strike the enemy. Such early strikes gave the white soldiers time to prepare.

It took time for everyone to get ready. Each man had to find his favorite war horse. Each man had to make sure his protective medicine was right. Properly paint himself and his horse.

The sun was in the middle of the sky when they set out to find the white soldiers. They went where the Long Knife soldiers had been seen. They were no longer there. They searched all afternoon. They found no trace of the white men. When night fell, they made camp on the prairie.

Then, in the middle of the night, eight young men went out. They did just what the Dog Soldier chiefs had forbidden. They went looking for the enemy. Near dawn, they saw the light of fires. It was the camp of the white men. They were on a long sandbar in the same river that flowed to those villages. On one side of that sandbar the channel was wide. On the other side the river was narrow and shallow. That sandbar island had been long exposed. Willows and rushes and even a few cottonwood trees grew on it. The eight young men crept close. Waving their blankets and shouting, they ran through the horse herd to stampede it. But the horses were tied to picket pins. Only a few broke loose. The young men got away with seven horses.

Those young men came whooping into camp, driving the captured horses ahead of them. They were proud of what they had done. But Hook Nose shook his head.

"This is not good," he said. "They have given our enemies time to get ready."

He was right. By the time the main force of the people reached the white men's camp, the soldiers had dug like moles into the sand. They had piled up their packs as breastworks. The chiefs tried to hold everyone back. They were still three miles away from the camp. It would be foolish to start the attack. But the young warriors with them were too eager. It ended up with everyone charging in a long line. By the time they reached the island, all the soldiers were shooting at them.

Most of the warriors circled around the island, splashing through the river. But one Cheyenne man, Bad Heart, had bulletproof medicine. He rode straight through the scouts and up over the island. The white men fired at him many times. No bullets struck him. When he reached the other side, he turned around and rode through the white men a second time. He still was not hit by any bullets.

Other men, though, were not bulletproof. Some white scouts were concealed in the high grass and reeds. Dry Throat was shot by them and killed. As he shook his shield over his head, White Weasel Bear was shot by those scouts. He fell off his horse and was dead. His nephew, White Thunder, who was only nineteen, rode to try to help when he saw his uncle fall. He, too, was killed.

The fight had been going on for some time when Hook Nose arrived at the battlefield. He stopped on top of a hill, a mile from the fight.

"Hook Nose has arrived," people began to shout. The fighting stopped. Everyone stood back, waiting to see what he would do.

Several men rode up to him. He dismounted and sat with them on the side of the hill away from the fight.

"When are you going to fight?" they asked him. "You should lead the next charge."

Hook Nose shook his head.

"Something was done the other day at the Lakota camp," he said to them. "White Bull, who made my bulletproof medicine, told me I was told never to eat anything touched by iron. The bread I ate today was lifted with a fork. I learned that only after I ate it. My medicine will no longer work until I have it renewed. There is not enough time for that now. If I go into this fight, I will be killed."

White Contrary rode up. He was an old man but still a good fighter. So he had ridden out with the other warriors.

"Ah," he said. "Here is Hook Nose, the man we all depend upon, sitting behind this hill. Do you not see your men out there dying? Two fell just before I came up here. All those men feel they belong to you." White Contrary then made a wide circle with his hands. "All of them. They will do anything you ask. But here you sit behind this hill."

Hook Nose stood up. "I have done something I was told not to do. My food was lifted with an iron tool. I know that I shall be killed today. Still, I will fight."

He went back to his horse and took down the bundle with his paint and war regalia. He shook out his war bonnet and held it up and looked at it. That war bonnet was the one given him by White Bull to protect him in battle. Its medicine would work only as long as he never ate food that had been lifted with a metal tool. He carefully put the bonnet upon his head. He mounted his horse. He rode fast toward the white men, followed by many other Cheyennes and Lakotas. As he rode right past those white men hidden in the high grass and reeds, they shot him in the back. He fell from his horse. He had enough strength to crawl up to the bank, where others came and carried him away. But he died before the setting of the sun.

The fight there went on for another two days. Finally, because the white men were dug in so well, it was decided they had fought enough. Everyone left. Nine people were killed there. Six were Cheyennes, two were Lakotas, and one was Arapaho. In addition to Hook Nose, the Cheyennes who died were Prairie Bear, Dry Throat, White Thunder, Killed by a Bull, and Weasel Bear. The Arapaho was named Little Man, and he was a chief. Wolf could not remember the names of the two Lakotas.

An elbow poked Wolf again in his side.

"Brother," Horse Road said, "are we going to sit here all afternoon?"

Wolf looked up. Only he and Horse Road were still there. All the others were gone. Wolf had been so deep in remembering the story of Hook Nose's death that he had not noticed the white man finish his talk.

Wolf stood up. He shook his legs to bring them back to life after sitting for so long.

"Let's walk," he said.

Together the two of them walked to the edge of the camp. They stood side by side looking out at the prairie.

Wolf thought about what it meant to be one who protects the people. One who would face the enemy even if he knew it meant his death.

Would I be able to do such a thing? And what would happen then to my mother and my sister without me to hunt for them and protect them?

Wolf looked over at Horse Road. His friend longed to make his own name good, to have stories told about him.

Is that all I want?

"What were you dreaming about?" Horse Road asked.

"Hook Nose."

"Hee'he'e," Horse Road said. "How great it would be to be made bulletproof! Would you not like such medicine, Following Wolf?"

Wolf was silent for a time. "Perhaps," he replied. "But I would be careful who I got it from. Not everyone can make men bulletproof."

THE MAN WITH ONE EYE
LEARNS TO THANK GOD
WHEN HE MEETS A MAN
WHO IS BLIND.

BOWING TO ONE
WHO IS SHORTER THAN YOU
DOES NOT PREVENT YOU
FROM STANDING STRAIGHT AGAIN.

A MAN'S FAULTS
ARE LIKE A HILL.
WHEN HE STANDS ON THEM
HE SEES ONLY THOSE
OF OTHER PEOPLE
AND TALKS ABOUT THEM.

IT IS NOT THE EYE
THAT UNDERSTANDS
BUT THE HEART
AND THE MIND.

RAIDERS

Indians had attacked some of the settlers' homesteads. Bad attacks.
It was not just that cattle and horses were stolen. People were killed.
The latest dead were a man and his wife and their two children, bru-
tally murdered and then scalped in front of their own home.

Since arriving at Fort Griffin, the only Indians Wash had seen
were their Osages and the new Tonkawa scouts. But an attack like
that just had to have been Indians. Kiowas and Comanches. Or
maybe Cheyennes. Renegades leaving their reservations and raiding
down into Texas.

At the moment, Lieutenant Pratt was riding up front with some
of those Tonkawa scouts. Like a bear in a honey tree. A big grin on
his pockmarked face as he looked down his long nose at them. He
nodded and they agreed and followed after him like he was Moses
showing the way to the Promised Land.

It hadn't been that way when they first arrived. The Tonkawas
had been a problem. It was because of the very same thing that was
the curse of so many a man and woman in the West, but especially
so for the red folks: strong drink.

Whiskey was cheaper and easier to come by at Fort Griffin than
clean water. As a result, on any given day half of the Tonkawas were
useless as scouts or for any task other than lying about drunk as
skunks. Or so it was until Lieutenant Pratt took his usual direct way
of dealing with things. He called the Tonkawa chief to him.

"I have been told by our commanding officer," Lieutenant Pratt said, "that whiskey is a problem for your people. So I have made a road for those of you who drink, and I am going to make you walk it."

The old Tonkawa chief, not yet realizing the measure of the man he was facing, nodded his head.

"Right, Lieutenant. Whiskey no good. Whiskey bad. Me not like whiskey."

"Your judgment is right," Lieutenant Pratt had replied. He lifted up one long finger and drew a line in the air. "Now listen well. Here is the road I am setting before you. The next time you are drunk, you will be placed in the guardhouse until you are sober. Then, for the next seven days you will be given a wheelbarrow and go around picking up trash. The next time it happens, you will have to do this for fourteen days. And if it happens again, twenty-eight days. Each time the punishment will be doubled. That is all. Now go back to your camp."

Not long after, Lieutenant Pratt, Wash, and Charley were riding by the Tonkawa camp, just down off the mesa where the fort sat. From the woods they heard loud, inebriated voices. The lieutenant signaled them to tie their horses and follow the sound. There among the trees just behind the Indian camp, they saw the two drunk men who'd been fighting. One of them was the Tonkawa chief, who lay sprawled out on the ground. The second intoxicated Tonkawa, one of the tribe's big men, stood over the chief with a rock, threatening to kill him. Lieutenant Pratt knocked the rock from the big man's hand while Charley grabbed hold of the man. Wash tried to help the chief to stand, but he was too drunk and his weight too great for one man to lift.

"Leave him," Pratt ordered.

A few minutes later they entered the fort, the big Tonkawa man staggering in front of Pratt, who was riding his horse close behind to prod him along.

"Sergeant Brown," Lieutenant Pratt ordered, "you and Private Vance get a cart. Then collect the chief and bring him back up to the guardhouse, where we are taking this man."

Although the chief was still so drunk, the sergeant and Wash managed to flop him up into the wagon bed like a sack of flour and then roll him out into the guardhouse.

The next day, when both Tonkawas were sober, Lieutenant Pratt repeated his talk about not drinking to the man who had held the rock.

"I shall not warn you again," the lieutenant said, sending the man back to the Tonkawa camp.

The chief, however, was told to stay and was given that wheelbarrow to push. Not an hour passed before a delegation of old men from the tribe arrived at the gate of the fort.

"Our chief no work that way. Not right." they said.

Lieutenant Pratt nodded. "Your chief," he said, not raising his voice but speaking in a tone that brooked no disagreement, "chose to do that work. I told him that if I found him drunk, he would push that wheelbarrow and pick up trash for seven days. Since he was drunk, that told me he wished to do that sort of work. So neither you nor he can complain. The commanding officer says that your whiskey drinking must end."

The little delegation went back down the hill mumbling. Presently, a crowd of old Tonkawa women came up the hill. They stood outside the fort wailing and carrying on so loud they could be heard all around the post. Lieutenant Pratt again came out and gave them the same talk. Then he surveyed their ranks.

"A woman," he said, a grim smile playing over his mouth, "may push a wheelbarrow just as well as a man."

The women went away.

Next to show up was Johnson, the chief's son and head sergeant of the scouts. He held thirty dollars in his hand, all the pay the scouts had earned for the past month.

"Lieutenant, sir," he said, "I give you this money, you let my father go?"

But Lieutenant Pratt was solid as the rock Moses stood on.

"Your father's release will come when his sentence is served."

And that was just what happened. At sunset on the seventh day, Lieutenant Pratt had the chief brought to him.

"You are chief over these people," Lieutenant Pratt said. "I have been put in charge to help you any way I can. I cannot help you unless you Indians help yourselves. The bootleggers who sell you whiskey get your money and keep you poor and degrade you. They take away your health and your manhood. When those bootleggers come into your camp late at night, you come quietly to me and tell me they are there. I will arrest them and ask the government to punish them as the law provides."

This time the old chief did not just nod. He put one hand over his heart and held the other one up, palm forward. "You are right, Lieutenant," the old chief said. "I will do as you say."

Sure enough, a few days later the Tonkawa chief came to the fort late at night while Wash was standing picket and asked to be taken to Lieutenant Pratt.

"Bootleggers in our camp," he said.

A detail was sent down to the Tonkawa camp straightaway. There they found two white men selling whiskey. The soldiers broke the bottles on the rocks, arrested the men, and threw them in the guardhouse.

Since then there had been no more trouble with whiskey in the Tonkawa camp. The old chief had become as tight to the lieutenant as a second skin, and Johnson showed more respect to Pratt than to any other white man.

The sun had moved only the width of two hands across the sky by the time the men of Company D reached the settlers' cabin where the massacre took place. It was a sad sight to see. The door to the small sod house was on the ground, torn off the hinges. A little wooden table that looked to have been nailed together from a packing crate had been tossed out onto the hard red earth and broken into pieces. Next to it was a rag doll with its head torn off. The rickety corral out back where the horses and cattle had been kept was empty.

Two men of Company D were waiting for them. They were with the four-man scouting party that had come upon the scene four hours ago. Private Henry Imes and Private Rufus Slade, both Virginia men like Wash. They'd stayed behind to give decent burial to that little family while the others galloped back to Fort Griffin. Wash could see that they'd been working hard. The only sign of the family that had lived here, aside from the blood darkening the ground near the soddy, were four mounds of dirt with rocks piled atop. Henry Imes, big and burly as a bear and nearly as strong, was hammering a rough cross into the ground at the head of the largest grave.

Imes looked up at them and shook his head.

"Black folks, just like us," he said. His voice was steady but as angry as the look on his face. He wiped his forehead with his kerchief, set his wide-brimmed hat back on his head, and took a slow breath. "You wouldn't want to have seen what the savages done to these poor folks. Every one of them scalped, even the two chillen."

Rufus Slade, an equally big, wide man with a deep voice, stood up from the last and smallest grave where he'd been kneeling. "Killing is too damn good for the bunch of renegade snakes done this," he rumbled.

Charley, sitting on his horse to Wash's left, pursed his lips and then swallowed back the tobacco he'd been about to spit onto the dry ground, realizing that it might seem like disrespect to the dead.

"Ana!" someone called. "Look here!"

It was the head Tonkawa scout, Johnson. Off his horse fifty yards out from the cabin, he'd been examining the ground and now was holding something in his hand. He brought it to Lieutenant Pratt, who nodded gravely, then put the small white object into his pocket.

Johnson vaulted back onto his horse and galloped off, the three other scouts fanning out behind him. Fine trackers that they were, in pursuit they would not even slow their horses down. Just keep going at a gallop, extended out in a line so if one lost the trail, another would pick it up, even on such hard and rocky ground as stretched around them in all directions.

The men of Company D, Imes and Slade included, mounted up and followed at a trot.

An hour later, Johnson came back into sight, gesturing for the troop to follow. He led them to the base of a great rock.

"Ana!" he said again, leaning down—without leaving the back of his horse or even slowing it up—to scoop something up. It was small and white like the first thing he had found back near the soddy. This time Wash was close enough to see what it was he handed to Lieutenant Pratt. The butt end of a paper cigarette.

Seeing it sent a chill down Wash's back.

Damn, he thought. *I do believe I know what that means.*

Wash kicked his horse to catch up to and ride next to Johnson.

"Ta-in," Wash said. He'd been talking with the chief scout, who had passable English, the day before and learned that Ta-in, which meant "friend" in Tonkawa, was a good way to start a conversation.

"Ta-in," Johnson replied with a nod.

"The Indians around here," Wash said, "they smoke tobacco only in a pipe?"

"Is so," Johnson replied. Then he kicked his heels into the side of his horse to catch up with the other scouts riding ahead.

Another two hours passed. Time for Wash to think back on the talk he'd had the day before with the chief scout. He'd discovered the simple fact that although white men usually believed that Indians did not have much to say, that was mostly because white men seldom shut up and gave them time to talk. If a man was patient and showed he was ready to listen, it might reach the point where you could hardly get an Indian to shut up.

The day before had been a Sunday. After morning services, when there was not much to do, Wash had been taking his leisure on a tree trunk just outside the fort, looking down on the little forest that edged the Tonkawa camp. When Johnson walked past, Wash had held up a hand and beckoned him to sit down.

Just then, a big greenbottle fly buzzed up and landed on the back of Wash's hand. Instead of slapping at it, Wash lifted his hand to look closely at it, studying how bright its eyes were and the way it cocked its head and rubbed its front feet together. Johnson said something Wash did not understand in Tonkawa. Then, leaning over, he gently blew the fly off Wash's hand. The two of them smiled. Johnson sat down beside him.

"I have been wondering about something," Wash said. "Why are all of you Tonkawas here?"

"How come we work for white man?" Johnson said.

Wash nodded.

Johnson looked at Wash. "How come you?" he asked, his voice deep as the beat of a drum.

Neither said a word for a while. Then the heavy-set Tonkawa man cleared his throat, and spoke.

"Long ago, time of my great-grandfathers, all this our land." He swung his hand in a wide circle. "Us Tickanwatic, Real People. Mayeye, Tohaha, Cantona, Emet, Sana, all of us together. Mexicanos come from south, push us. Comanches come from north, push us. We lose our land." He put his hand palm down on the soil and was silent for a moment.

"We ally with Apaches for a time. No good. We move down into Texas. Scout for Tejano Rangers, fight other Indians. Get paid. Then Tejanos say we must go to Indian Territory. It was when some white men put on gray suits and fight their brothers in the blue suits. We work as scouts for gray suits. Fight other Indians. Get paid. But blue soldiers attack agency, kill agent. We try go south, get caught. Not by white men but other Indians. Angry at us for helping white men all those years, fighting other Indians. Big war party attacks us. Half our people killed. Hard time then. Now we here, work for blue suits."

"Fight other Indians?"

Johnson had smiled. "Get paid."

There was, to Wash's eyes, no sign of any tracks on the hardpan soil. They were now winding their way past red alkali pools, over rocky ridges, and through stony valleys. But Johnson and the other scouts had been leading them on as if the trail was as easy to see as a wagon-rutted road.

Then, as they entered a stretch of softer soil, Wash saw just that. Wagon tracks.

Not many Indians hereabouts use wagons. None, in fact.

Johnson was gesturing from the top of a small hill. Lieutenant Pratt led the troop up to join him. Johnson pointed with his chin off to the east, the opposite direction of the raiding party they'd been following.

"More men come," Johnson said, shading his eyes and staring where a little dust cloud was barely visible on the horizon. "I see badge. Sheriff, I think."

"Raise up and wave the company flag to make sure they see us." Lieutenant Pratt said.

Being flag bearer, that is what Wash did.

It took half an hour for the men to reach them. Sure enough, as Johnson had said, it was the sheriff from a nearby county, accompanied by a posse of six dusty and well-armed men. Extremely well-armed. Rifles, shotguns, pistols. Every man also had on his belt an Arkansas toothpick, the big knives that Texans seemed to strap on as soon as they climbed into their britches every morning. They were a grim and determined-looking bunch.

As they reined up, they pulled down their kerchiefs. Though red dust coated their faces, Wash noted that, somewhat to his surprise, two of them were black men.

Maybe this sheriff is less prejudiced than some about folks of our color. Or it may be these negro cowboys are so handy with their guns that he is glad to have them along.

Aside from the color of their skins under that red dust, all six looked alike as cousins. Every one of the seven, the sheriff included, was wearing sheepskin chaps, had a red bandanna around his neck, and was sporting a thick mustache. The sheriff was the tallest in the saddle of his crew. Long and lanky, he appeared to be more rawhide than muscle. The bones of his cheeks stuck out on either side of his black handlebar mustache and looked sharp enough to cut bread.

"Sir," the lawman said in a high, raspy voice to Lieutenant Pratt, "I am Sheriff Bob Long. This is my posse. I wish to execute my office against a party of depredating cattle thieves. They are villainous horse rustlers, a desperate and dastardly crew whom we have tracked thus far. From the sign ahead it appears they have joined up with another party. Might we beg the help and assistance of you and your men?"

Lieutenant Pratt reached out and took the sheriff's hand.

"Sir," Pratt said, "you may count upon me and my soldiers. We have the same objective as you. If these thieves are white men or Mexicans, I shall gladly hand them over into your custody to take them back for trial."

For some reason the lieutenant's speech caused the sheriff some amusement. He actually started to laugh, then swallowed it back as he brought up his hand to stroke his mustache.

"I do understand. I thank you, sir," Sheriff Bob Long rasped.

Pratt looked over to Johnson. The scout held out both hands and then brought them together and pressed them forward.

Does that mean our two groups are now working together, or is he just saying that the two groups of raiders joined just ahead of us? Probably both.

As usual, Johnson and the other scouts kicked their heels into their ponies' sides and galloped ahead, disappearing into the folded hills. The men of Company D and the posse pushed on behind them at a slower pace.

The sun was just two hands above the western horizon when Johnson came back.

"Two corral. Many cattle, forty ponies. Two cabins on creek. Twelve men. They not know we come."

At Pratt's command, they divided up into three parties, Company D taking the center and the right while the sheriff's posse flanked left. As flag bearer, Wash stayed next to Lieutenant Pratt in the center. Soon they reached a vantage point where they could look down into the valley. Ten or so of the raiders were gathered around a fire, cooking their supper. Half seemed to be Indians, though the buckskin clothing and feathered headdresses looked bedraggled.

All of a sudden, from the left flank a barrage of shots sufficient to rival the fourth of July was let loose. The large black pot hanging over the fire went flying, spraying hot mush in all directions. The befeathered man closest to the cooking pot fell face down into the fire.

"Bugler," Lieutenant Pratt shouted. The men of Company D went charging in to arrive at the outlaw's campfire at the same time as Sheriff Bob and his men. Around the fire the remaining outlaws who'd not been mowed down by the hail of gunfire were cowering with their hands raised.

"Cease fire," Lieutenant Pratt yelled. To Wash's surprise, Sheriff Bob and his boys did as he said.

A smell like that of a singed chicken began to fill the air.

"Haul that dead man out that fire," Sergeant Brown growled.

Two of the other men in Indian garb tried to push the dead man from the fire with their feet, not willing to lower their hands and risk being shot by the Texans, who were staring at them like hungry wolves eyeing a flock of goats.

"Use your hands, you dang fools," the sergeant snarled.

The two lowered their hands to roll the dead man from the fire. They coughed so hard from the smoke as they did so that they both dislodged their headdresses, revealing dirty blonde hair. Wash was close enough now to see that their headgear had been roughly fashioned from chicken and turkey feathers rather than eagle plumes. Like the deceased outlaw at their feet, they were white men roughly dressed and poorly painted as Indians.

The Tonkawa scouts came into camp then. Each pushed ahead of him an outlaw with his hands tied behind his back. As sentries they had done as poor a job of keeping watch as their comrades' attempts to lay the blame for their deeds on renegade Indians.

Sheriff Bob sniffed. "You see before you the game of this vile gang," he said. "They disguise themselves as Indian. They go so far as to take scalps." He pointed his rifle at the bloody hair attached to the belt of the dead man. "After, with a washed face and a change of clothing, they may come openly in to town. There they do bemoan and complain loudly about the renegades who are depredating."

Lieutenant Pratt took a careful look at each of the eleven outlaws once they were well tied up. Wash looked them over, too. None of them was either a weasel-faced man with a beard or a New Orleans high yellow with a bugle. Though he'd heard nothing about Tom Key since getting into Texas, rumors had reached Fort Griffin of a light-skinned negro deserter among the Comancheros, those mixed gangs of Mexicans and Indians that dealt in slaves and illegal arms.

The lieutenant turned to the sheriff. "Can you bring them in to trial without our help?"

Sheriff Bob looked up from chewing. He and the other men in his posse had dismounted and were busy eating beans and bacon from the fry pans undamaged by their fusillade, one of the black cowboys sitting on the broad back of a dead outlaw.

"Yessir," the sheriff said, "I do believe that we can handle them on our own. Is that not so, men?"

Six heads nodded as one.

"Sure thing," one of the white cowboys said.

"Well and truly," one of the black cowboys agreed through a mouthful of beans.

Sheriff Bob eyed his men in a fond, fatherly way.

"So," he said, "you see. We have it under control. Thank you again, Lieutenant. You can head on back to the fort."

There was a fine full moon in the sky to light their way, and the men of Company D arrived back to the barracks shortly after midnight. The cooks had saved a cold supper for them, which they gratefully ate before falling into their cots.

Late the next morning, Sheriff Bob and his posse arrived at the fort. Just the seven of them.

Colonel Davidson came out to greet them, Lieutenant Pratt by his side.

"Sir," Sheriff Bob rasped, "I have just come by to thank and commend your good lieutenant. He and his men did one fine and professional job. They assisted in the apprehension of a desperate and dastardly crew."

"Thank you," said the colonel. "Your commendation is noted."

"Sheriff," Lieutenant Pratt asked, "where are the prisoners?"

A serious look came over Sheriff Bob's face, a look that might have been hard to hold due to the snickering from the men in his posse behind him.

"Well, sir," he rasped, "during the night they did foolishly try to get away. All were shot to death and killed, to a man."

To that neither the colonel nor Lieutenant Pratt had any reply.

WHOEVER COMMITS EVIL UPON ANOTHER,

IT SHALL COME BACK UPON HIM.

SO DO THE LEARNED MEN SING,

MAY ALLAH HAVE MERCY UPON THEM.

FOR TRULY, TRULY IT IS SAID

THAT WHOEVER SOWS EVIL,

IT COMES UP IN HIS OWN GARDEN.

—HAUSA PROVERB

SHOWDOWN

Charley Smith had gone down into the Flat. Knowing that Wash would not approve, he went without telling him. He'd heard there would be a place for him in the poker game at the biggest of the saloons. Some men with money were saying they had heard there was a black soldier thought he could play cards. They wanted to prove him wrong. Having Lem Smith and Little George Williams, two other troopers from Company D with him, and seeing as how he was going down during the day and planned to be back before dark, Charley had figured he would be safe enough.

But he figured wrong.

In the dark, Wash heard someone outside the tent. Then a scared whisper.

"Wash."

Wash sat up and lit a match. It showed him two faces. One was on the pocket watch by his bedside, telling him the time was only an hour after taps. The other was that of the man who had slipped into the tent and was looking down at him. Little George.

"What?" Wash said, slipping his suspenders over his shoulders and pulling on his boots.

"They done got Charley in town."

"You tell Sergeant Brown?"

"No. Said they'd up and kill him they saw me coming back with more'n jes' you."

"Why me?" Wash said. But even as he said it he thought he knew the reason.

"Man say he know you. Want his watch back."

Wash took one deep breath, then another. He felt as if he should say something to Little George. But for once there were no words coming to him except those in his head saying *Get ready*.

"You comin'?" Little George said, even more nervously.

Wash just nodded and put on his blue coat, fastening each button one by one. He strapped on his belt with the holster high on his right side. He'd seen a few cowboys and men who considered themselves gunfighters wearing their holster low on their hip, right where the pistol would get in the way and maybe even jolt out of the holster if you were trying to ride a horse. Drawing a gun fast might look pretty, but taking careful aim was more likely to ensure the shot you fired was going to hit something other than air.

He drew the hammer back to half cock, opened the loading gate to the side, and shook the metal cartridges from the cylinder of the .45 Cavalry Colt—a good solid gun with more stopping power than the M1860 Colt .44 the 10th had used before. He looked at each bullet to make sure it was clean, no grit or dust on it. Reloaded the first bullet, left the next chamber empty, then shucked in four more rounds. The Colt held six shots, but without a safety, leaving the hammer over a chamber with a shell in it was an invitation to an accident. He brought the hammer up to full cock and then let it down so that it was resting on an empty chamber.

"Hurry up," Little George said.

"Unh-unh," Wash shook his head. Methodical, careful, that was the ticket. Especially when a life was at stake.

"He said not to keep him waiting."

"Uh-huh."

That was another reason why he wasn't hurrying. A man made to wait gets more nervous. From what he knew of Tom Key, the more nervous he'd get, the more shaky he would be. He hefted the gun, then slid it into the holster with the butt forward. That made it a little awkward to pull out if you favored shooting with your right hand, but

Wash was good with either hand. He'd learned how to pull out the gun with a cross draw, reaching across his belly with his left hand after he unfastened the buttons that held the gun in place with his right.

He rubbed his fingers across the callouses on his thumb and palm. Callouses on his thumb from time after time thumbing back the single-action, first dry firing and then with rounds in the chamber. Callouses on his palm from the recoil of the gun butt against his hand as a .45 caliber slug burst from the barrel. He brushed imaginary dust from each shoulder, and settled his cap on his head.

"Let's go," he said. "You and me."

"And me," a voice said from the shadows outside. Josh ducked his head and came in, his carbine held across his chest. "Couldn't help but overhear."

The ride to the edge of the Flat was a short one. But it was long enough to allow Wash to think about more things than he'd intended. What would happen if he failed. What would happen if he succeeded and ended up in trouble for shooting a white man. But those were only two of the thoughts in his mind. Others troubled him just as much. Like what would his mother and sister do if he got killed. And if he did get all shot up, what could he possibly say to apologize to Bethany for not showing up tomorrow as planned for them to read Shakespeare together? He ran over that last thought in his head three times before he realized just how ridiculous it was.

Man who's dead doesn't do any apologizing, does he?

Wash chuckled to himself.

"Man," Little Bob whispered from behind him, "you hear that, Josh? Wash, he so cool about this, so sure he is going to shoot that skinny old white man, that he's jes' laughing."

That made Wash chuckle a little louder until he had a brief coughing fit and Josh had to pat him on the back.

Serious now, he thought. *Don't think of anything else, especially not Bethany's face.*

Which of course was all he found himself thinking of as they tied their horses to a rail at the far edge of town and began the long walk to the saloon that Little George pointed out to them.

They drew their rifles and carefully made their way past the
noise of music and loud voices coming out of the drinking parlors
that were as numerous in the Flat as fleas on a hound's back. Lights
shone out of the doors and windows, but the three men stayed in
the shadows and passed by unnoticed. As they neared the final
saloon, the one whose rough board sign read SILVUR DOLLER, they
noticed that it was quieter than the others. No music, no shouting.
Almost as if the place was holding its breath.

*A man with a drawn gun threatening to kill someone does tend to
spoil the party,* Wash thought.

Their eyes were used enough to the dark by now that the three
of them could clearly see each other, even though they knew they
would still be invisible to those inside. Josh tapped Wash on the
shoulder, put his hand on Wash's chest, and made a circling motion.

You go around, come in the back.

Wash nodded, tapped Josh and then Little George on their
chests, and pointed to the front door.

You two go in the front.

Holding his own rifle across his chest, Wash began to make his
way along the side of the building as Josh and Little George stepped
up onto the ramshackle porch nailed onto the front of the SILVUR
DOLLER. The sounds of their heavy boots on the wood and then
the creaking of the swinging doors as they pushed them open covered the noise he made as he passed through the alley. It was just as
bad smelling as it was packed full of debris, including what might
have been a dead cat and stuck to his right boot until he scraped it
off with a broken piece of plank.

It took him longer than he'd intended. But the wall of the
saloon was so poorly made that he could now and then catch thin
glimpses through the cracks in the siding of what was going on
inside. And he could hear what was being said. Said by Tom Key, his
voice as mean and pinched as if he'd just spit out a mouthful
of alum.

"Who the HELL is you! You ain't the ONE I want. Where's my
little darkie?"

"Now take it easy, sir." That was Josh's voice. Slow and calm as always, though without the joking tone that was so often there in whatever he said.

"NO SIR, DO NOT *SIR* ME, BOY. Go back and get me the one I want or I shall blow a hole in this man big enough to drive a wagon through. YOU HEAR ME? And don't you or your friend try nothing. I got two more men here just aching to kill them a Buffalo Soldier."

The next crack between the boards was wide enough for Wash to see inside, though he had to lift himself up on his toes to do it. What he saw made him want to cuss out loud. Charley Smith was sitting in front of a little table, but his hands were not in their usual place, dealing out cards or raking in his winnings. They were down at his side, tied to the chair legs. And behind him stood Tom Key. His beard was gone now, and Wash could see that the man's scrawny face was even more drawn than it had been the day when he ran off from the plantation and dry-gulched the Vances. There was a vivid red scar on his right cheek, and Wash could see that half the man's front teeth were gone. The life of an outlaw had been taking its toll on the man. But his eyes were as snake black and devil mean as ever. And the cut-off double barrel twelve-gauge shotgun in his hands was leveled at Charley's head.

Charley didn't move his head, but he did move his eyes. Moved them so he was looking right at that crack in the wall where Wash was watching him. And he saw Wash's eyes. Wash knew that for sure because Charley raised one eyebrow and then looked down, just with his eyes, drawing Wash's gaze to Charley's left hand. It held the razor that Charley had confiscated from their former bugler, the razor that Charley had carried in the top of his left boot since then. And Wash could see that with those long dexterous fingers of his that could shuffle a deck of cards one-handed, Charley had pulled out that razor and cut through the ropes that had held him to the chair. All that was holding those cut ropes from falling down was the pressure of Charley's big hand.

Tom Key was still talking, talking the way men who like to hear their own voice talk.

"You boys better LISTEN. You go back and bring me that little boy. You tell him I am going to WHIP him like I done his no-good lazy pappy."

Wash looked beyond Charley and Tom Key, trying to locate the other two men Key had mentioned. There were at least twenty other men in the room and two women that he could see. Then he made out what had to be one of the former overseer's partners in crime. It was a lumpy-faced middle-aged man of medium height standing twenty feet to Key's right. Thin red hair plastered over the top of his head, his right cheek was pressed against the stock of the Spencer repeating rifle he had raised to his shoulder. But where was the second one? Not there or there. Wash's calves were feeling the strain from standing so long on tiptoe, but he caught sight of the second one when the man shifted and took a step forward from where he'd been leaning against the very wall Wash was peering through. Wash caught a quick glimpse of a green-shirted arm holding up a muzzle-loading Springfield before the man moved back again out of sight.

And then, his legs trembling now, Wash caught sight of a dark face that looked familiar in the crowd. A man leaning lazily back in his chair, showing none of the strain Wash had seen in the others in the tense room where stray shots could be as likely to kill a bystander as a gunfighter. Intense eyes, mustache. Where had he seen him before?

Wash knew it was time to move fast. He dropped down and reached back with his right hand to open the flap that held his Colt in place. Then he pushed as quietly as he could through the trash-filled alley toward the back of the building, where he prayed there was a door.

Before turning the corner he dropped into a crouch that took him down about as low as that deceased cat would have crawled. It was a good thing that he did. Tom Key had mentioned having two other men with him. But there'd been three. As Wash looked around the corner and then looked up, he found himself staring first at a pair of trail-worn, dirty boots and then up at the man who'd been placed to guard the back entrance. But the man neither heard nor saw Wash, partly because Wash had come in so quiet and at such a low angle, but also because he was looking back over his shoulder to watch what was going on inside.

Wash didn't stop to think about what to do. He brought up the butt of his rifle so hard between the man's legs that it lifted him off the ground with no more sound than the soft thud of the wooden stock and the deep "Aggghh" that came out of the man's mouth as he folded over. Wash straightened up and swung the barrel so that it clipped the man across the back of his head, and he fell unconscious into the embrace of the low cactuses that grew next to the back of the building. Wash was pretty sure he hadn't hit him hard enough to crack the man's skull and kill him. But when he woke up he'd have a hell of a headache and a hide full of prickers.

He moved into the narrow doorway and looked in around the half-closed door that opened in and to the right. He could see the back of Tom Key no more than thirty feet in front of him. Key was agitated, stomping his feet now like a child having a tantrum

"What-all do I have to do to get you stupid brunettes to understand me? I wants that boy and I wants my watch what he stole. NOW! WHERE IS HE?"

"Here I am," Wash said.

Tom Key turned his head to look. As he did so, Charley Smith's big hand came up and grabbed the barrel of the twelve-gauge, pushing it away from his head and down as he rolled away to his left.

BLAM!

Both barrels of the gun discharged as one, blasting a hole on the table top but missing anything else.

Things began to happen so fast that they seemed slow. Tom Key turned around, pulling a Colt .44 from the holster he wore slung low on his hip. He pointed it with his right hand. Holding down the trigger, he fanned the hammer with his left hand.

BANG! The first shot hit the ceiling two feet above Wash's head.

Wash tried to raise up his rifle. The space was too narrow for him to bring it around. As he moved, the stock knocked against the door, making a hollow thump.

The man who had been standing and leaning against the wall, a long-jawed, blond-haired man that Wash now recognized as another of the gang of whiskey traders they'd arrested last winter, raised his weapon. But he didn't have a chance to fire it before being knocked flat by the chair that had still been tied to Charley's right hand but now was splintered over the man's head.

Tom Key fanned the hammer a second time.

BANG! The second shot splintered the half-open door to Wash's right.

The lumpy-faced man with the thin red hair was aiming his gun at Wash, more calmly and deliberately than the panicked Tom Key whose third shot—BANG!—went whining past Wash's left ear. But before the red-haired man could thumb back the hammer, another gun appeared to his left and the heavy barrel of that weapon was slugged across the man's head, dropping him like a pole-axed steer.

That gun was in the hand of the black man with the mustache, a man Wash recognized now.

One of Sheriff Bob Long's deputies, Wash thought as he pulled out his own .45 Cavalry Colt. Gripping it firmly, thumb against the recoil shield, he raised it and took careful aim, his index finger pointing at his target. He thumbed back the hammer.

POW!

A dark hole appeared in the middle of Tom Key's chest. His arms dropped like a puppet with cut strings and he collapsed to the floor.

Wash moved forward, not feeling his own legs as he walked. He stood over the dead man and looked down. He wasn't sure what he felt.

The black deputy was standing next to him, his gun still in his hand.

"Name is Anson Mount," the black deputy said through tight lips. "Appreciate the help you gave us back when we took that gang of murderers. Man and his family they killed was kin of mine."

Wash kept looking down at Tom Key, amazed at how small the man looked, almost as little as a sleeping child.

"I never killed a man before," Wash said in an emotionless voice.

Anson Mount pointed his gun at the floor near Tom Key's body. BANG! The slug dug into the floor board.

"Hell," Anson Mount laughed. "You still ain't killed no one." He held up his Colt .45. "That's my slug there in his chest. You missed him and put that hole in the floor. Ain't that right, Luke?"

A second black man with a mustache stood up from the corner and walked over. His build and face were nearly the same as Anson Mount's, though he was a bit shorter.

"Yessir, cousin Anse," the man said. "You killed him dead. And Mister Sure-shot here," he patted Wash on the shoulder in a friendly way, "he plum missed."

"So," Anson Mount said, "since you never killed this man, there is no reason for you to tell any of your superiors back up there at the fort about this little dustup."

Mount put his hand on Wash's shoulder. "And once again I have to thank you for your help, seeing as how we had been tracking this sorry crew for a while and just located them here this very night. We was waiting for the rest of our boys to catch up to me and Luke before we tried to take them. But now we don't need to wait no more."

"Thank you," Wash said. He looked around for his friends. Charley and Josh were standing together, Charley rubbing his wrists. Little George was next to them.

"There was no time for us to shoot or anything," Little George said. "We might have hit you or Charley. It all happened so fast."

"It's all right," Wash said, his voice calmer than he felt. "You did what you needed to do." He pointed at Tom Key's body. "But there's one more thing I need to do."

"Go right ahead," Anson Mount said, stepping back.

"Would you loan me your razor?" Wash said to Charley.

"Oh man," Little George said. "You not gonna scalp him or nothing like that?"

Wash said nothing. He pulled the whip from Tom Key's belt. Then, with the razor, he cut it in half, cut the halves into quarters, and threw the pieces on the floor.

As they walked back to where their horses were tied, Charley sighed. "Man," he said, "I had one of the best hands before that scrawny white man pulled that shotgun on me." Then he laughed out loud and flung one big arm around Josh's shoulders, almost lifting him off the ground. "A friend in need," he said, "a friend indeed."

Wash reached across to his pocket to put his hand against the watch that was now surely his. He wondered if the Vances would be smiling now in that picture of them inside the case. But he didn't take it out to look.

"I guess you have avenged your daddy," Josh said in his slow, deep voice.

"What do you mean?" Wash said, surprised at the sudden anger in his own voice. "Mr. Vance was not my daddy."

Josh held up his hands. "Whoa now, I was talking about the way that man whipped your father with that whip, which will never take a drop of blood from another black man's back."

"Oh," Wash said. "Oh."

Words Spoken by Porcupine Bear,
Chief of the Dog Soldier Society,
During an Argument with His Brother-in-Law
Over the Opening of Some Kegs of Whiskey

ONCE WE WERE A GREAT AND POWERFUL NATION.
OUR HEARTS WERE PROUD, AND OUR ARMS WERE STRONG.
BUT A FEW WINTERS AGO ALL OTHER TRIBES FEARED US;

NOW THE PAWNEES DARE CROSS OUR HUNTING GROUNDS
AND KILL OUR BUFFALO.
NOW WE CALL OTHER VILLAGES TO OUR ASSISTANCE,
AND WE CANNOT DEFEND OURSELVES FROM
THE ONSLAUGHTS OF THE ENEMY.

HOW IS THIS, MY PEOPLE?

WE KILL BUFFALO BY THE THOUSAND,
OUR WOMEN'S HANDS ARE SORE WITH DRESSING THE ROBES,
AND WHAT DO WE PART WITH THEM TO
THE WHITE TRADERS FOR?

WE PAY FOR THE WHITE MAN'S FIREWATER,
WHICH TURNS OUR BRAINS UPSIDE DOWN, WHICH MAKES
OUR HEARTS BLACK, RENDERS OUR ARMS WEAK.

IT TAKES AWAY OUR WARRIORS' SKILL
AND MAKES THEM SHOOT WRONG IN BATTLE.
OUR ENEMIES, WHO DRINK NO WHISKEY,
WHEN THEY SHOOT ALWAYS KILL THEIR FOE.

WE HAVE NO AMMUNITION TO ENCOUNTER OUR FOE,
AND WE HAVE BECOME AS DOGS,
WHICH HAVE NOTHING BUT THEIR TEETH.

WE ARE ONLY FEARFUL TO OUR WOMEN,
WHO TAKE UP THEIR CHILDREN
AND CONCEAL THEMSELVES AMONG THE ROCKS
AND THE TREES, FOR WE ARE FAMISHING.

OUR CHILDREN ARE NOW SICK,
AND OUR WOMEN ARE WEAK FROM WATCHING.
LET US NOT SCARE THEM AWAY FROM OUR LODGES,
WITH THEIR SICK CHILDREN IN THEIR ARMS.

I SAY LET US BUY FROM THE TRADER
WHAT IS USEFUL AND GOOD,
BUT HIS WHISKEY WE WILL NOT TOUCH.
LET HIM TAKE THAT AWAY.

I HAVE SPOKEN ALL I HAVE TO SAY,
AND IF MY BROTHER WISHES TO KILL ME FOR THAT,
I AM READY TO DIE.

I WILL GO AND SIT WITH MY FATHERS IN THE SPIRIT LAND,
WHERE I SHALL SOON POINT DOWN
TO THE LAST EXPIRING FIRES OF THE PEOPLE,
AND WHEN THEY INQUIRE THE CAUSE OF
THIS DECLINE OF THEIR PEOPLE,

I WILL TELL THEM WITH A STRAIGHT TONGUE
THAT IT WAS THE FIREWATER OF THE TRADER
THAT PUT IT OUT.

LOOKING FOR PEACE

It was his first ever visit to a town of the ve'hoes.

It was the same for Horse Road, who rode on his left. As they walked their horses down the middle of the wide dirt trail that ran between the buildings, Wolf looked over at his friend out of the corner of his eye. Horse Road's shoulders were hunched. He was moving his head back and forth, trying to take in all these strange sights.

"Close your mouth," Wolf whispered. "You look like a frog catching flies."

Horse Road straightened his back and turned his gaze forward. He yawned, trying to appear as if he was not awed by all he saw.

Wolf understood. He shared his friend's feelings, even if he was not showing them. The wooden buildings were so big. There was even wood on the ground, boards laid so that the white people could walk on them. He had never seen so many wagons rattling along piled with freight or such glittering windows—like thin sheets of clear ice, where all sorts of things for which he had no names were on display. Just the strange new things to see were too much for him to take in.

But he was most disturbed by the loud noises here, unlike anything ever heard in any Cheyenne village. It was not just the rattling of wagons and the screeching of their wheels, or the strange music coming out of the buildings, places the interpreter said were where ve'hoes would pay to sleep. That was hard as it was to believe. How could anyone have no homes of their own or relatives to stay with?

No, the worst sounds were the voices. The loud and harsh voices of the white townspeople. None of them seemed able to keep their mouths closed, not for even a heartbeat. The ve'hoes were all shouting, laughing, threatening each other. Wolf glimpsed one drunken brawl after another as they rode past the buildings. Leaning out of windows above them were women unlike any he'd ever seen before. They were brightly colored as birds, many of them wearing feathered caps on their heads. Their clothing—what little there was of it—seemed designed to show off their bodies rather than to keep them warm. They were as loud as the men. Their voices were higher and shriller, but they sounded just as aggressive, and their laughter was empty of real happiness.

The interpreter, seeing where Wolf and Horse Road were looking, leaned over toward them.

"Strange as this might sound," the interpreter said with an ironic smile, "white men pay money to be with those women."

Horse Road was shocked. He started to lift his hands to cover his ears. Then he remembered he was holding the leads for half of the horses they were bringing. He dropped his hands and pretended to relax.

Wolf knew how his friend felt. Seeing and hearing this place helped him understand something. He knew now why the ve'hoes acted as they did. Spending time in places like this would make any people crazy! But he would not let it affect him. He would maintain his dignity. By his example he would help Horse Road to do the same. They had an important job to do. They must not look like small, frightened children as they did it.

The two had been chosen. Their job was to travel with this group of soldiers, black men led by a white officer. Among these Buffalo Soldiers was the small one Wolf had seen before. Although there was no reason for that little Buffalo Soldier to recognize him, he had looked at Wolf. He had nodded several times during their long ride.

But Wolf had kept his face impassive. The little man's nodding in a friendly way had been pleasing. However, there was no way he could ever be friends with any ve'hoe soldier, black or white.

The seven horses they were leading had been carefully selected. They were fine animals for their six chiefs and their Indian agent to ride home. Their chiefs, they had been told, were to come in to this town. It was named Wichita, although it was home to none of the native people it had been named for. The six chiefs and the agent would arrive by iron horse. Wolf had never see a train close up. It would be interesting to get close to an iron horse without having to worry about being shot at by the white men on board.

The six chiefs who had been sent as a peace delegation to Washington were Stone Calf, Pawnee, Wind, White Shield, White Horse, and Little Robe. Stone Calf and Little Robe had been to the East before.

"What I liked best," Little Robe had said as they readied themselves for their journey, "was Harvard University. It would be a good place to send my son for an education."

"Maybe my son, too," Stone Calf had agreed.

As Wolf listened to that talk about being educated by ve'hoes, he had wondered what that would be like. He always wanted to learn things. Strange as the whites were, there was much they knew that the Indians did not know. But would he want to be taught by whites? Would they want to teach him? *Maybe if there was peace. Maybe I could go to a ve'hoe school*, Wolf thought.

Peace. They had been trying to find peace with the whites for so long. His grandfather Black Kettle had been a warrior. But that was when he was young. And he had never fought against the whites. Black Kettle had followed the way of peace more than half of his life. He had been living it when he was killed.

There was never a time when their chiefs were not trying to make peace with the ve'hoes. The first white men they met were Lieutenant Clark and his brother Lewis, who had been traveling toward the sunset, seeking a trail to the big saltwater. They and their men had been treated very well by the Cheyennes, who gave them food and shelter. In return, Clark and Lewis gave them medals bearing the face of the Great Father in Washington. We shall always be brothers and live together, the captains had said.

That was good. The Cheyennes had liked the captains and their men. They were powerful and good-looking. They were interesting people. They had strong weapons. Friends with strong weapons could help the Cheyennes against their enemies. Enemies were all around them then. There were the Pawnees, the Crows, the Utes. Farther south were the Kiowas and Comanches. Back then every tribe was an enemy except for the Lakotas and the Arapahos.

Gray Head had told Wolf about those days.

"We were fewer than those enemy nations," he had said. "But we were good fighters."

Fighting the white men, though, was something they did not want. The council of forty-four chiefs, those whose job it was to follow Sweet Medicine's advice, agreed to peace. They smoked the pipe with the whites who came after the captains. Let us be brothers. The pale-skinned men said they agreed.

It started well. The whites brought useful objects. They brought pots for cooking that did not break easily like those made of baked clay. They brought warm wool blankets. They brought sharp steel knives and arrowheads. They brought fine new guns. But it soon became clear that these new people wanted more than just trade. Their hide hunters began to kill all the buffalo. Their traders also brought the deadly poison of whiskey that made men crazy. White thieves stole their horses. When young men of any tribe raided the whites, every Indian was blamed. Horse soldiers came in and built forts. Then those soldiers attacked peaceful villages. Chiefs who tried to live in peace were shot dead with the American flag in one hand and the other extended in friendship. It seemed those pale-skinned people wanted more than just buffalo hides. They wanted all of the Cheyenne land.

"So we began calling them by another name," Gray Head said. "We gave those pale-skinned people the name of ve'hoe. Ve'hoe, the trickster. Ve'hoe, the one who allows his greed to control him. Ve'hoe, who is powerful but can never be trusted. Ve'hoe, the black spider. Beautiful to see but deadly to touch."

Now they were in the very middle of the white town. They were bothering no one as they rode down the middle of the trail.

But the closer they came to the tracks where the iron horses traveled, the more people came out of the buildings. Some pointed at them and shouted. Some brandished guns and made angry, threatening gestures.

"It is good we are not we alone," Horse Road said. "If we were, those people would kill us."

"We are safe," Wolf said. "The Buffalo Soldiers will protect us."

He spoke those words in a confident voice. But he was not all that sure he was right. He had never seen so many white people before. There was not a friendly face among them. He had never done anything bad to any ve'hoe. But he knew that to them, one Indian looked just like another. And if one Indian did anything bad, every Indian should be punished.

It was a crazy way to think. It was the ve'hoe way. It was just as crazy as the way ve'hoe soldiers were treated. Gray Head had explained it to him.

"Among the ve'hoes," Gray Head said, "if a white soldier disobeys, then his leaders have the right to beat or even kill him."

Wolf had thought at first that Gray Head was joking. How could any nation be held together if those who disagreed were treated that way? But then Gray Head had reminded him of something. Those white men had just spent many years killing each other for such reasons. They killed each other because some believed that all men born with dark skins were meant to be owned by those with white skins.

The most important thing that Cheyenne chiefs did was not to lead the people into war. It was to seek peace. You could not belong to the Council of the Forty-four unless you lived as a man of peace. Sweet Medicine had set it up that way. Each of the forty bands had one peace chief and then four more were chosen by all to help lead the council. All of them were brave. Many had been great fighters before they answered the call of the chieftaincy. But when they became a member of the forty-four, they no longer went to battle. No matter what. Little Robe's family had been killed at Sand Creek. Still he spoke and acted for peace.

Soon they would see Little Robe and the others. Their welcoming party was now at the edge of the town. They could see the iron rails running across the land and a small wooden house near the rails. But there was no iron horse. And there was no sign of the six chiefs and Agent Miles.

The white officer in charge of the party of soldiers got off his horse. He went up into that little wooden house. Then he came out. He looked unhappy. He held a piece of paper in his hand. He spoke a few quick words. Wolf could not catch any of them.

"What is it?" Wolf asked.

The interpreter, who looked as unhappy as the white lieutenant, shook his head.

"Dodge City," he said to Wolf and Horse Road. "That is where your chiefs are. We have come to the wrong ve'hoe town."

"Hah," Horse Road replied. "Is any ve'hoe town right?"

"This trip has been an unmitigated misadventure. A disaster! A debacle!"

Agent John D. Miles was mad as a wet hen. He stomped his feet and waved his arms as he stalked back and forth in front of the railway car where his six half-frozen and loop-legged chiefs had spent the night. November nights got deadly cold in Dodge City, and there had been no heat at all in that car, nor any extra blankets to keep them warm.

But that did not explain why his Indians looked the way they did. They were drunk and befuddled, every one of them.

Wash stayed sitting on his horse alongside the other eight men of the company and the Indians who had traveled with them. Best right now to keep their distance from the angry agent and his half-dead, intoxicated charges. It was not their fault that they'd not been there when the agent and his chiefs has arrived yesterday. They'd just been following the orders that sent them to Wichita, one hundred fifty miles east of Dodge.

So, instead of being on time, they ended up a day late. Their lieutenant, the only one dismounted, was still trying to explain it to the angry Indian agent.

Lord knows, Wash thought, *we rode like blue blazes to cover those hundred and fifty miles over rough ground and did damn well to get here as soon as we did.*

But that was not earning any sympathy from Agent Miles. He continued flapping his arms like a rain-soaked banty rooster.

"Wichita," Lieutenant Millen repeated again, his voice apologetic. "Our orders said Wichita and——"

"*Wichita* me not, soldier," Agent Miles spat. "Hold thy tongue. I do not wish to hear that name uttered again in my presence!"

"Yes, sir," the new lieutenant said, lifting his hand halfway up and then pausing, not sure if he should salute, the Indian agent not being an army officer. "I am deeply sorry, sir. Still our orders did state that Wi——"

"What!"

The lieutenant stopped himself halfway through the word, which was a good thing. Agent Miles no longer looked like an enraged rooster. He resembled an overheated kettle about to blow its stack.

"Er...," Lieutenant Millen said, then he bit his lower lip. Just out of West Point, he was not set for such situations as this, nor for a Nineveh like Dodge City, which was bigger than Wichita and the main railhead for cattle drives and the shipping out of buffalo hides.

As they'd ridden into town the lieutenant had looked down his snub nose in disbelief at the drunk cowboys and buffalo skinners slumped in alleys, the scrawny dogs licking slimy pools behind the saloons, the mean men sporting old Confederate jackets and handguns looking at them slanty-eyed.

Happy to kill them a negro soldier the first chance they get, Wash thought.

Josh had pointed to the rail yards and warehouses ahead of them. "A million buffalo hides sent back East jes' in the last three months alone." Josh had a head for such facts. "Ou-wah fair Dodge

City," he continued, changing his voice to sound like some boasting white city father, "it is a bustling center of commerce, a place of pure promise, destined for greatness."

Josh had chuckled and then inclined his head toward the front of a mercantile store across the street from them. The roughly printed sign in its window read CLOSED.

"Heard tell," Josh said, "two weeks ago the owner of the hotel down the street had a little disagreement with the other white man who run that store. Both got drunk as skunks and killed each other in a shootout right over there."

His gaze directed Wash's eyes to a horse trough whose usefulness for holding water had been lessened by the bullet holes in it.

"Both had to reload twice, but each of 'em finally managed to sling enough lead to kill the other," Josh had grinned.

And then, as they had turned down the street to the rail station, the sight of the outraged Quaker Indian agent had greeted them.

Right now, Wash thought, *if our Quaker friend had a gun in his hand, despite all of his peaceful beliefs I believe he would ventilate our green lieutenant, who is cogitating over the right approach to pacify a pacifist.*

"We are here now, Mr. Miles," Lieutenant Millen said at last, deciding to rely on courtesy and plain truth. "Please accept my most sincere apologies for the delay." He held out the telegraph message received in Wichita. "As you can see, we were told to proceed with all due haste to meet your party once we received this message in——"

"Where?" the agent asked. His voice was dead calm, but it was like the pause before a thunderstorm slams in.

"Ah...ah," our lieutenant stammered. "The other town."

From behind the mounted soldiers, someone let out a little bark of a laugh. Wash turned his head back to see both Indians innocently looking up at the sky as if expecting rain. The young Cheyenne men had been brought along with them so that the chiefs would be greeted by some of their own people. The taller one was mounted on a fine big roan. He understood and spoke a little English, and Wash suspected him of that laugh. That young Cheyenne had acted as if he knew Wash. But from where? Wash wasn't sure. Had he seen him at Camp Supply when Company D was stationed there? Or when they visited the agency? He did look a bit familiar.

"Me, him, we help Little Robe much," the Cheyenne had said when the two of them rode up with their string of horses. "Little Robe know me, feel good see me."

Not that the chiefs would have been aware of anyone greeting them in their present state. They were so drunk they would not have noticed a cannon shot off next to their ears.

Agent Miles looked again at his inebriated Cheyenne leaders, one of whom began vomiting green bile into the gutter next to the agent's leg. Miles took a quick step to the side and drew in a deep breath, raising his voice as if he wished to address not just those nearby, but all within the city limits.

"Of all the miserable, lost, and misbegotten locations on this green earth to be stranded! Hear thee my words, for I have no doubt! This flea-bitten, filth-ridden, forsaken town is the worst place in the world! It is Sodom and Gomorrah reborn."

"Amen," Wash and Josh said as one.

Agent Miles stared at them. They hushed up quick, like children caught talking in class by the teacher.

Miles turned back to Lieutenant Millen, who looked as if he would gladly dig a hole and crawl into it. The agent waved his hand at the six stretched-out chiefs who, in their miserable state, were perhaps the only ones within a hundred yards not hearing his declamation.

"We arrived here assured that mounts would await us. We found nothing, not even a message at the telegraph office. We made our way along the street, being jeered at by ignorant buffoons and having clods of dirt hurled at us by delinquent children. Upon entering the Dodge House," he pointed up the street with a finger quivering so hard Wash was surprised not to see a bolt of lightning shoot out of it, "I was told that the establishment did not wish to cater to Indians. It took all of my powers of friendly persuasion to convince them, plus my proffer of double the usual nightly rate—from my own funds—to pay for those wretched rooms."

Miles let out a sound half moan, half growl.

"I should have known from the bedlam among the ruffians at the bar downstairs that no good would befall us there. Sure enough, when we were all finally fast asleep, miscreants slipped into our rooms to place packages of red pepper and gunpowder in our stoves. We woke immersed in a black miasma of smoke that burned our eyes and blinded us. After we went tumbling downstairs and into the chill night, the doors of the hotel were then shut against us. Our only recourse was to make our way back to the railroad car, followed by the raucous laughter of the authors of our discomfort. Though the car was cold, the benches hard, I thought that at least we would be left in peace. Alas, 'twas not so. Whilst I slept, some of those same ill-favored louts made their way to the rail car. They brought with them what they assured the chiefs was hot toddy, a harmless drink to warm them against the cold. But that toddy was naught but a splash of warmed milk mixed with a great dose of whiskey. Thus thee do see them as they are now."

He gestured at the six befuddled chiefs stretched out now on the ground. Then he dropped his arms and his voice failed him.

"Help us," he whispered.

It took a good amount of walking around and strong coffee, as well as some further helpful vomiting, but the soldiers and the two young Cheyennes finally did get the six chiefs into a state where they were able to mount their horses. Then they started on the long and awkward ride to Camp Supply.

As the day wore on and the miles passed, the chiefs sobered up enough to begin to suffer from fearful hangovers. Sick as they were, it was clear to Wash that they were a formidable group. He could feel the power emanating from them. Every one of them a major chief. Stone Calf, Wind, White Shield, White Horse, Pawnee, Little Robe.

Little Robe, the only one of the chiefs who had smiled at Wash and who seemed honestly grateful for his help, appeared saddened but not angered by the turn of events.

Little Robe. Wash had heard his name. He was good Indian who talked peace more than most. Not that he was the weak sort. He seemed to Wash to be one of those gentle types with a spine of iron.

White Horse, though, was another sort. Iron all the way through.

"He Dog Man," said the taller of the two young Cheyennes, who was riding his roan to Wash's right. "White Horse he Dog Man Chief."

A Dog Soldier, Wash thought. *Oh my!*

Dog Soldiers were the most fearsome fighters on the plains. From what Sergeant Brown had told Wash, they were men who had made a sacred pledge to die rather than retreat from the enemy. White Horse was cupping his head with both hands like one might hold onto a cracked egg. Wash could not understand the words the Dog Soldier chief kept mumbling to himself in Cheyenne—except for one word in English that he frequently repeated, in the same tone as a curse.

"Washington!"

Wash didn't need an interpreter to gather that things had not gone well for the Indians there. Being in the army, that was no surprise to him. Every soldier, black or white, knew that nothing good ever came out of Washington. Just trouble.

Trouble, though, Wash thought, *always comes in threes.*

So say that one was the wrong destination. Two was the drunk chiefs. Had to be a third one coming along soon.

And Wash was not wrong. When they finally we reached the Indian camp, trouble number three was waiting for them. In the absence of Agent Miles, a whiskey seller had found his way to White Horse's village. There were drunk Cheyennes everywhere. Wash glanced over at the chiefs. Little Robe simply looked sadder. The other four were just shaking their heads. But White Horse's face looked like a thundercloud.

Lieutenant Millen seemed about to ride into the middle of it. Following Sergeant Brown's lead, the Buffalo Soldiers eased their ponies in around him to block his way.

"Sir," Sergeant Brown said, his voice as polite as could be, "Agent Miles has asked us to hold back."

Millen looked over his shoulder at Miles, who had stopped on his horse fifty yards back. Just sitting there. The agent held up his hand and shook his head. Millen nodded, pulling up on his reins.

Wash's new Cheyenne friend had come up quietly on his left. Close enough that Wash was able to see a brand on the horse's haunch. A brand on it like one he'd seen in Texas.

"Watch good," the tall young Cheyenne said. He had a grim smile on his face.

White Horse slid off his horse. He waved one arm and shouted something at the biggest of the Cheyennes who had been drinking, a man with a bellicose scowl.

"Bear Shield," the young Cheyenne said, pointing with his chin at the shield with a big bear paw painted on it hanging from the side of the tipi where the big Indian was leaning. "Big Chief Warrior Society."

Bear Shield, who seemed only slightly drunk, had positioned himself between White Horse and the whiskey trader, whose wagon was parked behind Bear Shield's lodge. The booze peddler, a red-headed, one-eyed, chubby fellow, looked happy as a pig in its sty, clearly figuring he was safe with Bear Shield and his warriors defending him. Bear Shield gestured. Half a dozen young men came up to stand behind him. Unsteady on their feet, drunk as the others.

Then Bear Shield spoke, making hand signs to emphasize his words. Wash had learned enough of Plains sign talk to understand what he was saying.

Trader friend. He stay. White Horse no drive trader away. White Horse go.

In response, White Horse turned but did not walk way. He shouted. His voice echoed through the camp. Then, one by one, from the other tipis, young men began to come out. One, two, three, four, five, six, seven appeared and strode purposefully over to stand behind White Horse.

"More Dog Men," the tall young Cheyenne said to Wash.

From their firm stance and the looks on their faces, they were among the few in the village who had not been drinking. White Horse smiled. It was not a happy smile.

Then he made his own gesture to Bear Shield.

Wait here.

White Horse disappeared behind another row of tipis. But he was not gone long.

In two shakes of a lamb's tail he reappeared, walking stiff-legged as a mad grizzly, a Sharps rifle cradled in his arms. No more words or gestures. He just lifted the big gun.

BLAM!

Shot between the eyes, Bear Shield's pony dropped like a bag of sand.

Bear Shield stumbled backward, his hands up, as White Horse calmly handed the Sharps to one of the Dog Soldiers behind him and accepted a Colt revolver in its place. The six drunk men who'd come to stand with Bear Shield turned and began running for their lives. So did the whiskey trader, leaving his wagon behind, while White Horse fired one shot after another at the ground behind his fleeing feet.

As White Horse and his crew began emptying kegs and breaking whiskey bottles, the tall young Cheyenne nudged Wash with his elbow.

"Much good," he said.

"Much good," Wash agreed.

It had been a wasted trip. Little Robe had realized that while they were still in Washington. He was the last of the chiefs to speak when they met with White Father Grant. He had listened to all the words spoken before it was his turn.

So, when Little Robe stood up, he took a slow breath. "I have come a good ways to see the Great Father," he said. "Now I see him. That is all I have to say." Then he sat down.

It was soon after their return from Washington that a Great Star appeared in the sky. Each night for two moons it burned. It was so bright you could see your shadow. Many were frightened as it filled the night with a strange blue light. They thought the world was about to end. But the oldest woman among the Cheyennes was not afraid. Her name was Makes Moccasins. She had lived through ninety winters.

"I have seen such a thing before," Makes Moccasins said. "It has come. It will go. All will be the same."

It was as she said. The Great Star burned. Then it was gone. But the people wondered if that star was a message. Was it a warning sent by Maheo that a hard time lay ahead?

And hard times did come. The white robe of Winter Man spread over the land. It was so heavy that people froze to death in their lodges. They starved for lack of food. They froze because they could not fight through the snow and find firewood. Each time the people reported to the agency for rations the story was the same. The rations from the government had not been delivered. Without being able to hunt buffalo and with no other game, there was only one other way to get food. People began killing horses for their meat.

The buffalo hunters from Dodge City swarmed onto Cheyenne lands in ever greater numbers. They were many as maggots on the body of a dead animal. Those hunters knew that the one last big herd of buffalo still roamed to the south. They also knew that the tribes would fight to protect those sacred animals. Their greed was greater than their fear of the tribes. The treaty had promised the white men would be kept out. The white hunters broke that treaty, but no one stopped or punished them. The sheriffs ignored them. The army tried at first. The Buffalo Soldiers arrested eleven white hunters they caught on Cheyenne land.

Those eleven were not punished. Their leader, holding his hat in his hand, apologized to Friend Miles. Then Friend Miles gave them back their guns. He allowed them to leave.

"They are poor men," Miles explained to Chief Little Robe. "They were hunting to feed their families. They have given unto me solemn promises that they will return to Kansas and not come onto your lands again."

Little Robe watched as the men rode off, laughing. His lips were pressed tightly together. He shook his head. He knew they would be back.

White men's promises were as empty of weight as the wind.

"Your people," Little Robe said to Miles, "make big talk. They make war if an Indian kills a white man's ox to keep his wife and children from starving. What do you think my people should do? How should they act when they see our buffalo killed by such men as those buffalo hunters who are not even hungry?"

Friend Miles turned and went back into his house.

Still, hard as the winter was proving to be, the Cheyennes tried to keep the peace. Hungry as they were, they held back. They did not want war. Even the Dog Soldiers waited. They would give the government another chance. Perhaps the white men would prove that the word of Washington meant more than dust blowing across the prairie.

There was little game to be found near the agency. The Indian hunters were not allowed to hunt beyond its borders. If they did so, they could be attacked by the ve'hoe soldiers.

But we have to eat, Wolf thought.

He stepped outside to greet the dawn. New snow had fallen. It was soft beneath his moccasins as he walked over to the lodge of Horse Road's family. Before he could scratch on the door, a strong arm holding a bow was pushed out through the flap. It was followed by Horse Road's head.

"Hunting!" Horse Road said. There was a determined look on his face. "A good day for hunting."

He was right. Though it was midwinter, the weather had changed greatly overnight. It was no longer so cold that the grass crackled underfoot. The trees no longer popped as they froze. The deep drifts of snow were melting away. The sun was warm on their shoulders and backs. It felt like the start of the Moon of New Grass.

As they walked to their horses, Wolf and Horse Road slipped their wool blankets off their shoulders. They would still carry them along. Winter Man might return at any moment. He could freeze the whole land in a few heartbeats with his harsh breath. But Maheo seemed to smiling on them.

Maheo is helping us. Our job is a sacred one. We are going out to bring back food for the people. It is a good day to look for game. And perhaps the ve'hoe soldiers will not see us.

Too Tall and Too Short called to them as they readied their horses.

"We shall come."

"Yes, we shall come along."

Wolf made the sign for *yes*. The two brothers joined them. It would be good to have his three best friends with him.

Sun moved across the sky as they rode. The warm air smelled of spring. They rode enjoying the sense of freedom. They had been confined so long by the cold and snow and by the boundaries of the agency. Wolf felt the muscles of his horse ripple beneath his legs.

"You are stronger than me," he whispered in Wind's ear. "But soon we will find game. Then my family will eat. Then I will eat and get strong again."

He smiled at that thought. He was hopeful. So were his three friends. But that feeling of hope began to fade by the time the sun was four hands high. They had ranged back and forth. They had studied the soft snow for tracks. They had watched the hilltops for the dark shapes of game animals. But there were no animal tracks. They saw no deer or antelope silhouetted against the sky. No hoofed animals had been out digging through the melting snow to graze on the buried grasses.

More of the good feeling left them as the day wore on. Before long, Sun was only two hands above the horizon. Would they have to turn back empty-handed? One more hill rose in front of them. It was the one called Trickster's Hill. The story was that a big rock had been balanced on top of it. Wihio had given that stone a present and then taken it back. Then the big stone had rolled after Wihio and flattened him out.

Horse Road was riding slightly ahead of the others. He looked back over his shoulder at Wolf. Some of the mischief that had been missing came back to his face.

"Race to the top!" he shouted, kicking his heels into his horse. "Soehoetse! Charge the enemy!"

Some of the energy they'd felt when they started out came back to Wolf.

"Whee-yah," he whooped, kicking his heels into Wind's sides. "Charge!"

Behind him he heard Too Short and Too Tall urging their horses on. They would not catch him. Wind was too strong! He passed Horse Road just before reaching the top. Then he stopped, staring at what he saw. He heard his three friends come up behind him. They, too, stopped as he had stopped.

The four of them looked down. Below was yet another empty valley. No sign of game animals. Not even a rabbit or a prairie grouse. But the hilltop across from them was not empty. A feeling as if he had swallowed a stone caught in Wolf's throat. Their hunt was over. There on that nearby hilltop were real enemies. They were not the pretend ones Horse Road had urged them to charge against.

Four mounted and well-armed men. They were close. Close enough for Wolf to see the darkness of their faces beneath their army caps. Buffalo Soldiers. Wolf held up his hand, signaling his friends to wait. Perhaps the army men would not attack. Perhaps they would just ignore them.

Then the smallest of the black white men raised his right arm. He held it palm out. It was not a signal to attack, but a greeting. And Wolf recognized him. It was the short Buffalo Soldier.

Wolf waved back, unsure of what would happen next. The small Buffalo Soldier kept his right hand up in greeting. He reached down with his other hand.

Going for his rifle? Wolf gripped Wind's reins harder.

But the small black white man's hand went past his scabbard. He reached behind him to untie something. A heavy-looking bag that hung from his saddle. He let it drop it on the ground. He waved. Then he and the others with him turned their horses. They disappeared over the crest of the hill.

"Shall we go see what he dropped?" Too Tall asked.

Before Wolf could answer, advising him to use caution, Too Tall was on his way. His horse chuffed out white clouds of breath. He galloped it down across the narrow valley and up the other hill.

By the time Wolf and the others caught up with him, Too Tall had already dropped from the back of his horse. He had grabbed the bag. He was dumping its contents out on the ground. Wolf shook his head in disbelief.

Food. Hard biscuits, dried meat, cans of food, each can with a picture of its contents on its top.

Beans and sweet fruit. A gift from a friend.

Wolf looked around. His friends were smiling as broadly as he was. The old and the weak would eat first. But there was enough for them as well. For this night at least, they would not sleep with their bellies cut in half by hunger.

THERE WAS THIS PLANTATION ON DOWN THE ROAD, MAMA SAID.
MASTER MANSON OWNED THAT PLANTATION AND WAS ABOUT AS
STINGY AS A MAN COULD BE. HE WOULD NOT GIVE ANY MEAT AT
ALL TO HIS SLAVES. HE TOLD THEM IF THEY WANTED MEAT
THEY WOULD HAVE TO GO OUT AND FIND IT FOR THEMSELVES.

SO UNCLE JOSHUA, THE OLDEST OF THE SLAVES ON
THAT PLANTATION, TOOK TO STEALING MASTER MANSON'S PIGS.
THAT WENT ON FOR A WHILE TILL OLD MASTER MANSON
NOTICED SOME OF HIS PIGS WERE TURNING UP MISSING.
SO HE DECIDED TO PAY A VISIT TO UNCLE JOSHUA.

AS SOON AS HE GOT CLOSE TO UNCLE JOSHUA'S CABIN,
MASTER MANSON COULD SMELL A STEW COOKING.
WHEN HE WALKED IN, UNCLE JOSHUA WAS BENT OVER
A BIG BLACK POT, STIRRING THAT STEW.
HE DIDN'T HARDLY LOOK UP WHEN MASTER MANSON
CAME IN WITHOUT KNOCKING OR EVEN SAYING HOWDY-DO.

"WHAT ARE YOU COOKING THERE?" MASTER MANSON SAID.

"THIS HERE IS POSSUM STEW," UNCLE JOSHUA ANSWERED BACK
AND KEPT ON STIRRING.

"IT SURE DOES SMELL LIKE PORK STEW TO ME,"
SAID MASTER MANSON.

"YES INDEED," UNCLE JOSHUA REPLIED. "POSSUM STEW SURE
DOES SMELL LIKE PORK, DON'T IT?"

"WELL THAT MAY BE SO, BUT I KNOW HOW POSSUM
TASTES AND IT DOES NOT TASTE LIKE PORK.
SO YOU HAD BETTER LET ME TASTE THAT STEW."

"OH MY, YES," UNCLE JOSHUA SAID.
HE STARTED FILLING A BOWL FROM THE POT.
BUT AS HE DID SO, HE WAS TALKING UNDER HIS BREATH.
"MMM-MM," HE SAID TO HIMSELF. "THIS HERE IS THE BEST STEW
I HAVE EVER SPIT IN. ALL THAT SPITTING IS GONNA MAKE
THIS STEW REAL GOOD."

THEN HE MADE TO HAND THAT STEW TO MASTER MANSON.
BUT MASTER MANSON DIDN'T TAKE IT.

"WHAT'S THAT YOU SAID ABOUT SPITTING?"
MASTER MANSON SAID.

"DON'T YOU KNOW ABOUT THAT?" SAID UNCLE JOSHUA.
"ALL OF US NEGROES, WE ALWAYS SPITS INTO OUR STEW
TO MAKE THE MEAT TENDER."

EVERY ONE OF US IN THIS CABIN, ALL TWELVE OF US,
HAS BEEN SPITTING INTO THIS STEW ALL MORNING
TO MAKE IT TASTE FINE."

MASTER MANSON NEVER DID TASTE THAT STEW.
HE WENT AWAY REAL FAST AND NEVER AGAIN DID BOTHER
UNCLE JOSHUA WHEN HE WAS COOKING POSSUM STEW.

I WAS HUNGRY

I was hungry and ye fed me. So it said in the Good Book, Wash thought as he stood waiting for the Indians to arrive at Fort Sill.

The officers and men of the 10th were about to put those words from the Bible into action at their new post. Company D had been shifted again.

Camp Supply, Fort Griffin, and now, in the spring of 1873, Fort Sill. We have been jumped around more than the pieces on a checkerboard.

They were now at one of the biggest of the army posts on the frontier. Fort Sill had been formed in conjunction with the new Kiowa and Comanche Indian Agency in 1869. It was located in a dry country of little mountains called the Wichitas that rose up out of the plain.

Just as at Darlington, there was a Quaker Indian agent. Friend James Haworth was the second Quaker posted here. Agent Tatum had given up the idea of peace after his Comanches and Kiowas had persisted in raiding. It reached the point where Tatum himself asked the army to chastise them. That did not sit well with his superiors, him having been told to always play the role of a pacifier, and so he had had to resign.

Haworth was a true lover of President Grant's peace policy. That had earned him the out-and-out hatred of Colonel Davidson, commander at Fort Sill as he had been at Fort Griffin. It seemed to Wash that their colonel wanted nothing more than to be given free rein to punish the Indians as he saw fit. Subjugation, Davidson said more than once to his troops, would be the only solution to the Indian problem. He was pleased that the buffalo hunters were killing off those big animals the Indians depended upon. Starve them out. That might force them to come in, or, better yet, to take up arms in a war that would not just offer their colonel a chance to pacify the savages but also lead to his own advancement. Few officers ever moved up in rank in peacetime, and Davidson was eager to get back the generalship he had lost.

If our old colonel was here today, Wash thought, *and not off on a three-day excursion, I have no doubt that what is about to happen would not be going on. He would regard it as useless tomfoolery or worse.*

But Wash didn't think that. What they were doing could mean the difference between war and peace, at least for a little while. There were some of the frontier who believed there were but two kinds of Indian—those who were shooting at you and those who were not. But Sergeant Brown had been more subtle in his assessment of the different tribes.

"Kiowas," he said, "are touchy. If our Cheyennes is like dry prairie grass, easy to set ablaze, our Kiowas is more like gunpowder. Twenty years or so ago, they was at war with every other tribe. Moreover, Kiowas is clannish, with all different ranks and classes amongst themselves. Lowest are them who was originally Mexicans, stolen as boys, then raised Kiowa. The highest are sort of like lords and always the big leaders." The sergeant shook his head. "Umm-hmmm. That makes them even more fierce fighters. Them Mexican Kiowas is always trying to prove themselves to be just as good as the ones born Kiowa."

Yet another element made Kiowas volatile. That was a nearly superstitious dread of being counted. Getting put on a list never troubled either the Cheyennes or the nearby Comanches. But a Kiowa saw getting counted as one step away from getting dead. Taking down their names and noting how many of them there were was like kicking a hornet's nest. Kiowas would fight or run before allowing anyone to enroll them.

"Man plans to count Kiowas," Sergeant Brown said, "best count his ammunition first."

Still, despite their history of being warlike, the Kiowas now seemed to have made up their minds to follow the peace road. Much of this was due to their major chief, Kicking Bird. Kicking Bird was a tall, slender man with an affable bearing, always ready to reach out his hand to Agent Haworth or whatever military officer he had to meet with when he went to the fort. Even Colonel Davidson seemed to grudgingly respect Kicking Bird.

For his part, Kicking Bird had formed a company of Kiowa scouts whose job it was to ride out among their people and see that things were peaceable and that no young warriors were slipping away to do such things as to murder surveyors. Even more than census takers, surveyors were hated by the Kiowas. Putting marks on the land troubled them as much as being counted. So doing what he could to protect even such detested people was a strong indication of Kicking Bird's deep devotion to peace.

Soon after Wash and Charley and the other men of Company D arrived at Fort Sill, Kicking Bird had come to visit. As they watched Kicking Bird shaking hands with the newly arrived officers and warmly welcoming them to his land, Charley had leaned over toward Wash.

"I swear," Charley whispered, "if that old chief been born a white man, he would be a United States senator."

But even with Kicking Bird endeavoring to keep things calm, the peace they had been enjoying was tenuous at best. Another of the tribe's big leaders, Lone Wolf, had nothing but bitterness in his heart about the army. His favorite son, Tau-ankia, Sitting in the Saddle, had been shot and killed in December by men of the 4th Cavalry. Tau-ankia and a little party of Kiowa and Comanches had been on a raid into Mexico and were bringing back a string of horses when the 4th surprised them. The officer in charge, Lieutenant Hudson, had opened fire as the Kiowas were peacefully resting their horses. One of Hudson's first shots killed Tau-ankia. On getting word of his son's death, Lone Wolf had gone crazy with grief. He'd cut off his hair, killed his best horses, and burned his lodges, his wagon, and his buffalo robes, all as a show of how deep his mourning was. Then he had ridden off to find his son's body and bring him back for a proper burial. But to add insult to injury, even though Lone Wolf did locate Tau-ankia's body, he was attacked by another group of soldiers and forced to abandon his son's remains among some rocks.

"Think we'll see Lone Wolf today?" Josh said as he put down another box.

"Not likely," Wash replied. "His mind is on revenge for his boy."

"Little late for that, ain't he?" Josh said.

Wash nodded. One of the ironies about Lone Wolf's desire for vengeance was that fate had already taken it on the man who'd killed his boy. Lieutenant Hudson had been shot and killed by accident at Fort Clark not long after that fatal encounter with Tau-ankia. Hudson's roommate was cleaning his Spencer rifle and it went off by accident, as Spencers were prone to do. So the man who killed Lone Wolf's boy died even before Lone Wolf got the news.

Wash put that out of his head. Thoughts of death or revenge were not the things to focus on now. Instead, like the rest of the post he should be thinking of the big feast about to happen. He smiled at the thought of that.

I would a sight rather feed an Indian than be fighting him. Some might declare that the only good Indian is a dead one. But they are mostly the same folks who venture a similar opinion about black soldiers. Nor have they reckoned the cost of making just one bad Indian into what they would call a good one.

Hard as it was for some to realize, when all things were taken into account, the cost to the United States in 1874 for killing one Indian in a military campaign had reached about a million dollars.

Providing Indians with rations was far more than charity. Nor was it just honoring the bargains made by promising in writing to provide the tribes with their basic needs in exchange for them giving up the bigger part of their land. It also meant peace, which was far cheaper than war.

Keeping that peace had been harder in recent months. The incursions of the buffalo hunters had doubled and then doubled again. They had even set up a big camp at Adobe Walls in the very center of the Kiowa and Comanche hunting grounds, which was like waving a red flag before the face of a bull. The only thing to keep them pacified had been providing them their promised rations. Lately, though, despite the real danger of bloody conflict, rations for the Kiowas and Comanches had not materialized. No herds of cattle had been driven in to the agency. No wagons full of flour and sugar had appeared. For more than two months the rations had been late.

A week before, Wash had thought that was about to change. A wagon had pulled in packed with boxes for the Indians.

"Hallelujah," Charley had exclaimed. "Food at last."

"Wait and see," Sergeant Brown had said.

Wash, Charley, and Josh had been detailed to escort the wagon in to the agency and to help unload those boxes.

"Oh my Lord," Charley had said when he saw the words on the boxes.

Not flour or sugar or even coffee.

"Soap," Wash said. "Every box. Big white bars of soap."

Sergeant Brown had nodded wearily as Josh held up one of those bars of soap to show him.

"Been more promises made to the Indians and broken," Brown said, "than stars in God's own sky. And it will be one of the Lord's own miracles if this all don't end up in another war afore this year is out."

"Amen," Josh said.

"Praise the Lord and pass the ammunition," Charley added.

Wash said nothing.

Feeding Indians was not the army's job. Still, on his own part, whenever possible, Wash had been quietly borrowing canned food from the commissary—with the help of a certain sympathetic sergeant—and then, when far enough away from the post to not be seen by their superior officers, dropping it where the Indians could get it.

But now the drawn faces of those starving Indians in their camps seemed to have touched the hearts of every person at the post, aside from the absent commander. It was especially true of the army wives, most of whom were mothers and had seen the swollen bellies of the Kiowa children.

Despite the lack of treaty rations, the post commissary had remained well stocked with food. Officers and men alike agreed to chip in whatever they could. By the time the soldiers had finished buying food, the commissary's tills were filled with gold eagle coins and rolls of "shinplasters"—the new paper currency issued in twenty-five and fifty cent denominations. And a great stock of food was amassed. The better part of it was canned goods—tomatoes, pears, peaches, and meats, as well as sacks of sugar and rice and dried beans and box after box of hardtack.

All was now stacked in great piles around the flagpole in the middle of the parade ground where Charley and Wash, the day's duty officers in charge of raising and lowering Old Glory, stood at attention next to that flagpole. Though a crowd of people had gathered, it was quiet, everyone listening. It was so silent you could hear the soft flapping of the flag on the small breeze blowing in off the prairie. It was a day clear as crystal. The only clouds were those few that always linger around the top of Mount Scott in the distance. Overhead there a bird was circling that Wash thought at first might be a turkey buzzard. But as it floated lower, he saw it was an eagle, cocking its head to look down at the throng of waiting soldiers and their families.

Then Wash began to hear the sound for which everyone was waiting. The solid beat of drums coming from outside the fort. But not the drums of war. Voices, too, a solemn sort of singing, repeating the same words again and again. Women's high ululations were cutting in with piercing notes, along with the men's deep voices, strong and solid as the beat of their drums. It stirred Wash's heart in a way beyond words. He felt as if he should be moving his own feet. But he remained at attention.

And here they came, a long procession of Kiowas and Comanches marching—no, dancing—from their villages ten miles away. Every man and women was wearing his or her finest clothing. The leaders wore eagle bonnet headdresses, so long they trailed down to the ground. All their faces were painted, but not for the path of war. Every single Indian, from the littlest toddler holding a mama's hand on up to Kicking Bird himself, was holding up a green willow branch and waving it back and forth in time to the drumming as they entered the fort.

Stiff at attention, Wash couldn't move his head, but he cut his eyes over toward where Bethany was standing with Sergeant Brown's wife and the other colored women of the fort. Her face looked as excited as he felt. She turned her gaze his way. Wash knew that the smile on her lips was meant to tell him how thrilled she was to be sharing that moment with him.

More and more danced on in. Some were men who had surely seen hard fighting in their lives. They bore on their bodies the marks of battles they had survived. Healed wounds from bullets and spears and knives showed on their arms and legs and shoulders and chests. One tall old man had a half-moon scar on his forehead, perhaps from where some enemy tried to scalp him.

They danced in to form a great circle around the flagpole, tromping down the colonel's beloved grass. Then, as one, they raised their willow branches up and, pointing them at the flag, all joined their voices in one long shrill cry that made the hair stand up on Wash's neck. Then they lay those willow wands down on the ground in front of all the foodstuffs piled before them.

They were so close that Wash could see how thin most of them were, their faces drawn with hunger. But not one rushed in to grab any of the food. They had too much dignity for that. Instead, the drumming and singing kept on as they danced in place. Finally, at a signal from Kicking Bird, it stopped. The men remained standing as the women and little ones sat down on the ground next to them.

Right on that green grass that will be matted and yellow tomorrow from all those dancing feet. Good thing Colonel Davidson is away.

But the colonel's wife was there and had been one of the women at the fort who had done the most to push the idea of feeding the Indians. So had the wife of Lieutenant Pratt. The two, along with most of the other women of the fort, stood together and watched in approval. Sergeant Brown's wife, Martha, and Bethany were there as well. Even though he was at attention, eyes forward, he could see Bethany's face. Had she placed herself so he could see her? It might be so, for her eyes were on his and a brilliant smile was on her face. She nodded at him. He almost forgot himself and nodded back, but stopped at the last second. Her mouth shaped a word. Good? Was that it? Then another. Idea?

It suddenly came to Wash. Bethany had helped him put together that bag of food he had dropped off for the Cheyennes before their transfer here to Fort Sill. It had been both her idea and his after he'd told her how starved the Indians were getting to be. It had reached the point where he wished he could share his own rations with them. But that was impossible.

"Nothing we can do," he'd said. "We are under orders not to go into the Cheyenne camp."

"No," she had replied. "There is always something that can be done. Even if it is small."

"Well," he'd said, "we could get some food and I could just accidentally drop it if I do run into any Indians whilst out on patrol."

Had Bethany passed that story on to Lieutenant Pratt's wife? Or had the idea simply come from the pity and goodness in the hearts of the officers' wives? No way to tell, Wash supposed. But there was a warm feeling in his chest as Bethany looked at him and nodded again.

Wherever it had come from, that idea of feeding the Kiowas had met the approval of Davidson's second, Major Schofield, the acting commanding officer. The major stepped up and gestured with his right hand. Two dozen enlisted men stepped forward and started prying the tops off the boxes, portioning out bags and cans of food to the waiting Kiowas and Comanches.

It was all done in good order. Each Indian man came up one after another—no pushing or shoving—to be given his share of the food. Wash noticed how the head chiefs and their families were the last to take their rations. Kicking Bird, in fact, was the very last, waiting until everyone else had their food handed to them before he came forward.

Sergeant Brown came up to where Wash was still at attention with Charley.

"See them two there," the sergeant said, jerking his thumb to indicate a pair of tall Kiowa men with big war bonnets. "Known hostiles. Last week they was at war, riding with Lone Wolf. But as long as the bellies of their families is filled they shall not be quick to go back on the war path."

Although the army might still end up fighting the Indians they were feeding, on that day there was a feeling of good will worth more than any paper treaty ever signed.

Wish our government was able to see just how simple it is, Wash thought. *Just make a promise and then keep it.*

The sun was close to sinking by the time all the food was distributed to the happy families of Kiowas and Comanches. The order was given for the bugle to sound retreat. The cannon was fired, signaling the end of the day.

As Wash and Josh lowered the flag and folded it, the last of the Indians filed out of the fort and disappeared into the dark.

Wash, he said to himself as he dropped into his bunk, *today was one of the finest days you and the 10th has ever seen.*

At least he thought he just said it himself. But he must have been saying his thoughts out loud, for a voice spoke up from the bunk next to his.

"A-yup," Josh said. "I do agree. Today was a fine day indeed. But what about all them buffalo hunters who are still killing off the herds? What will happen when our Indians have gone and eaten all of that food, which will not last them more'n a week at best? Today is fine. But what about tomorrow?"

What about tomorrow?

LONG AGO THE BUFFALO WERE MUCH STRONGER THAN THE PEOPLE.

THE PEOPLE HAD NO WEAPONS,
AND THE BUFFALO HUNTED THE PEOPLE AND ATE THEM.
THE BUFFALO BOASTED THAT
THEY WERE THE STRONGEST BEINGS ON THE EARTH.

MAHEO, THE GREAT MYSTERY, HEARD THOSE BOASTING WORDS
AND KNEW THEY WERE NOT GOOD.

SO MAHEO SENT A DREAM TO A CERTAIN MAN.
WHEN THAT MAN WOKE, HE DID AS THE DREAM TAUGHT HIM.
HE MADE A BOW, STRUNG IT WITH SINEW,
AND MADE ARROWS. HE PRACTICED HARD
TILL EACH ARROW HE SHOT STRUCK WHERE HE AIMED.

THEN HE WENT TO THE PEOPLE, WHO WERE SURROUNDED
AND TRYING TO FIGHT OFF THE BUFFALO WITH CLUBS.

HE FIRED ONE ARROW AFTER ANOTHER.
EACH ARROW BROUGHT DOWN A BUFFALO.

RUN, THE BUFFALO CRIED, THIS ONE KNOWS HOW TO KILL US.

SO, FROM THAT DAY ON, THE BUFFALO
HAVE NEVER AGAIN HUNTED THE PEOPLE,
AND THE BUFFALO RUN WHEN THEY SEE A HUMAN.

AND AS LONG AS HUMANS DO NOT BOAST
THAT THEY ARE THE STRONGEST ON THE EARTH,
THEY MAY HUNT THE BUFFALO.

UNEXPECTED NEWS

Petersburg, Virginia
March 23, 1874

Dear Private Vance,

As I am sure you have gathered by both my salutation and the fact that this letter is not in her handwriting, your sister is not writing this letter. Allow me then to introduce myself. My name is Henrietta Ames, and I am the new schoolmistress for the school that was recently built to serve the colored children of your community. It is a job that I hold in large part or perhaps entirely because of your father. But I shall explain that later in this epistle.

Your mother asks me now to tell you that she is well and that all is well. They have planted the fields and hope for a harvest as good as last year's. They have received the money you have generously been sending from your pay. Because they have done so well with their crops, they have not had to spend all of the money and they have begun to put some of it aside so that when you return home you will have your own money to use however you wish.

She and your stepfather are proud of you. They and your sister eagerly read every word in your letters again and again and imagine you are having a great adventure. They fear for your safety but are glad that you have good friends. I, for one, admire your attitude toward the Indian. At home in Boston, my father is a member of the local Friends of the Indian and works in his own way to bring peace and civilization to our red brethren.

Although your mother asked me not to mention it, I feel it is necessary to explain why I am writing this letter and not your sister—who has been one of my finest students. Your sister is too ill to write. She came down with a fever and for a time it was uncertain whether she would recover. It was a long struggle. Now, however, she is improving. I am sure the next letter you receive will be one that she writes. Your mother and stepfather were by her side every minute, and she could not have had better care. I admire your stepfather, Mr. Moses Mack, for his devotion to your family. And it is very pleasing to see how much he and your mother care for each other.

Before I close I should explain my rather mysterious reference to your father in the first paragraph of this missive. Like your father, my own father was a Union soldier. He was a lieutenant, and your father served under him. In the Battle of the Crater where your own father perished valiantly, my father lost his arm. But he would have lost his life had it not been for your father defending him and shielding him with his own body. All of the negro soldiers in my father's company fought with incredible bravery and honor, but your father was the best of them all, a man of both courage and intelligence with whom my father enjoyed discussing great literature.

When my father returned to us and told his story, I vowed, though I was but eleven years old at the time, to find some way to repay your family and those brave negro martyrs. I decided to become a teacher and travel to the South to teach negro children. It took me some years to gain my education, but I did not waver in my vow. I sought out the community where your family lived and took up my post four months ago.

I shall close by sending you my best wishes and my prayers for your continued health and safety. Your mother says to tell you that she loves you. She hopes all is well between you and Miss Bethany Brown. She is proud of you.

I remain most sincerely,
Henrietta Ames,
Schoolmistress
Hope School for the Colored

Wash put down the letter. Then he picked it up and read it again from start to finish. He shook his head and then read it a third time. There were so many conflicting emotions in his mind that he felt as if a hive of bees had taken up residence between his ears.

"You all right?"

Wash turned to look up at Charley, who had come into their tent without his noticing it.

"I reckon."

"Bad news from home?" Charley asked.

Wash let out a deep breath. "Well," he said, "my sister Pegatha been real sick for a while and nobody told me about it."

"That's bad."

"But she is getting better."

Charley grinned. "So that's good."

"My mama is married to Mr. Mack, the man who was my father's friend."

"You never told me that," Charley said.

Wash sighed. "Just like my mama never told me. I wouldn't know it now if it hadn't been for this letter written by the new schoolmistress, who must have figured I already knew about it."

Charley opened his mouth as if to say something, then closed it. He sat down next to Wash and put a hand on his shoulder. "Families is funny things," he said. "Sometimes our mamas just don't tell us everything. Like my own mama. She always say, 'What you don't know won't hurt you, son.' And most of the time she's right."

"I suppose," Wash said. "It just seems as if I think I know what is right, and then the next thing I just don't even know what I know."

The next evening was a Sunday. It had become Wash's favorite day of the week, for every Sunday now he was invited to dinner at Sergeant Brown's. The food was better than anything served in the mess hall. A far cry from Cincinnati chicken, as they called salt pork, or Stars and Stripes, the troopers' name for beans and bacon. But Mrs. Brown's home cooking was far from the best thing about those Sunday evenings. When dinner was over and the dishes cleared, he and Bethany would be left alone in the little combination dining room and sitting room while Sergeant Brown and his wife repaired to the third of their house's four small rooms—leaving the door open between them, of course. The door to the outside and the few windows in the small building were left open as well, for it was one of those hot nights in early summer where every evening breeze was like a blessing.

Wash bit his lips, looked up at Bethany in her chair not three feet away. Noticed a small bead of sweat on her perfect brown forehead. Then, even more quickly, he looked down. Some of the shyness he'd felt back when they first began to talk had come back to him. He didn't know what to say.

But Bethany smiled and broke the ice.

"So," she said brightly, "we are in the midst of Act Two, Scene Two, are we not, Private Vance?" Then, leaning close to him, she whispered, "Just read, Wash."

And, taking a breath from the air that suddenly seemed even warmer, he read:

> *"See, how she leans her cheek upon her hand!*
> *O, that I were a glove upon that hand,*
> *That I might touch that cheek!"*

His voice failed him, and he found himself squeezing the book tighter than he'd ever held the reins of any horse.

"Go on, Private," Bethany said.

Wash took a breath that was almost a sob. He knew he was speaking but couldn't hear his own voice or the words of the Bard who'd always delighted him. *How can I be saying this to her, to her!* he was thinking. *Does she understand how much these lines echo my own thoughts?*

"Ay me!" Bethany replied.

Wash sat up straight, as startled as if he'd been jabbed with a sharp stick.

"Ay me." Bethany repeated. "That's Juliet's line. Now go on with Romeo, Private."

Wash swallowed hard and began to read again:

"She speaks:
O, speak again, bright angel! for thou art
As glorious to this night, being o'er my head
As is a winged messenger of heaven..."

Wash closed the book. "Can we just stop there?" he said in a soft voice.

"You wish to leave now?" Bethany said. She sounded uncertain.

"No, not at all. But...can we just talk some?" As he spoke those words it was with a double worry. One was that, overhearing what he was saying, the sergeant or Mrs. Brown would step into the room and order him to leave. Or worse, that Bethany would be the one to say no. But neither happened. Instead, her long elegant hand reached across and touched him lightly on his right wrist.

"Go on, Private Vance," she said, her voice as soft as his own.

Wash sat there in silence, a confused but somehow happy silence despite his uncertainty about what he wanted to say or even why he'd said he wanted to talk. And then it came to him. He believed somehow, without knowing how, that Bethany would understand the confusion he was feeling about every part of his life that had seemed so simple and clear mere months ago.

"I got this letter from back home," he said. "It confused me."

"From a sweetheart, I suppose," Bethany said, straightening up a bit, her voice more careful than before.

"No," Wash said, "not at all. I never had a girl back home. There was always too much work to be done. It is from my mother."

"Oh," Bethany said, leaning forward again, "is it bad news?"

"Well, yes it was and, well, no it wasn't. That is what has me confused. And it was not from my mother. She never learned to read and write, so my sister usually wrote the letters. Except my sister was sick, very sick, and so this letter was written by the new schoolteacher." He took a breath. "From Boston. I mean the teacher is from Boston. Now why did I tell you that?"

Bethany smiled briefly, then quickly returned a serious look to her face. "That doesn't matter, does it? So just tell me about the letter, Wash. And your sister."

"Right," Wash said, rubbing his thumbs over the raised lettering on the book in his hands. "My sister was sick, but she is much better. The letter said my mother and my stepfather had been taking good care of her. My stepfather, Mr. Moses Mack. And she said, the teacher said, that my mother and my stepfather are proud of me."

The smile returned to Bethany's face. "Why, that is lovely, Private Vance," she said. "How nice to know that. And I could see why they would be proud of you." She paused and lowered her voice. "From what my uncle has said of you. He never praises any of the men as highly as he does you, Wash."

That stopped Wash. He had to take another breath on that thought, then realized it was probably just that the sergeant was being polite to his niece seeing as how she was enjoying talking about books so much with him. Nothing more than that.

"So," Bethany said, "what confused you in that seemingly lovely letter?"

Wash looked up at her. "I didn't know any of that before the letter."

"Any of what?"

"That my sister was sick or that my mother had gotten married again. That teacher just assumed I knew. But I darned well did not!"

"Oh," Bethany said.

"Why would they do that, keep all that secret from me?"

Bethany looked over her shoulder. The silence coming from the room on the other side of the open door was eloquently still. She shook her head, then placed both of her hands on top of Wash's where they rested palms down on Shakespeare's works.

"Sometimes," she said, "people who love you, truly love you, do not tell you everything because they do not wish to worry you or burden you. I think that is what your mother and sister were doing. I think that is what you have probably done in your letters to them."

"Maybe so."

"Did you know Mr. Moses Mack?

"Yes."

"A good man?"

"He was my father's best friend and took me fishing. I liked him well enough. But when my father died in the war, Mr. Mack went away for a good many years before he ever came back. I didn't even know he'd come back. My mother never told me he'd come back."

Bethany looked at Wash for a moment without saying anything. Then she folded her hands together and tapped her chin with them.

"Private," Bethany said, "have you ever killed anyone?"

It shocked Wash. He stared at her.

"Have you?"

An easy thing to deny, but not to Bethany, not with the way she was looking at him. Plus he had no doubt that word of what had happened in the Flat had long ago reached every corner of Fort Griffin, even though no official mention was ever made. And Bethany had been at Fort Griffin.

"Yes," Wash said.

"Was it justifiable?"

Wash nodded. "He would have killed my friend and me. He certainly tried." He found that he was holding something in his hand, holding it out to Bethany. It was his watch. The Vance watch. He had not realized he'd taken it from his pocket.

Bethany took the watch and opened it, looked at the picture inside. "These people," she said, "you knew them, didn't you?"

"The white Vances," Wash said, taking back the watch and studying the picture, wondering as he often did now if those faces had always been smiling up at him like that. "They owned us, me and my family. And the man I killed used to be our overseer. He whipped my father. And when the Yankees were coming, he dry-gulched the Vances and killed them all and stole this watch from them."

"Ah," Bethany said. "Your owners. It is interesting how often we look a bit like the white people who owned us, isn't it?"

Wash started to say something, but Bethany held up her hand. "But we are not them, are we? We have our own lives and our own destinies. Just as your mother has a life of her own. And do you know why I asked you if you ever killed a man?"

Wash shook his head.

Bethany held her index finger up to her lips and then moved it forward. "Because I intended to ask you this question next. Did you write home to your mother and sister about killing the outlaw Tom Key in a gunfight? Or do you ever intend to do so?"

"No," Wash said. "I did not. And I do not." And then, in spite of himself, he had to laugh. "You made your point."

Bethany nodded. "I certainly did," she replied.

It was the same now for all of the tribes. After years of resisting the call to turn from the old ways, it was over. Their only chance to survive was to accept life at the agencies. A few had tried the path of raiding into Mexico. If they avoided the American settlements, they might not stir the anger of the army. But it did not work. When they took horses and cattle from the Mexicanos, they were attacked on their way back across the border by American soldiers.

Among the Kiowas, only Lone Wolf would not give up. His heart still burned over the death of his son Tau-ankia and his nephew Gui-tain. Lone Wolf stayed out with a little band of his relatives and followers.

The Comanches were ready to quit—aside from the Quahadis. They were being urged on by Quanah Parker. He was half-white, the son of the Nokoni chief Peta and a captive white woman. But his mother had loved his father. She had become as much a Comanche woman as any born to their nation. She and Peta raised their son to be a fierce and intelligent fighter. When the Nokonis came in to the agency, he refused to join them. He joined the Quahadi band because they were not ready to accept quiet ways. Soon he had risen to be their war leader.

The Cheyennes, too, did not want to quit. But it seemed hopeless. By the end of the Moon of Drying Up, they realized what they had to do. If they wished to live, they had to come in to the agency.

Winter Man had finally let go his strangling grasp. Now they could travel. Gray Head, Heap of Birds, all of the chiefs of the Council of Forty-four came in with their many lodges. Into Darlington came one hundred forty lodges led by White Shield, Old Wind, and Eagle Head. Most of the people were walking and limping behind the few who still had horses. White Horse, the head chief of the Dog Soldiers, was with them. His return to the agency showed that even the fiercest fighters were ready to accept peace if it meant food for their family. The war leaders came in—even those who had urged the people not to rely on government rations. All they asked for now was food in exchange for peace. They knew that the rations they might receive would be small. But they also knew that some food was more than the nothing they had before.

They all waited to be fed. Seven hundred lodges in all. They waited. Day after day.

Just feed us. We will not fight.

Still they were not fed. Still they waited.

"My son!"

Wolf looked up from the piece of wood he was carving with his knife. At first he had been whittling to pass the time. It kept his mind off his empty belly. But now the shape of a buffalo calf was beginning to emerge from the soft cottonwood.

"Mother," he said. He looked up. There was a hopeful smile on his mother's face

"Come along! Our agent is calling us to gather. It must be that the rations have arrived."

A crowd had gathered in front of the home of Agent Miles. But there was no smile on his face. The soldiers who stood to either side of him were not smiling.

Wolf held on to his little sister's hands on one side, his mother's on the other.

No, he thought. *No. Let the news be good.*

"My friends, my dear friends," Miles began. His voice caught, as if there was a hook in his mouth. He raised his hands. "I am sorry." He looked down at his clenched hands and then held them open. "There is no more food for you. I have been told that there is none coming soon. There is nothing I can do. I am sorry."

No one in the crowd spoke, even after the interpreter finished translating. A few shook their heads, as if not understanding the words, but no one spoke.

Agent Miles looked over at the army man next to him, whose yellow stripes on his shoulder showed him to be an officer. The officer nodded his head.

"The army understands how hard this is for you," Miles said. "So they have given you permission to leave. You may leave the agency to go and hunt. You may leave," Miles said again. "Go. Find your buffalo herds. Hunt. You have my permission and that of the army to leave." He turned, went into his home, and shut the door behind him.

People began looking at each other and talking.

"We came here believing their promises of food and peace," a woman named Red Beads said. "Now we are worse off than when we arrived. Their promises are as empty as our stomachs."

But her words were not spoken with anger. If anything, her voice sounded tired.

Wolf and his mother and sister turned away to go back to their lodge. Their possessions were few. Still, they needed to get them together so they could leave with the dawn.

"My son," Wolf's mother said to him, "our hope now rests with our sacred herds. I know you will do your best to find them."

Early the next morning, the women took down the lodges. They tied the tipi poles to the oldest horses. The chiefs divided up the strongest of the young men into small scouting parties. They were given the best of the remaining horses. That way they could range as far as possible when they fanned out over the prairie.

Wolf looked at his own scouting party. Himself and his three best friends.

"Now that the hard winter is over," Too Tall said, "hunting will be good."

"We will surely find our herds," Too Short agreed.

Horse Road nodded and kicked his heels into his pony's sides.

As they rode south they felt hopeful. And it seemed their hope was rewarded. On the second day, they found the tracks of a small buffalo herd.

"Look," Too Tall said, poking at a buffalo chip with a stick. "They passed through here no more than a few days ago."

"I am hungry enough to eat a horse," Too Short said.

"Eat your brother's horse, then," Horse Road said.

"No," Too Tall said, "my horse is skinny."

"That is true," Too Short agreed. "We should eat Following Wolf's horse first."

Wolf smiled. There was little chance of that. His horse, Wind, was strongest. It had been agreed that he would be the one to ride back once they saw a herd of their animals. While his friends kept track of the herd, he would lead back the lodges of women and children and old people. They would set up the hunting camp. As the young men hunted, the women would skin the sacred animals. They would butcher them with respect and care so that nothing would be wasted. All would give thanks to Maheo as they ate together.

Wolf's smile grew broader as he thought of that. Real food to eat. So much better than rotten beef from sick cows. The bellies of the sacred ones—the hungry children and the starving old people—finally would be filled again.

The warm air tasted good as they rode. The tracks grew fresher as they trotted along. They knew they were moving faster than the buffalo. If there was good grass, a herd would move along slowly, grazing. And the grass had been good. It had been grazed down low all around them by the herd, but it was clear that the new grass had been green and tall. Deep winter snow always made for good grass when the spring came.

Sun was in the middle of the sky. It was late spring. The days were long. Unless something had stampeded the herd, they might make up the distance between them before the end of the day. The sun moved across the sky as they rode. The width of one hand, two, three, four. Though the land seemed flat, there were folds in the prairie and small hills. Those folds and hills could hide even a large herd from sight until they were close.

Horse Road began to sing. Too Tall and Too Short joined in with him.

A good day to be alive
a good day to be alive
we are hunting for the people
a good day to be alive…

Wolf held up his hand. His friends stopped singing. They pulled up their horses. They were at the foot of a range of hills. The hoof marks of buffalo led up it, through a small pass at the top.

Dismount, he signed.

They did so quietly. Then they moved up the hill slowly. They didn't want the sudden sight of hunters to disturb the herd that they would soon see on the wide plain stretching out on the other side.

A meadowlark burst up from the dry grass in front of them as they climbed. It fluttered so close to Horse Road's face that he almost fell down. He looked over at Wolf and grinned. Wolf grinned back.

They all dropped down low to crawl.

They reached the hilltop.

Together, in silence, the four young men looked down across the plain.

Before them were many buffalo. So many. They would have been enough to feed every lodge of their people for many days. The herd had been bigger than expected.

Wolf and his three friends stood. The walked down among the herd. They walked in silence. Wolf began counting the animals. Ten, twenty, a hundred, two hundred. There were buffalo everywhere as far as they could see.

But Wolf's counting soon stopped. It was not because the number was too great. It was because his eyes filled with tears. He could no longer see clearly.

Two ravens ka-awked. They flapped up from the remains of the stinking buffalo carcass closest to Wolf. Only the hides and tongues had been taken by the hunters. Even after the prairie wolves and ravens had taken their share, there had been much meat left. But now that meat was no longer good. The weather had been warm. The buffalo hunters had not taken out the insides of each animal. They had not done as the people always did, finding a use for every part of this sacred gift. What meat was left was rotten.

That awful waste showed who had done this terrible thing. That and the way the buffalo had been skinned. When Indians skinned a buffalo, they took the whole hide. But the white buffalo skinners were always in such a hurry that they cut around the legs.

"We will stay hungry," Horse Road said. The hard anger in his voice was like a stone.

No one else had anything to say.

LISTEN TO ME CAREFULLY,
SWEET MEDICINE SAID,
AND TRUTHFULLY FOLLOW MY INSTRUCTIONS.

YOU CHIEFS ARE PEACE-MAKERS.
THOUGH YOUR SON MIGHT BE KILLED
IN FRONT OF YOUR LODGE,
YOU SHOULD TAKE A PEACE PIPE AND SMOKE.
THEN YOU WOULD BE CALLED AN HONEST CHIEF.

YOU CHIEFS OWN THE LAND AND THE PEOPLE.
IF YOUR MEN, YOUR SOLDIER SOCIETIES,
SHOULD BE SCARED AND RETREAT,
YOU ARE NOT TO STEP BACK
BUT TAKE A STAND TO PROTECT YOUR LAND
AND YOUR PEOPLE.

GET OUT AND TALK TO THE PEOPLE.
IF STRANGERS COME, YOU ARE THE ONES
TO GIVE PRESENTS TO THEM AND INVITATIONS.

WHEN YOU MEET SOMEONE,
OR HE COMES TO YOUR LODGE
ASKING FOR ANYTHING,
GIVE IT TO HIM. NEVER REFUSE.

GO OUTSIDE YOUR LODGE
AND SING YOUR CHIEF'S SONG
SO ALL THE PEOPLE WILL KNOW
YOU HAVE DONE SOMETHING GOOD.

QUANAH'S SUN DANCE

The sun had risen and set twenty times since Friend Miles had
released the Cheyennes to hunt. Their scouting parties had gone far
and wide. They had ranged across the lands where the great herds
had always grazed at that time of the year. But no one had found
a single living buffalo. Instead of living herds, they found only
skinned bodies. In some cases, the killing had been recent. So a
little meat had been salvaged from the fresher carcasses. It had been
enough to feed the people for only a few days.

The leaders gathered.

"There are herds farther to the south," White Horse suggested.

"But there is danger there, too," Gray Head said. "Buffalo hunters. Stinky white men who would shoot an Indian as quickly as they
would an animal. Perhaps more quickly. And there are not just a few
of those stinky white men to the south. There are many."

"Those stinky white men," White Horse said, "they broke the
law against coming onto our buffalo grounds.

"But the army did not stop them," Heap of Birds said. "It has
turned a blind eye toward them. Now they have built a big camp.
It is near the old white man's abandoned fort the ve'hoes call Adobe Walls. They even have their own store there. It supplies them
with goods and buys the skins from them. They will stay there
until every buffalo left in the world has been killed, skinned, and
left to rot.

Wolf walked away from the little council. He walked for a long time through the hills. His feet kicked up swirls of dust as he walked. The snow was gone, but this moon brought no rain. No rain at all. First the killing cold and now this drought.

When the sun was two hands above setting, he returned. His mother had set up their lodge near a small streambed. There a trickle of water still flowed. His mother and sister were not there. He saw they had taken their digging sticks. They were looking for roots for food. It was so dry they'd had little luck at that. Still, they kept trying.

Wolf slid down against the wall of the lodge. The dry leaves in the nearby grove of cottonwoods rattled in the breeze.

"Is there nothing we can do?" he said to himself.

"There is something we can do!" Horse Road sat next to him.

"Henova'eto? What?"

"We can go to the Comanches."

"Henova'e? Why?"

"They are having a Sun Dance. They sent a messenger, who came while you were off walking. All are invited."

Wolf looked hard at him. "It is not yet the time for the Sun Dance. It is only the Spring Moon. The Sun Dance is done when the days are long and the sun is high."

"That is true," Horse Road said.

Wolf thought about the Sun Dance. It was a great and sacred ceremony. It was always done carefully and in a sacred way. They would build a great arbor and put up a sacred tree. Cheyenne men who had pledged themselves to sacrifice would put on holy paint. They would dance for several days facing the sun. They would take neither food nor water as they prayed to Maheo. They prayed for health and help for the people.

"There are many sacred steps that must be taken to do the Sun Dance properly," Wolf said.

"That is also true," Horse Road said. "Also, as far as I know the Comanches have never done a Sun Dance before. But has not knowing how to do something ever stopped a Comanche from trying to do it?"

Horse Road smiled at his own joke. It was a thin smile that did not go beyond his lips. The laughter that used to be in his eyes as they joked with each other was gone.

"Anyhow," he continued, "whether they know how to do it or not, they are going to do one now. Quanah has invited all of the nations to come. He says that his little prophet, Isa-tai, can make us all bulletproof."

Isa-tai. Wolf knew who he was. Like Quanah, Isa-tai was Quahadi. He was not a fighter. He had not accomplished any deeds of war. But he had done other things. Or so people said. He foretold the coming of the Great Star before it began to burn its path across the sky. Night after night, that strange star lit up the dark like a second moon.

Isa-tai had not feared that burning star.

"The star is a good omen," he had stated boldly. "It will disappear in five days' time."

When it did just that, many were impressed. His next prediction had been about the season to come.

"There will be terrible cold!" Isa-tai had prophesied loudly. "Great blizzards will come. It will be worse than any winter in memory."

Indeed, that past winter had been as dreadful as Isa-tai said. Most Comanches now believed that his power was real.

"So," Horse Road said. "Shall we go to Quanah's Sun Dance?"

"Hea'e," Wolf replied. "Maybe."

There was a strange, tight feeling in his chest. He could not tell if it was excitement or dread.

Four days later it was a warm and beautiful day. The sun was shining. A small wind was caressing the long grasses about the Comanche Sun Dance grounds. Swallows were dipping down to the surface of the nearby river. They dappled the water with their beaks as they scooped water to drink in midflight.

The Comanches had chosen a good spot for their Sun Dance. It was near the boundary of their reservation, on the banks of the north fork of the Red River. As Wolf expected, they had stripped away much of the ceremony. They had not used sacred paint. Many other important things had been left out.

"Why is there no Sacred Woman?" Wolf asked a young Comanche man who looked about his age. His name was Ta-a-way-te. Buffalo Scout.

"Ours is a big Sun Dance for warriors," Buffalo Scout replied. His tone indicated he thought that was a foolish question.

I will ask no more questions.

Their Sun Dance was, indeed, a very big one. They had made a huge circular lodge, placing twelve poles around it connected to a forked center pole. From the top of that center pole hung the skin of a newly killed buffalo, stuffed with willow twigs. The ceremony had been simplified, but the Comanches had worked hard to prepare.

They had sent invitations far and wide for others to join them. Come, help us pray for the return of the buffalo and the survival of all our nations.

There were more people gathered in one place than Wolf had ever seen. All of the Comanche bands had come. So, too, had many of the Cheyennes. There were Arapahos, Wichitas, Delawares.

Surprisingly, Wolf saw few of the closest allies to the Comanches, the Kiowas. The only Kiowas at the Sun Dance were Lone Wolf and his small band.

There was also whiskey. Plenty of whiskey. Too much of it. Most of the Cheyennes were staying away from that firewater. But others were drinking and behaving as men do when they are drunk. The tight feeling in his chest came back.

How can there be whiskey at a Sun Dance? How can whiskey help when we are praying for help from the Creator?

Buffalo Scout smiled and beckoned for Wolf to come join those about to be pierced before they would dance facing the sun.

Wolf shook his head. He meant no disrespect to their ceremony, but he would not take part.

This whole ceremony was far different from any Sun Dance ever done before on the plains. Its purpose was different, too. Rather than just praying for help, it seemed to be meant to be the prelude to a war council.

On the next day, that was made clear. A council was called. Quanah rose first to speak. He called Isa-tai to his side.

"I believe in this man," Quanah said in a strong voice. He stared out across the crowd. "We must do as he says."

Although Quanah spoke in Comanche, all of those gathered understood him. Comanche was the easiest of the Plains languages to speak. It was the one most often used when there was more than one nation gathered.

Isa-tai stepped out in front of Quanah. He lifted up his skinny arms. "Hear me," he proclaimed, in a voice that seemed too big for his body. "I have talked with the Great Mystery. I talk with him every day. He has promised to aid us if we join together to fight."

"We do not have enough ammunition for a war," one of the Wichitas said. "The American soldiers are too well armed."

"Hah! I can make bullets come out of my stomach," Isa-tai boasted. "I can make all of you bulletproof. I will paint you with sacred paint that will protect you. Then, if I wave my hand, bullets fired at you will fall to the ground and not touch you."

The Wichita man shook his head in disbelief. He turned without another word. He walked over to his horse. The other Wichitas followed him. They all mounted and silently rode away.

I, too, have my doubts, Wolf thought. *There is something about Isa-tai that I do not like. Maybe it is his name. Isa-tai means "Coyote Dung" in the Comanche language. What if what he is saying is no more than that?*

Horse Road grabbed Wolf's right arm.

"Wait," Horse Road said. "He is right. Together, something great could be done. We should join together, ride out, and strike the enemy."

"Which enemy we ride against?" someone with a Delaware accent called out from behind them.

"Tonkawas," Quanah replied. "They help the Tai-bos fight us. They killed my friend, the one who grew up with me. There by the Double Mountain fork of the Brazos. Then they ate him. It makes my heart hot to think of them."

Fighting the Tonkawas. Many began to nod their heads. That would be a good thing to do. The Tonkawas were a common enemy to all of those gathered.

Then someone called out. His voice spoke pure Comanche. It was loud and clear as the beat of a drum.

"Quanah! These old men want to see you over here!"

Wolf turned. There stood two old Comanche men, White Wolf and Old Man Otter Belt. They were respected Comanche elders.

Quanah walked over to them.

"You are a good fighter," White Wolf said to Quanah. "But you do not know everything."

"That is so," Old Man Otter Belt agreed. "We think you should take the pipe first against the white buffalo hunters. They have broken the treaty and come onto our lands. Lead us to attack them. That will make your heart good."

"Yes," White Wolf said. "After that, when we come back you can take the young men to Texas against the Tonkawas."

Quanah nodded. "Your words are good. We should make war on the buffalo hunters. Do all here agree?"

In response, hundreds of voices joined together in a loud shout. "YES!"

But even though his friend was one of those shouting, Wolf was silent.

Perhaps together we might drive away the buffalo hunters. But will it end there? What then will the army do?

Out on the wide plains, you could see a storm coming from a long way away. It was not like it was back in Virginia, where a rain would just wash in without warning. On the plains, you could watch clouds forming on the horizon a hundred miles away before they reached you. You could see the flash of lightning long before the thunder came. Then, as those clouds came closer, getting bigger and darker, a tightness grew in the air and you knew that storm was going to strike hard as a hammer hitting an anvil.

That was how it felt at Fort Sill. Friendlies from the various tribes had been coming in great numbers. All told stories of trouble brewing. No one was fooling himself any longer that things were going to be quiet. A storm would be coming. But this one would not be dropping rain and hail. Arrows and bullets would be flying.

"Lordy, Lordy, here they come! Wash, Wash?"

Charley stuck his head into the tent as Wash looked up from his third try at writing a letter to his mother, his sister, and his new stepfather. Every word he wrote and every line kept coming out wrong. He crumpled the paper and tossed it aside.

"Come on," Charley said, grabbing Wash's arm and practically carrying him outside. "You have got to see this."

It didn't take more than a glance for Wash to understand what the commotion was. Big chiefs were arriving. Kicking Bird of the Kiowas and Quirts Quip of the Comanches were riding into the fort at the head of a small party of ten or twelve warriors. All of their faces were as serious as if they were a funeral procession. Agent Haworth, looking just as morose, was riding among them. The warriors reined up at the entrance while the two chiefs and the agent kept going, past the enlisted men's tents and straight on into the fort. Wash and Charley, not being not on duty, followed at a respectful distance. The two chiefs and the agent dismounted in front of the commander's quarters, tied their horses, and walked past the guard, who stepped aside to allow them into the commander's office. The door shut behind them.

Charley looked over at Wash.

Wash shrugged his shoulders, sat down, and pulled out his knife and the piece of wood he'd been working on. He hadn't been sure when he'd started, but it now looked like it was turning into a buffalo calf. "Nothing else to do till roll call. Might as well just wait and see what is cooking."

Ten minutes passed. The voices were muffled by the closed windows, but it was plain that serious business was being discussed. Half an hour. The chiefs came out, looking even more depressed than before. Agent Haworth was not with them. The two Indian leaders silently mounted their horses and rode off, neither looking back.

A minute later the agent emerged. He strode after the two chiefs for a few paces, then stopped, staring at the backs of the departing Indians as if he was trying to decide whether to follow them or not. Finally he shook his head like a bereaved relative realizing it was far too late to do anything for the dearly departed.

Wash and Charley stood up and turned around at the sound of booted feet thudding on the porch. Colonel Davidson and Major Schofield emerged. Along with the guard at the door, Wash and Charley came to attention and saluted. The two officers did not even turn their way. The major's face was as serious as the chief mourner standing by a grave. But there was a little smile on the colonel's lips. His look was that of someone who'd just heard the will read and finally got what he'd long been awaiting.

Colonel Davidson chuckled. Funeral over. He walked back inside whistling a tune. Major Schofield gritted his teeth, took a deep breath, and as soon as the colonel's door was shut let out a string of cuss words. Not loud enough for anyone else to hear except for the guard still standing at attention—and except for Wash and Charley.

It surprised Wash. Major Schofield was a man of measured speech and not one to take the name of the Lord in vain. The major sighed and straightened his back.

"Drat," he whispered. Then, as if waking up, he turned and noticed Wash and Charley, still standing at attention, eyes front.

"At ease," he said. Then he motioned to Wash. "Private, take this message to the officers. The colonel wants all officers assembled in his quarters at 1400 hours."

"Yes, sir!" Wash snapped a salute and took off on the double.

It took Wash longer than he'd expected, largely because Lieutenant Pratt was hard to find. Wash finally located him outside the walls, palavering with a group of Kiowa scouts. Wash recognized them as being among the honor guard that had ridden in to the fort with the two chiefs and stayed waiting outside for them.

He quickly got the gist of what the Kiowas were telling Pratt from the hand signs they made.

The Comanches have called together all of the tribes of the southern plains. Quanah Parker is going to lead them to battle against the buffalo hunters.

Little groups of soldiers not on any specific duty were gathering around the parade ground in front of the colonel's quarters as Wash returned following Lieutenant Pratt. As Pratt went inside, Wash joined the others, wondering like every other soldier at Fort Sill about what was being decided inside.

A few phrases were loud enough to be heard outside the closed room.

"War with…"

"Attack at…"

"Buffalo hunters are NOT…"

"General Pope's explicit orders forbid…"

But what they all heard loud and clear were the colonel's final words that ended the meeting. Words shouted out loud and clear.

"Assemble the men!"

A second later the officers came boiling out like hornets from a nest hit by a stone. Wash tried to keep calm, but his heart was pounding. It was hard to catch his breath. War! They were finally going to war! Any minute it would be boots and saddles and they'd be charging out the gate.

But that did not happen. When they were all assembled in ranks, all they heard was a speech from the colonel telling them that the situation was grave.

"All must be prepared," he finally said. And that was it.

By the time they went to mess, everything was back to normal. People ate silently, looking around at each other. No one was quite sure what would happen next, but in the end it was what always seemed to happen when you were a soldier. You waited. And then you waited some more.

That evening, Wash made his way quietly to the bunkhouse. He stepped inside, went to the back left corner, looked around, stepped onto the nearby chair, and then reached up as high as he could. Charley Smith's long right arm reached down, grasped his wrist, and hoisted him up to the secret hiding place between the roof and the rafters known only to the enlisted men. Colonel Davidson had forbidden all games of chance. But telling soldiers not to play cards or roll dice in their spare time was about as likely to succeed as ordering the sun not to come up at dawn. It had been, of course, Charley's idea to shove aside the loose ceiling boards and explore the space above. The tallest men had to hunch a bit, but there was plenty of room. A single lantern that hung from a nail on the highest beam shed more than enough light for the five card players gathered around the barrel serving as a card table.

Wash settled down to watch as Charley retook his place and shuffled the deck.

"You fellas hear 'bout the local sodbuster with a fast team?" Josh said as he picked up his cards. "He was hauling a load of hogs when he got caught in one of them prairie rainstorms. Man drove so fast that when he got home, only the back of his neck was wet. But ever one of them pigs in the back of his wagon was drowned."

One of the new recruits, a gangly young man from Tennessee who Wash guessed was about to lose a week's pay, opened his mouth as wide as a catfish about to swallow a hook.

"My, my," he said, "must have been some rain."

"Uh-huh," Josh replied as he studied his hand. "Must have been."

"Are we not going to get no action?" another new recruit groused.

"That is right," said the first one. "I did not join up just to sit about. I wants to shoot me some Indians."

"Two cards," Josh said.

"Here you go," Charley replied, dealing him two kings.

"My pot," Josh said, raking in his winnings.

Normally Wash would have smiled. But not that night. He was thinking about what those new recruits just said and how a man needed to be careful about what he wished for. They feared that all they had to look forward to was more boring drill and weather so hot you could fry an egg on the stone wall of the fort. But what Wash feared was that the storm brewing just might hold more thunder and lightning than any of them could handle.

Meetings had been held in the days following the Comanche Sun Dance. The decision to attack the stinky white men had been agreed upon. Invitations were sent out to attend a medicine and war council. Those invitations were sent to all of the Plains tribes except for the hated Tonkawas.

The council met at a place on the north fork of the Red River by the mouth of Elk Creek. Wolf was there with his best friend. Despite his uncertainty, Wolf had chosen to accompany Horse Road.

Hundreds of men from many nations were there. Wolf and Horse Road stood among the Cheyennes, who were the largest group. Quanah Parker and Isa-tai were sitting together in front. Everyone was waiting. For a moment all was silent. From the tallgrass meadow behind them, Wolf could hear a meadowlark singing. It seemed as if he could understand what the bird was saying. He heard it as clearly as if it was singing in Cheyenne.

> *You will sing sad songs.*
> *Lodges will be empty.*
> *Your songs will be sad.*
> *There will be empty lodges.*

Isa-tai stood. He stepped forward. He held a pipe carved from the red sacred stone. Long ago that stone had been the blood of powerful beings.

"Accept this pipe," Isa-tai shouted.

His voice was loud. To Wolf it sounded hollow, like wind through a reed. He looked around. Three young men next to them were trembling. Was it with excitement over Isa-tai's words? Or was it just that they were suffering from hangovers? That was true of far too many of the men gathered for this war council. Wolf shook his head. So much drinking had been going on over the past days. The Comancheros, those Mexicano traders and slavers who presented themselves as Quanah's friends, had brought three wagons full of guns and ammunition to trade. They had also brought one wagonload of whiskey. By the time they left, all four wagons had been empty of their original cargo. They had been filled with buffalo robes. All but one of the traders had left. He had attached himself to Quanah's Quahadis.

Wolf peered over at that man. A strange man. His skin was not brown or pale. It was an almost yellow color. He had been a Buffalo Soldier. So Wolf heard it said. It might be true. The yellow man carried with him a shiny metal horn. Wolf had seen such horns carried by ve'hoe soldiers. Quanah seemed quite pleased to have this man with him. Apparently that yellow man and his horn would play some part in Quanah's big battle plans.

Many had come to the Comanches' war council. But not as many as Quanah hoped. Many fighting men from several tribal nations were gathered here. But even more had stayed away. Some did so because they wanted no part of the whiskey drinking. Others thought the war a foolish idea or a waste of time.

That had been especially true of the Kiowas. Aside from Lone Wolf and his little band, no Kiowas had joined Quanah's army. It would soon be time for the Kiowa Sun Dance to take place. Preparing for that sacred ceremony was more important to the Kiowa Nation than going to war against the buffalo killers. But not to Lone Wolf.

He strode up to Isa-tai and held out his hand.

"My men and I accept the war pipe," he said in a firm voice.

The Kiowa war leader's eagerness troubled Wolf.

His wish for revenge is so strong. Is it blinding him? Can we really drive off the buffalo hunters? Or will we just kill enough white men to bring the army down on us? Will Isa-tai's magic work against the army's bullets and big guns?

Wolf watched Horse Road out of the corner of his eye. He had not yet moved. More came forward to take the pipe. Horse Road stayed where he was. Was he, too, uncertain about this idea of going to war? Wolf hoped so.

After the Kiowas, it was the turn of the Arapahos. Few of them were there. There was only one Arapaho leader in attendance— Yellow Horse, a lesser chief. The other members of their tribe had followed the counsel of their peace chief, Powder Face. They had stayed at their agency. Yellow Horse strode forward, his back straight, to grasp the pipe. His twenty-two men followed him.

The next to be offered the pipe were the Yapparika and the Penateka Comanches, led by their chiefs Quirts Quip and Ho-weah.

"Take this pipe," Isa-tai said, thrusting it at them.

"No," Quirts Quip replied in a calm voice.

Isa-tai was shocked. Other Comanches refusing him?

"You must take it!" Isa-tai said. He showed his teeth as if he was about to bite.

Ho-weah held up his hand. He made a pushing motion. "We want no part of your foolishness."

"We will shoot your horses!" Isa-tai screamed. "We will make you walk back to the agency like the cowards that you are!"

Quirts Quip looked down his nose at the little medicine man.

"Hunh!" Quirts Quip snorted. He turned to Ho-weah, who nodded. Then, as one, they and all their men turned their backs to Isa-tai. Without looking back, they mounted their horses and rode slowly out of the encampment.

Straight back to the Kiowa and Comanche Agency at Fort Sill, Wolf thought. *They will tell their agent what is being planned. He will tell the army.*

The feeling in Wolf's chest, like two hands squeezing together, grew tighter.

Isa-tai stood staring after the departing Comanche bands. His hands were trembling.

"Let them go," Quanah said. "We will have enough without them. Look at our Cheyenne brothers just waiting to be offered the pipe."

The Cheyennes. Wolf's own people. For a moment Wolf's eyesight blurred. He found himself looking into the white heart of winter. It was a winter deeper and colder than the one just past. He shook his head. The bleak vision faded. But it was replaced by another sight. Horse Road stepping forward.

"Come on," Horse Road said.

Wolf stepped forward with him.

Horse Road took the pipe in both hands. He touched it to his lips. He passed it to Wolf. The day was hot. But the pipe felt as cold as the ice in his vision. It took all his will to keep his hands from shaking.

"Peheva'e," Horse Road was saying. Wolf passed the pipe to another Cheyenne. All around them Cheyennes had come forward. So many of them. Too many of them.

"It is good," Horse Road said. "Very good. We have the new repeating rifles. We will be part of a great force of strong warriors. Quanah and Isa-tai will lead us to victory. We will wipe out the buffalo killers."

So Horse Road said.

But would it be so?

WIHIO WAS OUT WALKING AROUND.
HE WAS HUNGRY.

HE CAME TO A GREAT STONE UP ON A HILL.

GRANDFATHER, HELP ME, HE SAID TO THAT STONE.
HE TOOK OUT HIS KNIFE AND PUT IT ON THE GROUND.

I WILL GIVE YOU THIS KNIFE
IF YOU HELP ME FIND FOOD.

THEN WIHIO WALKED ON, ON DOWN INTO THE VALLEY.
AND THERE IN THAT VALLEY LAY A FRESH-KILLED BUFFALO.

AH, WIHIO SAID, LOOK, I HAVE FOUND FOOD.
BUT WHERE DID I PUT MY BEST SKINNING KNIFE?

THAT'S RIGHT, I DROPPED IT
BACK UP BY THAT OLD STONE.

HE RAN BACK UP THE HILL.
HE PICKED UP HIS KNIFE AND RAN BACK DOWN.

BUT WHEN HE GOT THERE, ALL THAT WAS LEFT
OF THAT BUFFALO WAS OLD DRY BONES.

THEN HE HEARD A SOUND, A RUMBLING SOUND.
HE TURNED AROUND TO LOOK
AND HE SAW THAT OLD STONE
ROLLING DOWN THE HILL RIGHT TOWARD HIM.

HE BEGAN TO RUN AS FAST AS HE COULD,
BUT HE COULD NOT OUTRUN THAT GREAT ROLLING STONE.

IT RAN OVER WIHIO AND LEFT HIM THERE,
SQUASHED AS FLAT AS YOUR HAND.

RIDING WEST

"You see," Horse Road said. "Isa-tai was right. It has been easy."

Wolf had to agree. It had been easy thus far. They had needed horses in better shape than the few left after the hard winter and the constant raids on their herds by white thieves. So they had gone to where they knew good mounts would be.

For the Comanches it had been the corral at Fort Sill. Their night raid was so fast and silent that they came away with eighty horses. Not even one shot was fired. No one had pursued them. At the same time, the Cheyennes, Wolf and Horse Road among them, had made a quick visit to the army herd at the Darlington Agency. They, too, had encountered no resistance. They drove off fifty fine fat horses.

The peace chiefs Little Robe and Stone Calf were going to take no part in Quanah's and Isa-tai's war. But they were not displeased about such taking of horses. It was only fair. The army had promised to protect their herds. It had not done so. Little Robe's own son had been wounded just a few days before by a group of white horse thieves who took a big part of the Cheyennes' remaining herd. Gray Head and Little Robe had gone to the Darlington Agency. They had asked Agent Miles to send the army.

"We want you to bring back our stolen ponies," Gray Head said.

"The army has better things to do than bring back Indian horses," Agent Miles had said.

Of course, soon after the horse raiders reached the Cheyenne camp with those fifty horses, the interpreter from the agency paid them a call. He carried a message from Agent Miles

"You must bring back the horses you took," the interpreter told Gray Head.

Gray Head laughed. "Tell Friend Miles," he said, "that he can have these horses back when the army men bring back our horses. Unless they have better things to do."

Each night there were more men around the campfires of those readying for Quanah's war. One was the oldest son of Stone Calf.

"My father's road is not mine now," Stone Calf's son said. "I am ready to fight."

As yet, though, there had been no fighting. Instead, they had to listen to Isa-tai brag each evening about how his power would protect them.

"The Great Father above has told me that we are going to kill many tai-bos. I will stop the bullets from their guns. Their guns will not pierce your shirts. We will kill them all as if they were old women," Isa-tai boasted.

"Hear what he says," Quanah said. "The Great Father above has told him the truth."

The former Buffalo Soldier with the bugle stood near Isa-tai and Quanah, puffing out his chest as they talked. Loud Voice. That was the name they all now called the yellow-skinned man. It was only partly because of the horn he carried. Four moons ago, he had joined the Comancheros. Now, with Quanah and the Quahadis, he was always boasting in the broken Comanche he had learned.

"I teach how ve'hoe soldiers fight as one. Then we defeat them easy!"

Wolf looked at the man with distrust. How could a man desert his own people and join their enemies? Of course Loud Voice had his own answer to that question.

"Why me here? Bad. Them treat me bad. Them treat Indians bad."

But Wolf thought there was another reason Loud Voice had joined them. Greed. In return for his help, Loud Voice asked for a big share of whatever was won in battle. Loud Voice smiled like a hungry coyote when Quanah promised he would be given much, much.

Wolf looked back over his shoulder as he rode. The great mass of people from several nations moving across the land did not look like an army. They were not marching swiftly and alone as white men did. The fighting men were accompanied by their families. They set up their camp circles each night, re-creating their own villages.

Wolf's sister waved to him. She was sitting on the back of her mare. It was an old animal, too old for battle. So it was dragging the lighter of the two travois with their possessions. His mother's even older horse plodded next to it. It was dragging the tipi poles as Wolf's mother led it along.

That night he would sleep in his mother's lodge. He would eat by her cooking fire with her and his sister. He would be home each night. Even though each night they moved far from where they had been the night before. Despite his worries about the fighting to come, that made him feel good. Not just being at home, but being able to travel. He felt free, so much freer than when they were confined at the agency.

He looked along the line of horses and travois. Each travois was accompanied by the women and children and old people who did not ride ahead with the younger men. His gaze paused for a moment at a certain white horse. One girl was on its back and another walking by its side. Both were attractive and about his age. Both had about sixteen winters. They were no farther away than a man might throw a lance. As he looked at them, both girls turned their heads. They looked his way and smiled. Wolf turned his eyes upward. He felt his face grow as warm as if he had just leaned toward a fire.

If times were not so crazy, he thought, *I would think about bringing horses to their father. But which one would I ask to consider me as a husband?*

If only that was all he had to worry about. But such easy problems as choosing a girl and hoping she would choose him were far away. As far away as the possibility starting a family. All that was close was war.

That morning they had practiced horn fighting like white men. They had lined up on their horses two by two. Loud Voice had played the horn sound that meant to start. Together, they had walked their horses forward then. That had gone well. Then he had made the sound to stop. That, too, went well. Everyone had been pleased. Some had laughed and joked. It was easy. But Quanah had not laughed.

"Listen," he had shouted. "Be quiet."

Loud Voice had made the horn sound to start. Again, all started together. Then he made the sound to attack. All started galloping. They went faster and faster. Some were shouting war cries, kicking their heels into the ponies' sides. It did not go well, though, when he played the horn call to turn back. No one was ready to retreat. But between his horn and Quanah's shouting, everyone finally did so.

Wolf turned his eyes to the front. He had seen something. Dust was rising. A rider was coming their way fast. It was Buffalo Scout, one of the men who had been told to ride ahead.

"Tai-bos!" Buffalo Scout shouted. "Tai-bo soldiers ahead!"

Quanah signaled to Loud Voice. The yellow man lifted the horn to his mouth and played the call to assemble.

"We attack," Quanah shouted.

"At last," Horse Road said, raising the new rifle in his hand.

Wolf kicked his heels into Wind's side as they moved forward together.

It was not long before they reached the soldiers, who were on horseback and moving at a trot toward the north. The soldiers saw them and began to move in their direction. Wolf counted them as best as he could through the dust. There were at least sixty of them, maybe more. His heart began to pound.

"Now we confuse them," Quanah said. "Watch. Do not move."

Loud Voice rode forward and lifted his bugle. He played the white man sound that meant to retreat. Many of the white soldiers heard that sound. They turned their horses and began to ride away.

"Now we attack," Quanah said.

The battle that followed was a good one. The sounds of Loud Voice's horn kept confusing the enemy soldiers. The sun moved two hands across the sky as both sides fought like white men, forming up, charging, and retreating.

Wolf fired his new gun many times. So did Horse Road. They all had plenty of ammunition. The ve'hoe soldiers shot many times too. But no one was hit on their side. Perhaps Isa-tai's medicine really was working. Finally, the white soldiers rode off. None of those ve'hoe soldiers seemed to have been hurt, either, although two white men had fallen off their horses when the bugle calls confused them so much they ran into each other.

It was a good battle. All fought well together. They rode back to their camps to tell the women and children and old ones about the fight. Everyone was in great spirits

"Maybe we will fight again tomorrow," Horse Road said. There was a big grin on his face. Even Wolf had to smile. If war was like this, it was not such a bad thing.

The next morning they rose early.

"More white soldiers are camped over that hill," Quanah said. "Today we will fight them."

It turned out to be just as good as the day before. They had another fine battle. It was the same group of white soldiers. It was easy to recognize them. Their soldier chief who had led them before was a burly man with dark hair and a feather in his hat.

Just as before, Loud Voice's horn calls kept their side together and confused the white men. Finally the soldier chief led the ve'hoes off the field. He wanted no more of this kind of fighting. Just as before, no one had been hurt. Some on both sides waved goodbye as the white men rode off.

It would have been enjoyable to fight that soldier chief and his men again the next day. But Quanah decided that they had better things to do.

"We still need to find the buffalo hunters and wipe them out," Quanah said that evening when they all met to talk about their plans. "Tomorrow we turn to the west."

Wolf and Horse Road stayed sitting by the fire as the others drifted away. They were feeling happy. Then they heard a loud voice coming from the direction of Quanah's tipi. It was an easy voice to recognize. The former Buffalo Soldier, Loud Voice.

In his bad Comanche he was complaining. He was not pleased about the way the last two days of fighting had gone.

"No good," he whined to Quanah. "Why we no kill 'em soldiers? Me want kill all. Me want get horses, money, sugar, coffee. Me no get anything."

Horse Road smiled and made the sign for *foolish*.

Wolf shook his head. "Our yellow Buffalo Soldier does not want honor. All he wants is to fill his saddlebags."

The next day, Wolf and Horse Road were among those sent out to scout along the Canadian River.

"Find the stinky white men's camp," Quanah said. "We know they are near here."

They went with a party of six others to find the buffalo hunters' camp. Old Man White Wolf was the leader. They had searched all day and were almost ready to turn back when Wolf saw something.

"Look."

The others squinted their eyes to peer in the direction of the sunset. A small, thin column of smoke was rising from beyond the farthest hill. They rode to that distant hilltop and looked down over the other side, into a wide valley. And in that valley was what they had been seeking.

Four log houses surrounded a big corral filled with horses and mules. The smoke Wolf had seen was coming from the chimney of the biggest house. Wagons were pulled up behind the two houses at the far end of the corral. A dark mountain of hundreds of buffalo hides was piled by the wagons.

And beyond their camp was nothing but death. The skinned and rotting bodies of buffalo stretched south as far as their eyes could see.

"Ahhh-ahhh," Old Man White Wolf said. His voice was filled with disgust.

All of them shared that feeling. Any pleasure from having found the place was mixed with sorrow. What those evil men had done to their sacred animals was awful.

"We ride back now," Old Man White Wolf said. "We ride through the night."

It was dawn when they sighted their lodges. Old Man White Wolf made a signal, and all six of them fired their guns in the air. They galloped in a great circle four times around the big camp. That told everyone that they had met success and gave time for those in the camp to make ready for their entrance.

Old Man White Wolf led them in. Single file, they rode into the village. Because Wolf had first seen the telltale smoke, he rode in second place.

In their camp, all the men and women had formed a long line. The women were ululating. Their voices were high and sweet as the cries of eagles. The men were lifting up their guns and bows, shaking them and crying out loudly.

"HAI! HAI! HAI!"

It lifted Wolf's spirit. He felt as if there were wings beating in his chest.

"HAI! HAI! HAI!"

They walked their horses slowly.

"HAI! HAI! HAI!"

Their heads were up. Their eyes were forward until they came to the center of the big camp.

"HAI! HAI! HAI!"

There, Old Man Black Beard stood with Quanah and Isa-tai at his side. As they reined up their horses, Quanah raised both arms. Everyone became silent.

"Tell the truth," Old Man Black Beard said. "What did you see?"

"I shall tell you the truth," Old Man White Wolf answered. "We saw four log houses. We saw horses moving about. We saw buffalo hides piled high and many dead buffalo."

"All right," Old Man Black Beard replied. "Soon we kill some stinky white men."

WIHIO WAS OUT WALKING AROUND.
HE SAW SOME FAT RABBITS. HE WAS HUNGRY.

YOU RABBITS, HE CALLED OUT TO THEM,
CAN YOU LEARN A NEW SONG?

YES, THE RABBITS REPLIED. WE ARE GREAT SINGERS.
WE CAN LEARN ANY SONG FAST.

THAT IS GOOD, WIHIO SAID. I WILL CHOOSE JUST FOUR OF YOU.
THEN I WILL TEACH YOU A GOOD SONG.
THOSE OF YOU WHO LEARN IT
WILL NEVER HEAR A BETTER ONE AGAIN.

WIHIO CHOSE THE FOUR FATTEST RABBITS.
HE TOOK THEM WITH HIM OUT ONTO THE PRAIRIE.

NOW, HE SAID, HERE IS THE SONG.
BUT WHEN YOU SING IT YOU MUST KEEP YOUR EYES CLOSED.

THE RABBITS CLOSED THEIR EYES. THEN WIHIO SANG.
EYES CLOSED TIGHT, CAN'T SEE A THING.
EYES CLOSED TIGHT, CAN'T SEE A THING.

THE RABBITS SANG IT BACK TO HIM.
EYES CLOSED TIGHT, CAN'T SEE A THING.
EYES CLOSED TIGHT, CAN'T SEE A THING.

KEEP SINGING, WIHIO SAID, KEEP YOUR EYES CLOSED
THE RABBITS DID AS HE SAID. AND AS THE RABBITS SANG,
HE KNOCKED EACH OF THEM ON THE HEAD
AND THREW THEM INTO HIS BAG.

NEWS

Petersburg, Virginia
June 24, 1874

My Dear Son Washington,

This is your mother writing to you (with the help of your bright and talented sister). Did you receive the letter written on my behalf by Miss Henrietta Ames? I hope she told you that I am in good health and spirits and that your sister (me, of course) has recovered from her illness.

Mama is still talking, Wash, but I think it is better for me to just write what I think you would like to hear and not worry about taking her words down exactly as I tried to do in my earlier epistles.

My dear brother, when I think back on those early letters I wrote to you, I am a bit embarrassed. I have become so much more adept (is that not a fine word?) at expressing myself thanks to the tutelage of Miss Ames. I just love her. She is the kindest person, but very strict about our being the very best students that we can be. She told me just today that if you are as talented as I am, then whatever you do will be a credit to our family and to our entire race. She is very eager about doing whatever she can to help our race rise above the past and the indignities of slavery that were inflicted upon us by callous representatives of her own race. That is how she talks. Is that not wonderful?

I should let you know that a good deal has happened in the time you have been gone. Some of it is rather a secret, and Mama has asked me not to speak of it. So I shall honor her wishes. But let me simply say that I have not seen her so happy in years and that you need not worry yourself as much as you have in the past about being the man of the family and caring for all our needs.

I am now at least three inches taller than you! I am also the best student in Miss Ames's school. I simply mention these two things as factual details, not to brag in any way. We love and miss you.

> Your loving mother,
>
> Mama
>
> (and, of course, your exceedingly brilliant and well-educated sister Pegatha)

Wash read the letter for the third time.

Pegatha, he thought. Then he laughed out loud.

Despite the colonel's call to readiness, they had not marched right out against the hostile Indians, even though Kicking Bird had informed Colonel Davidson that an attack on a big camp of buffalo hunters was imminent.

A rider with orders from General John Pope himself had arrived no more than an hour after the colonel had begun to assemble the men. Those orders contained explicit instructions from the general, the head of the western armies.

Stay put. Do not ride to the defense of those men.

The buffalo hunter camp had been set up deep in the heart of Indian lands—where whites were forbidden to trespass. The buffalo hunters and the traders with them had put themselves into a position like that of setting up a honey shop inside a bee's nest. As far as General Pope was concerned, anything that happened to them was just what they had coming.

Surprisingly, Colonel Davidson seemed not all that bothered about the stop to his plans. Josh thought he knew why and voiced his opinion to the small group of men gathered in the barracks after the last bugle call—Wash, Charley, Private Henry Imes, and Private Rufus Slade.

"Our colonel," Josh said. "I imagine he knows that it is just a matter of time now. Sooner or later war will get here. Then he can kill him some Indians. Or, to be more accurate about it, have us kill them for him."

Despite the raid they'd made on the fort's horse herd, it seemed that most of the Comanches and nearly all of the Kiowas had resisted Quanah Parker's call to go on the warpath. But that was the only good news. A considerable number of hostiles had taken up the war pipe. Among them were the most deadly and dangerous of every tribe, Lone Wolf and his followers among them. And word had been brought to Fort Sill that nearly all the Cheyenne tribe had left the agency at Darlington.

"Pretty soon," Charley said, "someone going to drop a match on this here powder keg. 'Specially now that it's about fighting time."

All Wash could do was nod his head in reply. It was the time of year when war parties always ventured forth, the time when the horses were getting fat from the spring grass and strong enough again to carry their riders on long raids. And some of that raiding had already begun. They'd just heard the grim news that two buffalo hunters were killed by the Indians and left out on the prairie near Adobe Walls. Those unfortunates had not just been scalped. They had been staked to the ground and their bodies cut up bad. No one said it out loud, but everyone knew those murdered men must have been kept alive for a long time while being cut up piece by piece. The thought of that happening to one of their own had brought down a silence upon them as thick and dark as a buffalo robe until Josh had finally broken it.

"Adobe Walls," Henry Imes said. "Did I ever hear tell anything about that place?"

"Yes, indeed," Josh said. He paused and looked around at the other men sitting on their bunks, studying the floor of packed red dirt at their feet. "Adobe Walls," Josh repeated, a little louder this time. "Any of you all know what happened there just about ten years ago?"

"No," Wash replied before Josh could say the name a third time. "I have not heard of what happened there just about ten years ago. But I would bet a handsome sum that you are about to tell us whether we want to hear it or not."

Henry and Charley chuckled.

Rufus, ever the serious type, just looked grim. "Don't know as I want to hear no more about Indian massacres," he said.

Josh paid no heed. Like a man tilling a field whose blade has bumped over a stone, he plowed on. "Adobe Walls," he said, "was a fight for the ages. Kit Carson and about three hundred soldiers held off three thousand Comanches and Kiowas. Indians was buzzing around the adobe walls of that fort like mad hornets. Bullets flew thicker than hail stones in a prairie downburst. But Kit Carson stayed cool. Yes, indeed. Colonel Carson and his men killed half of them Indians and retreated without losing a man. Now there was a fight you will never hear the like of again."

"P-tah!" Charley let loose a splat of tobacco to knock down a red-eyed horsefly that was unwise enough to land on the tent post nearest him. "Adobe Walls? Know what I reckon?"

He pulled his right foot up into his lap and began to rub it between his palms like an Indian starting a fire with a stick. It was the same foot from which the toe had been removed after the frostbite of the previous winter. That foot was always bothering him. It seemed that poor Charley's foot always felt cold now, even in the heat of summer.

"I reckon," Charley said, his voice slow as molasses dripping, "that we have heard the last of any tale of heroism attached to Adobe Walls. Next thing we are like to hear of will be the massacre of all them buffalo hunters and traders fool enough to venture out there."

"Amen," Rufus said, his voice as deep as a well.

WIHIO WAS GOING ALONG.
OVER HIS BACK WAS A SACK.
IN IT WERE FOUR FAT RABBITS.
WIHIO HAD TRICKED THEM.
HE WOULD EAT WELL THAT NIGHT.

AH, WIHIO SAID, IT IS GOOD TO BE SMART.
NO ONE CAN FOOL ME, FOR I AM WIHIO.

THEN HE SAW COYOTE.
COYOTE HAD A BAG.
IT WAS BIGGER THAN WIHIO'S.

WHAT DO YOU HAVE THERE?
WIHIO SAID.

I HAVE ONLY OLD DRY BONES,
JUST DRY BONES IN THIS SACK,
COYOTE REPLIED.

AH, WIHIO SAID TO HIMSELF,
COYOTE IS TRYING TO TRICK ME.
THAT SACK MUST BE FULL
OF SOMETHING REALLY GOOD.
MAYBE FRESH BUFFALO MEAT.

COYOTE, WIHIO SAID, LET US TRADE.
I HAVE FOUR FAT RABBITS HERE.

NO, COYOTE SAID, THAT WOULD NOT BE FAIR.
ALL I HAVE HERE IS OLD DRY BONES.
YOU WOULD NOT WANT THEM.

BROTHER, WIHIO SAID,
YOU CANNOT REFUSE ME.
COME, LET US TRADE.

COYOTE SHOOK HIS HEAD.
YOU WILL NOT LIKE WHAT IS IN MY BAG.

BUT WIHIO INSISTED.
HE ASKED FOUR TIMES.
SO COYOTE TOOK WIHIO'S SACK
AND GAVE HIS BAG TO WIHIO.

OUR TRADE IS DONE, COYOTE SAID.
THEN HE RAN OFF.

AND WHEN WIHIO OPENED COYOTE'S BAG
ALL THAT HE FOUND THERE WERE OLD DRY BONES.

THE TEST OF ISA-TAI'S MEDICINE

They left their camp behind. They had followed the south bank of the river throughout the day, and now dusk began to settle on the plains. They were getting close to the brutal town of the buffalo hunters. Close to the place where the skins of their sacred animals were piled higher than the tops of the tallest lodges.

"We stop now," Quanah said. "We get ready."

Everyone got off their horses. They made bundles of everything that would not go into battle with them. They tied those bundles high up in the branches of the nearby trees. It was a necessary thing to do. The prairie wolves were always watching the curious doings of men. If they left their possessions on the ground, they would return to find everything torn apart. That is what those prairie wolves always did, whether searching for food or just making mischief.

Wolf chose a cottonwood four times his height. He tied his bundle in a crotch near the top of the tree. Then he climbed down to where Wind was patiently waiting for him.

Although Wind was a very big horse, he was strong and agile. He was as swift as the name Wolf had given him when he rescued him from the white horse thieves. Before that, judging by the brand on his hip and the spur scars on his sides, he had been the mount of some cavalryman who had not treated him well. But as soon as Wolf saw him and he saw Wolf, it was as if something passed between them. They were made for each other.

Wind nuzzled Wolf as he uncoiled his riding rope. He passed the rope around Wind's body a few hand widths behind his front legs. He secured the second loop to keep it from slipping back across the big horse's chest. Around him, other men were doing the same. Another, smaller loop of rope was already braided into the horse's mane.

Those ropes would be put to good use. With one leg under the longer rope tied around Wind, he could lean so far over that he would no longer be seen from the other side. Shielded by the horse's body, he could fire his gun or shoot his bow from underneath the big animal's belly. Then he could grasp the mane loop to pull himself back upright. Many times in battle, white men were fooled by that move and thought that they had shot a man off his horse. If Wolf was actually knocked from Wind's back by a bullet, his horse would stop and walk back, waiting for him to remount.

Wolf checked his arrows. He counted his bullets. He made sure that the straps of his shield were fastened properly. The firelight was bright enough for him to see the circle of men getting ready around him. To his left, Gray Head and others who had won many eagle feathers in war were shaking out their bonnets. They were making certain each feather was straight and securely tied. Every man had put on his best war clothing.

But this is not the end of our preparations, Wolf thought.

Until then, everything he had done had seemed right. But he was not so sure of what they were to do next.

"Come," a loud nasal voice shouted. "Come be made bullet-proof!"

Wolf went to join the others answering Isa-tai's call. Isa-tai stood there with the yellow paint he had prepared. He stood next to the fire. His eyes reflected the flames and glowed red. He wore nothing but ochre paint, the paint that was to be put on all the men and all the horses.

"No bullet will pierce through this sacred paint," the little prophet shouted in his squeaky voice as the yellow color was spread on one man after another.

Finally, everyone was painted. As the paint dried on Wolf's face, on his arms and chest, it pulled at his skin. He moved his mouth and felt the paint on his cheeks crack.

The Comanches, headed by He Bear, Tabanica, and Quanah, led them out. They went by fours. They walked their horses instead of riding them. That made the sound of their horses' hooves striking the earth much quieter.

They crossed the shallow river and moved up toward the hill. Their attack would come from above. Slowly they moved. Slowly, slowly. Wolf's breath felt thick in his throat. He squeezed the lead rope tightly to lessen the shaking in his hands. He could smell the sweat of many men and horses around him in the dark.

It took a long time to reach that hilltop. But it was still before dawn when they got there. Some men simply lowered themselves to the ground by their horses. The lead ropes wrapped around their wrists, they returned to sleep. Others were too excited to close their eyes.

"Who among us will be the first to strike the enemy?" Too Tall whispered.

"I think it will be Horse Road," Too Short whispered back.

Wolf looked over toward his best friend. He was only a few hand widths away. But all Wolf could see was his silhouette against the stars. Wolf began to sing a strongheart song under his breath.

A soft wind was in their faces. It was blowing away from the buffalo hunters' camp. He Bear and Tabanica were seated to Wolf's left. He watched as they checked that wind by holding up wet fingers. Then they took out small pipes. They could smoke tobacco without the scent carrying down to the white men below.

It was quiet, so quiet Wolf could hear the chuffing of the many horses. He listened to them breathe and scrape their hooves on the ground. Like most of their riders, those horses were not sleeping. They knew something would happen soon.

Will dawn ever come? Wolf thought. Calm as the night was, there was no calm within him. He felt like a bowstring drawn back so far that it was about to break the bow. Too Tall and Too Short were silent. But they kept wrapping and unwrapping their blankets as they tried to sleep.

Horse Road slid closer to Wolf. "The little medicine man said they would all be asleep," he whispered.

"So he said," Wolf replied.

"He said the fight would be quick and we would kill them all."

"Hee'he'e," Wolf said. He didn't feel like talking. His throat was too dry. The yellow paint made his face feel as tight as a drumhead.

Horse Road shook his head. "A fast fight would not be good. Let us hope that the fight will not be too quick. I hope enough of them will fight. Then there will be a good battle tomorrow."

Wolf lay back. He looked up at the dark sky and closed his eyes. He knew he would not be able to sleep. But when he opened eyes again, Horse Road was gone. The first light was starting to show itself in the east. Gray Head was leaning over him.

"Nomo'ke," Gray Head said. "Let's go."

As he spoke those words, a meadowlark flew up behind him, singing to greet the day.

Wolf rose. Leading his horse, he followed Gray Head to the place where everyone was gathered. Isa-tai was there. He was sitting on his horse just below the crest of the hill, out of sight of the camp of the buffalo hunters. He was still naked. But now he had added a little crown of sage stems to his head.

"Hear me," he said dramatically. "I must not move from this spot. For my medicine to work, I must stay away from the battle."

That does not surprise me, Wolf thought.

Isa-tai raised his arms over his head. "The guns of the stinky tai-bos will be useless," he said. "The bullets from your guns will find their hearts. Their bullets will not reach us."

Wolf wondered about that. He knew what guns were carried by white buffalo hunters. They were long-barreled big .50s. He thought back to the time when he had watched his little Buffalo Soldier shoot one such gun. He had shot it a long way with great accuracy.

Wolf looked at his own rifle. It was a Spencer, a short-barreled gun for close fighting. So were the Winchester rifles that other men were carrying. It was true that they were repeaters. Each gun carried six or seven bullets. But their range was short. It would be hard to hit anything farther away than they could reach with arrows.

Leaving Isa-tai behind, all the others rode to the hilltop. The only thing moving below was a thin wisp of smoke from the chimney of the biggest building. Even the horses and mules in the corral were standing still. Perhaps the buffalo killers were sleeping. Perhaps it would be as Isa-tai had promised. Perhaps his medicine would work.

Or perhaps not.

Wolf looked to his right and then his left. At least two hundred fifty men were ready to attack. They would outnumber the stinky white men ten to one. The dawn wind picked up, bringing the rank scent of the camp up the hill.

"Ahe!" someone said next to Wolf. It was one of the Comanches, Timbo, the son of He Bear. He was Wolf's own age. He had joked with Wolf the day before. "I am worried about those white buffalo hunters," he had said. "I have heard they smell so bad that their odor may knock us off our horses!"

Now Timbo grinned at Wolf. "Ahe!" he said again, pinching his nose with his fingers.

"Yes," Wolf agreed. "Nasty."

"We will have to bathe a lot after we wipe them out."

Wiping out those stinky white men in the camp below. That was what Quanah and Isa-tai wanted.

What do I want? Wolf thought. *To count coup? To be among the first to touch an enemy with his hand, a coup stick, a quirt, or a bow?* He knew that was what was in the heart of Horse Road. It was so for many of the other young men around him going into their first big battle. They were eager for nothing more than to win honor.

All I want now, Wolf thought, *is for this battle to start.* He squeezed his knees tight against Wind's sides as he walked him forward. He felt sweat dripping down his wrist. His breath was shallow and shaky. He could smell his own sweat. It still held the scent of the sweetgrass that they had placed on the hot stones in the sweat lodge. Before leaving camp the day before, all of the Cheyennes had gone into the sweat lodge that was run by Gray Head.

Nearly everyone was on the hilltop. Horses were stomping their feet. Some were breathing hard. Their heavy muscles rippled as if currents of water flowed beneath their skin.

Gray Head pushed his pony in front of the Cheyenne men. He held up his left hand, palm toward them.

"We will charge in a line together," he said. "Wait for the sound of the war horn." He pointed with his chin to their left, where Loud Voice sat on his horse next to Quanah and Timbo. The yellow Buffalo Soldier had on more of Isa-tai's bright ochre paint than anyone else. His mouth was open. His narrow face wore a twisted grin.

"Now!" Quanah shouted.

Loud Voice lifted his horn. His cheeks puffed out. He blew, and a shrill high sound came from the horn. Charge!

As one, all two hundred fifty men charged headlong down the hill in one wide line. Dust flew up in red clouds. Hooves on the hard ground sounded like thunder. Some men began making high, ululating war cries.

We will sweep through the camp of the stinky white men like a fire through dry prairie grass! Wolf thought. *Nothing will stop us!*

Then something did.

Their minds and eyes fixed on the battle ahead, no one had noticed what lay at the base of the hill. Horses and men began falling around Wolf as if they were struck by the clubs of invisible giants.

Out of the corner of one eye, Wolf saw them, saw the mounds and holes of the prairie dog town they had just ridden into. Saw them too late. Wind's foot caught in one of the holes, and the big horse stumbled. Wolf found himself flying through the air. He ducked his head but still landed with a thud on the hard earth.

He sat up, slowly. His back and side felt like one great bruise. Somehow he was still holding onto his Spencer.

Wind! he thought. *Has his leg been broken?*

He rose to his knees, turned. Wind was there, unhurt. The big horse came up and bumped Wolf with his head. Wolf grasped the rope around the horse's chest and pulled himself to his feet. He looked around. Others who had hit the ground were rising, limping downhill. Twenty or more had been thrown. But no one seemed badly hurt. Nor had even one horse broken a leg. That, at least, was good.

But the rest of those who had been charging were now far ahead. Wolf shaded his eyes with one hand. Horse Road was among those who had avoided the prairie dog holes. He would be among the first to reach the buffalo hunters' camp. Wolf's heart sank. He would not be by his friend's side when the fight began.

Wind nickered, bobbing his head up and down as Wolf held onto the chest rope. Wolf straightened up. He felt stiff and sore as a man of eighty winters. But he could not stop now. As he pulled himself up onto the big horse's back, he heard the first sounds of war below. Many guns being fired.

He kicked his heels into Wind's sides, urged him into a trot. As they went the rest of the way down the hill, he could see what was happening. It seemed the white men had not been asleep as Isa-tai had promised. Spurts of flame and smoke were bursting from all the windows. Guns were even being fired from between chinks in the walls of the log and sod buildings. The cracking of rifles was like the noise cottonwood trees make when struck by the club of Frost in deep winter. Among the sound of the rifles was also the popping of handguns. And, now and then, another sound, a thudding boom, its voice as deep as thunder. The sound of a big .50 buffalo gun.

Their military line had broken like a snake cut into pieces by a knife. Wolf heard Loud Voice's horn sounding the call to fall back and re-form. No one paid any attention to it. Men and horses were on the ground. Some men had been shot. Others had dropped off their horses to take shelter among the wagons outside the corral or to crouch behind buffalo carcasses. Most of those still on horseback were trying to make themselves harder to hit. They were staying in motion and dodging. They were galloping around and back and forth, firing from horseback into the four buildings.

There was so much confusion. So much smoke, so much noise. The shouting of the men as they made war cries. The screams of wounded horses. As he rode closer, Wolf tried to find his friends. With the yellow paint on everyone's bodies, it was difficult to tell men apart.

Then he noticed one group of young men who were not taking shelter or riding back and forth. They were trotting right toward the biggest building. They were riding right up, ignoring the shots being fired at them.

"Stinky white men," the one in front shouted. "Come out and fight!"

Wolf knew that voice as well as he knew his own. Horse Road. He was at the head of that small spearhead of brave men. Blood flowed down his chest from a wound high in his shoulder. It made a red line through the worthless yellow paint. That red line went straight toward his heart.

"Horse Road." Wolf called. "Brother! Wait for me!"

Horse Road did not respond. The sounds of battle were so many and so loud. And Wolf was still far away. Perhaps his friend did not hear.

Horse Road vaulted off his horse. His legs almost failed him as he hit the ground. He staggered. Then he straightened himself. He walked up to the door in front of him. He banged on it with the butt of his rifle.

"Cowards," he shouted, "come out and fight."

Voices did not answer him. A volley of gunfire from inside did. The rifle fell from Horse Road's hands. He turned, leaned back against the wall. Then he slumped into a sitting position like someone overcome by exhaustion.

Wolf saw all this as he galloped forward. Bullets buzzed around him. He heard them whistling past his ears, yet he paid less attention than if they had been gnats. All he could see ahead of him was a small circle of light. In the middle of that circle of light was his friend.

And now he had reached the big building. He slowed his horse as they came up along the wall of the building. There below him, Horse Road sat. His hands were open. His left arm was across his chest. Wolf held tight with one hand to the rope around Wind's girth and reached down with the other to grab Horse Road's wrist. He tried to heave him up, but his friend's body was too limp and heavy. Bullets kept flying past him, whining like hornets.

Wolf refused to let any of them strike him. He pressed his knees into Wind. The big horse obeyed his command, turning and trotting away from the building. Horse Road's heels dragged across the ground, leaving two lines behind in the dry red earth. Ahead was a big mound of buffalo hides. Wolf circled behind it and stopped.

The lifeless skins of our sacred animals are giving us shelter from death, he thought.

He slid from Wind's back and dropped onto his knees. He pulled his best friend up into his arms. He felt his chest. There were many bullet wounds there. None of them were bleeding. He knew what that meant. No heartbeat. He leaned his face close to Horse Road's mouth. No breath.

Wolf lifted Horse Road. He slung his friend's dead body up across Wind's back and vaulted up behind him.

"Run," he said to Wind.

Bullets kicked up dust around them as they burst out from behind the hill of skins. Wolf paid no attention to them. He heard nothing but his own breath and the thudding of Wind's hooves as he rode back up to the hilltop. As he rode, he wiped the yellow paint, moistened with tears, from his face.

He arrived at the hilltop at the same time as Quanah. The Comanche war leader was also carrying the body of one of his people over his horse. Quanah looked at Wolf. For a moment sorrow crossed his stern face like a cloud crossing the sun. But he said nothing. He turned his horse to ride down the other side of the hill. There he could put the body of his Comanche comrade in a place where it would be safe from the tai-bos. The white men were known to do terrible things to the bodies of dead Indians.

Wolf rode down the other side of the hill, too. There were some Cheyennes there, men who had been wounded but were rescued or stayed on their horses. They were being cared for by men who knew medicine who had come along not to fight, but to help those who were injured. But some were beyond being cared for. As he lowered his friend's body to the ground, Wolf saw that Horse Road was not the only dead Cheyenne.

On the other side of the hill, the battle was continuing. The cracking of rifles had been joined by the booming of even more big .50s. Wolf rode back up to the hilltop and looked down at the battle scene below. More men and their horses had fallen. But others were still sweeping around the buffalo hunters' buildings and corral and firing. From the bodies of horses and mules scattered inside the corral, it seemed that all the mounts the ve'hoes might have used to try to escape had been killed. But Wolf saw no dead white men. Nor any live ones. He saw only the flame and smoke, heard only the crack and boom of their gunshots.

He started down the hill again. This time he did not go straight. He rode back and forth at a quick trot. Soon he came to a wagon far from the buildings where the white men were hiding. Three Comanches were crouched behind the wagon, leaning over something. As Wolf came closer he saw what it was. The bloody bodies of two white men.

One of the Comanches turned toward Wolf.

"You see," he shouted, waving a bloody blonde scalp. "We got them."

"Ah-hey!" the second Comanche agreed, waving another bloody trophy. "They could not escape us."

Wolf did not know the names of those first two Comanches. But he recognized the third one. It was Timbo, the son of He Bear. He also held a scalp in his hands, a strange one. It was a wide strip of thick bloody black fur. Then Wolf saw the body of the one it came from. A big dead dog lay behind the wagon.

Timbo grinned. "That one fought more bravely than his tai-bo owners."

Wolf nodded, then rode past. He wanted to get closer to the buildings. He was not feeling frightened. He was not angry. He was not sure what he felt. The loss of his best friend was with him as he rode. He had swallowed it like a stone.

I must reach those buildings, he thought. *There the white men are hiding like turtles inside their shells.*

His hair had come loose and hung down around his shoulders. Bullets whizzed by so closely that they clipped off little strands of it. He did not stop. As he came to the place where Horse Road had died, he raised his rifle to his shoulder. He shot it again and again. He shot into the doors, the windows, the walls of logs and sod. He did not know if he hit anyone. He did not care. It was as if he was within a cloud.

Wolf turned his horse and walked it away. Bullets still flew. None touched him or Wind. He passed the wagon where he had seen Timbo and the two other Comanches. They were no longer there. Only the pathetic bodies of the two whites and their black dog remained. Wolf continued on toward the nearby hill of buffalo skins. There he saw Timbo. He and his friends had joined a group of others, sheltered by the thick hides from the white men's guns. They gestured for Wolf to hurry, to join them. He continued walking his horse. Bullets hit the ground around Wind's feet.

When he was close enough, hands reached out for him. They grasped the ropes around Wind's back and grabbed Wolf's right arm. He did not resist. He allowed them to pull him and his horse behind the hides. Wolf slowly climbed from Wind's back. Timbo took him by his arms. He turned him around, ran his hands across Wolf's back, his chest, his shoulders. He wiped off the blood on his legs.

Not my blood, Wolf thought. *The blood of my dead brother.*

"No bullet holes," Timbo said. "Good! Not like me."

He tapped his finger on his leg, where a bullet had gouged a deep bleeding line across his thigh. "Where our little medicine man's paint was thickest!" he said. "But not thick enough, huh?"

Timbo coughed out a bitter laugh. He squatted down with his back against the buffalo skins, patted the ground next to him. Suddenly Wolf's legs felt weak. He sat down next to the young Comanche man just before he fell.

Timbo pointed with his lips at the wagon where they had killed the two men and their dog. "Too hot there," he said. "Too many bullets. Had to leave before we got any goods in that wagon. Many goods there."

Wolf closed his eyes. Goods of any kind held no interest for him now.

"What in wagon? What?" asked someone. That person's command of Comanche was poor. His accent was strange. Wolf opened his eyes. It was Loud Voice leaning over them, his horn now tied to his waist.

"What in wagon?" he asked again

"Canned goods," Timbo said, "sugar, coffee——"

Before Timbo could finish talking, Loud Voice was running toward the wagon. Wolf leaned out to watch, ignoring those trying to pull him back. Loud Voice was a fast runner. He covered the distance to the wagon quickly and dove under the canvas that covered the piled goods. A moment later he emerged. He had a big can of coffee under one arm, an equally large can of sugar under the other. There was a wolfish grin on his face as he leaped down from the wagon bed. But as he jumped, a loud boom came from the big cabin. The runaway Buffalo Soldier's legs went to sleep beneath him. He pitched face forward. There was a hole in his back from the bullet that came from the big .50. As he hit the ground, the cans of coffee and sugar he would never taste went rolling out of his grasp.

The sun rose higher. The fight went on. No one was on horseback anymore. They were just shooting from whatever shelter they could find.

Midday.

Afternoon.

Men began to pull back. They followed little ravines and dips in the land that hid them from the deadly guns. And gradually all the shooting stopped. No targets were in sight.

The leaders gathered on horseback in a hollow behind the crest of the butte. It was not yet dark, but they were out of sight of the buildings where the buffalo hunters were holed up. Other men, Wolf among them, came close enough to hear what they would say.

Isa-tai raised his hands from where he sat on his pony's back. "You will all be safe here," he proclaimed. "This is a good place for us to plan our next attack."

Gray Head stared at him. "Our next attack? What happened to your promise that the white men would all be sleeping and none of us would be shot? Too many of us have been killed or wounded."

"The only losses those stinky buffalo killers suffered were two white men and their brave dog," Medicine Water, another of the war leaders said. The anger on his face made him look like a storm cloud.

Hippy, not a chief but one of the bravest fighters, stood by Medicine Water's side.

"Hunh," Hippy said, "that is true. More of our people have been killed or wounded than the men from all the other tribes put together. You said the whites would be as easy to kill as rabbits. All we had to do was hit them over their heads."

"It is not my fault," Isa-tai whined. His voice was now even more like that of the animal whose dung he was named for. He lifted his yellow-painted hands to adjust the cap of sage stems still riding neatly atop his head. "It is your fault. My medicine was spoiled by you foolish Cheyennes. I have just found out that one of your men killed a skunk before the battle. That is what spoiled my medicine. If you had not done such a stupid thing, those bullets would have bounced off you."

As soon as he finished those words, Isa-tai realized he had made a mistake. The look in Medicine Water's eyes had become dark as a thundercloud. Hippy began slapping his riding quirt into the palm of his hand.

Isa-tai began to move his pony back behind Quanah. Quanah did not look, though, as if he was ready to protect his little medicine man. Quanah himself had been struck in the battle. It was not bleeding, but Quanah's left arm was hanging dangling and useless. He had been far away from the long guns when his horse was shot out from under him. Then, as he crouched behind a buffalo carcass, he had been struck between the neck and shoulder. Whatever hit him did not pierce his flash, but it paralyzed his arm.

As Hippy walked his horse toward the little medicine man, Isa-tai raised his hands.

Does he plan to threaten us with his power? Wolf thought. *Or is he about to plead for mercy from us?*

SPLAT! The sudden sound was like that of a big bird's egg being dropped on a rock. Isa-tai's pony, coated like its owner with the magical yellow paint meant to keep it safe from all harm, staggered. It dropped to its knees and then pitched onto its side. Isa-tai went rolling in the dust. From the other side of the hill, the distant boom of the big .50 that had been fired reached them. The heavy slug from that gun had traveled all the way up and over the hill. It had struck Isa-tai's horse in the forehead and killed it.

His paint streaked with red dirt, his crown of sage stems broken, Isa-tai struggled back to his feet. His mouth was still open but had been emptied of words.

Medicine Water glared down at him. "Coyote Dung," he growled, "where is all your power now?" He turned to Hippy. "Beat him."

Hippy leapt off his horse, raised his quirt, and reached for Isa-tai.

Gray Head rode his horse in between them.

"Leave him," Gray Head said. "Look at him. His disgrace will shame him for the rest of his life."

Perhaps the bullet that had killed Isa-tai's horse had been only a stray one. Still, that shot made no one eager to test the white men's powerful guns again. Everyone moved farther down the hill. They counted their losses. Thirty men had been badly wounded or killed. All of the wounded men and the bodies of some of the dead had been brought back. But twelve others remained on the field of battle, too close to the deadly guns to be retrieved. Among them was Quanah's yellow bugler.

Night came. Wolf found a place back in the hills that would be hard for the white men to find. There he dug the grave for his friend Horse Road. Too Tall and Too Short, who had survived the fight unharmed, stood by and watched. Wolf would not let them help him. He made sure that his friend was dressed properly and saw that all of his weapons and his medicine were with him. They would accompany him on his last journey to the Sky Land.

After he had covered Horse Road's body with earth, he motioned to his two friends. Together the three of them gathered rocks. They piled them on top of the grave to make it hard for any of the animals of the plains to dig down to his body. Then they covered it all with brush. Unless one knew it was there, no one would find his friend's resting place. Above them, in the clear sky, the great Wolf Road stretched across the heavens. Wolf sat by his brother's grave. He stayed there through the night, singing softly one of the strongheart songs they had learned together when they were initiated into the Kit Fox Society.

When dawn came, Quanah's arm had regained its strength. So had his spirits. He was ready to talk about plans for another attack. Wolf rode up to the place where the Comanche war leader and a group of twenty headmen from the gathered tribes were meeting on the top of a second butte. The white men's cabins could be seen far off, tiny as little piles of sticks, in the valley below. This hilltop was much farther away from the one where Isa-tai's horse was killed. Surely no bullet could reach them.

Aside from Lone Wolf of the Kiowas, all of the leaders were Comanches.

"Listen," Quanah said. "We all know what we must do now."

Just then, Wolf saw a puff of smoke from the window of the biggest building far below.

THUD!

To-hah-kah, the Comanche war leader sitting closest to Quanah, fell from his horse. The boom of the big gun whose bullet had struck him came rolling across the valley like thunder.

Quanah leapt off his horse. He lifted up To-hah-kah, whose limbs were as slack as those of a dead man. Everyone else—Wolf included—turned their horses and rode back down out of sight of the buffalo killers. They stopped a good distance from the crest to wait for Quanah. He came walking down. With one hand he led his horse. With the other he held up To-hah-kah. Though he moved like a drunk, To-hah-kah was almost able to walk on his own. The distance had been so far that the heavy slug that struck him in the chest did no more damage than a rock when it knocked him out.

It was enough. The expressions on the faces of Quanah and the other war leaders told it all. They were shocked and disheartened. That one shot had ended any desire to continue the fight.

WIHIO WAS GOING ALONG WHEN HE SAW THE EARTH
STIRRING BENEATH HIS FEET.
IT WAS MOLE, MAKING HIS WAY BENEATH THE GROUND.

AH, WIHIO SAID, I NEED TO KNOW WHAT MOLE IS DOING.

SO WIHIO TOOK A STICK, THRUST IT INTO THE GROUND,
AND FLIPPED MOLE UP OUT OF THE EARTH.

MOLE ROLLED OVER AND SAT UP,
CONFUSED BY THE BRIGHT SUNLIGHT.

WHO DID THAT? MOLE SAID, SHIFTING TO ONE SIDE
THE LITTLE LEATHER BAG HUNG AROUND HIS NECK.

IT IS ME, MY FRIEND, WIHIO SAID.
I JUST WANTED TO SAY HELLO.

OH, WIHIO, MOLE SAID. HELLO. NOW I MUST GO.
THEN HE TURNED TO DIG HIS WAY
BACK UNDERGROUND.

WAIT, WIHIO SAID, GRABBING HOLD OF MOLE'S TAIL.
FIRST TELL ME, MY FRIEND,
WHAT YOU HAVE IN THAT BAG AROUND YOUR NECK.
IS IT FOOD?

NO, NO, MOLE SAID,
AS HE TRIED TO ESCAPE FROM WIHIO'S GRASP.
THESE ARE JUST SOME THINGS I NEED TO THROW AWAY.

BUT WIHIO REACHED OUT AND GRABBED THAT BAG,
FOR WIHIO NEVER TAKES ADVICE
AND ALWAYS TAKES WHAT IS NOT HIS.

DON'T UNTIE IT, MOLE SAID.

BUT IT WAS TOO LATE. WIHIO TORE OPEN THE BAG.

THEN ALL OF THE FLEAS MOLE HAD PUT IN THAT BAG
SWARMED OUT AND GOT ALL OVER WIHIO.

TAKE THEM BACK, WIHIO HOWLED,
AS HE JUMPED AND SCRATCHED.
I DON'T WANT YOUR FLEAS.

BUT MOLE HAD ALREADY DUG BACK INTO THE GROUND.

AND SO, TO THIS DAY, WHEREVER HE GOES,
WIHIO IS ALWAYS BEING BITTEN BY FLEAS.

THE ARMY
SHALL FOLLOW

It was just past daybreak. Charley and Wash were standing guard outside the room where Lieutenant Pratt, the officer on duty, was meeting with an overexcited visitor. Soon it would be Independence Day, but Wash suspected they would not be doing much celebrating. That was thank to the news from the events of last week, which had just reached them.

Messages never arrived quickly at Fort Sill. The nearest telegraph station was in Kansas. So what news they received came in either by dispatch rider or by word of mouth from visitors to the fort. Word of mouth was what it was today. And the mouth was that of a young Englishman by the name of Fisher, or maybe it was Fletcher. Wash wasn't certain which. The man's excitement and his British accent had made it hard for him to be sure, though the Englishman was so het up that, even though the door was closed and Wash was out on the porch, it was easy to hear every word he was saying.

He had come to America to find excitement and to make his fortune shooting buffalo. The place to do it, he'd been told, was a new camp out in the buffalo country—which they neglected to tell him was also Indian country. That camp was the one at Adobe Walls. Fletcher had heard that the Walls was where Kit Carson fought that big battle with the Indians ten years ago, but surely such troubles were all in the past.

Except they were not. What the Englishman found was neither fortune nor buffalo hunting. Even before he reached the buffalo hunters' camp, he had been passed by a wagonload of men heading lickety-split in the opposite direction. They had not paused to greet him. They had just kept whipping their team like the devil was after them.

When Fletcher got close enough to look down into the valley, he thought he saw lots of little hills around the buildings of the buffalo camp. He also took note of a number of black lumps atop the corner posts of the corral. When he got closer, he realized that those hills on the level ground around Adobe Walls were the carcasses of horses and half a dozen or more headless bodies of Indians. And those black lumps stuck on stakes atop the corral's corner posts were the heads of those dead Indians.

Everything there stank of death. There were more swollen bodies of dead horses and mules inside that corral—all with so many arrows still sticking out of them, they looked like porcupine quills.

As Fletcher came closer, he saw four graves.

Two men were sitting on chairs in front of the store, resting after having helped load up a wagon with buffalo skins.

"Wondering whose last resting places those might be?" the younger of the two men asked. He was cradling a Sharps rifle in his lap. His companion was twirling a .45 Colt.

"Ah, yes," Fletcher answered, not knowing what else to say.

"Those were the four unfortunates who fell during the last three days of fighting," the other man answered, switching his gun from one hand to the other. "Three to the arrows and bullets of the Indians. Fourth man shot and killed himself while climbing a ladder after the fighting ended."

"Ah, I see," Fletcher replied.

"I guess you do," the second man said with a little smile. "But I am forgetting my manners. This here is Mr. Billy Dixon, the finest shot with a long gun in the West. And my name is Mr. Bat Masterson. And you are...?"

"Fletcher," the young Englishman replied. "I came out to hunt the buffalo."

"Not exactly the best time." Billy Dixon said, shifting the gun in his lap.

"Yup," Masterson agreed. He held his revolver to one side and squinted as he looked down the barrel.

"What happened here?" Fletcher had then asked.

And in a few words, Masterson had told him. Just as Fletcher was now about to tell Lieutenant Pratt. Wash leaned his ear closer to the door.

"No fewer than a thousand Indians attacked them at dawn," Fletcher said. "A great horde of screaming savages! Savages!" His own voice was pretty near a scream. From the sound of a chair scraping back and the brief silence that followed, Wash imagined the lieutenant moving over to try to calm the near hysterical Fletcher.

"Go on," Lieutenant Pratt's calm voice said.

A moment later, his voice more under control, Fletcher continued his tale. The hero of it, it seemed, was that same Billy Dixon. Dixon had known something was up even before the attack. He'd scouted the Indians and knew they were on their way. So he had been waiting long before sunrise with his big .40 loaded. His accurate shooting had put the fear of God in the Indians.

"His last shot that ended it all," Fletcher said, "was taken from more than two miles away, and it killed the great chief of all the Indians."

Wash smiled at that. He was well aware of just how far away a good shot might hit the mark with a Sharps. But he was as skeptical of that two-mile shot as he was of Fletcher's next claim, that more than five hundred Indians had been slain in that fight.

"Still, despite their losses," Fletcher continued, "it had been a dreadfully close thing, with hundreds of red Indians beating on the walls and doors of their buildings. Mr. Masterson opined it was the sturdy log walls absorbing the rain of bullets and arrows as much as their guns that saved them from slaughter."

There came a pause. Then, polite and unconcerned as if all that young Englishman had been talking about was the weather, Lieutenant Pratt's voice broke the silence.

"Might we offer you a night's hospitality here, sir?" he asked.

Fletcher's first answer was a nervous bark that might have been meant to be a laugh but sounded more like a sob. Then, as he controlled himself, he answered more politely but with no less emphasis. "No, kind of you to ask. Not at all, no, sir. Have to go. Do have to depart."

Feet began to approach the door. Wash quickly stood back at attention. He watched as the young Englishman awkwardly mounted and galloped away, heading north as fast as he could.

I reckon that he calculates up there in Kansas there will be considerable less chance of losing his scalp. Especially with the war that is sure to come.

War. It was what everyone talked about now, most of them with excited anticipation. Wash could understand why. A war would bring a change from the everyday routine of drilling and drudgery that was the life of a negro cavalryman. In the months that had passed since he had arrived on the frontier, things had not gone as he had thought they would. His plan of proving himself to be a man, making something of himself, and providing for his family had been complicated by more things than one. First were the changed circumstances of his mother and sister. Second was the relationship growing between himself and Bethany. He'd never worried about his own safety before. He reckoned that he was still not all that afraid of death. But the prospect of losing his life in battle and never seeing her face again was too much to bear.

And there was a third thing as well. The prospect of shooting Indians was no longer thrilling. He'd come to see them as men, not faceless enemies. He now found more sympathy in his heart for their Indians than for the buffalo hunters. He felt a sort of tie with them, in fact. In some ways, a Buffalo Soldier, despite the fact that he wore the uniform of the United States Army, was closer to the Indians than to the white men—who despised them both.

It wasn't just the unreconstructed rebels or the civilians in the towns. A great many of the white officers and enlisted men viewed all negroes, soldiers or not, as inferior beings. They called them apes or worse. They doubted the courage and intelligence of every colored soldier, even those under their command.

There were exceptions. Lieutenant Pratt, more than almost any other white man, always treated his black troops with firm respect. But far too many white men would not mind seeing every Buffalo Soldier killed in battle. Wash had no doubt that in any Indian fight, it would be Buffalo Soldiers pushed to the fore, to kill or be killed.

At dawn on July 4th, Wash stood at the gate of the fort looking out onto the plain. In the past few days, more word had reached them about the events at Adobe Walls. Though the number of slain Indians had been considerably fewer than the excited Fletcher had claimed, there was no doubt that the Indians had retreated with serious losses. And the long-range shooting of Billy Dixon had been verified by every survivor's story. It seemed as if he and his friend Mr. Masterson were on their way to becoming legends of the West.

One of the most interesting pieces of news, to Wash at least, had been that there was a light-skinned negro fighting on the side of the Indians. Moreover, that negro had been playing a bugle and leading the charges. Though dressed as an Indian, it was suspected that he had been a Buffalo Soldier based on the evidence of that bugle. But the man had not survived. He'd been shot, it was said, while grabbing a can of coffee from one of the wagons. His head had been one of those stuck up on the poles at Adobe Walls.

Wash shook his head as he watched the rising sun. *My, my. So now we know what befell Old Landrieu.*

Contrary to expectations, they not been sent out to provide any help to the buffalo hunters at Adobe Walls. The opinion of General John Pope, their overall commander, had remained the same. Those buffalo hunters got what they were asking for. Not a single soldier would be wasted in their defense.

Wash had the nagging feeling, though, that sooner or later conflict would find them. He lifted his hand to shade his eyes as the sun just cleared the hill to the east of the fort. Something coming. A cloud of dust that resolved itself into white man on a little sorrel. As he approached the gate, Wash saw the man's horse was so lathered up it was about played out. It looked to have been ridden through the night.

"Hold on," the rider called out. "Hold on!"

Wash slung his rifle over his back and stepped forward to take hold of the reins.

"Johnny Murphy," the rider panted as he slid off his horse.

Wash recognized him as one of the civilian workers at the Darlington Agency, seventy-five miles away. His legs were so cramped up by the hard ride that he almost dropped to his knees. Wash took his arm to help him steady himself.

"Cheyennes," Johnny Murphy wheezed. "Oh Lordy. Cheyennes. Take me...to your officer."

Wash handed the sorrel off to the other man on guard at the gate and half-carried Murphy to Colonel Davidson's quarters.

"Cheyennes," Murphy said as soon as he saw the colonel, "Cheyennes..." Then his voice and his legs failed him.

"Over here," Davidson said, pulling out a chair and steering the exhausted messenger into it. "Drink this." He handed him a cup of warm coffee.

After the first sip, some color returned to Johnny Murphy's face. After the second sip, he took a deep breath and sat up straighter. And though his breath was still labored, he was able to get out his message.

"Near...the...entire...Cheyenne...Nation...has...bolted," Murphy panted. "They have...painted up...and gone off...on the war path. Close to...three thousand of 'em."

Three thousand Cheyennes on the war path. Only three hundred or so Indians had chosen to remain at the agency under the leadership of Little Robe and two other friendly chiefs. The hostiles had already begun raiding all around the agency. They had not only stolen horses. They had also killed several settlers. Agent Miles feared for the lives of himself and his staff. His message was a plea for help to be sent at once.

Early as it was, it did not take long before they were in action. No time for chow, as men grabbed whatever biscuits and bacon they could stuff in their saddlebags.

"Mount up," Sergeant Brown barked.

And just like that they were on their horses and the whole of the company was on its way and proceeding north posthaste.

But at the end of the daylong ride, there was no fight to be had. The hostile Indians had all slipped away. Colonel Davidson was fit to be tied. But Lieutenant Pratt seemed not at all upset. He turned to the men and raised a hand like an orator.

"Each time they run," Pratt said, his voice ringing like a preacher's, "the army shall follow. These plains may be theirs now, but the day of their rule is almost done. We shall harry them as the hound does the hare, drive them from their places of refuge and defeat them utterly."

Johnson, the head Tonkawa scout, reined in his horse next to Wash, leaning close so that no one else could hear him.

"Longnose likes to hear his own voice," Johnson said, his voice low as the humming of a bee.

Wash managed not to smile. Longnose, he'd learned, was what the Tonkawa scouts called the lieutenant. Pratt's nose being big and hooked like that of a bird of prey, Wash could see how the moniker suited him.

Lieutenant Pratt was now quoting the Bible. Wash recognized it. One of the lesser known parts of the Good Book: Zechariah, Chapter Ten, Verse Five.

"We shall be as mighty men, who tread down their enemies in the mire of battle," the lieutenant intoned, "and we shall fight because the Lord is with us, and the riders on horses shall be confounded."

Unlike most of the Bible-thumpers Wash had heard, Pratt got only one or two words wrong. Wash turned to look again at Johnson, who had been listening intently to the lieutenant's words. But there was no amusement on Johnson's face now, only sorrow. The Tonkawa scout shook his head ruefully. "Longnose is right about that. The time of all of us riders on horses will soon be done."

CHEYENNE VILLAGE, August 29, 1864

Sir:

We received a letter from Bent, wishing us to make peace. We held a consel in regard to it. & all come to the conclusion to make peace with you, providing you make peace with the Kioways, Commenches, Arrapahoes, Apaches and Siouxs.

We are going to send a messenger to the Kioways and to the other nations about our going to make [peace] with you. We heard that you have some in Denver. We have seven prisoners of yours which we are willing to give up, providing you give up yours.

There are three war parties out yet, and two of them are of Arrapahoes. They have been out some time, and exspect now in soon. When we held this council, there were a few Arrapahoes and Siouxs present. We want true news from you in return, —that is, a letter.

BLACK KETTLE, and other chieves.

MEDICINE WATER'S WORST

Never again would so many of their people from so many of their tribes join together in battle. Wolf felt that in his heart as he watched the great war party scatter like a great flock of birds startled by an eagle.

The Kiowas were riding off to the west. They had a place to go where they believed no one would ever find them, the great canyon of the Palo Duro.

"If you need a safe place," Mamanti said, "you Cheyennes come and join us. We will be protected by the canyon's great stone arms. We can strike from there, make the stinky white men cry, and then retreat within its walls. No white men can ever enter there."

Mamanti. Sky Walker. He was a man Wolf felt he could trust. It was said that he could truly see the future. Far more of a medicine man than Isa-tai. But in Wolf's heart he wondered if even the stone arms of the Palo Duro could protect them now.

The Quahadi Comanches were heading south. They were still following Quanah, whose disgraced little medicine man was trailing behind them.

"I will fight and keep fighting even when all others quit," Quanah vowed. "In Texas and Mexico, we will keep warring on our own."

But what of us? Wolf thought.

The Cheyennes were divided about what to do. They had suffered the heaviest losses from the long shooting guns of the buffalo hunters. Those among them who had died were Walks on the Ground, Horse Road, Spotted Feathers, Stone Teeth, and Coyote. Others were so badly injured that all they and their families wished for now was to find a quiet place where they might either recover from their wounds or die peacefully.

But there was one who still had war burning in his heart. Medicine Water. The death of so many at Adobe Walls had just added wood to the fire within him. His grudge against all whites went back a long way. His brother had been killed by white men. Although it was twenty winters ago, Medicine Water had never forgotten. He had been the first Cheyenne to take the war pipe from the Comanches.

"I will keep fighting," he growled. "I will make all the whites cry."

"And I will be beside you," his wife, Mochi—Buffalo Calf Woman—said.

Wolf saw the determination in her face. She seemed even fiercer than her husband in her desire to keep striking the enemy. Again, it was easy to understand why. She had lost her first husband and all the rest of her family at the Big Sandy River. It had turned her into a warrior woman. She did not stay with the other women when fighting took place. She joined in with the men. When they had attacked the buffalo hunters' camp, she had been among the fighters. She had charged down the hill. She had fired her rifle and dared the cowardly white men to come out and fight like men.

"My husband and I will kill any ve'hoe we see," she declared. "Who will join us?"

She and Medicine Water looked straight at Wolf. He read the question in their eyes.

Am I angry enough to ride with them?

There was much anger in his heart. He, too, remembered the Big Sandy. He had just seen his closest friend die. The white men took so much and kept taking. But he worried about his mother and sister. Would they be safe if he went off with Medicine Water and Mochi?

Wolf also suspected that the burning anger of Medicine Water and Mochi would not just be turned toward their real enemies. It would be directed at all ve'hoes, even innocent ones. He did not want to be a killer of women and children.

He made the sign for *no*. He turned Wind's head back toward the camp where his family was waiting. Mochi called something out at him. He paid no attention to her insulting words.

He had not gone far before he heard someone riding behind him. It was Gray Head. The old chief drew his horse so close that their knees touched.

"Nephew," he said. He put his left hand on Wolf's shoulder. He said nothing further. He understood all the feelings of despair and confusion and anger fighting inside Wolf. *The losses he has experienced in his long life have been even greater than mine,* Wolf thought. *Yet still he tries to follow the road of peace.*

They rode together for a time without speaking. Then they came to a small stream. It was one of the few still running in the drought that was strangling the land. They paused to let the horses drink.

"What will we do now?" Wolf asked.

"The best we can," Gray Head answered.

Gray Head's band of a few dozen families did not return to the agency. They feared they would be punished by the army. But they did not try again to make war. They avoided fighting. For horses, at night they raided the corrals of white men with big herds. Those white men would not suffer from the loss of a few ponies. They hunted as best they could. Most of the game was gone from the land. When they could find nothing else, they took cows from large herds. A few animals might not be missed. They did not attack any white settlers. When soldiers tried to attack them, Gray Head knew the ways to escape. They knew their own land better than anyone else. Their land helped them.

"Perhaps," Gray Head said, "if we do not hurt any ve'hoes, they will see that we are just trying to survive. Then they will not be angry with us. Then maybe there can still be peace."

The summer moons passed. Though life was not easy, their small band remained free. However, with the coming of the Cool Moon, terrible word came about Medicine Water's band. Although those with Gray Head had done the best they could, Medicine Water had done the worst.

The story was pitiful. It was difficult to tell. Medicine Water and Mochi and the twenty with them had come across a wagon driven by a white man. He had with him his wife and their seven children. The only weapons those innocent white people had were two muzzle-loaders. Those guns were so bad that Medicine Water's band just left those old rifles on the prairie. What Medicine Water's band did take were the lives of five of those people. They killed the man. They killed his wife. They killed three of the children. Then Medicine Water's band took the remaining four girls as captives.

Many terrible things had been done by the ve'hoes, more than could be counted. But it did not make it right to do the same. Medicine Water and his band had not behaved like real human beings. When Mochi split the head of that poor ve'hoe father with an ax, her heart had been as bad as that of the worst white man.

Five days had passed since they had heard of what Medicine Water and Mochi did. Gray Head had led them to a sheltered valley, a good place for their camp. There were trees for firewood and a spring of sweet water. And Wolf had seen a small herd of antelope out on the rolling plain. He knew that no game animal was more curious than the antelope. So that morning he had tied a white cloth to a stick and placed it where it would wave in the wind. Then he had hidden in a small dip in the land and concealed himself with brush. His plan had worked well. The antelope were drawn by the white cloth. From his hiding place Wolf was able to bring down two fat antelope with his arrows.

Now the smell of cooking meat was drifting through their camp. That night they would eat well.

I wish that we could stay here for a long time, Wolf thought. *But if we do so, there is a greater chance that the army's Tonkawa scouts will find us. We must move.*

Gray Head had said that they would be safe here for two more days. Then they would move camp. Or maybe they would have to do so sooner.

Wolf saw hand signals being made by the sentry who had been placed among the distant boulders near the valley's entrance. It was Too Tall. He was out of sight from anyone coming across the plain, even though he was visible to those in the camp.

People coming, Too Tall signaled.

Enemies? Wolf signed back to him.

No. Real People.

Others had seen Too Tall's signal, so everyone in the camp was watching as the riders entered the valley. It was as Too Tall had said. They were Real People. Striped Arrow People. Cheyennes. But it was not good that they had come. The two who rode in front were Medicine Water and Mochi. A dozen men, ten women, and four girls followed them. All had the worn and tired look of people who had traveled far without food or rest. But as they got closer, Wolf saw that the four girls were not just tired from travel. Their faces were frightened. Their expressions were those of ones who had just seen a bad ghost. Their horses were being led by Medicine Water's men. The travel dust had darkened the girls' faces. They were the four sisters who had survived the killing of their family members.

Medicine Water slid off his pony and walked up to Gray Head. He held out his hands. Gray Head said nothing, made no move to welcome him.

"My friend, are you not going to invite us to eat?" Medicine Water said. "We have had no real food such as we smell cooking here. All we have had to eat is what we have taken from ve'hoes."

White people he killed, Wolf thought.

There were many of them now. Medicine Water had vowed to take ten lives for every Cheyenne who fell to the buffalo hunters' guns. He was well on his way to fulfilling that promise. Some were buffalo hunters. Medicine Water's warriors caught them as they were leaving Adobe Walls. Despite the fact they had held off Quanah's attacks, that place had now been abandoned. But most of those he and his band had killed were as innocent as the four captive white girls.

Gray Head sighed. Trouble had come to him. But he still had to show proper hospitality. "Come," he said. "Eat."

As they moved toward the cooking fire, Wolf looked into the eyes of the captive girls. Two of them were not little girls. They were young women.

"You see this one," one of Medicine Water's men said. His name was Rising Bull. He squeezed the arm of the taller of the two young women. "I think I will make her my wife."

Wolf said nothing. It was true that captive women often ended up being married to Cheyenne men. But they were adopted when that happened. They were treated with as much honor and respect as any woman born Cheyenne. He could see that those two young woman had not been treated that way.

The one who seemed to be the oldest seemed to notice that Wolf was looking at her in a kindly manner. She tried to smile at him. Mochi walked over, and the smile vanished from the white girl's face.

"This one is Gah-dlin," Mochi said. She slapped the girl hard on the back of her head. "She tries to help. She is stupid. But maybe she will make a good wife." Mochi slapped her again. "Or maybe not. Maybe I just kill her like I did her father, hah?"

Wolf could see that someone—probably not Mochi—had braided the hair of the four captives. They had been put into proper clothing to look like women of the Striped Arrow People. But there were many bruises on their faces and arms.

Mochi named the others, pointing at them as if they were dogs. "Tso-fia, Choo-lee, Ah-dleyt."

They cringed back as she swung her hand toward each of them.

Wolf felt such pity for those girls. When Mochi walked away, he cut off a piece of liver. He handed it to the oldest girl, the one Mochi called Gah-dlin.

"Thank you," she said.

But when she tried to feed it to her littlest sister, Mochi came back around the fire. She pushed Gah-dlin down, snatched the piece of liver away from the littlest girl, and ate it herself.

"Foolish girl. Why waste food on one who is too small to do any work?"

No one did anything to stop Mochi. The captives belonged to her and her husband. But Wolf could see from the look on Gray Head's face that he, too, was pitying those pathetic girls.

"Uncle," Wolf whispered to him. "I have an idea. Let us trade for these captive girls. If we have them with us, the army may not attack us. Then if we give them back to the their own people, maybe the ve'hoes will treat us better."

Gray Head looked at the four girls. The two little ones were almost dead from hunger. They were like puppies that had been beaten so much they no longer dared to raise their heads. They would not survive much longer being treated this way. Gray Head nodded. He turned to Medicine Water.

"What will you take for these four ve'hoe girls?" Gray Head asked.

At first Medicine Water refused to trade at all.

"Those two bigger ones useful," he said. "They are strong enough to help around the camp." He pointed with his chin at Gahdlin. "That taller one is skinny, but she can carry more firewood than you would imagine. Rising Bull has been thinking that he might take her as his wife."

"What about the little ones?" Gray Head said.

Finally a deal was struck. When Medicine Water and his people rode away, they took only two captives with them. The two little ones, Choo-lee and Ah-dleyt German, stayed. In exchange, Medicine Water had accepted four blankets, a parfleche bag of dried meat, one horse, and two knives.

Still, even though she remained a captive, there was something close to a smile on the face of Gah-dlin as she was taken from Gray Head's camp. The look that she gave Wolf and Gray Head was one of gratitude. She knew they had saved the lives of her little sisters.

AFTER BRINGING THE BUFFALO, SWEET MEDICINE WENT TO DO
ANOTHER THING FOR THE PEOPLE. HE AND HIS WIFE TIED THEIR
TRAVOIS TO A DOG AND WENT TOWARD THE BLACK HILL TILL THEY
CAME TO A GREAT BUTTE. INSIDE THAT HILL WAS A BIG LODGE.
THE PEOPLE OPENED THE DOOR FOR SWEET MEDICINE.

"GRANDSON," THEY SAID, "YOU HAVE COME BACK AGAIN. COME AND
SIT IN OUR LODGE."

SWEET MEDICINE AND HIS WIFE ENTERED.
THEY SAT JUST INSIDE THE DOOR. SWEET MEDICINE LOOKED
AROUND AT THOSE GATHERED WITHIN THE BIG LODGE.

THOSE INSIDE THAT LODGE WERE ALL OF THE BEINGS THAT GROW
AND EXIST UPON THE EARTH. THEY WERE MAI-YUN, SPIRIT PEOPLE.
THEY WERE THE ANIMALS AND BIRDS, THE TREES AND THE GRASSES
AND THE ROCKS. ALL OF THEM SEEMED TO BE PEOPLE AS SWEET
MEDICINE ENTERED. FOUR OF THOSE PEOPLE, THOUGH, STOOD OUT
ABOVE ALL THE OTHERS. TO THE RIGHT OF THE DOOR SAT A MAN
WHO WAS ALL BLACK. AT THE BACK OF THE LODGE TO THE RIGHT
WAS A MAN WHO WAS BROWN. BESIDE HIM, TO HIS LEFT, WAS
ANOTHER MAN WHO WAS ALL BROWN. TO THE LEFT OF THE DOOR
WAS A MAN WHO WAS ALL WHITE. THOSE FOUR MEN WERE
HANDSOMER THAN ANYONE SWEET MEDICINE HAD EVER SEEN
BEFORE. HE LOOKED AT ALL OF THEM FOR A LONG TIME.

"NOW," SAID THE CHIEF MAI-YUN, "WE HAVE BROUGHT YOU HERE TO
GIVE YOU SPIRITUAL POWER TO TAKE BACK TO THE PEOPLE. BUT
FIRST YOU MUST CHOOSE ONE OF THESE FOUR MEN YOU WOULD
MOST LIKE TO RESEMBLE."

AS HE SPOKE, THE CHIEF SPIRIT PERSON POINTED WITH HIS LIPS,
INDICATING THE MEN TO EACH SIDE OF THE DOOR.
BUT SWEET MEDICINE PAID NO ATTENTION TO THAT.

"I HAVE CHOSEN," HE SAID. "I WILL BE LIKE THAT BROWN MAN
THERE AT THE BACK OF THE LODGE."

AS SOON AS HE SPOKE THOSE WORDS, EVERYONE INSIDE
THE LODGE GROANED. ONE OF THE SPIRIT PEOPLE STOOD UP.
"THAT MAN IS A FOOL," HE SAID, AND THEN HE LEFT THE LODGE.

"GRANDSON," THE CHIEF SPIRIT PERSON SAID, "YOU HAVE MADE A
MISTAKE. LOOK." AS SWEET MEDICINE LOOKED,
THE WHITE PERSON AND THE BLACK PERSON BECAME STONES.

"IF YOU HAD CHOSEN THEM," THE CHIEF SPIRIT PERSON SAID,
"YOU WOULD HAVE LIVED FOREVER. BUT NOW, THOUGH YOU WILL
LIVE A LONG TIME, YOU WILL DIE. AND THE ONE WHO IS NOW
ENTERING THIS LODGE WILL ALWAYS BE AROUND."

AS THOSE WORDS WERE SPOKEN, A THIN MAN CAME INTO
THE LODGE, SAT DOWN, AND BEGAN TO COUGH.

"THAT MAN IS SICKNESS," THE CHIEF SPIRIT SAID.
"NOW HE WILL ALWAYS BE AROUND YOUR PEOPLE. HE BELONGS
TO WINTER MAN AND WILL COME EACH YEAR TO YOUR LODGES."

"IS THERE NOTHING I CAN DO TO HELP THE PEOPLE?"
SWEET MEDICINE ASKED.

BUFFALO BULL SPOKE. "FIRE WILL HELP THE PEOPLE.
IT WILL GUARD AGAINST THE COLD BROUGHT BY WINTER MAN.

"I CAN BRING FIRE WITH MY LIGHTNING," SAID THUNDER.
"BUT THE PEOPLE WILL NEED TO KNOW HOW TO MAKE FIRE
FOR THEMSELVES."

BUFFALO BULL GAVE SWEET MEDICINE A DRY BUFFALO CHIP AND A
STICK. "WITH THESE YOU CAN MAKE FIRE."

THEN THUNDER SHOWED SWEET MEDICINE HOW TO MAKE FIRE BY
RESTING THE POINT OF THAT STICK ON THE BUFFALO CHIP AND
TWIRLING THE STICK BETWEEN HIS HANDS.

ONE BY ONE THE OTHER SPIRIT BEINGS TAUGHT SWEET MEDICINE
OTHER THINGS TO HELP THE PEOPLE. LAST OF ALL, THE CHIEF SPIRIT
SPOKE. "NOW YOUR WIFE MUST TURN AWAY AND CLOSE HER EYES"

THEN HE SHOWED SWEET MEDICINE EIGHT ARROWS.
FOUR WERE FLETCHED WITH HAWK FEATHERS.
FOUR WERE FLETCHED WITH EAGLE FEATHERS.

"WHICH FOUR ARROWS DO YOU CHOOSE?" THE CHIEF SPIRIT ASKED.

SWEET MEDICINE LOOKED CLOSE. HE TOOK HIS TIME TO MAKE HIS
CHOICE. "THESE FOUR," HE SAID, CHOOSING THE FOUR EAGLE FEATH-
ER ARROWS.

THE CHIEF MAI-YUN SMILED. "THIS TIME YOU CHOSE WELL.
THESE ARROWS ARE THE MAAHOTSE. THEY ARE THE MEDICINE
ARROWS. THESE TWO PAINTED RED ARE THE BUFFALO ARROWS.
THEY WILL BRING FOOD AND NOURISHMENT FOR THE PEOPLE.
THESE TWO PAINTED BLACK ARE THE MAN ARROWS.
THEY WILL BRING VICTORY OVER YOUR ENEMIES."

THEN THE CHIEF MAI-YUN MADE A QUIVER FROM A COYOTE SKIN
AND PLACED THE ARROWS WITHIN IT. HE SHOWED SWEET MEDICINE
HOW TO WRAP THE ARROWS IN THE HIDE OF A BUFFALO. WHEN THOSE
ARROWS WERE SAFELY HIDDEN FROM SIGHT WITHIN THE BUFFALO
SKIN, THE CHIEF MAI-YUN TURNED TO SWEET MEDICINE'S WIFE.

"ALTHOUGH NO WOMAN MUST LOOK AT THESE ARROWS OR TOUCH
THEM, AS THE WIFE OF THE ARROW KEEPER, SHE WILL BE THE ONE
WHO CARRIES THEM," HE SAID. THEN HE PAINTED HER WITH SPIRITUAL
PAINT, WRAPPED A ROBE AROUND HER, PLACED THE ARROWS ON HER
BACK, AND GAVE HER A CANE TO LEAN UPON.

SO IT WAS THAT SWEET MEDICINE AND HIS WIFE BROUGHT
THE SACRED ARROWS TO THE PEOPLE.

DEATH SONG

Fort Sill,
Indian Territory
September 22, 1874

Dear Mother,

I hope all is well. Things here have become quite hot. By this I mean
not only the temperature, but also the situation with our Indians.
Sadly, circumstances have led to what I know the eastern newspapers
are calling a general uprising. I would not mention this if it were not
for the fact that I know you have likely read some of the highly colored
accounts in the newspapers. I know you may be fearing for my safety.

Please do not worry. Our Cheyennes have left the agency. But
they are more eager to flee than to confront us. Our forces are far superior, and they are well aware of that fact. It is now our job to round
them up and bring them in. Rather than heroism, what is called for
on our part is to be rather like truant officers charged with bringing in delinquent students. Hardly a gun has been fired, and when
weapons are discharged they are almost always our own. Please do
not worry that I am in danger.

How are things at home? How of Mr. Mack? How of my sister who is certainly reading this to you? (Pegatha, I enjoy your asides in the letters you have written. They are quite amusing. However, I hope that your next letter will include just as much truth as humor. I hope you understand my meaning.)

I have become quite close with Bethany. I now dare to think and hope that after my time in the army we might have a life together. But I have not yet gone further than thinking and hoping. Still, she treats me with such kindness and affection that I believe our feelings to be mutual and that our minds truly meet as one.

I continue to enjoy the confidence of our Lieutenant Richard Henry Pratt. He has indicated he wishes me to remain at his side in all of our engagements. I am usually the company flag bearer, which is a considerable honor.

I send my love and warm wishes and await your next letter.

Your loving and obedient son,
Washington Vance

The past months had seen one long march after another, hard on the heels of the hostiles. The 10th had done little actual fighting with the Indians. But what they had accomplished had been as good as victories in battle. Whenever they came across an abandoned camp—tipis standing empty with smoke still rising from their cooking fires, a sure sign that the hostiles saw them coming and took to their heels— they had made use of a weapon more effective than any gun.

The match.

Every deserted lodge. Every camp. Clothing, food, shelter, blankets, every possession that had not been lugged away was sent up in flames. Now and again they did corral an actual Indian. Most often it was some old man or woman too weak or slow to manage to get away. They found them sitting on the prairie, their hands held up, singing.

This time it was an old man that they had caught.

Though I don't rightly know if caught is the right word to describe a rabbit hopping into your pot, Wash thought.

The three of them riding point, Wash, Charley, and Josh, had almost trotted past him where he sat. He had been nigh invisible. What with his legs out in front of him, his brown skin and stick-thin arms and legs had blended in with the dirt and dry brush around him. When he had started to chant, it had been so sudden that Josh's horse had reared up.

"Jehosophat!" Josh yelled as he grabbed at the reins, barely staying in the saddle.

"Watchit," Charley chuckled. "If that old fella was a snake he'd have bit you." Josh had his rifle out and was pointing it at the old man. The old fellow paid him no mind, singing even louder.

He has been here some time, Wash thought. *His lips are cracked from not having any water to drink. Voice is still strong, though.*

"Lower your weapon, Josh," Wash said. "We are in no danger here."

"What in blazes is this old Cheyenne lizard chanting?" Josh asked as he craned his neck at the Indian.

"He is Kiowa," a deep, familiar voice said from just behind them. It was Wash's turn to jump. Johnson, the Tonkawa head scout, had come up so quietly they had not heard him.

"Kiowa he is, then," Charley said, a big grin on his face. "And you just about jumped out of your skin, Wash!"

That strange sense of humor of Charley's was a bit unsettling at times.

He is like the man in the old story my father told me, Wash thought. *About a man who found it funny when his friends were in trouble. That man was out hunting when he heard a call for help. He climbed a hill and looked down into the valley below, where he saw a friend of his being chased around a big tree by a bear.*

"Help me!" the man being chased by the bear yelled as he ran around and around that tree.

"You want to catch that bear," the man with the sense of humor yelled down, "you need to run a mite faster."

"What's he chanting?" Josh asked.

Wash thought he knew the answer, and Johnson's reply proved him right.

"Death song," Johnson said. He leaned closer to look at the old man, then turned back to Wash.

"Remember him?"

Wash shook his head.

"Last time you see him, you feed him. Skinnier now."

A lump formed in Wash's throat. He did recognize the old Kiowa. That half-moon-shaped scar on his forehead. He was one of those who'd been fed that day at the fort. Only a handful of Kiowas, led by Lone Wolf and Mamanti, had taken part in the fight at Adobe Walls. And even after Adobe Walls, no more than another eighty or so of their people had been convinced to take the war path with them. Just about all the enrolled Kiowas had stayed at the agency. They had wanted no part of another war. This old man, though, maybe because he was one of Lone Wolf's relatives, had joined up with the hostiles.

Although it seemed like it was years ago, only a few months had passed since that day when the chanting Wash had heard was not a death song but one of thanks for gifts of food. This dried-up old Indian had appeared tall and strong then, dressed in his finery as he danced before them. But now he looked a hundred years old. His eyes were clouded. He was on his last legs for sure.

"What do we do with him?" Josh asked.

"Can't take no prisoners now," Charley said, the laughter gone from his voice. "We need to push on."

Charley is right, Wash thought. *Even if we were able to get this old man up and onto a horse with one of us, he probably would not survive to the end of the day, starved and dehydrated as he is.*

"We should give him what he sings for," Johnson said.

There was no emotion in the scout's voice. Just a matter-of-fact suggestion that they shoot the poor old man or save a bullet by cutting his throat.

As one, the scout and Wash's friends turned to look at Wash.

And why should I be the one to decide anything?

The old man was not chanting so loud anymore. Maybe he was listening to the young men converse. Or maybe he was just getting weaker.

Wash unslung his canteen and dropped it to the ground next to the old man. "Some of his people might just circle back for him," Wash said.

Then they moved out.

Everywhere they went, the ve'hoe soldiers had pursued. So the forty-four chiefs had met. They had sent out word. The best chance for their nation to survive would be to break up into even smaller bands.

Wolf and his family left Gray Head's camp circle. They joined with his old friend White Horse, the Dog Soldier chief, and his six lodges.

"We will go to Palo Duro," White Horse said. "Mamanti said it would be safe. I trust him."

And so that is where they went.

Perhaps we will be safe here, Wolf thought.

He looked around again at his new surroundings. The great canyon, with its sheer stone walls, was in the middle of the Staked Plains. No one could find their way across that vast plateau without following the marker sticks stuck into the earth. And the canyon was invisible until one came close. Surely no one would find it without a guide.

He turned to look back at the way they had come into the Palo Duro. It was a narrow trail winding down among great stones. The only other way in—or out—was an even narrower trail at the other end. Within the wide canyon there was good grass for the horses. The river that flowed through had clear, sweet water. The trees that grew within the canyon were tall and straight, perfect for lodge poles. There was lots of firewood. The hunters of the various nations sheltered there had found no buffalo on the surrounding plain. But there were many deer and antelope nearby. The people were well fed.

I like this place, Wolf thought.

He liked Mamanti, too. The Kiowa medicine man was both a brave leader and a modest but accurate prophet. Unlike like Coyote Dung, the things Mamanti said always seemed to come true. He carried a sacred stuffed owl with him everywhere. It spoke and gave him good advice.

As Wolf walked past, Mamanti nodded to him. Wolf took this walk from one end of the Palo Duro to the other every day if it was a day when he did not go out hunting. He hunted only every third or fourth day. He and his family owned only one horse strong enough to use to hunt. His horse, Wind.

As he walked he thought about what he saw. More than a hundred lodges of the three tribal nations were now living in the Palo Duro. They were in several camps that were strung the length of the canyon along the river like beads on a piece of sinew. Wolf passed the lodges at the lower end of the canyon. The grazing was best near those lodges. The canyon was at its widest. It was space and grass that the Kiowas needed.

The Kiowas' horse herd numbered more than a thousand animals. Those Greasy Wood People had the most lodges. Their lodges were the biggest, tall, painted tipis covered with sacred symbols. They possessed many buffalo robes, piles of blankets, many bales of calico, many guns, and much ammunition. They had all sorts of canned food and dry goods. Some of them even had stone china to eat their food on. Their possessions had come from many successful raids. They were wealthy people.

Next to them, in the middle of the canyon, were the Comanches. Those Snake People were not as rich as the Kiowas. Still, they had fine lodges and several hundred horses. Their lodges, too, were full of goods. Again, just as Mamanti and others of the Kiowas had done, Comanche men nodded to Wolf as he walked past. They looked a little amused. They did not look worried. They did not wander back and forth as he did, worrying.

They were not Cheyennes.

Wolf had come now to the narrowest part of the great Palo Duro. He had come to the place where the Cheynnes were camped.

Only twenty lodges of our people.

They were led by White Horse and Iron Shirt. All but a few of the Cheyenne horses were gone, some of them stolen by white thieves, others eaten when food ran out. Some had been run to death as they fled the ve'hoe soldiers. The Cheyennes had only the horses they rode in upon and a few pack mules. They had almost no possessions.

Wolf stopped when he came to their small lodge. Wind lifted his head as Wolf came close to pat his neck. Behind him their other animal grazed. It was a small, scrawny mule. Wolf counted up their possessions in his head.

One cooking pan, one wooden bowl, two spoons, three knives, my gun and one bandolier of ammunition, my bow and arrows, and the clothing we are wearing.

His mother smiled at him. He had not said a word yet. Still, what she spoke was in answer to his thoughts.

"The more people have," she said, "the more those people have to lose."

Then she bent back to her task of scraping an antelope skin.

Wolf sat down next to her.

"What is the news?" she asked.

"Scouts say that Three Fingers and his troops are nearby."

Three Fingers. That was the name the Kiowas had given the ve'hoe chief called Colonel Ranald Mackenzie by his own people. He had lost two fingers during the big war the white men fought against each other.

"How near?"

"A day's ride from here. Some of the Snakes and the Greasy Wood People had a little fight with him. Then they rode off. They left the ve'hoe soldiers behind. They say no one followed them. They say those white men are too blind to find the Palo Duro."

"Ah," his mother said. She bent back to the task of flensing the hide of the antelope he had shot with an arrow the day before. Some of its meat was cooking over their fire. Then she looked up at Wolf.

"What do you think, my son?"

Wolf reached into his pouch. He pulled out the little figure he had made of dark wood. It was a perfect figure of a buffalo calf. He had thought to give it to his little sister when he finished. But for some reason he had kept it. He sighed.

"I am not so sure. The ones who scout for them—they are not white men. They are Seminole negroes. They are the best scouts the ve'hoes have. Even better than the Tonkawas. Almost as good as our own Wolves."

It was still early in the day. Wolf climbed to the top of a big rock. It was far below the canyon rim but still high above their lodge. Wolf sat down where the first rays of the sun were just beginning to touch the flat place on top of the rock. It was peaceful. A wren perched on the branch of a mountain juniper near Wolf's head. It opened its throat to greet the new day with song. Then it stopped. It cocked its head. It fluttered away as quickly as the thought that came to Wolf.

It heard what I heard.

It was a noise like the sudden breaking of a dry branch, a cracking sound. It came from the direction of the Kiowa camp at the mouth of the canyon. He recognized that sound. Not a branch. A gunshot. He stood and cupped his ears to hear better.

Maybe there is nothing to fear. There are deer in that part of the canyon mouth. Maybe a Kiowa hunter shot one.

Then the noise came again. And again. Wolf's heart began to pound. His breath came fast. He ran headlong down from the rock to their lodge. He needed to warn his family. He needed to tell them to run.

But his mother had heard the shots. She and his sister were already packing.

"Eat this," she said, handing him the wooden bowl. It held some of the antelope that had been cooking. Wolf ate. He knew that he could not be sure when he would eat again. She had already packed away the rest of the antelope meat and the metal cooking pan and the spoons. Her face showed no emotion, but her voice was tense.

His mother and sister began to take down and roll up the lodge skins that covered their home. As they did so, Wolf tied their few belongings onto the pack mule, fastened the travois. His mother and sister left the lodge poles standing. One could always cut new lodge poles. One could not cut a new life. All around them, other Cheyenne women were doing the same.

They moved quickly, but not frantically. If the attack was coming from the other end of the Palo Duro, they would be safe for a little while. The distance and the resistance of the Greasy Wood warriors would protect them. The gunfire coming from the direction of Kiowa camp was now steady. It was the sounds of full battle. The cracking of hundreds of rifle shots echoed off the rock walls. Wolf also heard shouting. He heard the distant screams of Greasy Wood women and children.

Wolf vaulted onto Wind's back and looked around. Other Cheyenne men were also mounted. One of them was White Horse. Wolf caught his eye and pointed with his chin toward the lower end of the canyon. Toward the sounds of fighting.

Should we ride to the fight?

White Horse shook his head. He nodded toward the trail that led in the opposite direction—out of the narrow upper end of the Palo Duro.

"We follow them," White Horse said.

Wolf understood. It was more important to make sure those women and children were safe. His mother and sister were already on the trail. They had joined a stream of other Cheyenne women and children and their pack animals. All were silently making their way out of the canyon that had become a death trap.

White Horse and half a dozen men rode past the women. They would go first on the trail and would make sure no enemies waited at the trail's end out of the Palo Duro.

Wolf joined the other men who covered the retreat. They walked their horses backward, holding their guns and bows and arrows ready. The trail was narrow and long. The retreat was slow. They could hear the fight in the canyon below as they climbed. Wolf listened nervously for the sound of gunfire ahead. But there was only the sound of the feet of the people and their animals scrambling up the trail.

The sun was high when they reached the canyon rim. White Horse and his Dog Soldiers were there. They nodded to Wolf. They had found no enemies waiting for them. The ve'hoe soldiers were all at the other end.

The canyon was filled with the sounds of battle. Smoke rose from below them in the middle of the Palo Duro. The white soldiers were still being slowed by the Greasy Wood warriors. Wolf could hear other people coming up the trail now. He heard voices speaking Comanche. It was the women and children of that tribe escaping by that same trail.

Four days passed. The Palo Duro was now far behind them. The canyon floor had been covered with the shells of countless bullets, but the only ones who lost their lives were three brave Kiowa men. No Cheyenne or Comanche had been killed or even wounded. The fierce resistance put up by the Greasy Wood warriors had held back the soldiers long enough for everyone else to escape unharmed.

But the Cheyennes' allies had suffered greatly in other ways. They had had to leave behind all of their lodges and most of their possessions. The Kiowas' and Comanches' big herds of horses and mules had been captured. The Greasy Wood People had gone from wealth to poverty in less time than it took the sun to rise to the middle of the sky. The wives of the Tonkawa scouts had been allowed to rummage through and take whatever they wanted. Then Three Fingers had ordered the burning of the lodges and possessions left behind. The soldiers took a few hundred of the best horses and killed the rest of the herd. More than a thousand innocent animals were slaughtered by the pitiless guns of the ve'hoes.

And, once again, the allies scattered. The Cheyennes went north. Mamanti and his Kiowas went west while the Comanches went south. All that anyone hoped to do was survive.

NOAHA-VOSE IS THE SACRED MOUNTAIN,
THE PLACE OF ORIGIN FOR ALL THE SACRED POWER.

MANY CALL IT BEAR BUTTE, FOR ITS SHAPE IS THAT
OF A GREAT SLEEPING GRIZZLY BEAR.

NOAHA-VOSE IS THE PLACE OF ORIGIN
FOR ALL THE SACRED POWER THAT MAHEO POURS OUT
UPON THE PEOPLE AND THEIR WORLD.

IT WAS THERE INSIDE THE SACRED MOUNTAIN
THE ALL-FATHER FIRST REVEALED HIMSELF
TO SWEET MEDICINE.

IT WAS THERE THAT MAHEO GAVE THE SACRED ARROWS,
MAAHOTSE, TO SWEET MEDICINE.

IT IS FROM NOAHA-VOSE THAT HOLY POWER
STREAMS IN AN ENDLESS FLOW, POWER THAT BLESSES
AND RENEWS THE PEOPLE WHENEVER THEY FAST
OR PRAY UPON ITS SLOPES.

THE PEOPLE KNOW THAT NOAHA-VOSE
IS THE MOST HOLY PLACE UPON THIS EARTH.

HOOFPRINTS

Wolf breathed in the clean scent of late autumn sage crushed under the horse's feet. The sweet voice of a meadowlark came from somewhere in the bushes along the small creek. The hoofprints led upstream. He followed them quietly.

War was still all around them. Any bluecoat soldier who saw him would not hesitate to shoot. The only Indians not being attacked were those who had come in to the agencies and turned in their weapons. There they were safe from bullets. And just as safe to starve on the poor rations provided to them.

After the flight from Palo Duro, Wolf and his mother and sister had found their way back to Gray Head's camp circle.

"Grandchild," Gray Head had said, embracing Wolf as he got down off Wind's back. "I feared you had not survived."

There were tears in his eyes as he looked at Wolf.

I had not realized how much he cares for us. Perhaps it is because we have survived so many terrible things together.

"The army is angry," Gray Head had said. "It is very angry. It is like a big dog whose meat has been snatched from its mouth. I think it would not be wise for us to go in now to the agency. Maybe if we take care, if we do nothing to hurt anyone, the army will leave us alone. Maybe we can still remain free."

Wolf had nodded at his words. They were words that Gray Head had spoken before. But in his heart, Wolf feared that peace would not be easy to find. The hope that the ve'hoes would to leave them alone was a thin one.

Whatever happens, Wolf had thought, *I will take care of my family.*

The attack on Gray Head's camp had come four days later. Again, they had to run. The ve'hoe soldiers were so angry. After months of trying to catch the Cheyennes, those angry white men probably would not let them surrender. Even if they put down their weapons and raised their hands, they might be shot.

Wolf had not taken flight right away as many did. As the big wagons with guns firing from them rumbled toward them, he had made sure his mother and sister were on their way to safety.

He had also stayed back to do another thing.

The two little white children had still been with Gray Head's camp. Though Stone Calf's niece and her husband had been caring for them and had done their best to be kind to them, those sad little ones were not well. They were weak. Stone Calf's niece had fed them as well as she could. But there was almost nothing to eat for anyone. It had become clear to everyone that the two little girls might not survive.

So as the wagon guns rolled toward them, Wolf went to the lodge of Stone Calf's niece and her husband. Gray Head, always calm in the face of danger, was already there.

"Uncle," Wolf had said. "Is it time for us to try again to give them back?"

"Hee'he'e," Gray Head agreed. "That is my thought. Maybe this time the ve'hoe soldiers will not be blind."

He paused then. There was a great sorrow in his eyes. His gaze seemed as sad as that of a man seeing his own death. Then the moment passed.

"Hurry!" Gray Head said. He pulled out his only blanket. It was a fine wool one given to him by the agent when they were at peace.

Stone Calf's niece hugged each of the little girls and pressed his cheek to theirs. Then she let her husband pull her away. They mounted their horses and rode away.

Wolf picked up one of the little girls. She was as light as a bird, all skin and bones. The other little girl held up her arms to Gray Head. He lifted her into his embrace. Then they ran, carrying the little girls. They ran to the lodge edge of the camp circle farthest from the attack. There they would be safer from guns.

Gray Head spread out his blanket in front of the lodge. They sat the two little girls down on it.

You stay here, Wolf signed to them. *Wait. Your people come.* Choo-lee, the bigger one, nodded her understanding. The littler one, Ah-dleyt, just clutched a doll to her thin chest. That doll had been Wolf sister's before she gave it to the little white girl.

Wolf mounted Wind. He galloped hard, leaving the sound of gunfire behind. He soon caught up with his mother and sister. Knowing that the army would be in pursuit, his clever mother had split off from the main group of fleeing people. She was leading the pack mule down into the shelter of a small grove below a hill. It was a good place to hide. In the distance Wolf could see one group of ve'hoe soldiers chasing the rest of the people off toward the north.

Wait for me, Wolf signed down to his mother.

We wait, she signed back up.

Wolf circled back to their deserted camp. He tied Wind to a small juniper. Then he crawled up a small rise. Two of Gray Head's young men, Bull and Horns, were there. They were waiting in a little hollow on that rise above the camp. They were well concealed, but they could still see the two little girls. They sat as they had been told.

Soldiers were walking now into the empty camp.

"Will they be blind again?" Horns whispered.

"Wait and see," Bull whispered back.

The three young men watched the approaching soldiers. Their job was to be sure that this time Ah-dleyt and Choo-lee were noticed by the white soldiers.

Two moons ago Gray Head had tried to return the little girls to their people. He had left them on a blanket for the soldiers to find. But those blind soldiers had galloped right past them. They left the little girls sitting on the prairie, where they might have starved.

Luckily, three Cheyenne scouts had happened across them days later. The girls had wandered back to the deserted camp site and were half-starved, eating wild fruit and left-behind scraps of food.

"Why are ve'hoes so stupid?" Horns asked now. He was one of the scouts who found the little girls the first time Gray Head tried to give them back.

"Be thankful for their blindness," Bull replied. "If they were able to see as well as an owl in the daytime, our lives would be harder."

The first of the mounted soldiers had reached the far end of the camp. Amazingly, he rode right past the little girls. He did so even though Ah-dleyt was standing up, waving at the man with one hand. Her other hand still clutched the doll Wolf's sister had given her.

Horns looked at Wolf and rolled his eyes. "Not again," he said.

"No," Wolf said, "not again. Look."

One of the Indian scouts, a Delaware, had gotten off his horse. He was walking toward the little girls. All three of the young men sighed with relief.

The Delaware scout turned quickly. He looked up at the rise, looked right at the place where the three were hidden. He raised one eyebrow. A thin smile came to his lips. Then he made little signs with his right hand.

Good. Go now.

The Delaware scout turned back to the little girls. He went down on one knee. Ah-dleyt reached out her hand toward his.

Bull, Horns, and Wolf crawled backward to their horses. Despite the fact that once again they had been forced to flee, one good thing had been done that day.

As he followed the tracks into the twisting coulee, Wolf reached one hand up to the bandolier slung over his shoulder. His fingers counted the bullets. Twelve. Twelve more than most other Cheyenne men had now. Everyone was short or out of ammunition. If there were no ve'hoes nearby, he might use those bullets to hunt for game.

But he did not dare not risk the sound of a gunshot. Ve'hoe soldiers were too close. A party of black white men led by Tonkawa scouts had been chasing them for days.

Wolf was not sure now where those Buffalo Soldiers might be.

The Buffalo Soldiers were not as foolish as Bearcoat. Bearcoat was the Cheyenne name for General Nelson Miles, the white chief leading the largest group of ve'hoes trying to catch Cheyennes. Bearcoat fired off his cannons every morning and every night. That made Wolf smile. It seemed as if he was trying to tell them where he was so they could avoid him.

With the Buffalo Soldiers, the only sign of where they were was the small smoke from the cooking fires of their camps. And sometimes they made no such fires at all.

Wolf thought this place might be safe to hunt. It was a long ride in the opposite direction of where the Buffalo Soldier campfires had last been seen. He leaned forward and ran one hand along the scabbard that hung on Wind's right side. His rifle was not a good one. But this scabbard was one of the best ones he had ever made. He had spent a long time decorating it. He had cut the fringe just right. He had painted the leather with symbols that came to him in dreams. He felt as if it protected him. He trusted it more than his rifle.

No man had ever been killed by his own scabbard. But Wolf had already seen two men shot dead by their own rifles. They had guns just like his. Stone Boy had been careless. He was killed when he allowed his gun to fall to the ground. It had bounced off a stone and fired, and the bullet struck him in the heart. It had killed him right away. Mouse, though, had been careful. He had gently placed his rifle on a cottonwood tree that had fallen across the trail. Then he had started to climb over the trunk. He got only partway across. He was not even touching the gun when it discharged, sending a bullet into his throat. It took some time for Mouse to die. After they buried Mouse, Black Horse and Wolf had broken that gun into pieces and scattered the pieces to the four directions.

"A bad way to die," Black Horse had said. "Better to be shot by ve'hoes than killed by your own weapon."

Wolf had not said anything. He had not even nodded his head in agreement. It was bad luck to speak about being shot.

Probably bad luck to think about it, too.

Wolf turned his attention again to the trail. The tracks along the stream were very fresh. He took his big war bow into his hand and nocked an arrow to the sinew string.

The wall of a red cliff rose just ahead. Because the ravine turned and twisted so much, he could not see very far ahead. He had never been to this place before. Still, something about it felt familiar.

I will get meat here. I will bring it back to my family. We will eat and be happy.

Then maybe the heavy sadness he had been feeling would leave him. Then maybe he would sleep peacefully. Maybe his dreams would not take him back to the sounds of guns. He would not choke on the smoke of burning lodges. He would not smell the sweat of fleeing people. He would not see his best friend pierced by bullets, dying. He would not imagine his family suffering that same fate.

A small brown bird was playing in the stream. The sun glistened off its back. Wolf paused for a moment to watch it. It ducked into the water and came out with something in its beak. A water insect. The bird tossed its head back to swallow, cocking one bright eye up at Wolf. Then it flew right past his face. Its wings spread a little rainbow of mist in front of him. Some of that moisture touched his forehead. He took it as a blessing.

He continued on up the little canyon. The tracks were very fresh. Large tracks and small ones. Two animals at least. More food for their camp. He rounded another sharp bend, and Wind planted his front hooves and stopped. A big buffalo bull stood there, facing them. It was almost close enough to touch with a long lance. Its massive head was lowered. It snorted and pawed the earth.

The old bull turned its head so that one of its great dark eyes was staring up at Wolf. Foam dripped from its mouth onto the yellow soil. Wolf raised his bow. If it charged, Wind would leap aside. Then Wolf could aim for that spot between the bull's ribs. His arrow would bury itself up to its feathers and pierce the heart.

But the bull did not charge. It began to walk backward, never turning its gaze away from Wolf, even as it backed around three small cottonwood trees. It reached the bend where the stream wound back into the narrow canyon. The buffalo went around the bend and was lost from sight.

Wolf sat there for a moment. Why had it seemed as if that old buffalo was about to speak to him? He shook his head.

"Let's go," he said. He kicked his heels into Wind's sides and held his bow ready.

They rounded the bend. The old bull was not there, but its fresh tracks were clear in the soft earth. So, too, were the tracks of other buffalo. More than two. The canyon had widened some. It looked as if it would widen out even more around the next bend. And there it seemed the canyon would end. Wolf could see where the stream was coming out high on the farthest wall. It was a box canyon. Whatever animals were here would be trapped ahead of them. The cliffs were not that high, but they certainly were too steep for buffalo to climb. Unless they were spirit beings.

Wolf could now hear the voice of the waterfall. Another sharp turn. The canyon opened up, and there was the waterfall. It trailed down the face of the cliff like an old woman's white hair, unbraiding itself near the bottom into a wide fan. The pool of water below the falls was larger and deeper than Wolf had expected. And the buffalo were there.

There were seven of them. The great bull, three cows, and three calves. One calf was brown. One was yellow. The third was as black as the carving Wolf carried in the pouch at his waist. All of them had their sides toward him. Their heads were turned in his direction. He had enough arrows. During his seventeen winters he had killed more than fifty buffalo with his arrows. It would be easy to take all seven of them here.

Then Wolf saw a movement at the top of the cliff. He looked up and saw the soldier. He must have come from the opposite direction and climbed the slope of the hill that ended at the cliff edge over this box canyon.

The man saw Wolf at the same instant Wolf saw him. Their eyes met. The man's rifle barrel turned in his direction.

Wolf recognized the man. It was his little Buffalo Soldier. Wolf thought of the long shot that man had made the day they caught the horse thieves.

I will be dead before I can lift my bow.

A STORY, A STORY. LET THE STORY COME.

THERE WERE TWO YOUNG MEN WHOSE FRIENDSHIP WAS SO
GREAT THAT THEY REGARDED EACH OTHER AS BROTHERS.
THE MAIDENS THAT THEY LOVED WERE SISTERS WHO LIVED IN
ANOTHER VILLAGE.

ONE DAY, THE FIRST OF THOSE YOUNG MEN WENT TO GET
THOSE TWO SISTERS. BUT AS THEY TRAVELED ALONG,
A GREAT LION SPRANG FROM THE FOREST AND ATTACKED
THEM. IT LEAPED UPON ONE OF THE GIRLS AND KNOCKED HER
DOWN. BUT THAT FIRST YOUNG MAN WAS A GREAT WARRIOR.
HE PULLED OUT HIS SWORD AND THRUST IT INTO THE LION'S
HEART, KILLING IT WITH ONE BLOW.

WHEN HE ROLLED THE LION'S BODY OFF THE GIRL
HE SAW SHE WAS NOT HURT, EVEN THOUGH HER BODY
WAS COVERED WITH THE LION'S BLOOD. AN IDEA CAME TO HIM.
HE WOULD TEST HIS FRIEND'S LOYALTY.

"GO," HE SAID TO HIS FRIEND'S YOUNG WOMAN.
"TELL MY FRIEND THAT YOUR SISTER AND I HAVE BEEN
ATTACKED BY A LION."

THEN, AS SHE RAN OFF, HE HAD THE FIRST YOUNG
WOMAN LAY HERSELF DOWN UPON THE GROUND
BENEATH THE LION. HE WIPED MORE OF THE LION'S BLOOD
ONTO HIS OWN BODY, CRAWLED BENEATH
THE LION, AND CLOSED HIS EYES AS IF DEAD.

WHEN THE SECOND YOUNG WOMAN REACHED THE VILLAGE,
SHE RAN STRAIGHT TO THE FIRST YOUNG MAN'S FRIEND.

"MY SISTER AND YOUR FRIEND HAVE BEEN ATTACKED
BY A LION."

AS SOON AS SHE SPOKE THOSE WORDS,
THE SECOND YOUNG MAN LEAPED UP.
HE DID NOT TAKE TIME TO GRAB ANY WEAPON
BUT RAN AS FAST AS HE COULD TO THE PLACE WHERE
THE LION'S BODY LAY ON TOP OF HIS FRIEND
AND THE OTHER YOUNG WOMAN. HE LEAPED UPON THE LION.
IT WAS NOT UNTIL HE BEGAN TO WRESTLE WITH IT
THAT HE REALIZED IT WAS DEAD.

THE FIRST YOUNG MAN ROSE UP AND EMBRACED HIM.

"MY BROTHER," HE SAID, "YOU ARE A TRUE FRIEND INDEED."

AND IF YOU DO NOT KNOW WHICH OF THEM
WAS THE BETTER FRIEND, THEN I CANNOT TELL YOU.

OFF WITH THE OLD RAT'S HEAD.

ON THE CLIFF

It had been quite a struggle making his way up the slope, picking his way through prickly pear and bushes with branches like bayonets. Nothing new about that, though. That last week, half of every day had been taken up with scrabbling through brush on a landscape where Old Nick himself might have felt at home.

To say it was unfriendly country was an understatement. There was cholla cactus everywhere, so vicious it seemed to jump up and grab you as you tried to ride or walk past. Rocks big as boxcars were strewn about everywhere, so many that to see more than fifty feet around you, you had to get some height. But the rocky outcrops and ridges were mostly too steep for any horse to climb, even one as fine as Blaze. Thus, day after weary day they had to sweat and cuss their way up one hill after another in futile attempts to catch a glimpse of their Indians. Climbing, descending, picking the prickers out of legs and hands, then climbing yet again. Doing it so many times a man might expect to meet himself coming up whilst he was going down.

"I figure it is your turn to climb and take a lookout, Wash," Josh had said when they reached the base of the broad hill. "I will wait here and watch your back."

Then he had grinned, waiting to see if Wash would give him any argument about it, knowing full well that Wash was the one who had undertaken such a chore the last two times in a row. And also knowing that, despite how steep the slope might be, Wash liked reaching those high places better than anyone else did.

So Wash had just slid off his horse and begun the climb without protest.

However, as he paused to take a breather, fanning himself with his sombrero, he did think again about how it came to be that he was lucky enough to end up on those desolate Staked Plains.

He had been a model cavalryman for the last ten months, so much so that he'd been praised by Lieutenant Pratt more than any other man in his company. And the lieutenant had rewarded him by keeping him close, trusting him as flag bearer, even engaging in man-to-man conversations with him. Treating him not like a negro servant, but as a soldier and a man. And that had been gratifying to Wash.

But not as gratifying as he had expected. At the start, his mind has been set on doing his best, making his way up in the ranks, having enough of a career to provide for his family back home in the South. It was different now. More different than he could ever have imagined. After hearing of how well his mother and sister were doing without him, he no longer fooled himself that he and he alone could provide for them. Why, they hardly needed him at all now! And after meeting Bethany, he'd begun to think about a life other than one in uniform. In fact, nothing had made him happier now than those moments they had shared together at the fort. Those moments were now gone.

As Charley often said, in the army no good deed goes unpunished. Wash's outstanding conduct had meant that—along with Josh and Charley, who though they complained more than he did were actually fine soldiers themselves—he'd been hand-picked from the various companies to go with Lieutenant Pratt and his Indian scouts to maintain pursuit of the elusive Cheyennes. As always, it had been like trying to lasso the wind. The ones they were after had been moving fast since two weeks before when Lieutenant Frank Baldwin had hit Gray Head's camp and started them all to running.

That bold assault of Baldwin's, outrageous as it was brave, must have been a sight to see. When Baldwin came upon Gray Head's camp, it had been wholly by accident. Lieutenant Baldwin had been escorting an empty train of twenty-three wagons back to the Washita for supplies. He had with him but one mounted troop, Company D of the 6th, a handful of infantrymen, and four Tonkawa scouts. Gray Head still had fully a hundred warriors.

"Baldwin, though," Sergeant Brown had said, "is a staunch fellow with considerable grit. He drew up them empty supply wagons into two columns, put one infantry man in every other wagon alongside the driver. Then, dividin' his scouts and cavalry so as that they spread wide on either flank, he told the bugler to sound the charge. What with them few men firing their rifles, the wagon wheels rumblin' across that hard-packed soil, and them scouts and cavalrymen screamin' like wildcats, it was some show. My, my."

Seeing all those wagons and horsemen coming at them, Gray Head's camp had been fooled into believing they were set upon by a large force. Those hostiles were so taken by surprise that they broke and ran out onto the Staked Plains, leaving just about everything behind. Every tipi was full of all sort of belongings—robes, food, even ammunition. And in front of one of those lodges was the biggest prize of all. There on a blanket sat the youngest of the two white girls who had been taken by the Indians.

And now, most likely, all those fleeing Cheyennes are a hundred miles from here and still running.

Wash wiped his face with his bandanna and looked back down. Josh, who was holding the reins of both his horse and Blaze, waved and motioned for him to go higher. Wash avoided the temptation to make an impolite gesture back at him. Climbing the hill had been something he'd wanted to do. But Lord, it was hot. The air rising off the Staked Plains behind him rippled like the heat from a cooking fire. Hot as it was, though, he knew that when night fell it would be cold enough to freeze the fires of Hades. Winter was coming on. If it was as bad as it was the previous year, their poor Cheyennes would be hard-pressed to survive. All that was left for them to do was surrender or perish.

Halfway to the top. Wash paused again to wring out his kerchief. He let his eyes drift over the yellow and brown of the wide plain. Nothing like old Virginny. And though his life there had been mostly as a slave, Wash realized now just how much he missed it. Missed the land itself. Grass so green that it almost stopped your heart to see it. The sweet taste of ripe peaches in late summer. The heaven-bright blue of its lakes and ponds. Were it not for the curse of slavery, Virginia might have been the Garden of Eden.

And might I be there one day with my own Eve beside me?

The thought was a sweet one, even though he feared it was far from realistic. A month had passed since Bethany had departed for the East. And he had yet to receive a letter from her. It had broken his heart to see her go.

Their friendship had progressed to the point where, with the permission of the sergeant and his wife, he had been making regular visits to sit, like a proper gentleman, in their little parlor and engage in conversation with their niece.

But Bethany had not planned to be a servant for anyone—not for her relatives or for a well-off white family. Her time in the West had been but a way station for her.

Another of her uncles, the brother of Sergeant Brown's wife, was involved in politics in the South, one of the new breed of black politicians. He had just been elected to the United States House of Representatives. And he had kept his promise to help his bright niece gain an education. She had been granted admission to the Hampton Institute, a new normal school for former slaves and their children.

Established in my own state of Virginia—not far from the very plantation where I was born.

"Washington," she had said to Wash two days before she left.

"Yes, Miss Bethany?" he had replied.

"You do know that it is only through education that we may help ourselves and our people?"

"Yes, I do."

"So why do you not aspire to the same?"

He had felt his face grow warm. It was the last thing he had expected her to say. He'd been hoping for a fond farewell, a touch of her hand. But he had swallowed hard and managed a reply.

"Perhaps being a soldier is enough for some," he'd said, more brusquely than he intended.

"Hmmph," was her answer to that.

She had said no more that evening about his going to school. He thought his quick reply had scotched all thoughts in her mind of him being more than just another black cavalryman. But that had not been the end of it.

The next day, the day before she was to leave, he had been invited to dinner with the Brown family. He had gone, even though his heart had sunk lower than a snake's belly. He sat, tongue-tied, hardly touching the food before him. He wanted to beg Bethany not to go as much as he wanted to congratulate her on the grand adventure upon which she was about to embark.

He finally managed the latter.

"I know you will do wonderfully well, Miss Bethany," he said.

She nodded without even a smile, and his heart dug itself a hole six feet deep.

But then near the end of the evening, after Sergeant Brown had left the room, called to the back of their small shack by his wife on the pretense of helping her find something, the two of them were alone. Inwardly, Wash thanked them for the privacy while cursing his own inability to speak the words filling his mind.

"I...will miss you," he managed to choke out, after taking a deep breath.

"Washington," her voice had been so serious, yet with a surprising warmth in it. She had reached out her hand and placed it on his. "Will you write to me?"

The touch of her fingers had nearly reduced him to idiocy, but he choked out one word at least.

"Yes," he whispered.

"Listen," she said. "I see your future. I do. It is not here. Your mind is too fine to be wasted so. Others of our people are not only gaining education, they are changing this country so that our children will have a grand future with none of the impediments that held us back."

She pressed something into his hand in place of her warm palm. It was her dog-eared copy of *Romeo and Juliet*.

"Washington," she said in a husky voice, "we are not star-crossed lovers. There is a future for us, together. There is no need for me to ask, 'Wherefore art thou?'"

That copy of *Romeo and Juliet* was in his breast pocket now. As he paused again in his climb, just short of the summit, he patted it with his palm. Then he shook his head.

Not the time to be lost in daydreaming. Keep your eyes open. It's when you least expect him that old Death'll be waiting for you over the hill. Wash, you are not yet ready to put on your traveling shoes and head for those Pearly Gates.

He'd now almost reached the top. But he did not stand up straight. That might make him a target silhouetted against the sky. He dropped down to crawl up behind a big rock and peered around it.

It was a grand view, almost as surprising as finding the Garden of Eden. Instead of the dreary worn yellows and reds and dull grays of the land behind, this was a sight as colorful as a rainbow. Below him was a box canyon, lush with growth. Green trees, still holding their leaves, rose all along a winding streamed of blue-green water flowing over stones that sparkled like gems. A misty waterfall sprang from the rocks below the crest and coursed down the mossy face of the cliff. The pale veil of water cascaded down to a deep blue pool below. In this unexpected oasis Wash saw dragonflies and other insects buzzing back and forth. He heard the songs of birds.

Then he saw motion. Something dark was coming around a bend in the canyon that hid whatever lay farther within its depths. Wash raised his rifle.

But it was no enemy. It was a yellow buffalo calf on long gangly legs. The very same color as the one Wash had carved from that piece of pine he'd picked up behind the carpenter's shed. He'd planned to give that little carved buffalo to Bethany but had forgotten to do so. As a result, it still rested in the top of the ammunition pouch strapped to his side.

Head raised, the yellow calf's big, innocent eyes took in the canyon and the waterfall before it, but it did not lift its gaze to where Wash was perched like an eagle on a pinnacle. A buffalo. The first buffalo he'd seen in many months, aside from the dried bones of those left on the plain by the hunters.

But it was not alone. Two more buffalo rounded the bend—a cow and another calf, a black one this time. More coming? Sure enough, a second cow and her brown calf appeared, the calf playfully butting its head against its mother. The yellow calf stopped drinking from the water of the stream and loped loose-legged over to butt heads and play with the other two. A wide smile came to Wash's lips as he watched them rollicking back and forth, sending up sprays of water as they chased each other through the shallow end of the pool.

Suddenly a loud sound halfway between a snort and a bellow came from downstream. Even as high as he was, Wash could not make out what it was because the trees and the shoulder of the winding canyon cut off his view. The three cows swung around to stand side by side and face the direction of that warning cry. The calves trotted in to stand behind them. Wash's hands tightened on his rifle.

Then what appeared around the corner almost made him laugh. It was the back side of a big bull buffalo. Pawing the earth, its head lowered, it backed toward the other animals. It was a comical sight. The front of the buffalo, with its massive hairy head, its dark eyes, its flaring nostrils, and its gleaming horns made its near-naked backside look weak and comical.

But why is it backing up?

Just one reason a bull would be acting like that. It was seeing a threat. Something or someone dangerous was coming that way. Wash raised his rifle to his shoulder, leaned his cheek against it, and took in a steadying breath, his finger firm on the trigger.

A lone Indian on his pony, bow in hand, came round the bend, following the buffalo. Wash did not move or make a sound, but somehow the Indian sensed something as the small Buffalo Solder sighted in on the center of his chest.

He lifted his head like a wolf sniffing the air, scanning the cliff top. Their eyes met.

A little smile came to the Indian's lips. He sat up straighter on his horse. A warrior, ready to accept the lead gift Wash was about to give him. But instead of sending a .45 caliber bullet his way, Wash eased off on the trigger. It was his Indian, the tall one he'd first seen that day when they went after the horse thieves. The same young man who'd been with them when they met the chiefs coming back from Washington.

I am some kind of fool if I do what I am thinking of doing.

But he did it anyway. He turned the barrel of his gun to the side. He raised his right hand in the sign for peace. The Indian nodded up at Wash. He slung his bow over his shoulder and raised his hand, too.

Then the young man's eyes dropped and he pointed the way Indians point. Not with his finger but with a little jerk of his chin. Wash turned his eyes that way. The little buffalo herd was making its way around the pool on a path so narrow a squirrel would have a hard time following it. They were heading straight for the waterfall. And they did not stop when they reached it. As water sprayed off their backs, they walked right into the falls. One after another, they went in.

The last to disappear was the big old bull, still walking backwards, keeping its footing even though it knocked free a few little stones that rolled down and fell off the edge into the pool. The last sign of it Wash saw was its massive head being pulled back through the curtain of the falls, water spraying off the tip of one horn before it was gone.

Wash realized his hands were trembling and he was breathing deep. It felt as if some kind of powerful magic had just happened. Like something from one of Great-Grampa Hausaman's tales from long ago.

Did this really happen?

His brain told him that there had to be a cave of some sort behind the waterfall. Yet the only thing that told him what he'd seen was real were the ripples crossing the blue pool from the stones knocked in by the big bull's hooves. He looked back at the Cheyenne. Was he going to try to follow the buffalo, seeing as how he'd been hunting them?

But the young Cheyenne did not move. He just sat on his big horse, watching without twitching a muscle. A man might think them a statue were it not for the horse's tail swishing back and forth.

Finally Wolf turned his head to look up at Wash. Even from fifty yards away, Wash could see that his Cheyenne friend's cheeks were wet with tears.

Wolf patted his chest and then made a motion backward with his hand.

I am going, he was saying.

Wash made the *yes* sign with his index finger. *Go.*

Travel good, Wolf signed.

Travel good, Wash signed back.

The young Cheyenne man turned his pony and rode around the bend in the canyon without a backward glance.

Wash descended the way he had come.

As he hopped off the last big rock, he noticed for the first time that there were shapes packed into its face. Seven shapes like buffalo. Two men, one with a lance and one with a bow. A curving path in front of them.

"See anything?" Josh asked as he handed over Blaze's reins.

"Nothing worth talking about," Wash replied.

LONG, LONG AGO THERE WAS A YOUNG WOMAN
WHO FELL IN LOVE WITH THE BRIGHT STAR.

SHE CLIMBED TO THE TOP OF THE TALLEST TREE.
THAT TREE BEGAN TO GROW UNTIL IT REACHED THE SKY LAND.

BRIGHT STAR WAS THERE. HE TOOK HER AS HIS WIFE.
AND FOR A TIME THEY LIVED WELL TOGETHER.

BEFORE LONG IT BECAME CLEAR THAT BRIGHT STAR'S WIFE
WAS SOON TO HAVE A CHILD.

THEN ONE DAY AS SHE WAS DIGGING ROOTS,
ONE BIG ROOT CAME UP AND LEFT A HOLE.
THROUGH THAT HOLE, SHE SAW THE EARTH FAR BELOW.

SHE THOUGHT OF HER MOTHER AND HER FAMILY ON
THE EARTH BELOW. SHE BEGAN TO GO OUT EACH DAY
TO GATHER GRASS TO BRAID INTO A ROPE.

ONE DAY SHE DECIDED THAT ROPE WAS LONG ENOUGH.
SHE TIED THAT ROPE TO A STICK, PLACED THE STICK ACROSS
THE HOLE, AND BEGAN TO CLIMB DOWN.

BUT THAT ROPE WAS NOT LONG ENOUGH.
SHE COULD NOT REACH THE GROUND.
SHE WAS TOO TIRED TO CLIMB UP AGAIN.

FINALLY, SHE LET GO AND FELL.
THAT FALL BROKE HER TO PIECES, BUT THE CHILD
THAT WAS IN HER DID NOT DIE. HE WAS MADE OF STONE.

A MEADOWLARK TOOK PITY ON STONE BOY
AND TOOK HIM TO ITS NEST.
THERE HE WAS RAISED WITH THE YOUNG BIRDS.
AS THEY GREW STRONG, HE, TOO, GREW STRONG.

THEN THE TIME CAME WHEN THE LEAVES BEGAN TO FALL.
THE MEADOWLARKS PREPARED TO FLY SOUTH.

MY SON, THE FATHER MEADOWLARK SAID, WE MUST LEAVE,
AND YOU CANNOT COME WITH US.

MY FATHER, STONE BOY SAID, WHAT MUST I DO?

GO TO YOUR OWN PEOPLE, THE MEADOWLARK SAID.
THEN HE PULLED OUT SOME OF HIS OWN FEATHERS
AND MADE STONE BOY FOUR ARROWS AND A BOW.

NOW GO DOWNSTREAM. YOUR PEOPLE ARE THERE.
THERE ARE THINGS THAT YOU MUST DO FOR THEM.

THERE ARE MONSTERS THAT MAKE LIFE HARD.
BUT THOSE CREATURES WILL NOT BE ABLE TO HARM YOU.
YOU WILL DESTROY THOSE MONSTERS.
YOU WILL HELP THE PEOPLE.

CALLING
OUT NAMES

The winter was the worst one Wolf had ever seen. It was terrible because they had lost their good lodge and blankets. It was made harder because food was so scarce. Their bodies were always exhausted because they had to keep running. Day after day they ran. Even when Cold Maker's breath was heavy with ice and snow, the ve'hoe soldiers still kept after them.

At times, all that kept him going was the memory of that day of the seven buffalo. He would dream of that canyon. Sometimes in his dream he would ride into the waterfall after them. Rather than finding a cave, he would come out into a land as green and new as it had been in the first spring after Maheo made the world. Everywhere were great herds of sacred animals, eagles circled overhead, and the air was filled with birdsong. In that dream his whole family was with him, not only his mother and his sister but both of his fathers and his grandparents. Then he would sense someone beside him. He would turn to see his friend Horse Road there, a big grin on his face.

But then he would wake. He would find himself in the small, torn tipi that was all they owned. His mother and sister would be there shivering beside him. All four of them cut in half by hunger. And he would reach out then. He would wrap his arms around his sister shivering there between him and his mother. And somehow, sharing their warmth, they would live through another night.

At last, the Leaf Moon came. As they stumbled through the melting snow Wolf saw smoke. They rounded a small hill and saw many Cheyenne lodges. They had found their way back to their people.

An old man with a straight back and a smile on his face walked forward to greet them.

"My nephew," he called. He opened his arms. It was Gray Head.

There were more than a hundred lodges in that camp. Gray Head, Heap of Birds, and Stone Calf had joined forces. But they had not done so to fight. They would never fight the ve'hoes again. They had joined together to surrender.

"We have sent messages to the soldier chiefs," Gray Head said. "We have said that we will all come in. We have asked only that they do not kill us."

Not all of the Striped Arrow People were trying to surrender. A few had chosen to go far to the north. There, northern cousins lived who were still strong enough to try to resist. Stone Forehead, Keeper of the Sacred Arrows, was among those who had decided to make that long journey north. He did not do so for his own safety. He did so to keep the Sacred Arrows away from the hands of the ve'hoes. That was a good thing. Those Sacred Arrows had long blessed their people.

"We are tired now," Gray Head said. "Our few ponies have become too weak to run."

Soon his mother and sister were speaking with girls and women they knew. Wolf watched them in admiration.

He had never heard his mother complain. She and his sister had seen so much sorrow. They had suffered so much. Yet now they were laughing and talking. His sister was cuddling a baby that had been born that winter. Somehow that child's mother had kept the little girl alive.

How strong our women are. Without their strength, how could we men survive?

Wolf began to walk around the camp. He saw the faces of people he knew.

"Brother," a familiar voice shouted. Then Wolf was caught in the tight embrace of two young men whose familiar faces made his heart feel good. It was Too Tall and Too Short. They sat and spoke of small things, of good times they remembered. They did not talk about friends who were gone. Then his friends told him the big news.

"The two ve'hoe sisters are with us," Too Tall said.

"Stone Calf talked Medicine Water into giving them to him," Too Short added.

"He did more than talk," Too Tall said. "Stone Calf asked him if he was willing to fight the army on his own just to keep them."

Many messages had been sent by the army to Stone Calf and the other peace chiefs. They had been told that no surrender would be accepted until the captive girls were returned. Now they could finally do so.

We have arrived at a good time, Wolf thought. *Maybe we will finally find peace now. Maybe.*

The next day an army scout arrived. To Wolf's surprise, it was one of their own people. He had surrendered some time ago. Now he was working for the agency. His message was simple.

"The army men will come to your camp. They will arrange how you must surrender."

"That is good," Stone Calf replied. "Tell them we are ready."

When Lieutenant Colonel James Neill and Agent John Miles arrived, Stone Calf rode out to meet them.

"We will give up our weapons and horses," Stone Calf told them. "We will come into the agency and attend daily roll call. I will accompany a soldier ambulance back to the village to bring in the two white women."

Agent Miles nodded. He was pleased. But Lieutenant Colonel Neill showed Stone Calf neither respect nor trust. The white soldier leader's face turned red as he started to speak, and his words were as rough as the barking of a dog. He spoke so fast in English that Wolf could not catch all his words. But his tone was clear. He wanted to punish every Cheyenne. Punish them hard.

The war between us may be ending, Wolf thought, *but what is coming now may not really be peace.*

Several days passed. The Cheyenne camp was moved. They went to the place they were told to go, three miles from the Darlington Agency on the north fork of the Canadian River. White Horse and his Dog Soldiers were already there. They had come in along with their families two moons before. Their lodges were set up on the other side of the river.

A big band of ve'hoe soldiers was also there. Their camp was an arrow shot away along a hillside. There they had been living in dugouts that were cold and drafty and that looked much less comfortable than the Cheyenne tipis. The ve'hoes never spoke to an Indian unless they were giving orders. They never smiled.

Maybe they resent us for how they are being forced to live, Wolf thought. *They are not happy to have to watch our every movement.*

And that is what those soldiers did. They were always watching. Any time any Cheyenne tried to leave, the soldiers stopped them. They could not even go in to the agency for rations. Whatever food they got was doled out by those unfriendly soldiers. Things were not as good as Wolf had hoped.

He sat in front of his mother's lodge. There was nothing else to do.

But at least, he thought, *we have some food. At least no one is chasing us and trying to kill us. Perhaps we are finally safe.*

Or perhaps not.

Armed ve'hoe soldiers were marching into the camp.

"All men," they shouted. "All men!"

Wolf was pulled to his feet, pushed by a rifle barrel thrust into the middle of his back. All around him other men are being pushed ahead.

"We have done nothing wrong. Where are you taking us?" a young man next to Wolf shouted. His name was Black Horse.

In answer, Black Horse was pushed harder. Women and children were crying. Some held out their hands as if to pull their husbands and sons back to them. But no one resisted. What good would it do? Everyone wondered what was about to happen. Would they be herded together and then shot like the horses had been at Palo Duro?

Wolf saw something ahead. A large group of ve'hoe soldiers had gathered around a tent that had just been set up. The Cheyenne men were pushed inside the circle made by those white soldiers. A dark-skinned man came toward them. It was the Mexican man named Romero. He had long acted as an interpreter. He did not speak Cheyenne all that well. But everyone knew him to be a good man. They knew he tried to do his best.

Wolf had spoken often with Romero. He was beginning to consider him a friend. There was a worried look on the interpreter's face. Still, his voice was steady as he spoke.

"Ovana'xaeotse'. Calm down. Must all form line."

The men did the best they could to move into a line. It was a long one, made up of all the men and teenage boys from the Cheyenne camp.

One of the white soldier chiefs called out something. Two big hairy soldiers stepped forward and strode up purposefully to the line. They went straight to the place where Medicine Water stood. Without hesitating, they grabbed his arms. They pulled him so quickly out of the line that his feet scraped along the ground.

"What are they doing?" Medicine Water cried to Romero.

The Mexican interpreter shook his head. There was nothing he could do. The soldiers dragged Medicine Water to the door of that new tent and shoved him inside. Romero walked over to wait outside the closed flap.

Are they going to beat him in there? Torture him?

But Medicine Water was not in the tent long enough to be tortured. The two big soldiers shouldered their way out. They held Medicine Water even more roughly than before. They lifted him up so high that his toes could not touch the ground and carried him to face the long line of uncertain Cheyennes. They lowered him enough so that he could stand. But they did not let go of his arms. Medicine Water stood there on weak legs. He was shaking. He stared at the tent they had just dragged him from.

What fearful sight is in there?

The flap opened. Three people came out. One of them was the red-faced soldier chief Neill. His expression was grim as death. The other two were young white women. They wore cloaks as red as blood and hats with tall plumes. They approached the long line of Cheyenne men. None of the men recognized them at first. But some of the Cheyenne women did. They had followed as the men were dragged away and were watching from a little rise above them. They knew those two white women right away, despite their new clothing.

"Ah-ah-ah-ah! My daughter!" the wife of Long Back cried out.

That was when Wolf realized who they were. They were the two older white sisters who had been captives. Gah-dlin and Tso-fia.

Gah-dlin heard that cry. Wolf could tell by the way she stiffened for a moment. Maybe she remembered how well Long Back and his wife had treated her. They had adopted her as their daughter to protect her from Mochi.

But Gah-dlin did not turn toward Long Back's wife. She and her sister kept their eyes straight ahead. Their faces stayed still as stone as they walked toward the line of men.

"They are going to choose which of our men are to be killed," another woman shouted. It was Medicine Water's wife, Mochi. As one, all of the women except for Mochi began to moan and weep. They were fearful of what was about to happen.

Lieutenant Colonel Neill walked by the side of the two sisters. He had a piece of paper in his hand. But he was unsteady on his feet, and as he passed, Wolf could smell the whiskey on the white soldier chief's breath. His face was angry as a storm cloud. Another white man not in uniform walked up to join him. It was not Miles, the Indian agent. It was his assistant, a man whose name Wolf had not heard.

Romero came over to stand not far from Wolf. He whispered something out of the corner of his mouth. For a moment Wolf did not understand what had been said. Then it came to him.

They choose now.

The sisters walked down the long line of Cheyennes, peering closely at first one man and then another. Then Gah-dlin stopped.

She pointed her hand at Rising Bull. When she spoke her voice was loud and shook with emotion.

"She say he one help kill father," Romero whispered.

Neill barked an order. Two more soldiers stepped forward and marched Rising Bull over to stand by Medicine Water.

Once again, the sisters started walking. Then Gah-dlin stopped in front of Wolf. It seemed as if she was about to reach out her hand to touch him. Seeing her pause, several of the soldiers started forward, ready to pull him from the line.

Wolf looked up and caught her eyes. There was recognition in her gaze. But there was no anger. She turned back toward the soldiers and spoke a few words. The soldiers stepped back.

"She say you not one," Romero said softly in Cheyenne.

When the two red-cloaked young women had finished walking up and down the line, they had singled out no one other than Medicine Water and Rising Bull. Still red faced, Lieutenant Colonel Neill had asked them a question.

"Whose lodge did you stay in?"

In reply, Gah-dlin had pointed out Long Back. She had looked upset when Long Back was grabbed and taken over to stand by Medicine Water. But because she had identified him, he was now in the punishment line.

Then the sisters walked away from the men and pointed out Mochi among the women. Mochi had not turned away or tried to run. She had simply walked over to stand beside Medicine Water. Mochi's face was defiant as she stood by her husband. He still looked frightened, but her eyes were hard as black stones. It had not been hard for the sisters to pick her out. As soon as her husband was brought out of the tent and made to stand under guard, Mochi had moved up in front of all the women. Her arms folded, she had waited defiantly. She had not been wailing or crying like some of the others. She had been ready to share whatever punishment was to be given her husband.

Only four people had been identified. It was not enough to satisfy Neill. He looked angrier than before. He spoke to the two young women, his voice slurred by the whiskey.

Wolf watched, wondering what would happen next. Black Horse, who was standing to his right, tilted his head in Wolf's direction. The sun had moved far across the sky since they were first lined up. Black Horse was swaying slightly. His voice was dry as he whispered through cracked lips.

"I think Red-face wants them to choose more. But they will not choose innocent men like you and me."

Even as Black Horse softly spoke those words Tso-fia and Gahdlin shook their heads. They walked away from Neill and went back into the tent.

"He say pick more, they say no. They done," Romero whispered from behind Wolf.

Neill turned back toward the Cheyenne men. He held up the paper in his hands. Again he growled words so slurred with whiskey that Wolf could not understand them.

"No good," Romero said. "Need thirty-three men."

The red-faced lieutenant studied his list. Then he called out names. They were not the names of men who had done bad things. They were the names of leaders, of honorable men who spoke first for peace.

"Gray Head! Lean Bear! Heap of Birds! Eagle Head!"

Each man stepped forward when his name was called. Each walked with quiet dignity, head held up. Each joined those who were to be punished. Eight now. Still not enough to fill Red-face Neill's list.

Neill shouted out more barking words. The two white soldiers holding Medicine Water pulled him. Neill leaned close to Medicine Water's face. Then the lieutenant turned. He motioned to Romero.

"Come," Neill growled. "Translate."

Then he began to shout words at Medicine Water. Romero translated them into Cheyenne loud enough for all to hear.

"Medicine Water, you point out men who were with you. Now! Point out ones who kills ve'hoes! Men who takes horses! Men who burns wagons! Do now or we punish you bad."

Sweat formed on Medicine Water's brow. He nodded. The two soldiers let go of his arms. Medicine Water began his own walk along the line. He looked down as he did so. With his left hand on his forehead, he reached out with his right hand. He touched the shoulder of one man after another.

Lame Man, Chief Killer, Bear's Heart, Hailstone, Big Moccasin. All of them had been with him during the attack on the German family. Left Hand, Bear Killer, Soaring Eagle. Those three had taken part in the killing of a white man near Fort Wallace last year.

Then Medicine Water stopped. Red-face Neill snarled more dog words at him. Medicine Water shook his head.

"Hena'haahnehe," Medicine Water said in a soft voice.

"He say," Romero translated, "that is it. Finished."

Seventeen. Much fewer than the thirty-three the paper had told him to take. The lieutenant shouted and waved his arms. But Medicine Water did not look up at him.

Perhaps, Wolf thought, *I will not be among those chosen to be killed after all.*

It was growing dark. Wolf no longer felt his legs beneath him. He had been standing still a long time, longer than he had ever stood without moving. He looked over at Black Horse. He, too, looked ready to collapse. But the look on his face was hopeful.

Red-face Neill was unsteady, too. He swayed in the growing dark like a tree being moved by the wind. He staggered forward a step. Then he caught himself. He nodded, straightened his shoulders. Once again he barked out words. Then he made a sweeping gesture with his left hand and walked away.

More ve'hoe soldiers stepped up. They moved down the line and pointed fingers at one man after another as if counting horses or cows. One of them tapped Wolf's shoulder. Another placed his palm on Black Horse's chest. The two of them were grabbed. Next to them other men were being pulled out. As they were marched toward the line of condemned men, Romero spoke to Wolf.

"I sorry," Romero said in Cheyenne. "He say just cut off sixteen from right of line."

DEATH WENT TO THE SINNER'S HOUSE.
COME AND GO WITH ME, DEATH SAID.
AND THE SINNER CRIED OUT, I'M NOT READY TO GO.
I GOT NO TRAVELING SHOES.

DEATH WENT TO THE GAMBLER'S HOUSE.
COME AND GO WITH ME, DEATH SAID.
AND THE GAMBLER CRIED OUT,
I'M NOT READY TO GO. I GOT NO TRAVELING SHOES.

DEATH WENT TO THE PREACHER'S HOUSE.
COME AND GO WITH ME, DEATH SAID.
AND THE PREACHER CRIED OUT, I AM READY TO GO.
I HAVE GOT MY TRAVELING SHOES.

AND OLD DEATH, HE SAID,
PREACHER, I WILL SEE YOU LATER.

THE FAT HITS
THE FIRE

Hampton Academy
March 3, 1875

My dear Washington,
I trust that you are well. I received your last letter. It was as fine an epistle as any maid ever received from her knight. Some of your words are pure poetry.

Be assured that I am tip-top and as happy as can be. Indeed, I am more pleased with my life as a student than I had dreamt I would be. Each day in classes new vistas open to me, and I feel as the poet Keats must have felt on his peak in Darien.

The rules are quite strict about the separation of the male and female students. We have our own dormitory. So you need not worry about some dusky Othello stealing my heart, my dear friend. Of course that would not happen under any circumstance.

Now we must each follow our paths until they come together, as I know they shall, in the future we can share together. You shall pursue your life as a cavalryman and I as a student. Though I foresee a time when the student life shall also be yours.

Oh, so many, many things are now possible in this new land our nation has become.

Do you realize what it means that on March 1st, a Civil Rights Act was passed by Congress and signed into law by our president? We are now guaranteed equal rights in public places. It even prohibits the practice of excluding negroes from jury duty! Think of what this fine new law shall mean for us and for our children.

I will close now. Take care of yourself and know you are ever in my thoughts.

Always,
Your Bethany

Our children!

Wash sat on his cot in the barracks and read those lines again. He held the letter in his hand as reverently as he'd hold a Bible. Bethany actually wrote those words. And though he had more than a year to go before his hitch in the 10th was over, a whole new future suddenly seemed so close. The thought of raising a family of his own with Bethany was not just a distant dream. It could be real. And it would be in a land where new laws meant that a black man had as many rights as any white man.

That put so broad a smile on Wash's face that Josh leaned over from his own cot and poked him.

"Man," Josh said, "you look like the old cat that swallowed the canary bird. Why you so happy?"

Before Wash could answer, Charley came running in.

"They are chaining up the Cheyennes! Come on, boys. Let's go watch the show."

The thirty Cheyenne men selected for the punishment of exile to far-off Florida were being led to the post blacksmith just outside the guardhouse. The 5th Infantry under Captain Andrew Bennett was in charge of the band of prisoners.

Wash bit his lip. Those white boys of the 5th seemed bored by the goings-on. They were joking with each other, hardly even looking at their prisoners. That was a fool way to act. They might figure the downcast Indians were no more than whipped dogs. But any Buffalo Soldiers who'd chased those Cheyennes to hell knew that was far from true. Every one of those those pitiful-looking Indians was tough as leather. A hell of a lot more wolf than dog. And while you might easily tie a dog, a wolf could prove to be a whole different animal to chain.

The thought of those men being chained troubled Wash. It brought an image to his mind, one that had been conjured up by his father's stories of how their ancestor came to this land. Great-Grampa Hausaman placed in shackles on the banks of the River Niger and then thrown into the stinking hull of a slave ship.

Here the one waiting to do the chaining was named Wesley. Just Wesley. That was the only name anyone ever called him. The post blacksmith, Wesley was a black man like the troopers of the 10th. But he was a civilian employee with no fighting experience, a man who knew little of Indians and seemed oblivious to the tension that Wash could feel in the way those men were holding themselves. You'd think Wesley was just about to shoe a bunch of docile old nags rather than hammer chains onto the legs of some of the fiercest fighters these plains had ever seen.

But as the blacksmith put the chains on the first man in that line of thirty, Wash had to admit to himself that Wesley knew his job. There was a quiet economy of movement in the way Wesley worked. He handled his tools with an ease of motion that came only from long years of doing that sort of work. A skinny Cheyenne man who looked to be made of brown leather stretched over bone was brought up to the blacksmith. As Wesley tapped his hammer on the anvil with one hand, he fitted the manacle around the ankle with the other. Without looking back, he grabbed a rivet, positioned it. Then, with one swift hard hit, he drove it home.

"Recognize that Indian just got chained?" Charley said.

"Lean Bear?"

"Ah-yup," Charley nodded. "Don't look like much now, does he?"

Lean Bear. One of the big chiefs. Despite his being so small and thin, he looked dignified. His back was straight. But the look on his face was such a mixture of sorrow and pride it made Wash want to cry.

Lean Bear bent over and picked up the big iron ball linked to his leg iron as if it was no heavier than one of the baseballs the men threw around in their games at the post. Then the old chief shuffled back into line as the next man stepped up to be shackled.

All the while Wesley kept a rhythm going with his hammer against the anvil.

Like some old song from Africa, Wash thought.

It made a strange sort of music along with the clanking of their chains as men shuffled off.

Did Great-Grampa Hausaman hear this same music when he was chained and marching down to the coast where the slave ships waited, holds like open mouths, hungry to swallow him and his people?

The knot in Wash's stomach felt big as a fist.

Far as Wesley was concerned, he was just doing his job. No irony about a black man putting slave irons on a brown-skinned man.

Another Indian was being led up. Wesley grasped his leg to position it.

Could it be?

It was. That Cheyenne now having his ball and chain fastened on was a young man Wash recognized. For a moment Wash felt as if he was back in that canyon, sharing the sight of those seven buffalo disappearing like spirits into the waterfall.

Wash blinked his eyes and the vision faded. But Wolf still stood there, his gaze now meeting Wash's. It was like seeing the face of someone you know in the window of a train on another track, knowing you're both about to be carried off in different directions by forces over which you have no control.

Wolf lifted one eyebrow. It was almost as if he was about to laugh at the strangeness of it all. Wash almost raised a hand in greeting. Wolf looked down as Wesley drove in the pin to fasten the irons. Then he shuffled off, not looking back.

And now there was just one last prisoner to put into irons. From the look on his face, he was more than just unhappy at the prospect. He looked to be one of those young warriors who would sooner die in battle than be chained. One who would gladly trade a ball and chain for a bullet in the breast. He was trying to hold back, digging his heels into the dirt. The two big men of the 5th on either side of him pushed him forward.

"Look at that one," Josh said. "Like a horse that's caught the scent of the branding iron!"

Black Horse. That was the man's name. Wash had heard it called out. The group of Cheyenne women who'd been watching from a distance were getting more upset as Black Horse struggled. Up to then those women had just been moaning and wailing. But now they were starting to sing. Wash had no idea what the actual words were, they being in Cheyenne, but he could guess the meaning. Some sort of warrior song, the sort that urges a man to fight like a wolf rather than be tied up like a dog. The white soldiers were paying the women no mind—and that was foolish. Nothing could get an Indian man stirred up to a boil faster than being embarrassed in front of his women.

Couldn't any of the white officers lolling about and smiling with Lieutenant Colonel Neill see what was going on? Wash thought about speaking a word of warning. But what good would his saying anything do? He was no more than a private, a man who was supposed to keep his mouth shut in front of his superiors, to say nothing of the fact that he was a colored soldier and therefore expected to be doubly silent. Plus the fact that the lieutenant colonel disliked and mistrusted black soldiers only a little less than he did the Indians.

That was one of the reasons why no black man was now on guard, just the bored and complacent white soldiers of the 5th—despite the fact that the two companies of Buffalo Soldiers, D and M, were the ones who'd been sent there to escort those same prisoners back to Fort Sill.

I just hope nothing goes wrong, Wash thought.

And then something did.

As Wesley raised his hammer to drive in the rivet, Black Horse pulled his leg free of the manacle. With that same leg he booted the surprised blacksmith in the chest, knocking him head over heels. Quick as a panther, Black Horse leaped over the man and began to run. The singing of the Cheyenne women turned into ululating cries as the fugitive sprinted toward the river. Cross over that and he'd get to White Horse's camp, only half a mile away.

But, Wash thought, *he'll never make it. All you need is a few men on horses to head him off.*

Black Horse was only one man, fleeing in fear of being chained. It should have been easy to catch him. Unless someone did the wrong thing.

And then someone did. More than one someone. Those surprised white men of the 5th Infantry raised their guns and started shooting. That was bad enough. But even worse, the white soldiers were so excited that their bullets mostly flew over Black Horse's head. And where were those rounds heading? Right toward White Horse's camp.

A bullet from a .45 rifle could travel a mile and still be lethal. And that was just what those stray rounds did. They ripped through the lodges of Dog Soldiers, the fiercest fighters of the Cheyennes. Not knowing what was going on, what were the people of White Horse's camp to believe? Just like those in many a peaceful Cheyenne village in the past, they assumed they were under attack. The angry shouts and desperate screams coming out of White Horse's camp were proof of that.

But the soldiers of the 5th paid no attention. They just keep reloading and firing at Black Horse as fast as they could, still sending most of their shots right into the Dog Soldier camp. Black Horse suddenly fell, finally struck by what surely must have been a mortal wound. His legs kicked, and then he lay still. The fight was over for him.

An arrow came arcing out from White Horse's camp. It dove like a hawk and *thunk!* hit a soldier of the 5th in the shoulder. A flock of arrows followed the first. Those Cheyenne Dog Soldiers had turned in their guns, but some had kept their war bows. They were taking the fight to the men they believed were trying to wipe them out like they had at Sand Creek and the Washita.

Wash, Josh, and Charley watched it all, stunned. They were far enough back to be out of arrow range, so they didn't move. Better in the middle of the craziness to stay still and wait for orders.

Most of the men of the 5th were still firing or ducking arrows. Some of the white soldiers, though, were showing enough sense to herd the manacled Cheyennes back into the stockade. At least those chained-up Indians would not be taking part in the fight begun for no good reason.

But I'd bet a million that is not going to be true for us, Wash thought.

And sure enough, just as he thought that, a bugle began sounding boots and saddles.

"Come on," Josh yelled, grabbing Wash's arm.

The three of them ran for the barracks.

By the time they had formed up with their companies, the fight had moved across the river. The Buffalo Soldiers rode toward White Horse's village. The Dog Soldiers had retreated, the women and children going first, the men following behind, keeping their faces to the army and firing as they fell back. The only weapons the Indians used were their bows and arrows. But even though they were outgunned, they had managed to slow the advance of the 5th Infantry and the 6th Cavalry.

Wash's hands were trembling—not from fear but from the tension that came before going into a fight. He held steady to the reins as he guided Blaze down the bank into the water. With Charley to his right and Josh to his left he splashed across the North Canadian in good order with the other men of Companies D and M.

They trotted through the deserted village, empty save for the body of a single Cheyenne warrior, his hands empty of any weapon, lying dead halfway out the door of a lodge. The acid odor of gunpowder was in the air, as was the smell of burning. One of the lodges they passed was on fire, flames licking up its leather sides. Volley after volley of gunshots could be heard from the sand hills ahead of them.

Wash found himself wishing that Sergeant Brown was with them and not back at Fort Sill. He felt nearly naked going into a fight without the sergeant's good sense to guide them.

"Up there," Charley hollered.

In the distance where the sand hills started, they could see men of the 6th dismounting and advancing on foot toward where the Indians had to be hiding. Unlike the nervous guards who had started the whole ruckus, the 6th cavalrymen were holding their guns at the ready and not yet firing. And no arrows were coming toward them.

"Dang it," Charley said in a disappointed voice. "Just when I thought we was going to have a real fight for once. Them Cheyennes must be out of arrows. This shindig'll be over before we get a chance to get into it."

Suddenly a dozen flashes of fire came from the hills. The sounds of those gunshots fired by the Cheyenne Dog Soldiers reached them a second later.

"Appears they did not turn in all their rifles after all," Josh said in a laconic voice.

The 6th cavalrymen had been totally taken by surprise by the fact that the Indians had dug up more than the hatchet. In those sand hills away from their village they had buried as many rifles as they had turned in when they surrendered. The men of the 6th quickly retreated, firing back at their hidden enemies.

When they reached the position where the men of the 10th waited, the cavalrymen of the 6th were shaken but appeared unhurt. Not a one of them seemed to have been hit. That didn't surprise

Wash. Taking careful aim never seemed to be a strong point in any battle, whether those shooting were Indians or army men.

"We are in it now, boys," someone shouted. It was Captain Alexander Keyes, one of the two white officers in command of companies D and M. "Dismount. Form up with the 6th."

Things began to happen fast. Private Hamms blew the signal to charge. And just like that they were running hard at the sand hills, bullets whickering around them, everyone hollering at the top of their lungs and shooting. Then, almost at the same moment, they were answering the call to retreat, taking withering fire from the Cheyennes, whose aim had improved. Captain Keyes took stock. A dozen men wounded, though none that serious. Six of them still able to keep up the fight while the others were taken to the rear.

"Get ready again, boys," Keyes yelled.

Wash looked around. Josh to his left, Charley to his right. All three of them untouched.

So far.

Hamms sounded the bugle once more. They charged on foot again, shooting at enemies where all they could see were rifle barrels. The Dog Soldiers were well dug in to pits in the sand, unlike the black cavalrymen, who were out in the open. And this time the response from the Cheyennes was even more accurate. Four more men were wounded, two so bad that they had to be carried back when retreat was sounded once more.

Wash spat sand out of his mouth. He wiped it from his eyes where the grit was being carried down with the sweat now soaking him from head to boots. Charley and Josh were still by his side, none them hurt but all of them bone tired. Though it had seemed to happen in a matter of heartbeats, the fight had now been going on for hours. The sun is was just a double hand's width from setting.

"Here come the coffee mill!" somebody yelled.

Wash turned to look. Lieutenant Colonel Neill had finally arrived and brought with him a Gatling gun, the kind of weapon that could spit out a stream of bullets as fast as the gunner could turn the crank.

Wash ducked down as the gun's barrel was swung to fire over the heads of the members of the two Buffalo Soldier companies.

"Fire!"

BAT-TAT-TAT-TAT-TAT-TAT!

Raking the dunes, .45 caliber rounds sent spurts of sand ten feet into the air. Impressive as it looked, Wash suspected those bullets were doing little more than rearranging the surface. The Indians had to all be scrunched down low in those deep holes they'd dug.

"Advance on foot," Neill shouted from his position back by the gun, waving his saber.

What?

Captain William Rafferty and his men of the 6th began to stand and start forward. Neill gestured for the white troopers to stay put.

Charley poked Josh with his elbow. "Guess who they goin' to send in instead of them white boys?"

Rafferty looked back toward Neill.

"More suppressing fire, sir?" Rafferty called out.

A second longer burst answered him from the Gatling gun. It raked back and forth, back and forth across the Indians' lines, sending sprays of sand into the air.

BAT-TAT-TAT-TAT-TAT-TAT! BAT-TAT-TAT-TAT-TAT-TAT!

Wash doubted that it had any more effect than the rounds fired before. The sand was absorbing most if not all of the rounds.

Lieutenant Colonel Neill waved his arms to get the captains' attention. He shouted so loud that Wash could see his face turn red—even from as far away and safe from the fighting as Neill was standing.

"Stand up the 10th! Move them forward!"

Moving again, moving past the 6th into the heat of the battle. More and more flashes came from the Cheyenne guns in the dunes. But the men of D and M companies didn't stop. They ran faster as more bullets came at them.

Then a bullet whizzed past Wash's head—in the wrong direction! Others followed. The shots were coming not from the Cheyenne guns in front, but the rifles of the white 6th cavalrymen behind him.

Charley was just ahead of him. Wash tried to call out a warning, tried to tell him to get down. The bullet hit Charley in the back and spun him around. He fell awkwardly on his side twenty feet away.

"Josh, Charley's hit!" Wash yelled.

Then a bullet with his name on it thudded into the back of Wash's hip. It was like being struck by a giant hammer. It dropped him to his knees, but he still managed to crawl forward to reach Charley's side. He rolled him over. Charley's eyes were open, but all the laughter was gone from them. The wound in his chest where the bullet had exited was as big as Wash's fist. No blood pulsed out of it. The big happy heart that the .45 bullet had passed through was no longer beating.

Wash tried to say something, tried to call Charley back to life. But no words come out of his mouth. Instead, something hit him hard on the side of his own head. The whole world turned gray around him as he fell forward into a hole so deep that it had no bottom.

He opened his eyes when he heard the sound of thunder. The sandy battlefield was gone. He was on a cot. When he tried to move, a pain stabbed him in his hip that felt like he was being pierced by a bayonet. Still, he tried to sit up.

Two hands gently pressed him back down.

"Wash, you stay still," a voice said. It was Josh. "You got hit twice. One was just a crease on your head. That knocked you out. Other was a bullet hit you low down, right where you sits. Old Saw-bones dug that one out. Says you might be stiff a while, but you can get back in the saddle in a month or so. So you going to be all right."

"Charley?" Wash asked.

Another roll of thunder from outside made Josh pause before he answered. "You know," he said.

"I know." Wash's voice caught in his throat. He swallowed, took a breath. "Wasn't Indians."

Josh sighed and nodded. "Them white boys in the 6th never did like us darkies. Captains say it just happens sometimes. Accidental-like. We stood up when we should have kept down." He shakes his head. "Not a thing we can do about it."

Rain began beating hard on top of the roof. Wash looked around. A dozen or more other wounded men lay in the cots around him. It was hard to tell by the lantern light whether they were black men or white.

"How many?" Wash asked.

"Nineteen casualties," Josh said. "Most from our 10th."

They listened to the sound of the rain.

"Want to know what happened in the fight?" Josh finally asked.

"I suppose."

"We never was able to break through. Old Neill, he called up every available man, had us all dig in around the Cheyennes' positions. By then it was dark and the storm was coming, way bigger than this little one hitting us now. So much thunder you'd a thought the sky was going to war. Rain so hard you could not make out your own hand at the end of your arm. Next morning, Neill orders us to charge. And all we find is empty rifle pits."

Josh let out a bitter chuckle. "Ever' one of them Indians snuck out during the night and got away. Most of them just went back to the other Indian camps near the agency. And even with all that shooting, looks as if there was not but three Indians killed."

Of that I'm glad, Wash thought. Then the thought of his best friend with his heart blown out came to him once more. His eyes filled up with tears.

"Goddamn it all," he managed to choke out.

"Yessir," Josh said. "That does about sum it up."

AS LONG AS THE SACRED ARROWS WERE TREATED
WITH PROPER RESPECT, THEY PROTECTED THE PEOPLE.
THEY WERE CARRIED ON THE BACK OF THE WIFE
OF EACH ARROW KEEPER WHO CAME AFTER SWEET MEDICINE.
WHEN THE PROPER CEREMONIES WERE CARRIED OUT
AND THE ARROW RENEWED, THE PEOPLE HAD PLENTY OF
BUFFALO. WHEN THE PROPER RITUAL WAS DONE BEFORE
GOING INTO BATTLE AGAINST THEIR ENEMIES AND
THE ARROWS WERE CARRIED IN A CERTAIN WAY ON THE LANCE
OF A CHOSEN WARRIOR, THEY BROUGHT THE PEOPLE VICTORY.

THEN CAME THE SUMMER OF THE YEAR THE VE'HOES CALL 1830.
THAT SUMMER, IN THE MOON WHEN THE WILD CHERRIES WERE
RIPE, THE PEOPLE WENT TO TAKE REVENGE AGAINST THEIR OLD
ENEMIES THE PAWNEES. WHITE THUNDER WAS ARROW KEEPER.
HE AND HIS WIFE HAD THEIR HANDS AND FACES PAINTED RED WITH
THE SPIRITUAL PAINT. HIS WIFE CARRIED THE BUNDLE WITH THE
SACRED ARROWS UPON HER BACK. ALL WAS AS IT SHOULD BE.

BUT WHEN THE CHEYENNE WARRIORS CAME UPON THE PAWNEE
VILLAGE, THEY WERE IMPATIENT TO ATTACK. THEY DID NOT GIVE
WHITE THUNDER TIME TO DO THE PROPER CEREMONIES THAT
WOULD HAVE BLINDED THE ENEMIES. THERE WAS NO TIME FOR
HIM TO REVERENTLY PLACE THE SACRED ARROWS ON THE BED
OF WHITE SAGE, TO CHANT THE SONG:

THERE YOU LIE HELPLESS, EASY TO BE WIPED OUT.

THE WARRIORS WERE IN SUCH A HURRY THAT
THE ARROW KEEPER WAS UNABLE TO DANCE WITH HIS LEFT
FOOT EXTENDED, KEEPING TIME TO THAT CHANT, WITH ALL OF
THE WARRIORS BEHIND HIM IN A LINE AS HE THRUST THE POINTS
OF THE SACRED ARROWS TOWARD THE ENEMY.

NONE OF THAT WAS DONE, NOR ANY OTHER PARTS OF
THE ANCIENT RITUAL SWEET MEDICINE HAD TAUGHT.

INSTEAD, BULL, THE WARRIOR PRIEST CHOSEN TO LEAD
THE CHARGE, RODE UP TO THE ARROW KEEPER.
HE WAS IN A BIG HURRY. HE SHOULD HAVE BEEN LEADING,
BUT THE OTHER CHEYENNE WARRIORS HAD CHARGED AHEAD
OF HIM AND NOW HE HAD TO CATCH UP.

HE THRUST HIS LANCE TOWARD THE ARROW KEEPER.
"QUICK! TIE THE BUNDLE TO THE END OF THIS," HE SAID.

THAT, TOO, WAS WRONG. THE ARROWS SHOULD HAVE BEEN
TIED IN TWO SEPARATE PAIRS, THE MAN ARROWS TOGETHER
AND THE BUFFALO ARROWS TOGETHER. INSTEAD,
ALL FOUR SACRED ARROWS WERE TIED TOGETHER
AT THE END OF THE LANCE.

THEN BULL RUSHED INTO THE BATTLE.

A SINGLE PAWNEE MAN SAT ON A BUFFALO ROBE
IN FRONT OF THE OTHER ENEMIES. HE WAS SICK AND
HAD DECIDED THIS WAS A GOOD DAY TO DIE.
HE WAS SINGING HIS DEATH SONG. OTHER CHEYENNES
HAD ALREADY STRUCK THAT SICK MAN WITH THEIR COUP STICKS
AS THEY RODE BY HIM. THERE WAS NO NEED FOR
BULL TO RIDE AT THAT MAN AND TRY TO COUNT COUP.
BUT BULL DID JUST THAT, AND AS HE SWUNG HIS LANCE
AT THE PAWNEE, THE SICK MAN TURNED HIS BODY TO AVOID
BEING HIT, GRABBED THAT LANCE TIGHT, AND TORE IT
OUT OF BULL'S GRASP, TAKING THE SACRED ARROWS.

"COME HERE AND TAKE THIS," HE SHOUTED TO
THE OTHER PAWNEES. "HERE IS SOMETHING WONDERFUL."

HEARING HIS WORDS, THE OTHER PAWNEES RACED UP
TO SURROUND HIM. THE CHEYENNES COULD NOT GET THERE
IN TIME. THE SACRED ARROW BUNDLE WAS PLACED IN
THE HANDS OF BIG EAGLE, THE PAWNEE CHIEF, WHO BRANDISHED
THEM AS HE CHARGED AT THE DEEPLY SHAKEN CHEYENNES.

THE SACRED ARROWS AND THAT BATTLE BOTH WERE LOST
THAT DAY. AND THOUGH THE PEOPLE MOURNED THE DEATH OF
THE MEN WHO FELL THAT DAY, THEY MOURNED THE LOSS OF
SWEET MEDICINE'S GIFT EVEN MORE.

NEW ARROWS WERE PREPARED TO TAKE THE PLACE OF
THOSE FOUR THAT WERE LOST. BUT MANY FELT THAT
THEY WERE NOT THE SAME. YEARS LATER, WHITE THUNDER
RISKED HIS LIFE TO TRAVEL WITH ONLY HIS WIFE, OLD BARK,
BY HIS SIDE, TO THE LODGES OF THEIR ENEMIES.

HE BEGGED THE PAWNEES FOR THE RETURN OF THE SACRED
ARROWS. BIG EAGLE TOOK PITY AND GAVE BACK ONE OF
THE BUFFALO ARROWS. BUT HE KEPT THE OTHER THREE.
TWO YEARS LATER, THE GREAT FRIENDS OF THE CHEYENNES,
THE LAKOTAS, ATTACKED A PAWNEE VILLAGE AND RECOVERED
ONE OF THE MAN ARROWS, WHICH THEY BOUGHT BACK TO
THE PEOPLE. BUT THE OTHER TWO ARROWS REMAINED IN
THE HANDS OF THE PAWNEES AND ARE THERE TO THIS DAY.

FROM THAT DAY ON, THE CHEYENNE PEOPLE BEGAN TO SUFFER
BAD LUCK. WITHOUT THEIR SACRED ARROWS, MANY SAY,
THEIR WAY OF LIFE WAS DOOMED TO END.

FORT MARION

"How is this?"

Wolf added a few more lines to the picture he was drawing and then held it up for Zo-tom to see.

The stocky young Kiowa man leaned closer to study the picture carefully, tracing the outlines of the large black horse with the star on its chest and the small dark-skinned man in a cavalry uniform on the animal's back.

"This is a well-rendered drawing," he finally said—in English, of course. "Quite commendable, George."

"Thank you, Paul," Wolf replied, using his friend's American name just as Zo-tom had used his. "That is most kind of you."

One of the first things that they had been told to do after arriving at their place of captivity in Florida was to accept white man names. Each of them had been offered several choices. George was the one Wolf took. It appealed to his sense of humor. He had learned by then that George was the name of the first of the White Fathers, the one for whom the city of Washington had been named.

It pleased Wolf, or rather George, to hear such words of praise from his Kiowa companions. Though he had not known him before they became prisoners of war, Zo-tom—Paul, that is—had become one of his best friends. The two of them sat together often as they did now, high on the battlements of the old fort, their feet dangling over the side, the sandy beach and the endless stretch of saltwater below them.

Paul was perhaps the best artist among the seventy-two Indians being held at Fort Marion. When it had been suggested to them months ago that they might like to draw pictures of their experiences, he had been one of the first to pick up the crayons and paper and begin. His pictures of their strange journey, of the train in which they had ridden, the cities they had passed through, were as clear and accurate as any of the images held in Wolf's own memories of that painful trip.

And like Wolf, Paul had been proving himself to be a good student. Their new ability to speak and write English pleased their teacher, Miss Sarah Mather, so much that she often praised them to Captain Pratt.

Paul gently placed the side of his hand on the central figure Wolf had drawn, a young Cheyenne man clutching his side and falling as white soldiers fired their guns at him.

"Who is this fellow here?"

"His name was Black Horse."

"Did he succumb to his injuries?"

Wolf shrugged his shoulders. He did not know. Black Horse falling to the ground was the last he saw of the fight that took place on the day he was chained. He had been hustled away with the other Cheyenne prisoners too quickly to know if Black Horse had lived or died there. All he could do was listen to the sounds of guns being fired, the shouts of men, the galloping of horses' hooves as White Horse's Dog Soldiers fought like grizzly bears. It had been much later—just before they started the train journey to Florida—that he was told of how they fought. Only three Cheyennes had been killed there. A Gatling gun had been fired at them that shot off thousands of bullets, but the sand hills had swallowed up those bullets. The land itself had been determined to protect his people.

Many ve'hoe soldiers had been hurt in that battle, struck by Cheyenne arrows and bullets. Wolf hoped his little Buffalo Soldier was not among those hurt or killed. He wondered sometimes what had happened to him. It was strange how their lives had kept meeting.

As he and Paul sat together silently, Wolf thought about what had happened after that fight at the sand hills.

One of their camps, about sixty people led by Little Bull, heard the fight at the agency and fled north. The army was sent after those poor frightened people. Red-face Neill and his soldiers, guided by three white buffalo hunters, led the pursuit. They attacked Little Bull's camp at daybreak near Sappa Creek. Half of the people got to the pony herd and escaped. Those who were left, seven men and twenty women and children, did not get away. They were massacred near that creek of dark water.

The hide hunters and the soldiers stripped their bodies of what few valuables they had. They set fire to the lodges and threw in the bodies of the people. Some of the women and children were still alive when they were thrown into the flames. It was a terrible thing.

Word of what happened at Sappa Creek had reached them as they were being chained into wagons with the other condemned. Sixty-nine men in all. Kiowas, Comanches, Arapahoes, Cheyennes, and one unlucky Caddo. With them were two women and one small girl. Mochi was one of the women. The other was Pe-ah-in, who was not a prisoner. But she and her nine-year-old daughter had refused to be parted from her Comanche husband, Black Horse.

At that time, as the interpreter Romero was telling them the story of Sappa Creek, they were all sure that they were being taken to be hung. Instead, they had been loaded on a train. Then, through the interpreter, a soldier chief had spoken to them. He was a man some of them had seen before, a white officer of the Buffalo Soldiers.

"This man," Romero said, "he say name Captain Pratt. He say he be fair with you if you behave good. He also say tell you this. You be sent far away. So far even if you escape no way you ever find way back home."

No one had taken the news of the deaths at Sappa Creek harder than Lean Bear and Gray Head. Some of those who had died had been in Gray Head's camp. Wolf saw the despair on the faces of the old peace chiefs.

"I have lived too long," Gray Head said.

Wolf had understood his words. Young as he was, there were times when he found himself wishing that he, too, had died. All he had known since he was young was war. All he had known were hard times, times of running and starving and seeing those closest to him suffer and die. Yet he loved his land and his people. To be sent away from those things he loved was worse than dying.

The first place they had been taken was a big army camp called Fort Leavenworth. There they had been placed in cells. On Wolf's second day there, he had been walking through the cell block with Eagle Head, another of the Cheyenne leaders, when they had heard the sound of choking. Gray Head was trying to hang himself from the iron bars of the cell window. Wolf was the one who lifted him up while others untied the strip of blanket he had used as a noose.

"Uncle," they had begged him, "please do not leave us."

"I hear what you are saying," he had replied. But the look in his eyes was no less sad than it had been. Gray Head no longer wished to live.

Two days later, Lean Bear stabbed himself many times with a small knife he had managed to find. The soldiers took the knife from him before he killed himself, but his wounds had been so many he had not been put back on the train to continue the long journey into exile. And not long after that, whether from his wounds or his wish to join his loved ones in the next life, Lean Bear had died.

The rest of them had been on the train for many days. By the seventh day they had traveled so far that the land and the trees outside the partly open windows were strange to them. The air was so humid that it was hard to breathe. The sweat never dried on their faces, even after darkness fell.

Wolf was sitting next to Gray Head when Captain Pratt came walking through their car. Captain Pratt's young son was with him.

Although the Indian captives had been forced to leave their wives and children behind, the captain's wife and his children were with him on the trip.

"My son," Pratt said to his boy, "this fine old man is a great chief."

Then he had addressed Gray Head.

"This is my son."

Gray Head had looked at Pratt's son. He gently touched him on the shoulder. "He is a fine boy," Gray Head said. "He is the age one of my grandsons would have been."

Pratt smiled at that. He had heard the compliment for his son. But he had not understood that Gray Head was comparing his boy with a grandson killed by white men.

"Mason will be with us all in Florida," Pratt said. "Seeing him will remind you of the family you have left behind."

Then he stood up and left the car with his son, leaving Gray Head alone with his thoughts of the family he would not see again in this life.

Gray Head waited until Pratt was gone. Then he leaned his shoulder against Wolf. "Nephew," he said, his voice too soft for anyone else to hear, "I am going to join my family." His hand rested on Wolf's arm for a moment. "Do not try to stop me."

Wolf's voice caught in his throat. Tears came to his eyes as the old man lifted his hand from his arm. Wolf covered his head with his blanket. He did not see him squeeze through the open window, but he knew what was happening. He knew what would happen next.

Almost immediately, cries came from first one soldier and then another.

"Prisoner escaping!"

"Prisoner escaping!"

Wolf did not move. Nor did any of the other prisoners. He felt the train stop. He heard other white soldiers shouting. Among them, Captain Pratt's voice was the loudest of all.

"Do not shoot," he was shouting. "Do not shoot!"

There was much commotion. The soldiers could not find Gray Head. He was concealed somewhere in the palmetto trees along the track. Maybe he would escape. Maybe, even though they had traveled more than a thousand miles, he could find his way back home.

The train started up again. Wolf felt more hope. It seemed they were giving up the search. But he was wrong. Captain Pratt had ordered a small group of soldiers to get off the train and wait.

The sound of a rifle shot came before the train picked up much speed. The train stopped again. More voices were shouting.

"We have him!"

"We got him!"

Two soldiers came into the car carrying a limp body between them. It was Gray Head. He had been shot through the chest but was still breathing.

Everyone had been ordered to stay in their seats, but Wolf was close enough to hear.

"It is good," Gray Head whispered, his voice weakened from the great wound. "I have wanted to die ever since I was chained and taken from home. Send a message to my wife and daughter."

Then he died.

Because of Lean Bear and Gray Head, the soldiers became more vigilant. When the Indian captives finally arrived at the great stone house by the sea, the soldiers kept close watch. They were afraid others might attempt to escape.

And some did, though not by running. Sun, a Kiowa, killed himself not long after they arrived. Next was Mamanti, the great Kiowa medicine man. He had foretold his own death. Then Straightening-an-Arrow passed into the spirit world.

Captain Pratt had worried that more would follow them. So he had spoken words of encouragement "If you behave, if you are good, you may have a chance to see your families one day. But you can do so only if you walk this new road I have made for you. Do as I say, and you will be given more freedom."

They had tried then to follow his rules. They did so even though most of them doubted his word. What white man had ever made any promise that he kept? They worked to repair the old fort. They fixed its walls. They painted and cleaned it so that green slime no longer dropped from the ceilings and the floors were clean. And, to their surprise, just as he had promised, Captain Pratt allowed them more freedom.

They were allowed to walk on the sandy ground by the water that went on forever. There they picked up shells and sea beans. They were allowed to trade those shells and beans for money to people who made them into necklaces. They were then allowed to buy food and things to wear with the money they earned.

Captain Pratt had been pleased. Then he had taught them how to dress like soldiers. He gave them uniforms. He showed them how to march together and follow commands. To his surprise, Wolf had found it was fun. Moving together and stomping their feet on the ground was a bit like dancing. And to dress and act as a warrior again, even a ve'hoe warrior, was pleasing.

Captain Pratt had led them in Bible study. The elderly Miss Mather, who was brought in soon after when Pratt saw how quickly his Indian charges learned, was a kind and patient teacher. Soon the men were in the classroom every day, learning to read and write and do arithmetic. And then they had been given paper and crayons and told to draw pictures of what they remembered.

Like the one that Paul and Wolf were now looking at, the second picture Wolf had drawn that day. It showed an old Cheyenne man being shot by white soldiers.

Wolf held the drawing up in front of him. The warm wind from the sea made it ripple in his hand, almost as if the figure in it was trying to escape. He grasped the corners of the paper and pulled. The drawing tore in half.

Paul said nothing. Wolf put the two halves together and tore them again. He kept doing it until the pieces were smaller than the little seashells they collected from the beach. He opened his hands to the wind. He and Paul watched as the pieces of pale paper swirled away like snowflakes in the wind.

Wolf walked down the stone steps. A white soldier stood at the bottom, leaning against the wall. He simply nodded as Wolf, dressed in a uniform similar to his own, walked by and went through the gate.

Then Wolf heard a child's voice calling.

"George, George!"

It was Captain Pratt's daughter, Nana. She waved at him from one of the benches that had been placed for people to sit on and watch the waves.

"George! Come look."

Wolf walked over and sat by Nana Pratt's side. She was holding something in her lap, a board with a square hollow cut into it. Beside her were many small pieces of thin wood cut into all sort of shapes.

"Can you help me put this puzzle together?" she asked.

At first Wolf could not see the purpose. But as they put the small bits of wood into place, he began to see something. One edge would fit into another. Then the patterns painted on them began to make a picture. There were many pieces, and it took some time. But when it was done and the last piece was in place, the picture was recognizable.

Nana read the words printed at the bottom. "Castillo San Marcos. That is the old name for Fort Marion! We made our fort!"

"Yes," Wolf agreed.

"Wasn't this fun?"

"Yes," he said again.

Nana poked him with her elbow.

"George, do you always say yes to everything?"

"Yes."

They both laughed. But as Wolf watched Nana skipping back to their house farther up the beach, he thought about that puzzle. He thought of the many things that had happened to him and to his people as they fought to save their way of life.

Individually, the events made little sense. But when they were put together, the picture was a clear one. It showed the end of their lives as they had been. Their old ways had been broken. But another thought came to him then. Though they were in pieces now, could their lives be put back together like Nana's puzzle? Could they make a future for themselves and the children to come? Could the buffalo return? Could they keep the Medicine Arrows? Could they find a new way back to the way of life Sweet Medicine showed?

Those thoughts stayed in his mind all the rest of that day. As he lay in his cot and tried to sleep, listening to the endless crashing of the waves outside, those thoughts still ran through his mind. He closed his eyes.

And suddenly he found himself somewhere other than the old stone fort. He was standing on a high place over the plains. Below him were many lodges of people, great herds of buffalo. A clean river flowed nearby. Children played in the water, swam with their ponies.

From that great height, he saw the faces of people he knew. They were people who had walked the road of stars. There were his two fathers, Black Kettle, Gray Head, Lean Bear, Horse Road. There were many others whose lives on earth had ended. They were all looking up at him. All he had to do to join them was to walk down to them.

Was the dream telling him that it was time to give up life? Time to accept death as his only escape from confinement and loss?

He turned and looked the other way, down the other side of the hill on which he stood. There were others down there, too, and they too were looking up at him. They were people who had not yet passed from the life on earth. There was his mother and his sister. There were friends whose faces he last saw before being loaded into the wagon in chains. And behind them there were others, many others. Somehow, though he did not know them, they looked familiar. They were not dressed in the old way, but in the manner of the ve'hoes. Yet they wore that clothing with dignity and stood strong. And there, though it was not Stone Forehead, was the Keeper of the

Arrows. The Arrow Keeper smiled at him. Then Wolf noticed that his Striped Arrow People were not alone. They were staying close to one another, but they were among people from other tribes. There were also other people around them. Their faces were white and brown and black. Around them were great buildings and streets of hard stone. But when he looked closer, he saw that the sacred land remained beyond those cities.

His vision was now like that of an eagle in flight. He floated over the land. He looked down. He saw horses running. And farther in the hazy distance, as if seen through the flow of a waterfall, were herds of buffalo.

Then he was back standing on that high hill. He knew his vision was a true one. He knew he had to make a choice. He looked one way and then the other.

He walked down the hill.

A STORY, A STORY. LET THIS STORY COME.

LONG AGO, IN KABI, THERE WAS A KING WHO HAD THREE SONS.
ALL OF THEM WERE GOOD, STRONG YOUNG MEN.
ALL OF THEM HAD A LOT OF POWER.

SO, ONE DAY, THAT OLD KING, HE DECIDED TO TEST
HIS BOYS AND SEE WHICH OF THEM WAS THE BEST PREPARED
TO RULE AFTER HIM. COME WITH ME, HE SAID.

ALL FOUR OF THEM GOT ON THEIR FINE HORSES AND RODE OUT
TO WHERE A HUGE OLD TREE STOOD. I IMAGINE IT MUST HAVE
LOOKED MUCH LIKE THE GREAT TREATY OAK THAT STOOD
AT THE EDGE OF THE LOWER FIELD DOWN BY THE RIVER ON
THE VANCE PLANTATION, NOT EVER HAVING SEEN
ANY REAL AFRICAN TREES MYSELF.

THE OLD KING POINTED AT THAT TREE.
SHOW ME WHAT YOU CAN DO, HE SAID TO THE FIRST SON.

SO THE FIRST SON RODE HARD AT THAT TREE.
JUST BEFORE HE GOT TO IT, HE PULLED UP ON THE REINS,
JUMPED HIS HORSE RIGHT OVER THE TOP OF THAT TALL TREE,
LANDED ON THE OTHER SIDE, AND TROTTED BACK.
HOW WAS THAT, MY FATHER? HE ASKED.

BUT THE OLD KING SAID NOTHING BACK.
HE JUST TURNED TO HIS SECOND SON.
YOU SHOW ME WHAT YOU CAN DO, THE KING SAID.

SO THE SECOND SON RODE HARD AT THAT TREE.
BUT JUST BEFORE HE GOT TO IT, HE LIFTED UP HIS SPEAR AND
THREW IT SO HARD IT WENT RIGHT THROUGH THAT TREE AND
CAME OUT THE OTHER SIDE. BEFORE IT COULD HIT THE GROUND,

THE SECOND SON CAUGHT THAT SPEAR, HAVING RIDDEN
THAT FAST AROUND THAT BIG TREE. THEN HE TROTTED BACK
TO WHERE HIS FATHER AND TWO BROTHERS WAITED.

HOW WAS THAT, MY FATHER?

THAT OLD KING, THOUGH, AGAIN DID NOT REPLY.
HE JUST TURNED TO THE THIRD SON. YOUR TURN, BOY.
SHOW ME WHAT YOU CAN DO.

THE THIRD SON DID NOT RIDE HARD AND FAST.
HE JUST WALKED HIS HORSE UP TO THAT TREE, LEANED OVER,
GRABBED THE TREE WITH ONE HAND, AND PULLED IT
OUT OF THE GROUND WITH ONE HAND.
THEN, HOLDING THAT GREAT OLD TREE OVER HIS HEAD,
HE WALKED HIS HORSE BACK TO THE KING.

HOW WAS THAT, MY FATHER?

AND THAT WAS AS FAR AS THE STORY WENT.
INSTEAD OF SAYING WHICH SON HAD PROVEN HIMSELF WORTHY
TO BE KING, IT ENDED WITH THIS QUESTION.

NOW WHICH OF THOSE SONS DO YOU THINK DID THE BEST?
AND IF YOU CANNOT DECIDE, I GUESS WE WILL NEVER KNOW.

NEW ARRIVALS

It was a good day. He was walking pretty much without a limp. Not having been on horseback for several months had helped. That was yet another thing that had helped him accept the decisions he'd made. A man who couldn't ride for more than an hour without so much pain he was about ready to fall out of his saddle had no hope for a career in the cavalry.

It had been hard to not climb on Blaze's back as he had so often and feel that the two of them were one as they galloped across the prairie. Even a slow walk jolted his hip into fiery pain after the first few miles. The big horse had seemed to understand, and he had felt it try to modify its gait to keep from hurting him.

It'll get better, he had told himself.

But it hadn't.

"There's no shame in it, son," Sergeant Brown had said. "Sometimes a man just has to move on."

And finally he had accepted it and taken the offer to retire with his disability. The one good thing about it was that Sergeant Brown had helped, even though it was close to against regulations, to make sure that Blaze ended up in the right hands. Not those of another soldier, but the understanding hands of Baptist John. The big Osage scout had always been the only person other than Wash that Blaze cottoned to.

Wash reached up to feel the cross on a beaded necklace that hung around his neck, hidden under his shirt. It had been Baptist John's gift to him the day he had handed Blaze's reins to the Osage scout and then walked away without looking back.

So he had returned to his native Virginia on a government pension. It wasn't much, but more than the nothing his mother had ever gotten in exchange for his father's life.

On his own two feet, the pain pretty much went away. On a good day, like today, he was able to walk pretty much like anyone else. Thank the Lord for that. Wash did not wish to stand out any more than he already did. No other colored man at Hampton had gone from being a horse soldier to a scholar.

The pension for his disability was part of what had made it possible for him to attend school. The fact that neither his financial support nor, for that matter, his physical presence was much needed at home was another reason. His homecoming has been a mixture of joy and awkwardness. He'd been embraced by his mother and literally lifted off his feet and spun around by Pegatha, who had grown to the point of being a full four inches taller than he was. Moses Mack, his stepfather, had warmly shaken hands with him and assured him that there was always a place for him to stay in what had been his home long before Mr. Mack had become a family member. And he had found that old liking he'd felt as a child for Mr. Mack, with his quiet modesty and his gentle strength reinforced by the way his new stepfather clearly adored and did everything possible to please Wash's mother.

"Now there ain't no way I could ever come close to taking the place of your father," Mr. Mack had said. "He was the finest man I ever knowed. But I am hoping I can repay the debt I owe to your family for his friendship by helping out however I can."

In fact, it had turned out that Mr. Mack had been more than just helpful. He had amassed a considerable sum of money in the years he was away from Virginia as a prospector in the West. So much that it turned out Wash's mother had not spent a cent of the money he had sent to her while he was serving in the 10th. She had opened an account in the nearby bank and kept all that money, with interest, for Wash himself to use as he wished. And she would not hear him insisting that it was money he didn't want. Out west Wash had faced bullets and bad men, rattlesnakes and killing storms, but he was no match for his mother's determination.

"Schooling," she said. "That is how you should use that money, Washington Vance. You sweated and bled for it, and it is yours."

Things had clearly changed while he was away. Even their little cabin was no longer the same. With Mr. Mack's money they had built on two new rooms and a barn out back where they kept their two mules for plowing. They had even taken on more land to farm and were prospering.

And though Wash had been a bit flummoxed about it on the one hand, on the other he was relieved. Those savings would make life easier for him at the school he had intended to attend. He had returned East with not just the intent of returning to his family, but with the assurance that if he wanted it, a fine education could indeed be his at no less a place than Hampton Normal and Agricultural Institute, the famous school for the education of negroes not far from his home in the very same Virginia where he had been a slave.

He had two people to thank for that. One was his sweet, faithful Bethany. She was already a student there and had asked her uncle, by then in his second term in the House of Representatives, to sponsor him for admission. Apparently it had not merely been Bethany's words, but also the letters he had sent her—some of which she had shared with her uncle, that had convinced the Honorable Representative that Wash was worthy of a place at Hampton.

The second person to thank had been none other than his old lieutenant, now captain, Richard Henry Pratt. The letter of commendation Captain Pratt had sent on his behalf from Florida—where the captain was engaged in civilizing the Indian prisoners of war he had convinced the war department to place under his control rather than hang—was glowing in its praise. Far more than Wash felt he deserved, even though he kept neatly folded in his volume of Shakespeare the copy of that letter which the captain had sent to him.

As Wash walked across the green grass aglow with spring, he thought about all that had brought him to that place. It was still hard to believe at times that it was real, that the place itself was not a mere fantasy and his presence there a dream. But the clothing he wore, the books he carried, and the nods and greetings as he passed other dark-skinned young men and women—all assured him that it was true.

Most of the students were younger than Wash. They seemed, to his embarrassment, to view him as some sort of hero. He was one of their own race who had served as a soldier, fighting wild Indians on the frontier like some hero in a dime novel. More a legend than a man.

Wash shook his head at anyone thinking of him as heroic. How heroic were the fleas and lice in the barracks? Or the heat that made men drop like flies, the cold that froze feet and toes, the boredom that was their lot most of the time...or the terrible sorrow that still gripped him, like cold fingers digging into his chest, when he remembered the death of his best friend? Charley! He would never see his dear friend again until Gabriel sounded his trumpet and Saint Peter read Wash's name in his golden book.

But though Wash knew he was far from being a hero, he had not disabused his fellow students of their imaginings. He understood how important it was to have some sort of dream. And though he was far from the best of them, he had served among the best. There was no finer band of men than those he'd fought beside as a Buffalo Solider.

"Blue blazes, yes!"

He had said that out loud without intending to do so. Luckily, the nearest gaggle of students, chattering to each other like geese, was out of earshot. That was fortunate. He had to remember not to use the coarse language of the frontier.

Then he heard something. A commotion from the direction of the administration building. People were shouting as they ran in that direction. He pulled out his watch. Though his meeting with Bethany was in the opposite direction, he was still half an hour early. Time enough to have a look-see. He closed the watch, but not without a quick glance at the picture of the Vances. Not his family, but his former owners. But somehow it felt right that he'd been able to bring that watch back to the state they loved.

Wash followed the throng. Despite his wound, he was able to trot along at a good pace. That pleased him. But what pleased him more was what he heard the other students saying.

"Indians," a young man shouted. "Real Indians!"

"The Indians are here," another scholar whose face was flushed with excitement cried.

By the time Wash reached the crowd milling about the building he'd heard enough to understand what was happening. Some of the Indian prisoners held at Fort Marion had been deemed civilized enough after to be sent north for further education. And where better for that than Hampton?

My, my, Wash thought. *Could it be that I might recognize one of them?*

It was not through height that one sees the moon, as his Great-Grampa Hausaman said. But as he tried to see, Wash discovered that his shortness meant that nothing more was visible to him than the tops of the heads of the newcomers encircled by a mass of eager humanity.

However, Wash's arms were still stronger than most—even those who stood head and shoulders above him. He thrust his way through. And he found himself standing square in front of the new arrivals. His eyes swept over the thirteen tall, brown-skinned young men. They bore little resemblance to the Cheyennes and Kiowas and Comanches he had known. Every one of them had his hair cut short and neatly combed. They wore not the bright regalia of Indians at war, but carefully tailored suits. They might have been taken for mulattoes or well-dressed, sun-burnt farmers rather than Indians.

With one quick, agile move, the tallest of the Indians stepped forward. He stared down at Wash, a stern expression on his face. A hush fell over the crowd. Their Buffalo Soldier had been recognized! Was this tall Indian a former enemy? Would the two of them now leap at each other's throats?

"Wolf?" Wash said.

The tall Indian bowed. "George now," he replied, his English as cultured and correct as a schoolteacher's. He held his right hand. "It is fine to see you once more, my good man."

He paused and then chuckled. "My little Buffalo Soldier."

Wash grinned up at him. "Sir," he said, "it is just as fine for me to see you...my big Indian."

They laughed and took each other's hands.

LONG, LONG AGO, BACK IN AFRICA,
THREE MEN WERE TRAVELING TOGETHER.
ONE WAS THE KING OF THE ARCHERS.
ONE WAS THE KING OF PRAYER.
AND THE THIRD WAS THE KING OF WRESTLERS.

THOSE THREE MEN CAME TO A STREAM.
IT WAS WIDE AND DEEP AND THERE WERE CROCODILES IN IT.
THEY NEEDED TO CROSS TO THE OTHER SIDE,
BUT THERE WAS NO BRIDGE. THERE WAS NO BOAT.

THE KING OF PRAYER BENT DOWN AND PRAYED.
THEN HE TOOK HIS STAFF AND STRUCK THE WATER.
THE WATER PARTED, AND HE WALKED ACROSS TO
THE OTHER SIDE WITH THE WATERS CLOSING
RIGHT BEHIND HIM AS HE TOOK EACH STEP.

THE KING OF ARCHERS TOOK OUT HIS ARROWS.
HE SHOT THEM, ONE AFTER ANOTHER, SO THAT
THEY LAY IN A STRAIGHT LINE ALL THE WAY ACROSS THAT RIVER.
THEN HE WALKED ON TOP OF HIS ARROWS AND REACHED
THE OTHER SIDE.

NOW THE KING OF WRESTLERS HAD TO CROSS.
HIS TWO FRIENDS WERE WAITING FOR HIM ON THE OTHER SIDE.
HE WALKED BACK AND FORTH ALONG THE BANK,
MAKING HIMSELF ANGRY. THEN WHEN HE WAS ANGRY ENOUGH
HE GRABBED HIMSELF IN A POWERFUL WRESTLING HOLD
AND THREW HIMSELF OVER THE RIVER TO THE OTHER SIDE.

THERE IS ALWAYS MORE THAN ONE WAY TO SOLVE A PROBLEM.
OFF WITH THE OLD RAT'S HEAD.

Selected Bibliography

Adobe Walls: The History and Archaeology of the 1874 Trading Post by T. Lindsay Baker and Billy R. Harrison, College Station: Texas A&M University Press, 1986.

Afro-American Folktales: Stories from Black Traditions in the New World, selected and edited by Roger D. Abrahams, New York: Pantheon Books, 1985.

Battlefield and Classroom: Four Decades with the American Indian, 1867–1904, an Autobiography by Richard Henry Pratt, New Haven, CT: Yale University Press, 1964.

Battles of the Red River War: Archeological Perspectives on the Indian Campaign of 1874 by J. Brett Cruse, College Station: Texas A&M University Press, 2008.

Black Indian Slave Narratives, edited by Patrick Minges, Winston-Salem, NC: John F. Blair, Publisher, 2004.

Black Valor, Buffalo Soldiers and the Medal of Honor, 1870–1898 by Frank N. Schubert, Wilmington, DE: Scholarly Resources Books, 1997.

Buffalo Soldiers, 1866–91 by Ron Field, Oxford, UK: Osprey Publishing, 2004.

Buffalo Soldiers: The Colored Regulars in the United States Army by T. G. Seward, Philadelpia: A.M.E. Book Concern, 1903.

Buffalo Soldiers in the West: A Black Soldiers Anthology, edited by Bruce A. Glasrud and Michael N. Searles, College Station: Texas A&M University Press, 2007.

The Buffalo Soldiers: A Narrative of the Negro Cavalry in the West by William H. Leckie, Norman: University of Oklahoma Press, 1967.

The Buffalo War: The History of the Red River Indian Uprising of 1874 by James L. Haley, Norman: University of Oklahoma Press, 1976.

By Cheyenne Campfires by George Bird Grinnell, New Haven, CT: Yale University Press, 1926, Lincoln: University of Nebraska Press, 1971.

Carbine and Lance: The History of Old Fort Sill by Colonel W. S. Nye, Norman: University of Oklahoma Press, 1937.

Cheyennes at Dark Water Creek: The Last Fight of the Red River War by William Y. Chalfant, Norman: University of Oklahoma Press, 1997.

Child of the Fighting Tenth: On the Frontier with the Buffalo Soldiers by Forrestine C. Hooker, edited by Steve Wilson, Oxford, UK: Oxford University Press, 2003.

The Colonel's Lady on the Western Frontier: The Correspondence of Alice Kirk Grierson, edited and with an introduction by Shirley Anne Leckie, Lincoln: University of Nebraska Press, 1989.

Empire of the Southern Moon: Quanah Parker and the Rise and Fall of the Comanches, the Most Powerful Indian Tribe in American History, by S. C. Gwynne, New York: Scribner, 2011.

The Fighting Cheyennes by George Bird Grinnell, New York: Charles Scribners Sons, 1915.

The Forgotten Heroes: The Story of the Buffalo Soldiers by Clinton Cox, New York: Scholastic, 1993.

The Great Buffalo Hunt by Wayne Gard, New York: Alfred A. Knopf, 1960.

Hausa Folklore by Maalam Shaihua, collected and translated by R. Sutherland Rattray, Oxford, UK: The Clarendon Press, 1913.

The Peace Chiefs of the Cheyenne by Stan Hoig, Norman: University of Oklahoma Press, 1980.

People of the Sacred Arrows: The Southern Cheyenne Today by Stan Hoig, New York: Dutton Books, 1992.

People of the Sacred Mountain: A History of the Northern Cheyenne Chiefs and Warrior Societies, 1830–1879, Volumes I and II, by Father Peter J. Powell, New York: Harper and Row, 1981.

Quanah Parker by Len Hilts, San Diego: Harcourt Brace Jovanovich, 1987.

The Sand Creek Massacre by Stan Hoig, Norman: University of Oklahoma Press, 1961.

The Southern Cheyennes by Donald J. Berthrong, Norman: University of Oklahoma Press, 1963.

Sweet Medicine: The Continuing Role of the Sacred Arrows, the Sun Dance, and the Sacred Buffalo Hat in Northern Cheyenne History, Volumes I and II, by Father Peter J. Powell, Norman: University of Oklahoma Press, 1969.

A Treasury of African Folklore: The Oral Literature, Traditions, Myths, Legends, Epics, Tales, Recollections, Wisdom, Sayings and Humor of Africa by Harold Courlander, New York: Crown Publishers, 1975.

A Treasury of Afro-American Folklore: The Oral Literature, Traditions, Recollections, Legends, Tales, Songs, Religious Beliefs, Customs, Sayings, and Humor of People of African Descent in the Americas by Harold Courlander, New York: Crown Publishers, 1976.

Unlikely Warriors: General Benjamin H. Grierson and His Family by William H. Leckie and Shirley A. Leckie, Norman: University of Oklahoma Press, 1984.

Voices of the Buffalo Soldier: Records, Reports, and Recollections of Military Life and Service in the West by Frank N. Schubert, Albuquerque: University of New Mexico Press, 2003.

War Dance at Fort Marion: Plains Indian War Prisoners by Brad D. Lookingbill, Norman: University of Oklahoma Press, 2006.

ABOUT THE AUTHOR

Joseph Bruchac, coauthor of *The Keepers of the Earth* series, is an internationally acclaimed Native American storyteller and writer who has authored more than 70 books of fiction, nonfiction, and poetry for adults and children. His writings have appeared in more than 500 publications, from *Parabola* to *National Geographic* and *Smithsonian* magazines. He is the author of the novels *Dawn Land* and *Long River,* and other books for children.

He lives in the Adirondack mountain foothills town of Greenfield Center, New York, in the same house where his maternal grandparents raised him. Much of his writing draws on that land and his Abenaki ancestry. Although his American Indian heritage is only one part of an ethnic background that includes Slovak and English blood, those Native roots are the ones by which he has been most nourished.